The Cronkel Chronicles

Book one

Colandra's Quest

S.F. Barnes

authorHOUSE®

AuthorHouse™ UK Ltd.
500 Avebury Boulevard
Central Milton Keynes, MK9 2BE
www.authorhouse.co.uk
Phone: 08001974150

© 2009 S. F. Barnes. All rights reserved.

No part of this book may be reproduced, stored in a retrieval system, or transmitted by any means without the written permission of the author.

First published by AuthorHouse 11/21/2009

ISBN: 978-1-4490-2750-6 (sc)

Registered with the IP Rights Office
Copyright Registration Service
Ref: 832105976

This book is printed on acid-free paper.

Acknowledgments

Many thanks to all my friends for their encouragement and especially to Jean for her helpful advice and numerous pointers.

A special thank you to my sister, Felicity, for the creation of the cronkel and last, but certainly not least, to my husband, whose patience and love helped to spur me on.

Prologue

1666

    The spider had worked all night repairing his web, and now he had one rotation left to complete it. He had found the perfect spot, nestled between the oil lamp and the beam. The flying insects, of which there were many, were attracted by the glow of the flame, which was enclosed in a glass chimney. It was perfect. The lamp was lit as soon as the sun began to set, and was not extinguished until the dawn. Last night the spider had caught a vast amount of food and his larder under the eaves was full. In fact, so many insects had flown into his web, that they had damaged it quite extensively. There were more insects now than ever before, but that was as well, for the weather would soon change and then the spider would be less lucky.

    The spider had just finished his last circuit when the web started to tremble. He tensed; his eight legs poised, ready to pounce. However, it soon became apparent that the vibration was not caused by prey, but from the ground. The spider was no longer interested in what had caused him to be alerted now that he had established that his web was empty, so he went back to his repairs.

    A man with a cart, piled high with bundles wrapped in linen, was banging on the doors of the building and shouting to be let in. Once the doors were opened he dragged the cart inside. Other men came to help him unload the cart, throwing the bundles on to the floor, along one wall of the room. They grumbled to each other about the stench.

"People are complaining," one said. "The baker next door is moaning. He says the smell keeps his customers away. "

"Well, what do you want me to do about it?" asked the carter, the annoyance apparent in his voice. "I just do my job. I'm not responsible for the plague." Then he laughed. "Soon there won't be any customers left and then he won't have to worry about the smell."

The men all laughed with the carter.

Another man said, "I've never seen so many rats about. We've always had them, but not in these numbers before."

"It's the bodies," said the first man. "The smell attracts them. Still, it's only for another week and then we move to the other end of town. It will be much more convenient, being right next door to the cemetery."

The carter left, dragging his cart behind him, the doors were closed and the building became quiet once more.

It was late in the evening and the lamp had been lit by one of the men. The spider was very busy injecting his prey, wrapping it tightly in silk and carrying it to his larder under the eaves. He had so much food that he had had to extend his store and it now included an area inside the building along one of the roof trusses. He had made a temporary connection between the store and the web, so that he would be alerted, should another spider try to steal his cache while he was hunting.

He was in the process of winding a silk thread around his latest prey, a mosquito, when he felt the twitch on his web. Something was in his larder. With a rush, he ran across the web and into the eaves, still carrying the mosquito. As he entered the roof space, he was almost blown off his feet by the wind that swept the top of the room. No, it was not a thief that had caused the vibration; it was the wind, the same wind that blew in the building every night.

The first time the wind had come it had destroyed the web and blown away the spider's store of food. At that time the spider had built his web inside the building and the larder was attached to a roof beam. It had taken three more nights and three more winds for the spider to learn that he must move the web somewhere more secure. Then he built his web outside, first along the soffits, then under the light where the insects swirled around the gas lamp.

Now he had placed the cocooned insects behind the roof trusses which protected them from the force of the wind inside the building. The spider was no longer afraid of the wind; instinctively he knew that he was quite safe if he braced his legs and dug his tiny claws into the wood. Now the wind swirled in circles, moving faster and faster, down from the roof and into the room. It was like a small tornado, concentrating on the floor, but not picking anything up into its centre. As the wind spun round, it created a vortex that emitted a high-pitched, keening noise and spat lightning bolts down to earth. The noise was strangely hypnotic, and high up in the eaves, the spider looked on, not understanding what was happening, but swaying to the rhythm.

It was always the same. Things emerged from the vortex, strange, dark, shadows. They went up to the bundles along the wall and took something from them, carrying what they took, back through the vortex. When they disappeared, the vortex closed behind them with an ear-splitting explosion, the wind died down and all was still again.

However, this time was not the same as all the previous times. The black shadows emerged from the vortex, but instead of going to the bundles, they moved along the wall of the building and disappeared into the night through the cracks in the wooden panels. The vortex closed and the building was quiet once more. The spider waited, tense and alert, perhaps expecting more to happen, but nothing did. The night was still and quiet, the spider turned and went back to his store with the mosquito.

He had just finished securing his last fly to the edge of the roof truss when the wind rose up again. How could this be? Every night, for as long as the spider had lived, the vortex had visited the building, but always only once. This time the wind was the same, the vortex was the same, but now, instead of dark shadows, small lights appeared from the centre of the vortex. They darted around the room looking at the bundles, joining together and splitting apart. They made a musical sound as they moved about and had a sense of urgency about them. They whirled around the room, becoming brighter and brighter. Suddenly a shaft of fire burst from them, igniting everything it touched.

The straw on the floor caught fire first, burning fiercely, and this set the wooden building alight. The spider watched as more and more lights emerged from the vortex, disappearing from his view as they left the burning building.

The night was soon filled with the screams of people as the fire spread rapidly from house to house consuming all in its path, until soon the whole city was ablaze. The spider could see the glow of the fires from his vantage point up in the eaves, and even as the flames reached him, his last thoughts were for his larder, filled to the brim with tasty morsels that would keep him going all through the long, cold, winter months.

Chapter 1

All at sea

    The forest was always beautiful at this time of the year. It was nearing the end of spring and the sun was not yet strong enough to have burnt the leaves and dried out the soil. The undergrowth was still lush and the heavy scent of the woodland flowers was strong beneath the trees canopy. Animals scurried around among the tree roots, foraging for food. They had lived in this forest all their lives and knew no other place. This was their whole world. They hunted for food just as their parents had done and theirs before them. They knew which herbs and grasses were good to eat and where the safest places were to sleep. They were happy and carefree, enjoying a life of simplicity and innocence.

    However, their world was in danger. Unbeknown to them, beings from elsewhere were tearing down their trees and destroying everything.

    They heard the destruction before they saw it; a dreadful grinding, ripping noise, followed by a crash as the trees fell; crushing everything below. Fear passed among them as they ran around in circles not knowing what to do. The very ground was shaking as the noise came closer and closer. The creatures huddled together, petrified by fear, unable to fight or flee. Then a leader emerged from the group, bigger than the others, and started down a trail leading away from the noise and disaster. He turned and looked at the animals, and in response, they cautiously started to follow.

The noise was getting louder and louder. The ground was trembling and the air was filled with dust and debris. The creatures hesitated once more, and then as one, took off, running as fast as they could, trying to escape the devastation behind them. At first they followed trails that were familiar to them, but soon they were running along tracks that they had never used before. Slowly the trees started to thin out and the dirt track became a sandy trail. And then there were no more trees and the trail became a wide expanse of white earth. In front of them they could see water racing towards them with a roar and then, just as they began to back away in terror from this new monster, it receded, hissing and spitting, leaving white foam in its wake.

The leader stopped on the sand. Fear, and his race through the forest, had left him out of breath. He looked around as he rested. A feeling of puzzlement ran through his head. Everything was as it always was, but was it? Something was wrong; something, other than the catastrophe that had caused the animals to flee. He looked around once more. What was he doing on this beach? In fact, where was he? He looked down at his body and immediately froze.

"Oh my God! What has happened to me?" he shouted, but the only sound that came from his mouth was a shriek.

In that moment he remembered. He remembered everything! He was a bus driver in central Bristol! A suicide bomber had blown up his bus. He remembered the explosion. He remembered the pain. He remembered being right in front of the man, whose face was like a zombie's, his eyes huge and staring.

"No! No!" he screamed.

'I must be dreaming this,' he thought, as waves of panic surged through him. But he could feel the hot sun on his back and the grains of sand between his toes. He looked down at his feet and stood transfixed. These feet were nothing like a person's feet. They were small and grey, and at the end of each toe was a tiny, sharp claw. He walked unsteadily over to a rock pool and gazed at his reflection in the water. Looking back at him was a big brown rat! His eyes opened wide and he screamed, clawing at his head, trying to find his real self under the fur.

"No! No!" he screamed. "What is happening? Where am I? Help, help!"

The panic he had felt back in the forest was nothing compared with his panic now. Lumps of fur and flesh were ripped from his face as he raked his clawed hands through his head. The other rats ran to him and started licking the wounds, trying in their own way to soothe him. But he was beside himself, struggling free of their administrations and running up and down the beach screaming, "What has happened to me? Help! Help! Somebody help me! I am not a rat, I am a person! I shouldn't be here! Do something!"

At last he fell exhausted on the sand, weeping hysterically.

Slowly he became aware of a loud grinding, ripping noise, as the earth trembled beneath him. The big brown rat knew what it was now. It was a de-foresting machine, tearing down the trees to make way for some hideous concrete leisure centre or holiday resort! He didn't care. He would rather be dead than have to live the life of a rat!

He looked up at the circle of brown rats staring down at him, with their big ears, pointed faces and twitching whiskers. Just a moment ago he had known these animals intimately. They were his family, his friends, but now they were just rats. They were watching him, nervously grinding their teeth and making small squeaking noises. He took a deep breath and stood up, surveying the scene in front of him.

'Poor things,' he thought, 'it's not their fault that this has happened.'

Could he abandon them to the machine, just because of his dilemma? He might not want to live, but what about them? He needed time to work out what had happened, but time was in short supply just now. He would have to shelve his deliberations for the time being and work out a solution to their immediate problem.

'Somehow we must get off this island,' he thought. He looked out to sea, but he was too short to see beyond the water's edge. He climbed the nearest tree, cursing the fact that rats were so small and helpless. Far out, beyond the shallows, he saw a large cargo ship. A small rowing boat was slowly moving towards the shore.

'Ah! Our escape route,' he thought. He returned to the others and led them to a large log, digging a low trench behind it in which to hide. The other rats copied him and soon they were all hidden. Their big brown rat turned and watched them, fascinated, as they began to indulge in their normal behaviour. Some were washing themselves; others were digging in the trench for grubs and beetles.

'And to think, just a short while ago, I was doing those same things, and happy to be doing it. This can't be happening,' he thought. 'It really can't!'

His thoughts were interrupted by the rowing boat scrapping its hull on the sandy shore about one hundred yards to his right. The crew, a group of men with swarthy complexions and loud rough voices, clambered out and made their way into the interior of the island, arguing and shouting. The rats cowered down in their hiding place, making themselves as small as possible. Once the men had disappeared, the big brown rat jumped out of the trench and quickly went to the little boat. He ran along the rope that tethered the boat to a tree and hoped that the other rats would follow. Soon they were all safely ensconced among the various bags and sacks in the bottom of the boat. All they had to do was stay hidden until the men returned and rowed the little boat back to the ship, completely unaware that they would be carrying a few more passengers!

Chapter 2

Turmoil and storms

The ships hold was very big and cold, full of crates of food and water for the voyage. There were other rats living there, which had never been on land, and knew every crack and crevice of the ship. They showed the new comers the best places to sleep, where to get the tastiest morsels to eat, and how to avoid the numerous traps set by the crew.

The big brown rat had found a comfortable place in which to rest, high up among the oak ribs. He had managed to amass a store of food, which he had hidden in a small hollow where the rib joined the main hull and now he sat on one of the joists watching the activity below him and munching on a nut. Everything had happened so quickly that he had been concerned solely with survival, but now he had time to think. During the day the other rats were asleep in their various hidey-holes, only coming out at night when it was safe to wander about the ship, but the big brown rat was awake. He watched the crew below him as they moved boxes and provisions from one place to another, and he listened to them as they chatted to each other, perfectly able to understand all that was going on.

They grumbled about their rations, their lack of good, clean water and the fact that the captain kept the rum under lock and key. The rat cared little about the crew's complaints; he only cared about his own predicament.

Why was he a rat? He must have died in the explosion on the bus, he surmised, and was re-born into a new body. But why a rat? Perhaps God had deemed his life so bad that he had been born a rat as a punishment, but why was he aware that he was a rat? And why had he suddenly become aware of these things? And what would happen now?

These thoughts occupied his mind for the next four days. He could no longer remember being just a rat. When he looked at the other brown rats he only saw them as rats. He could no longer relate to them as family, even though they still saw him as their friend. He mechanically performed the usual tasks of a rat, but his heart was not in it. He was consumed by fits of anger that raged in him and caused him to fight with any rat that happened to cross his path. The black rats kept their distance and the brown rats slowly left him to his own devices. He spent more and more time in the company of the humans, keeping himself hidden from them, but listening and learning.

On the fourth day there was a terrible storm. The ship was battered by the wind and rain. Crates and boxes were thrown about in the hold and the rats had to be careful to hang on tightly to the nets that hung down the walls for fear of being squashed. They could hear the dreadful crashing of the waves and the clamour of the crew shouting on the decks above them. Water seeped into the hold and they were constantly soaked to the skin. The big brown rat had found a way into the locker where the captain had stashed the rum ration and now he was hidden among the barrels quietly nibbling on an oatmeal biscuit and listening to the first officer.

"The storm is getting worse," he was saying. "I have battened down the hatches and all the crew are on alert."

"Good!" said the captain. "Hopefully it will blow over tonight and we will make harbour by tomorrow afternoon."

Just then the ship lurched from side to side and the barrels were violently plunged against the wall. He was in real danger of being squashed, so he quickly jumped into a large empty crate.

He could no longer see what was going on, but he could hear a lot of shouting and banging.

Suddenly there was an almighty crash and the crate he was hidden in was smashed into pieces as it was flung against the wall of the locker. The big brown rat could see a huge gash in the side of the ship opposite him. Water foamed and frothed as it rushed into the ship and the rat knew he only had a few moments to make the decision of his life. Everybody was panicking, the rats, the ship's crew; even the sea gulls in the sky above seemed to realise that the ship was in real danger.

The brown rat flung himself onto one of the unopened crates and hung on with all four feet, his claws clinging to the wood. Suddenly the crate was thrown from the ship by a huge wave. It plunged beneath the water and the rat clung on, desperately holding his breath. Then, just as suddenly, it shot up to the surface where it was tossed about by the angry sea. The rat held on grimly, soaked to the skin and shivering from the cold. His crate was blown further and further away from the ship and the violent movement made him feel sick and disorientated. He sat up from his precarious position on the crate and looked back at the ship, as, with a loud creaking and groaning noise, it sank down into the depths below.

All around him was debris floating on the water, some with people clinging desperately to the sides, moaning and crying. Other crates and pieces of wood were covered with rats, some from the ship and others from the forest. Soon the raging sea separated the floating armada and the brown rat was alone in his crate, with only a few sea gulls for company. Night fell and the storm slowly blew itself out.

By morning the rain and wind had subsided, the sea was calm and the sun came out. The rat slowly started to dry out and he automatically started to groom his coat.

When he was satisfied with its condition, he appraised his situation. It was an impossible one. He was stuck on a crate, floating in the middle of the ocean, with no food and no water, completely at the mercy of the tide. At first he welcomed the sun as it warmed his flesh and bones, but it soon became stronger and stronger as the day progressed, until he prayed for something to shade him from its merciless rays.

As it became dark, dewdrops collected on the crate, which he drank eagerly, but the next day it became hotter and hotter, with no respite to his thirst. Each day was the same, hot and dry, and each night he tried to sate his thirst with the dew drops, but he needed more water than the dew could provide, and he grew thirstier and thirstier. As he became weaker and weaker he knew that he was doomed. He was finding it difficult to think coherently and he felt so tired. And so he curled up on the crate, pulled an imaginary coverlet over his shoulders and went to sleep.

When he woke, he felt surprisingly refreshed. The air was no longer oppressive and he felt neither hungry nor thirsty. The crate was still and he could not hear the crashing waves or the sea gulls overhead. Puzzled, he stood up and looked around. He was in a fog. He could see nothing in front of him, but a white mist.

'Where am I?' he thought.

"You are between here and there," said a voice. "In fact you should not be here at all!"

The rat fell down with fear.

"Who said that?" he said, terror making his voice a whisper.

"I did," said the voice.

"And who are you?" asked the rat, his voice trembling.

"I am Zoth." said the voice.

The rat started to shake, his breathe coming in short, sharp gasps.

"Where am I?" he whispered, "please will someone help me?" and he started to weep.

He wept for himself, for his terrible predicament, for the loss of his innocence, his friends, but most of all he wept for his despair. He desperately wanted answers, someone to soothe him and reassure him. He wanted to hear someone say, "There, there. Don't worry. Everything will be alright." But no-one did and so he wept.

Chapter 3

Zoth

Zoth watched the rat and felt his pain. He could feel the fear and bewilderment flowing from the little creature. He knew that the rat had many questions, but he was not sure how he was able to communicate so eloquently. Zoth also knew that the rat was not in the right state to be able to understand any of Zoth's answers to his many questions.

Zoth was a spirit and he took care of a being's soul after death. He was responsible for making sure that the soul was processed correctly and that its transition from material world to spirit world went as smoothly as possible. He had been in charge of this process for a long time and he had never before encountered a situation like this. Most beings died, and after some slight disorientation, they soon realised what had happened and accepted death as a normal state.

Occasionally humans failed to understand what was happening. They sometimes refused to believe that they were dead, particularly if their death had been sudden or they had unfinished business down on Earth. But even they eventually understood and accepted their new circumstances, but the soul of this rat was acting very strangely. Zoth suspected that all was not as it should be.

He tried to soothe the rat saying, "Do you know where you are?"

The rat looked up.

"All I see is a white mist. How can I know where I am?"

"Open your eyes." said Zoth, gently.

"I have my eyes open!" said the rat, annoyance evident in his voice.

"No. You have opened your physical eyes, but you no longer have physical eyes. You must open the eyes of your soul!" explained Zoth, patiently.

He had never had to teach a soul how to see. It should be automatic; an instinctive action.

"I do not understand," wailed the rat, and began to weep once more.

This entity was not behaving like a soul at all.

'How do I teach him to see?' thought Zoth.

The normal way was to meditate, then it was an easy step to go deeper, allowing the souls inner eye to take over, but this soul was a rat's soul. They were not capable of meditation, but then they were not capable of lucid thought either, thought Zoth. But this rat certainly did!

"I want you to close your eyes and imagine a candle burning in front of you. Do you know what a candle is?" asked Zoth, suddenly conscious that the rat may not be that aware.

"Yes, I know," said the rat quietly.

"Look into the heart of the flame. Watch it flicker. Look deep into the orange glow. Now step into the flame. Beyond the flame is the white light," said Zoth.

"I see it, I see it!" cried the rat, excitedly.

"Good. Now step into the light. Do not fear, it will not hurt you," continued Zoth, patiently. "Step into the light. Now you can open your eyes."

"I can see!" shouted the rat. "But where am I?"

Zoth knew that his work had just begun. The rat clearly did not understand anything of the spirit world and Zoth knew that he had a lot of explaining to do, and in a way that would not scare this little soul.

"First, I need you to describe what you see," said Zoth.

"Well, I am in an enormous room, with high walls and great white pillars from floor to ceiling. There are no windows, but the room is full of light and there is a sweet scent in the air, but I am still a rat!"

"Do you see me?" asked Zoth, not quite understanding the rat's last statement. "I am standing just behind you. Turn around and look," commanded Zoth, gently.

Slowly the soul of the rat turned around and stared at Zoth. He saw a tall, slim man, with kindly features and a flowing white beard. He wore a long, blue robe, tied at the waist with a dark blue sash. His feet were hidden by the hem of the robe, and all around him was an aura of purple and blue.

Zoth smiled at the soul in front of him and said, softly, "Welcome to the Celestial Hall."

Normally, when a being died and entered the Celestial Hall, they automatically knew all there was to know. With death came knowledge; the purpose of life, everything, no matter what that soul had been, and so Zoth was shocked to find that the soul of this rat had no knowledge of the after-life. Either he had lost his memory or something was drastically wrong.

Zoth sighed. "Being a rat clearly upsets you. What would you rather be?"

"A man of course! It is what I should be and what I was, before being a rat!" replied the rat, indignantly.

Zoth was astounded. If this was correct, it would certainly explain how the rat was able to communicate with Zoth. He was shocked to the core. Something dreadful had happened, the unspeakable. At sometime this soul had been inaccurately assessed!

"You were a man! Are you sure?" exclaimed Zoth.

"Of course I am sure! Why do you think I am so upset! I was a bus driver. My bus was blown up, in Bristol."

Zoth could sense the soul's anguish and the panic starting to rise in him and soothed him saying, "Do not upset yourself. I can sort this out. Just relax and imagine yourself as you would like to be, and you will become that being."

He saw the rat start to relax and watched as slowly his form changed. Instead of a rat, a man stood before him; tall and strong, with sandy coloured hair and blue eyes. He was dressed in the uniform of the modern youth, jeans and tee-shirt and, for the first time since Zoth had first met him, he seemed comfortable and happy.

Around the edge of the hall were soft, raised ledges and Zoth led the soul over to one and urged it to sit down and rest.

"Now that you are more relaxed I shall try to answer all your questions, but please bear in mind that it is complicated."

"You are in the Celestial Hall," went on Zoth. "It is a waiting room that all souls enter when they die. You died on the high seas, after the ship you were on sank during a storm,"

Zoth paused and waited for some reaction. When there was none he continued to speak.

"Normally, when a soul enters the Celestial Hall they know all that I am about to tell you. It is an automatic thing. For some reason you have lost that knowledge. I do not know why, but that will be addressed at a later date."

Zoth paused once more, took a deep breath and said, "All souls are processed in this hall and a determination is made as to where they move on to. Each soul lives over and over again in order to learn all it can, and once it has acquired all the knowledge available to it, it is taken to the Hall of Judgement and its life scrutinised. It is here that a determination is made as to whether the soul is deemed good or evil. If good, they pass into Celestina, to start their journey to Heaven, but if they are deemed evil they are banished to Hades, to start their decent down to Hell itself."

The soul before Zoth shivered at this statement, but was silent. It was difficult to tell whether this simplified version of Heaven and Hell was understandable to him or not.

Zoth prompted him saying, "Do you understand what I am trying to explain to you?"

"Oh, yes, Sir," said the soul eagerly. "What you have told me is very logical really. It makes sense. I always wondered what we were doing on Earth. I thought it would be a bit pointless if we just lived and died, especially as nature is, most of the time, very logical. But what happens when we get to Heaven?"

Zoth shook his head in bewilderment. It was usually so simple. Souls entered the Celestial Hall; he assessed them, decided where to put them and his job was done. Apart from occasionally checking up on them there was little else he had to do, but this new situation was proving very harrowing.

Chapter 4

Cronkel pots, Celestina and the Spirox

"Before I answer your question, I need to make you understand a bit more about life," he said. "As you know, my name is Zoth and I am in charge of all the souls as they arrive in the Celestial Hall. Every being develops a soul once it has started on its evolutionary journey. Before that, organisms live and die, giving sustenance to the Earth and the other beings on it. These organisms are made up of two components, material and spiritual. The spiritual part is pure energy and once the organism dies that energy returns to a great pot at the edge of the universe called the Primordial pot, ready to begin life once more. Every now and again the new life, a tree or an insect perhaps, makes an evolutionary change, which causes it to create a soul and start on its proper journey. The new soul amasses all the knowledge that it learns throughout its various lives and remembers this knowledge. We call this soul a cronkel, and like the energy of the non-evolutionary being, it too returns to a pot after death, but in this case it is called the Cronkel pot. The pot is itself made up of energy and this helps to revitalise the cronkel as it waits for re-birth."

Zoth paused again. He had been observing the soul throughout this latest disclosure and had been impressed with its air of concentration and thoughtful demeanour.

"So we live over and over again?" asked the soul of the rat, and Zoth nodded. "So now I must be cronkel?" he said innocently.

This was the question that was posing Zoth much angst. He was concerned about the fact that the cronkel did not know where he was or what he was. Once a being died and returned to their cronkel state, irrespective of what they had been on Earth, they should know all about their previous lives and retained all that they had learnt during those lives. Zoth had never heard of a cronkel losing its memory before and hesitated before trying to explain all this to the rat.

"Well, you should be a cronkel," said Zoth, "as a cronkel is the part of you that continues on after you die. You have just died and entered the Celestial hall, and as only cronkels can enter this hall, you should, theoretically, be a cronkel. My problem with this is why you do not remember anything. Cronkels should not only know all about their past lives, but also all there is to know about the very fabric of existence. I should not need to explain all this to you, you should just know it."

Zoth could see that the cronkel was getting tired. He had been in the Celestial Hall for some while without the support of the life giving energy of the Cronkel pot, and Zoth knew that it would only be a matter of time before the cronkel would be unable to benefit from its healing properties.

"I shall place you in the cronkel pot while I consult my colleagues," he said. "You will feel refreshed and better able to assimilate new concepts after it has healed you." The cronkel jumped up from the ledge, alarm registering on his face. "Please do not abandon me. I am frightened!"

"There is nothing to fear," soothed Zoth. "I shall be able to see you at all times. Nothing bad will happen to you. You will be among other human cronkels and perhaps they may be able to jolt your memory. You need to heal and become strong again and you can only do this from within the pot."

Reassured the cronkel followed Zoth to the end of the great hall where a door appeared. As Zoth approached the door it slowly opened before him. In front of them was a long white corridor, lit by a soft cream glow that radiated from the domed ceiling. Although there were no doors in the strictest sense of the word, a shaded outline of doors could be seen all along the right-hand side of the corridor.

"Wow!" exclaimed the cronkel. "This is beautiful, and so peaceful."

"This is the cronkel pot," said Zoth, leading the cronkel to the centre of the corridor. "Now you are standing directly below the top of the pot," he explained, looking up at the domed ceiling. "The pot is shaped like a large deep pan with all the rooms starting at this side of the corridor, falling away below us and coming back up to re-join the corridor on the other side. The bottom of the rooms all gather together forming the rounded base. The rooms don't connect at that point but their walls do, and although the cronkels in the pot are unable to see into the other rooms I can. In fact, if I was to place my head at that lowest point of the pot, I could see into every room at once! Only I and my assistants have access through these doorways to the rooms in the pot and we can look beyond the walls to observe the occupants of the rooms. It is difficult to understand if you have not seen it."

"Why are there so many rooms?" asked the cronkel, staring along the right side of the corridor.

"Each room is allocated to a different evolutionary state. Human, mammal, fish, bird etc." said Zoth. "It is better for the cronkels to associate with others at the same stage of their evolution, and for me when I am re-assigning them for re-birth."

Zoth led him back down the corridor and turned to look intently at the shaded patch on the right. Slowly an opening appeared, beyond which was a vast room, stretching away, far below them. Zoth paused for a moment and looked down, observing the many occupants of the room. It was full of other cronkels, but it did not seem crowded. They were of all shapes and sizes, colours and sexes. Some were grouped together talking quietly, while others flew around the room, imitating all manner of things. Zoth called softly to one of these and he came quickly to his side.

"Sorry sir, but I am so happy to have progressed to human that I cannot contain myself," said the cronkel, breathlessly.

"That is quite understandable, Sirtis. You have lived your nine lives as a cat most admirably. If anyone deserves to become human it is you," said Zoth, smiling indulgently at the cronkel,

Sirtis. "However, I now have a small task for you," he went on. "I want you to take care of this cronkel for me. He has lost his memory and I need to try and help him. In the meantime he needs to recuperate, so please look after him for me."

"Certainly Sir. It will be a pleasure. Come, little cronkel, step through the doorway. You will not fall. It is quite safe."

Zoth left the cronkel in the care of Sirtis, and as he stepped back, the door closed silently behind him. He walked down the corridor, away from the Celestial Hall, pausing every now and then to stare through the walls. At the far end of the corridor was a small room called the Primare Talis. This was a special room devoted to new cronkels. These cronkels were delicate, just venturing out on their lives of renewal and learning. Just a short while ago they had been unformed balls of energy, returning to the Primordial pot after death, with neither memory of their past lives nor any concept of existence itself. Now they were thrust into a new world of uncertainty and re-creation, frightened and confused, like a tiny baby without succour. It was important, therefore, to give these cronkels a good foundation and a support structure that would allow them to confidently begin their new journey. The first time the new cronkels arrived in the Primare Talis they were given a name for life and closely monitored by Zoth's colleagues. These cronkels would continue to return to this room after death, until Zoth was satisfied that they could cope in the main rooms of the Cronkel pot.

Zoth's first job was to find out about the rat who thought he was a human. It seemed extraordinary that a cronkel did not know even the most basic things, such as its name, and this confused Zoth and troubled him deeply. He had been in charge of the cronkel department for a long time, in fact he was nearing the completion of his spiritual journey and soon he would give up the department to his assistant, Trego. He could not remember a situation like this ever occurring before and he was worried that it was a symptom of a far greater problem.

Zoth walked back up the corridor and into the Celestial Hall, where many new cronkels were being assessed. It was always a busy vibrant place, with cronkels coming and going, but Zoth did not stop. At the other end of the Celestial Hall was a passageway between this hall and the Hall of judgement. A great door, called the Celestial Portal, was positioned about half-way along this passageway and was the only entrance into Celestina. Only spirits could access this portal, there being a spiritual mystic seal upon it. When you passed through the Celestial Portal you entered the Spirox, a corridor through the very centre of Celestina itself.

 Zoth stepped through the portal and stood for a moment at the bottom of the Spirox, absorbing the beauty and wonder that was Celestina. This was his world, his whole purpose for living. He always felt exhilarated every time he stood on this spot. From here he could see the whole of the Heavenly Kingdom, feel the presence of his God and marvel at the miracle of it all. He gazed upwards taking in the presence of the other spirits, each with their own auras, and felt their energy exuding from them. Celestina was solid, but not solid. Its walls were translucent and the whole kingdom had a luminescence about it, a brilliance that shone throughout. Celestina was a living structure, fed directly from the primordial pot and it, in turn, sent energy back to the pot, renewing it and keeping it pure. The walls of the Kingdom shimmered and pulsated, like a quietly slumbering womb, taking care of the spirits within it, feeding them, nurturing them and protecting them. Zoth could stand here forever, but he had work to do.

 Celestina was of a cylindrical shape with Heaven at the top and the Celestial Hall and the Hall of Judgement at the bottom. The Primordial Pot and the Cronkel Pot hovered just below these two halls, connected, but not connected.

 The Spirox was a vertical corridor, running straight up through the centre of the cylindrical kingdom and giving access to the various levels that made up the Heavenly Kingdom. There were six levels in all, the first three being dedicated to various activities to do with the universe. The remaining levels were devoted to learning. The edge of each level looked out into the Spirox, so it was easy for spirits to enter in order to ascend or descend to the different levels whenever they wished. Spirits were of different levels also, level one being the first level where new spirits began their spiritual journey. Level six spirits were at the end of their journey and ready to ascend into Heaven itself.

Each spirit was assigned work within their own level or of a level lower than their own, as it was not possible for a spirit to ascend above their own level. This meant that sixth level beings were the only spirits able to ascend and descend from the top of the Spirox to the bottom. The Great Lord of all resided in Heaven with the sixth level beings, and it was every spirits aim to reach that state and live forever with their God.

Zoth was a fifth level being. Once he had reached level six he would devote his time in learning and making himself ready for life in Heaven, but for now he was responsible for the Cronkel Department and preparing Trego, his assistant, to take over from him when his time to move on arrived. He looked forward to that time, but he knew that he still had a long way to go before he would reach that state. He knew that he had much work to do on himself before he would be judged ready to move up to the sixth level. He was too easy going and prone to accept things, even when he disagreed with them, rather than challenge the others point of view. Trego accused him of burying his head in the sand, which annoyed Zoth and made him feel inadequate, hardly the attributes of a sixth level being!

He found Trego too argumentative and overly confident. Traits that Zoth felt were not right for a Cronkel Assignor to have! One of his tasks was to prepare Trego for when he would become the Cronkel Assignor and Zoth sometimes found this more difficult than it needed to be by Trego's unwillingness to take criticism. Was he expecting too much of this young spirit? Zoth thought. Had he progressed so far that he had forgotten how difficult it was to change and grow? Perhaps he should spend more time getting to know his assistant better, but there were other more pressing things on Zoth's mind at present. Things that required his undivided attention!

Chapter 5

Assistant Cronkel Assignor, Trego

The cronkel department was located on the third floor and was light and airy, as were all the levels in Celestina. The office was quiet and orderly, each spirit knowing his or her role in the running of things. It was a large room with the same gentle lighting as was in the Celestial Hall. The walls were soft and the energy within them gently pulsated. There were no doors as such, one had but to think of the direction you wished to go in and the wall opened up for you. If one wanted to have a private conversation with someone, all you had to do was manipulate the energy in the wall with a series of thoughts and it would become firm. It would remain in that state until the manipulator released the energy and allowed it to revert back to its normal state. The furniture within the room was made from the same energy that formed the rest of Celestina. There was a high ledge around the edge of the room and in the wall above the ledge was a circular flat surface that resembled a pool of water. This was the called the Scrier and there were similar ones on each level of Celestina. It performed many functions, but its main purpose was to reveal information. It could also be used for communication. Spirits were able to communicate telepathically, but this was a learnt skill and first level beings were unable to use it. By the time a spirit reached the sixth level they were able to telepathically speak to any other spirit within Celestina.

The Scrier was also useful for looking at events that had occurred in the past and this was what the Scrier in the Cronkel Department was mostly used for.

Trego, a fourth level spirit, had worked in the Cronkel Department for some time now. He was the Assistant Cronkel Assignor and Zoth's second in command. He would eventually take over the department when Zoth moved up to the sixth level.

He had not really wanted to work in the Cronkel Department, preferring something a little more exciting and innovative, but he was here now so he had to make the best of it. He had really wanted to work in portal security, as he had a natural talent with magic and spells, but when Gabriel, the head of that department, approached him, he was already assigned to work with Zoth and was unable to change. He had to be content with practising his magic arts by occasionally conjuring up mystic protectors and sealing small rifts in the walls.

Of late he had not seen much of his boss, who seemed to be busy with other things, but that suited him, as he liked to work alone. He had been given an office adjacent to this one, but smaller. It opened directly onto the Spirox, so he was able to see the comings and goings of the other spirits. He would sometimes become so engrossed in watching, that he would fail to get his assignments done on time, much to the annoyance of Zoth. At the present time he was busy looking at ways to improve the system for assigning cronkels, but he knew that he would probably never have the opportunity to try them out, as Zoth was a stickler for adhering to the rules!

Trego was the complete opposite of his boss. Where Zoth was tall and slim, Trego was short and fat. He was rather self-opinionated, having very strong views on most subjects, but his heart was in the right place, happy to help anyone who asked. Trego was sure that Zoth must find him irritating and bossy, just as he found Zoth to be sometimes too soft and indulgent.

Now he looked up from his work as the Cronkel Assignor entered Trego's office. Zoth asked him whether he remembered a bus explosion in Bristol that occurred some time ago. Trego remembered it well because it was the first time that he had had so many souls to process all at one time. There had been many deaths, he explained. "You were not available and I had to ask Verda to help," he said in a slightly accusing way. Verda was a first level being who was often asked to help with cronkels. She had a gentle nature, which calmed down first comers to the Celestial hall.

"There were a great many cronkels to process. I had problems with one of them, Leticia, who had been a cat. She was very agitated, something about demonic possession, so I put her into an ante chamber in the Celestial Hall while she calmed down. Other than that, everything had gone well," explained Trego. "When we had finished putting all the rest of the cronkels into their respective compartments, we found one entity unplaced. It was strange, because it had been unable to tell me who it was, perhaps because of the trauma of the explosion, I don't know. I put it in with Leticia while I looked at the records. I discovered that this cronkel's name was Colandra, but he had not died in the explosion. His entity had been blown out of his body and the escorts had gathered him up by mistake and brought to the Celestial Hall."

"By mistake! Is that possible?" gasped Zoth.

Trego was surprised at Zoth's reaction. He felt that his boss was criticizing his judgement and immediately became defensive.

"I don't know!" he snapped. "I don't have control over the escorts! They do their own thing!"

"So what happened when you found all this out? Did you place him back in his body?" asked Zoth, trying to placate Trego.

Trego looked guilty, aware that he really should not rise to anger so quickly.

"No!" he said. "When I returned to the Celestial Hall his entity was gone. I assumed that his human body had woken up and his entity was pulled back inside his body by its golden thread. I never gave it another thought. It seemed the most natural thing to have occurred. Why, what has happened?" he asked, puzzled.

Zoth explained what had happened, "Somehow he was put into the cronkel pot, I don't know how or by whom. He clearly did not re-enter his body, unless he has died since the accident. Search the records to find out what lives Colandra has led since the explosion. Meanwhile he cannot stay in the cronkel pot as he is not a cronkel. He needs to go back to Earth, until we can decide what to do with him."

Trego followed the other spirit back down to the Celestial Hall. He watched as Zoth entered the Cronkel Pot and walked down the corridor, looking down into the human compartment. He quickly returned, but alone. "Trego, you must escort Colandra here so that I can talk to him," he said.

Trego was annoyed. Why couldn't Zoth call the cronkel himself? Why had he bothered coming all the way back here to tell him to do it?

Trego went down the corridor and opened the doorway into the human compartment, and then he stopped, astonished, as Colandra, in the form of a purple, fire-breathing dragon, cavorted about with a green lizard. Trego stifled a giggle. Someone had evidently shown Colandra that he could be whatever he wanted to be when in the cronkel pot! He watched indulgently as Colandra played. He remembered being a cronkel, and how exhilarating and revitalizing it was to re-enter the pot after completing a life. But enough was enough. He quietly called to the cronkel, introduced himself and escorted him back to the Celestial Hall.

Zoth looked Colandra over.

"How are you feeling now?" he asked gently.

"Okay. Much better, thank you," replied Colandra.

"Well, we have discovered a few facts, as Trego will explain." said Zoth, nodding at his assistant.

"I am the Assistant Cronkel Assignor. I help Zoth in the Cronkel Department," explained Trego.

"Oh, do get on with it!" interrupted Zoth, impatiently.

Trego glanced over at him, surprised at his tone of voice. It was not like Zoth to show annoyance, no matter how trying the circumstances.

"Your cronkel name is Colandra, but your body is not dead and therefore you are not actually a cronkel. In fact you should not be here at all!" continued Trego and he proceeded to explain to Colandra what had happened on that fateful day.

"I am truly sorry for what has happened to you and I sincerely wish to help you, however, as you are not actually a cronkel, you cannot stay in the cronkel pot any longer. We must establish what has happened to your body so that we can re-unite you with it, before it is too late. We will return you to Earth while we find out what needs to be done. You will not have a body while you are down there, but you can assume any identity as long as it already exists on Earth. Nobody will be able to see you, although some people may be able sense your energy, and you must conform to the laws of nature, therefore, no orange, fire-breathing dragons!" he added sternly.

"Oh! You saw then? Sorry." Colandra replied, contritely.

"Hmm. Have you any questions before you return to Earth?" asked Zoth.

Colandra had hundreds of questions, but none of them were answerable!

"No!" he said and before he could blink an eye he was hovering above the marble arch in the middle of London.

The next meeting Trego had with Zoth was a little tense, to say the least. Trego admitted that it might have been his fault that Colandra had been placed in the cronkel pot. He had failed to tell his colleagues that he had placed Colandra in the ante-chamber with Leticia and while he was up on the third floor looking through the records, one of them had asked him what he wanted to do with Leticia now that she had calmed down, Trego gave instructions for her to be placed into the mammal compartment of the cronkel pot. In order to simplify matters, a direct link had been created from the ante-chamber to the pot. No-one realised that Colandra had been placed with Leticia and so the two of them had entered the pot together. In so doing Colandra's life had been changed forever.

Colandra had been re-born as a mammal, "a lemur, as I recall," added Trego, and when the lemur died Colandra had entered the Celestial Hall, so it was naturally assumed that he was a cronkel. It seemed that Lysander had lived three more lives as a mammal since then, and at the end of each of these lives, placed in the Cronkel Pot. And so the circle continued and would probably still be doing so if Colandra had not remembered, while he was a rat, that he had been a man. Why he had remembered that he had been a man during this particular re-birth was a mystery.

"If his life as a rat had been very traumatic it might account for why he suddenly remembered being in another life," suggested Trego. "It's just a thought. It makes no difference really, but it is interesting, none the less."

"Hmm. Perhaps, but it was very fortuitous was it not?" said Zoth.

Trego squirmed a little at this comment. He had discovered that Colandra was not due to die for some years, but he had been unable to locate the bus driver's body. It was usually easy to keep track of human beings, because they had a thread connecting them to their entity. This thread was strong and elastic, allowing the entity a certain amount of freedom, but in Colandra's case this thread had been blown away from his body by the force of the explosion, making it impossible for Trego to find it.

"I have tried to find his body using the Obturama, but to no avail," he said, sadly. This was a device only available to those beings who worked in the Cronkel Management Department. It was like a flat milky stone, which was controlled completely by the being using it. One had only to look into its surface and visualize the place, the time and the person that you wanted to see. If you did not know one or two of these parameters, the Obturama could tune into your mind and give you various selections until it had found what you were looking for.

The fact that the Obturama was unable to locate Colandra's body was very worrying. This would indicate that the golden thread was missing completely. Trego had never heard of this ever happening before and he was concerned that this would make it impossible for them to re-attach Colandra's soul to his body.

"I don't think we will be able to find his body from here," said Trego, hesitantly, and Zoth agreed. The only way that Colandra's body could be found was from within the material world.

Colandra would have to find it himself, reclaim it and try to reunite with it.

"That will be very difficult," said Trego. "Colandra will only be able to speak to other entities and the chances of those entities having useful information will be very slim."

"Well, what do you suggest then?" asked Zoth.

"Perhaps we can allow him to have contact with humans. That would help. He could ask questions then," suggested Trego.

"In order to do that he would need to appear as human and he would expend too much energy if he was to do that for any length of time. If he does not receive the energy created by the golden thread, he will be unable to form a plausible image," explained Zoth. "I suppose we could narrow the field down to one human. He will have to return to his natural state every now and then, so that he can renew his energy, but I think that will work. You will need to choose very carefully though. Is there anyone in his past that you think would fit the bill?" asked Zoth.

"Well, actually, there is one," said Trego. "In two of his past lives he paired with a human female. They were never soul-mates, but there must be a strong link or they would not have found each other during different lives. The female's cronkel name is Tesserie, but her human name is Michelle."

Trego watched Michelle through the Obturama. Trego had been a spirit for a long while now, but even though he had not been in the material world for some time, he was still able to appreciate material beauty. He watched Michelle as she walked in the woods behind her house, her long fair hair shimmering in the evening sunlight and he marvelled at her lithe body and the way she moved effortlessly down the uneven trail. One of the advantages of the Obturama was that it not only showed the physical aspects of the scene, it also generated the emotional and psychological state of those persons being observed. Michelle was not depressed, but she was certainly not as happy as she could have been. Trego could sense the tension in her and the dissatisfaction with her life was very evident.

'It just might be the right moment for changes in Michelle's life too,' he thought, satisfied with his choice.

Chapter 6

Beginnings

Michelle walked through the woods, totally unaware that she was being observed by Trego.

She was not depressed, but neither was she elated. Her life did not seem to be going anywhere at the moment. She was looking for a change. She was thirty seven years old, single and a computer specialist. She did not dislike her job; on the contrary, she loved it. She worked in the local library's computer room and it was varied and interesting.

Her social life had much to be desired, however. In fact she had no social life at all. She distrusted strangers and found it difficult to mix with other people on a social level. Her knack of telling the truth often got her into trouble. This trait alienated people and this had been the reason that all her boyfriends had left. She was not unhappy about it as she liked her own company and disliked having to share her life with other people, but she felt at a crossroads in her life. She needed a change and she always found that walking in the woods was the perfect place for thinking.

Trego called softly to Zoth, "I think we have picked a good time. She is seeking some changes to her life, but does not know what or how to change it. I think she would be receptive to new ideas and as long as Colandra is careful and not too aggressive, I think she will accept him."

Zoth watched for a few moments and agreed. "Now is as good a time as any," he said. "Colandra are you ready to start your search?" asked Trego, gently. The cronkel had been recalled from Earth and Trego had explained all that they had found out about the day of the explosion, and of his life since that day. Now they were in the Celestial Hall and Colandra, though nervous, was eager to get started in the search for his body.

"Now remember," said Trego. "You will only be able to communicate with this one female. Her cronkel name is Tesserie, but her Earth name is Michelle. She will be the only human able to see you. It will be up to you to persuade her to help you, as we cannot do anything in that regard."

Colandra understood. He had been given some attributes of a cronkel and still retained the knowledge that he had acquired since his demise as a brown rat. Now it was up to him. He had been told that while his body was disconnected from its soul, it would be unable to function on a conscious level, but should return to normal once Colandra re-joined it. He had been warned, however, that he may experience some discomfort when actually merging. Colandra expressed some alarm at this news, but both Zoth and Trego had reassured him that they would do all in their power to help him.

Now, they placed him in the woods, close to where Michelle was walking.

Michelle loved the woods, but now it was getting late and she could feel the darkness starting to close in around her. It was autumn and there was a nip in the air as the sun started on its Earth bound path. The trees were clothed in gold and orange and the leaves had started to fall, covering the path in a colourful tapestry. As she walked along she kicked the leaves which made a rustling sound as she followed the path. She had not gone far when she thought she saw someone ahead of her. Surely she would have heard anyone who was walking in the woods. The leaves made it impossible to move undetected. She turned her head toward it, but all she could see were trees and undergrowth. She shrugged her shoulders and continued on her way. Then she saw it again, something over to her right, among the Hazel trees.

"Is anyone there?" she shouted, but there was no reply. The shadows were getting long and it was difficult to make out any definite shapes.

Again she thought she saw something, as if someone were hiding from her. Again she turned and again it was gone.

'Perhaps it is the late sun reflecting off moisture trapped among the bushes,' she thought, but even so, she picked up her speed, making her way towards the village and the safety of her house as quickly as she could.

It was unusual to encounter anyone else in the woods at that time of the evening. Sometimes in the daytime, particularly during the weekend, people came to take their dogs for walks or ramblers would visit the woods when the bluebells covered the ground, but never late into the evening.

Now she felt a presence. She instinctively knew that she was not alone. She was not far from her house now, but she was reluctant to show whoever was following her where she lived, in case that person intended her harm, so she stopped and listened. There was nothing, but on the edge of her sight she saw a movement. She turned sharply and there, just through the next row of trees was a tall, thin man.

"You there. Who are you? What do you want and why are you following me?" demanded Michelle, her heart thudding in her chest.

The man stood transfixed, like a startled rabbit caught in the beam of a car's headlights.

"Speak up, man!" Michelle shouted. She was angry and a little scared, her voice perhaps gruffer than she intended. The man slowly walked through the trees so that eventually he was able to emerge onto the path in front of her. Michelle just stood watching him, her heart racing and the palms of her hands sweating, despite the cold.

"I am sorry. I did not intend to frighten you," the man said. "My name is Colandra."

"You didn't frighten me," lied Michelle. "So, what do you want?" she asked, bluntly. All the time she was eying him up and down. He was thin, very thin, as if he had not had a good meal for some time. He had sandy coloured hair and he was wearing jeans and a tee-shirt, totally inappropriate clothing for a cold autumn evening.

But for some unknown reason she felt sorry for him! 'Whatever is the matter with me?' she thought. 'Some strange man appears from nowhere and I feel sorry for him! For goodness sake, pull yourself together!'

"So what are you doing here? It's rather late to be out walking isn't it?" she said out loud.

"I started my walk some time ago, but now I am completely lost," said Colandra. "I hesitated to approach you for fear that you might think I was going to attack you or something," he added, quickly.

"Hm," said Michelle, starting to relax a little. "Well you had better follow me then. I will show you the way to the main road."

Michelle and Colandra walked through the woods together and Colandra enthused as to the beauty of the trees. Michelle started to relax. Someone who could feel so sympathetic as to the beauty of the woods could not be all bad, she mused.

As they reached the edge of the wood, Colandra stumbled, catching his foot in a rabbit hole, and though Michelle made a grab for him, he seemed to slip through her hands, falling heavily to the ground.

"My ankle! Oh, the pain!" the man shouted, writhing on the grass, holding his leg.

Michelle bent down to look at his ankle, which was swelling around his shoe at an alarming rate.

"Oh, that looks awful! Can you stand?" she asked, anxiously.

"Maybe," he said, trying to get up. Eventually he managed to stand on his good leg, and with the help of a crutch fashioned from a fallen branch, he hobbled forward a couple of steps.

"Yes, I can hop with this thing," he said. "Just point me in the right direction."

"If you continued to the right," said Michelle, doubtfully, "you will eventually reach the main road. Are you sure you can manage?" she added, watching him as he tried to hobble along, one hand on the stick the other on the hedge that bordered her back garden.

"I'll be okay," he murmured, his face screwed up with pain.

"You can't be serious," she said, feeling sorry for the man. "It's late. Where do you intend to go?"

Something about him was very familiar, not what he looked like, more how he made her feel. She could only describe it as an itch in her head, but pleasant.

"If I can get to the main road, I can look for a bed and breakfast. There must be some in the village surely," said Colandra, deliberately not looking in her direction.

Michelle watched him trying to limp along the path, but it was very uneven and each step became shorter and shorter. It was obvious to her that he was not a murderer; just a man out walking. She knew that she could not abandon him and in that moment she made up her mind.

"It will take you hours at that rate," she said. "Why don't you stay at my house? If we continue along the left of the hedge we come to my back garden, where I have a private entrance. It won't be nearly as far as the road and you can stay the night in my lounge. I have a very comfortable bed settee, that way you don't even have to climb the stairs," she suggested.

"Oh, no, I could not impose myself on you," said Colandra.

"I insist. Now come on, it's not far," and Michelle led the way. They continued walking just a short way along the hedge until they had reached a gap, which supported a garden gate. The hedge had been neatly cut here and afforded a view of the woods to anyone in the house or garden.

As they stepped into the garden, Michelle looked up at the house with pride. It was a beautiful detached cottage, with a thatched roof. The windows were framed by wooden shutters, which were folded back against the cream walls. Around the door, and climbing above the first floor windows, was a wisteria, not in flower at the moment, but flush with leaves that had started to change from green to gold. The setting sun made shadows dance on the walls and bathed the garden in golden shafts of light. She led the way around the side of the house to the front. The front garden was a typical cottage garden, with lots of flower borders and a curving lawn. A cobbled path wound from the blue front door to the wooden gate leading out onto the road. Above the door was a small canopy with a hand-painted sign hanging from it saying 'Hazelwood cottage'.

Michelle unlocked the front door and ushered Colandra inside. It felt so right, as if it was all pre-ordained! She had no way of knowing how much this tall, thin man was going to change her life!

Chapter 7

Explanations

Once inside the house, Colandra hobbled behind Michelle to the lounge. Soon he was safely seated in a comfortable armchair on the right of the fireplace, his foot carefully placed on a stool. Michelle disappeared into the kitchen to make a cup of tea. 'Why is that humans always make tea whenever there is a crisis of some sort', thought Colandra, as he looked around the little sitting room. It was a typical cottage style room, with a log burner in the hearth and thick pile rug in front of it. The walls were a pale cream with a picture rail picked out in terracotta all around the room. The curtains were flowery, a little old fashioned perhaps, but they were in keeping with the style of the room. There were two armchairs, one on either side of the fireplace, with comfortable beige velour covers and a matching sofa opposite. A large screen television on a glass stand, complete with all the latest hi-fi and recording devices stood in the corner next to the bay window, the only concession to the twenty first century. There were several display cabinets along the wall opposite, each full of carefully chosen porcelain and ceramic ornaments. The walls were covered in pictures, mostly landscapes, and beautifully painted, vibrant and alive. The artist was obviously very talented.

Colandra could hear Michelle in the kitchen and wondered how he was going to introduce her to the idea that he was a cronkel! He had only just become used to the idea himself!

Just then she arrived back with two steaming cups of tea and placed one on a small table next to him and took the other to the armchair opposite. After carefully placing her own cup on a similar table, she sank into the chair and looked at him, expectantly. Colandra sat back and took a deep breath.

"Michelle, I am not as I seem," he said, anxiously watching her.

"How do you know my name? I don't remember telling you my name!" she said loudly, sitting forward in her chair.

"No, you did not tell me your name, but that is not important. I am sorry for deceiving you, but I did not hurt my foot."

Michelle sprang from her chair.

"Now I know that's untrue! I saw it, remember. It was swollen and red. Only a few moments ago, when you put your foot up on the stool, it was three times as big as the other foot, so don't tell me that!"

Colandra pulled up the leg of his jeans and Michelle gasped as she looked at his foot. It was perfectly normal. There was no swelling, no redness, in fact nothing to show that he had injured it just a short time ago.

"How did you do that? I know what I saw. It was swollen, I know," she said quietly.

"As I said before, I am not as I seem. I am sorry to have duped you, but it was imperative that I talk to you." He looked at her anxiously, hoping more than anything to appeal to her compassionate nature.

He was unsure as to how he should continue. Should he just blurt out his story or continue to beat about the bush in the hope that something would come to him. He had been a human such a long time ago, that he had forgotten how to communicate with them. In the end he decided to blurt it out and if she threw him out of the house, so be it. Michelle was staring at him, waiting for something, so he said, "I am not a human, I am a spirit, well, a soul actually," and waited for the reaction.

Michelle stared for a few moments longer and then burst out laughing.

It was not the reaction that he was expecting, but at least she had not dismissed his comments out of hand.

"I thought you were going to say that you were from outer space!" she said, sarcastically. "If you are a spirit, how come you are sitting in my armchair?"

"You only see me sitting here because you expect me to be sitting here. Like my foot. I told you that I had hurt it, so you expected to see a hurt foot. Come, help me up from the chair," and Colandra stretched out his hand to Michelle. She hesitated, then stood up and walked tentatively towards him. As she went to grasp his hand her fingers encountered thin air, nothing. She stared at his hand in hers, but felt nothing. She drew back her hand in alarm.

"Do not be afraid, I cannot hurt you. I cannot even touch you!" he reassured her. "That is why you could not save me when I fell. I am made of energy, nothing solid, and yet I will appear to you as a normal person."

It was obvious to Colandra that Michelle was shocked. She stood as if in a trance, staring at him, her breath coming in short gasps.

'Oh, no! She's going to die. She is going to have some sort of apoplectic fit and die! My only hope in the whole world and I have killed her!' thought Colandra, panicking.

"Michelle, Michelle! Please talk to me!" said a frightened Colandra leaping up from his seat. "I am so sorry. I did not mean to frighten you. Please, please speak to me!"

Slowly Michelle's breathing became normal.

She sat down, her hands shaking a little and whispered, "Its okay. I'm alright, I think. Perhaps you should start from the beginning."

And so Colandra sat back down and explained all about Cronkels and energy, Celestina and re-birth, Zoth and Trego, and everything else that he had learnt, until he had exhausted both himself and Michelle.

When he had finished, Michelle sat staring at him, "Wow!" she exclaimed. "Wow! I don't know whether to believe you or not."

"Supposing that it is all true, why have you come to me?" she asked

"I do not know why you were chosen, but I was told that you were the only person able to help me. I must find my body so that I can re-unite with it to make myself whole again," said Colandra.

"You make it sound very simple," said Michelle, "So why is it that I think it will be far from that?"

Just then Michelle heard a familiar "Clack!" ...Oh no! The cat-flap! She had forgotten about Thomas, her very large, grey Persian cat! What would his reaction be to the tall, thin man?

Colandra also heard the noise and looked up to see a large, grey, fluffy cat striding into the room. The cat paused for a moment and looked around. Colandra knew that the only being on Earth that was able to see him was Michelle, so he was surprised when the cat walked up to him, sat down in front of his chair and stared at him. Colandra opened his mind to the cat and immediately recognised him. It was Sirtis, the cronkel that had looked after him in the cronkel pot!

'Hi, Sirtis!' he thought to the cat. 'What are you doing here? I thought you would be re-born a human. How come you are a cat again?'

Colandra could, at once, feel the cats anguish streaming from him. Something was very wrong. Sirtis had been in the human compartment of the Cronkel Pot, so why was he a cat?

'Something is wrong!' the cat thought to Colandra. 'I should not be here!'

Colandra turned to Michelle.

"This is Sirtis," he said. "He is a cronkel, or was a cronkel. I met him just before I was sent here. He should not recognise me, or be able to communicate with me, but he certainly can. He is genuinely concerned that he is still a cat. He has already lived his nine lives and should have moved up a level to that of human. Perhaps more has gone wrong than even Zoth is aware of."

"Hang on! He is my cat Thomas. I have had him since a kitten! He is not a cronkel! Whatever are you talking about?" said Michelle indignantly.

"He is not a cronkel at the moment," said Colandra. "He was a cronkel when he died after his life before this one. From the cronkel pot he was assigned to one of the unborn kittens that were conceived by his mother. After he was born you adopted him and called him Thomas."

"Hmm. Are you sure he is the same cat?" asked Michelle, staring at the cat. "I must admit he does seem to know you. Sometimes he appears to understand what I say to him, but perhaps he is just a very clever cat? I thought it was because he is Persian and they are quite intelligent... for cats, that is," said Michelle, stroking Thomas, who was now sitting on her lap, purring very loudly. Thomas clearly liked being the centre of attention, and having two people taking notice of him was his idea of heaven.

"Well cats are right at the top of the mammal's evolutionary tree," said Colandra. "Most people think that apes are, but they are not spiritually as advanced as cats. Tigers and cougars are the highest cat form, but domestic cats are still considered advanced, because of their close relationship with humans. But he is definitely Sirtis. We have communicated with each other. He tells me that he has been on Earth as ten different cats, and according to him, a cat has nine lives, not ten."

Colandra sat back down in the armchair and proceeded to tell Michelle about his adventures as a rat and his sudden realisation that he should have been a man.

"When I died and met Zoth, I remembered being a man," continued Colandra.

"You are talking about re-incarnation. If we re-incarnate why can't we hold on to the things we learn during our lives? It seems a waste of time otherwise," said Michelle.

"We do hold on to what we learn, but only in our cronkel state. Once we are re-born, we become identified with our new lives and forget ever being a cronkel." said Colandra. "I suppose that if everyone knew about re-incarnation they wouldn't care what they did during their lives, they wouldn't bother to learn anything. People would just say that it doesn't matter, because there's always another life."

"When you met Zoth, did he tell you how he was going to make everything right again for you?" asked Michelle, hopefully.

"No, not really! I was taken back to the Celestial Hall and introduced to Trego, Zoth's assistant. Trego explained about the mistake that had happened when my bus exploded and how my soul was taken by the escort spirits. The explosion had killed eight humans, one cat, three rats, fifteen birds, ninety ants, two hundred and thirty flies, five thousand bacteria and forty two thousand viruses. Trego had been very busy making sure that he and his assistants put them into the right compartments and did not notice that there was one too many, me! Trego tried to question me apparently, but I was unable to answer him. When he had discovered that I was not actually dead and returned to the Celestial Hall to sort out the problem, I had disappeared. He thought that I had returned to my body, here on Earth, but unbeknown to him, one of his helpers had put me in the mammal compartment of the cronkel pot with another cronkel and so my life went slightly wrong from then onwards!" Colandra took a deep breath and relaxed back against the cushions. While he had been talking, he had watched Michelle's face. Many different emotions had flitted across it as he had spoken. Her brow creased as she concentrated on his story and astonishment had made way for understanding. He hoped sincerely that he had been able to convince her of the truth of his tale, because he knew that she was his only hope of helping him find his body and re-claiming his life.

Chapter 8

Acceptance

Colandra watched Michelle anxiously, wondering if he had told her too much.

"I don't understand all of this. You explained that a cronkel is the spirit that is released when you die. Now, if you did not die, how come you are a cronkel?" asked Michelle, quietly.

"A good question," said Colandra. "I am not a cronkel in the true sense, as I am not dead. I am the entity of the man I was. The part of you that makes you 'you', I suppose. My golden thread became detached from my body in the explosion and my entity was set free. When I was gathered up by the escort spirits, I was mistakenly placed in the Cronkel Pot, and so took on the attributes of a cronkel. I was re-born as a mammal over and over again. The error was only discovered when I realised that I had been a man and was able to tell Zoth."

"So Zoth knows who you were as a man?" asked Michelle.

"No." replied Colandra. "Unfortunately the spirits keep track of humans through the golden thread connecting the body to the soul and in my case the thread is broken. Zoth knew my cronkel name from the records and what I had been in my past lives, but no details of those lives. That is only known to the individual cronkel. This information is not shared by the spirits until the cronkel enters the Hall of Judgement at the end of their material existence," he added.

"So, if you don't know who you were, how can you find yourself!" asked Michelle, not completely sure if she had worded that question quite right.

"Ah! Therein lies the problem," said Colandra, looking intently at her. "Unfortunately I have not the foggiest notion to either question. I think that is where you come into it."

"Me! Why me? Your body could be anywhere. I am much too busy to search the planet for somebody that you don't know anything about. It will be an impossible task," she said indignantly.

"Well! I know that I was a bus driver and I know that I was injured in a bus explosion. There can't be that many bombs going off on Bristol buses, surely," said Colandra, fiercely.

"Well perhaps not, but why me?" she said, defiantly.

Colandra stood up and faced her. "You were chosen by Zoth and Trego as the only human that would be able to help me. They did not say why that was the case, just that it was so," he said quietly. "Perhaps there is something connecting you to the man. Perhaps finding out why you are the only person who can help me, is part of the solution."

"This is ridiculous." she said indignantly. "They made one huge mess up, so the chance of getting this bit wrong is probably very high! Anybody could have found you; someone walking their dog, a jogger, anyone."

Colandra interrupted her.

"No! That is not so! You are the only person on Earth that can see me and hear me. You are the only person who can help me!"

"Why do you need my help? Why can't you investigate the situation yourself? These days information is available to anyone."

Colandra sighed, sitting back down.

"Unfortunately I can only make myself look like something or someone. I am not solid, I only appear solid. You see me sitting on this chair, but I am not really. It is what you expect to see, so it is easy for me to persuade you that that is the case. I project the image to you and you see that image."

"Why can't you just wander about as a ghost and find this man yourself," she said.

"Yes I could. But I cannot interact with the material world. I wouldn't be able to look through data or stuff like that to find out names, addresses. If I wanted to enter a building, for instance, I would have to do so through an open door or window. Or I would need to wait for someone to go in, so that I could follow. Normally an entity is supplied by energy through its golden thread and this allows it to travel when its body is asleep. The constant supply of energy allows the entity to move through anything, solid or not. Because I am no longer attached to my body by the thread, I don't have that constant supply of energy. I can send thoughts through solid objects, but even then, the further away I send them or the denser the material I send them through, the less effective they are." said Colandra, patiently.

There was a long silence while Colandra anxiously watched Michelle. It was obvious to him that a battle was going on in her mind, between her heart and her head. It was a difficult situation for any rational person to find themselves in. Spirits, souls and the abstract world existed only in books and minds, so when confronted with them in your own home, it was a tremendous leap of faith, even when the evidence was there in front of you. His thoughts were abruptly interrupted with Michelle sitting forward in her armchair.

"Well what do you want me to do?" said Michelle in a business-like voice. As she uttered that question Colandra was relieved. He sighed and silently thanked the spirits for finding him this lovely, young woman to help him.

"Well we could start with noting down all the facts that are known about the day of the explosion," suggested Colandra.

Michelle jumped up and fetched a note book and pencil.

"Okay, fire ahead," she said, returning to her chair.

"I know that it was in Bristol and that it was winter time. I also know that there were some people killed and several injured, but I only know those things because Trego told me. He also said that it would have taken place about twelve Earth years ago, but that is only an approximation," explained Colandra.

"Can't you actually remember anything yourself?" asked Michelle. "You say you recalled that you were a bus driver, is there anything else?"

Colandra sat thoughtfully trying to remember. He visualised himself as a rat on the beach. It was his strongest memory, so perhaps in thinking back it might allow him to remember other things.

Suddenly he threw up his head, "Yes, I do remember something!" he exclaimed loudly. "It was an open topped bus, not the normal one, but the type used for sightseeing tours. Now there cannot have been many of those in Bristol."

Michelle wrote it all down in her notebook and looked up at Colandra.

"I work in the local library, so in the morning, I will look in the library's old newspapers, and see if I can find a reference to the suicide bombing." said Michelle. "As you say, it is not that common. I can also look on the internet. I don't remember it personally and I have lived in Bristol all my life, but I may have been away at the time." she said.

"You are tired," said Colandra, watching Michelle as she tried to stifle a yawn. "You need to sleep and I must return to my natural state in order to re-charge my energy,"

As he disappeared from her view and became a shimmer of light, he knew that she would help him in his quest, and hoped that it would be a simple matter of deduction. Little did he realise that it would, in fact, lead them both into a dangerous adventure, the repercussions of which would echo throughout the universe.

Chapter 9

The library

Michelle was woken by her alarm at seven o'clock. She sleepily stretched out her arm and flicked the disable switch, instantly silencing the intrusive noise.

She had thought that she would find it difficult to sleep when she had gone to bed last night. So many images had churned through her head, mind-blowing thoughts and unbelievable concepts. But she had seen him, passed her hand through his flesh and seen him disappear before her eyes. It was undeniable. She had to accept the truth, no matter how much her head wanted her to believe otherwise. Surprisingly, she had fallen asleep as soon as her head touched the pillow and she had had a long sleep, not troubled or plagued by nightmares. She awoke, refreshed and invigorated, ready to take on the world.

She got out of bed, put on her dressing gown and slippers and went downstairs to the kitchen to make herself a cup of tea. While she was making the tea, Thomas strolled into the kitchen from the utility room.

"Good morning, how are you?" Michelle said. Thomas rubbed against her legs and mewled. She bent to stroke him and he raised himself onto his hind legs to meet her hand.

"You are such a beautiful boy," she said affectionately and picked up his bowl from the floor. After washing it up and drying it, she filled it with dry biscuits and placed it back down on the floor for him. Thomas preferred his dry food, but Michelle insisted that he have meat as well, convinced that biscuits alone were not good for his kidneys. While Thomas ate his breakfast, she finished making the tea and took it upstairs to her bedroom. She got back into bed and switched on the television. This was her favourite time of the day. The bed was still warm and she relaxed back on the pillows to enjoy her drink and catch up on the news.

The newscaster was interviewing a politician about the general state of the country. He was a member of the green party and was talking about environmentally friendly houses. It all sounded very expensive, yet another reason why first-time buyers could not afford to buy their own homes!

The house Michelle lived in had been in her family for as long as she could remember. Her father had brought her step-mother, Elizabeth, to the cottage after they were married and Michelle had found it difficult to share at first. It was a beautiful old place nestled in the forest, surrounded by Hazel trees, oaks and copper beeches. In the spring the entire floor between the trees was covered with a sea of bluebells, and now, in the autumn, the gold, brown and reds of the leaves were breathtaking. The hedge, which separated her property from the wood, was planted by her father and hid a wealth of natural wildlife. Her garden was constantly trying to merge with the woodland and she had a steady job keeping the lawn a lawn. If she left the gate open, rabbits and deer would venture out of the trees and graze among flowerbeds, while Thomas watched from the conservatory windows. Michelle could not imagine living anywhere more wonderful.

When she focused once more on the television, the newsreader was reporting on a mass breakout of the inmates of the reptile house at London Zoo. Snakes and lizards had managed to force open cages and escape through a locked skylight. Now they were loose in the park. Michelle puzzled over this while she showered and dressed, wondering if this seemingly innocent piece of news could be connected to Colandra's dilemma. Perhaps she was reading something into this that wasn't there. Animals do escape from cages, it happens all the time, she thought, but reptiles? She decided to keep this information from Colandra, as he had enough to worry about, but she intended to investigate this further, and see if there were any other strange stories in the press that might have a connection to his little problem.

Michelle worked at the library at Clifton, and when she arrived, everyone was talking about the breakout. The theories put forward by the staff were so farfetched they were laughable. The library was an old Victorian building and the heavy oak doors opened on to a large vestibule with an imposing, granite staircase. Its wrought iron balustrade curved graciously, with ornate leaves and scrolls, topped with a beautiful oak handrail. On the ground floor, opposite the oak doors, was the very comprehensive lending library, with a large children's department and a computerised information system. The staff room and changing areas were located to the right, and the small manager's office was to the left.

Michelle took off her coat, hung it up in the staff cloakroom and climbed the stairs to the computer room on the first floor. It was a large room, with big bay windows, looking out over the street. It had bookshelves all along the three walls not taken up by the window and it was obvious that the room doubled up as a reference library. Down the centre of the room were three long tables with a computer and monitor on each one and a swivel chair in front of each screen. At the far end of the room, and opposite the window, was a desk which Michelle used for her own computer, and next to the desk were two more tables, with a scanner and large printer on them. In the hall outside, was a photocopier which Michelle turned on before she entered the computer room.

She walked to the windows and looked down onto the street below, scanning the people for a glimpse of Colandra. She had not seen him since yesterday evening and was disappointed that he had not been in the cottage when she had risen that morning.

'Perhaps it was all a bad dream,' she thought. She turned back to the room and there, standing by her computer desk, was the very man himself.

Michelle jumped and said, "Oh, you gave me a fright. Can't you call out or something, so I know you're there?"

"Sorry," he said contritely.

Michelle was having a problem with communicating with Colandra. "If no-one else can see you and I talk to you, people will think that I am talking to myself!" she said.

"Well, I can go back to being a cronkel and communicate telepathically if that would be better," suggested Colandra. "It will be far easier for me and that way you don't have to talk to me, you just need to think what you want to say and I will understand you. You will hear my reply in your head."

Michelle thought about his idea for a few moments and answered, "Okay, let's give it a try."

Once more Colandra disappeared, but this time Michelle looked closely at where he had been. She could detect a shimmer, not unlike the heat haze one sees above a fire, making the bookcases behind him distort and warp.

"How is that?" thought Colandra. Michelle jumped. His voice was in her head, but not only that she could sense an anxiety, as if she could feel him, as well as hear him.

"You are right," came the voice in her head. "When I am as now, my energy is radiated all around me. Not only do you see me, you feel me too."

"Oh." she thought. "I like it."

"You sound surprised," came the reply, but in her head. It was most extraordinary.

"Oh. Well! I am. Everyone should communicate like this. It's great. Do I need to be near you to communicate with you?" thought Michelle.

"No. But the further away you are the more difficult it is. It also depends what is between you and me. If there are thick walls or you were underground then it would be very difficult. I might still be able to convey something, but it would be more basic, like a feeling rather than a coherent message."

"If we communicate by thought, does that mean that you can read my mind?" asked Michelle, suddenly feeling threatened. She was a private person and her thoughts had always been hers and hers alone.

"Not really. I can only hear the thoughts you send me," answered Colandra. "However I am very receptive to feelings, so if you are in an emotional state, whether it is a happy one or a sad one, I will be able to pick that up. Rather like a very sensitive or empathic person would be able to," he added.

Michelle thought about this for a moment. Did she actually have anything private in her life that she would find uncomfortable sharing with Colandra? Not really, she decided. And it would be quite nice to share her feelings with some else, someone who was sensitive and considerate. And so Colandra became a cronkel once more and Michelle found this much the best way to converse with him.

Chapter 10

Slaves of God

    Now that they had settled on a satisfactory way of communication, Michelle went out into the hall to start on the search for Colandra's body. At the top of the stairs and opposite the door into the computer room, was the archive library. This was closed to the public, but Michelle kept the key in her desk. Now she unlocked the room and walked straight through to the back where non-current archives were kept. Several shelves were lined up along the back wall and these were stacked with boxes all neatly arranged in date order. She decided to start at 1997, as that was twelve years from now, and quickly scanned the labels. She found the relevant one and lifted the box off the shelf, placing it carefully onto the table that stood in the centre of the room. When she opened the box a cloud of dust was disturbed from the top and filled the air like a fine mist. She stepped back quickly to avoid breathing it in and waited for it to settle. Inside the box were magazines and newspapers and she carefully took the magazines from the top of the pile and placed them to one side. Then she took out a small pile of about ten newspapers and placed them on the table next to the box. They had been sorted by date, so it was easy to find the ones that she wanted. All the summer ones were put to one side and the rest were put into a pile. She continued to do the same with all the newspapers until the box was empty. She sat down with the pile of newspapers and started to read through them.

"Just look at the headlines first," said Colandra. "After all it was quite a big event."

Michelle took the newspapers one at a time, month by month, and read each front page. January, February, March, nothing much there. Then April the 7th said,

"Massive explosion rocks the city. Hundreds feared dead." The article went on to say that a huge explosion in the underground rail network connecting London to Heathrow was reported to have been detonated by a group calling themselves 'The Slaves of God.' More details were in the following day's paper, but it was apparent by then that this was not the explosion that she and Colandra were looking for. They were disappointed, but continued to search. When they reached October they decided to have a tea break. It was nearly eleven o'clock and Michelle's stomach was rumbling, so she got up and went out, careful to lock up before going down to the staff coffee room.

Two of the other girls were already having coffee, so she made hers, and sat down with them, listening to their conversation. Vera, the girl who looked after the children's section, was discussing the reptile escapees.

"'Ow come them snakes opened the winder?" she exclaimed loudly. "They ain't got no 'ands. Them snakes and things couldn't do that really. I bet it were a con."

"The police are still investigating that," said Janet, a tall slim woman who was in charge of ordering new books. She had a cultured voice and had been to university.

"You're right though, it does sound a bit farfetched. I suppose it is possible that a lizard could open a cage, if it was specially taught," she said.

"It's a load of rubbish, if you ask me," said Vera indignantly. "They ain't got no brains, so 'ow could you teach 'em."

Michelle smiled, noticing that the more excited Vera got the worse her grammar became.

"What do you think Michelle?" she asked.

Michelle was thrown by her question.

"Oh. I don't know," she stammered. "I suppose it's possible to train reptiles. After all, they have taught chimps to talk, haven't they?"

"What are they talking about?" asked Colandra in Michelle's head, making her jump and choke on her coffee.

"You OK?" asked Vera. "You don't look right. You gonna faint or somefink? 'Ere, sit by the winder and ge' a bi' of fresh air."

She took Michelle's arm and helped her to a chair next to the open window.

"I'm fine now, thanks." said Michelle, after taking some deep breathes. "I'll get back upstairs."

She got up and beat a hasty retreat, back to the sanctuary of her department.

She went in to the reference library and continued to look at the newspapers, but October had no more to offer than had the first four months of the year. Assuming Colandra's assumption was correct and the incident had occurred during a cold month, there were only two months left to search, however, there was still nothing. Michelle repacked the box and took down 1998. She repeated the search as she had done for 1997, but still found nothing. 1999 was the same and she was starting to lose hope.

"There doesn't seem to be anything," she said forlornly. "I will go backwards from twelve years instead, and see what that brings."

So she took down the box for 1996. She separated the magazines and the irrelevant newspapers, as she had done for the other years, but found nothing for the first few months, then, voila, she found it! November 28th 1996. There, in huge writing across the front page, was "The 'Slaves of God' strike again! Another explosion hits our city. Is nobody safe from these fanatics?"

It went on to say that a suicide bomber had boarded a double-decker, sightseeing, bus in Bristol City. According to eyewitnesses, he had walked to the front of the lower deck, tapped on the driver's window, and as the driver turned round to see who it was, he had detonated the bomb.

"No wonder I remember his face," said Colandra. "He was right next to me."

There was another article on page four, which stated that the separate compartment was the only thing that saved the bus drivers life. All the passengers were either injured or killed, and there was devastation over a quarter mile radius.

Michelle read all there was to read, and then turned to the next day's paper. The front page was again devoted to the explosion, stating that seven people on the bus had died and twenty three had been injured. Two cars were also caught up in the attack. One was a Vauxhall Cavalier that was being driven by a woman and she was critically injured. The other car was a small sports car being driven by a young man, who was taking his fiancée to visit his family. His car was pushed through a shop window by the blast and he suffered facial cuts and a broken pelvis. His Fiancée had been hurled from the car, and apart from cuts, she escaped injury. All the shop windows next to the bus were blown out and several people had suffered cuts from flying glass. Police were still investigating the claim that the explosion was committed by the group calling themselves 'The Slaves of God', but as yet they were not in a position to confirm that.

"Well, there you are," said Michelle. "Let's look at the next day's paper."

She opened the paper for the thirtieth and again the front page was devoted to the explosion. Three people were still critical in hospital, including the bus driver and the woman driver of the Vauxhall. The article continued on page five and named the victims from the bus, including the bomber, Simon Creasy. He had lived in Birmingham, and seemed to all his friends, as a perfectly normal person. His parents were devastated and could not understand why he had done this. They had never heard of 'The Slaves of God' and their son had never spoken about them. The police had searched his bedroom in their house on Claymore Street and taken several boxes of items away, including a computer and laptop.

The driver was in a critical, but stable condition, though they were unable to disclose his name until his next of kin had been informed of his accident, and as yet the woman driver, who remained in a coma, had not been identified.

The next three newspapers had nothing about the explosion in them and Michelle was about to discard the fourth, when a small article caught her eye. On page fourteen there was a photograph of a woman with the caption underneath which read "Woman driver remains in a coma, after bus explosion. Police are appealing for anyone who can help in identifying her."

Michelle spread out the page and looked at the photograph. It was very fuzzy, but something about it disturbed her. She read the paragraph.

"The woman injured in last week's explosion, known only as Jane Doe, remains in a coma and was transferred to a special unit today. She has had to undergo a live-saving operation to stop a bleed in her brain, and has a fractured pelvis, right arm and right leg. There is hope that, as her brain recovers, she will awaken. Anyone who can shed some light as to her name should contact Bristol Police department. She is believed to be in her fifties and not thought to be local."

There was nothing about any of the other survivors or the other dead persons. Michelle took the newspaper out to the hall and photocopied the article about the woman, put the copy on her desk, and then went back to continue searching for more news, but there was nothing else. She jotted down all the information that she thought had any significance to the case, put everything back in their right boxes, tidied up and went back to the computer department.

When she got back, Vera was standing in front of the main desk tapping on the surface. Michelle had a soft spot for the girl. She was about twenty, overweight and dowdy looking; however, she was actually a very pretty girl. Her auburn hair softly curled around her face, but she always had a worried look, as if something bad was about to happen. Michelle would dearly like to take her in hand and give her a complete make-over. Now Vera stood looking at Michelle accusingly and said, "Where've you bin? I've bin waitin' ages. There was a phone call for yer, but yer ain't answerin' yer phone. I've 'ad to come all the way up 'ere to give yer the message and when I get 'ere there you are, gone! What yer up to then, sneakin' around the place?"

"I am not sneaking around," said Michelle, chuckling to herself. 'If only you knew the half of it,' she thought. "I have every right to leave my department if I so wish," she continued, out loud. "Well what's the message then?"

"Oh yeah. Um. Janet wrote it down 'cos she thought I wouldn't remember it, cheeky basket! 'Ere you are." She passed a piece of paper to Michelle and stood there staring.

"That's all. You can go now. You must have plenty to do," Michelle told her.

"Oh yeah. I s'pose so," said Vera. She turned to go, and then looked around, as if seeing something in the room.

"'Ere, did you see somefink walk across the room just then?" asked Vera, a puzzled look on her face.

"What sort of something?" asked Michelle in reply.

"I dunno. I'm sure I saw somefink walk across there."

"No! I can't say I did," replied Michelle.

"Must 'ave bin a ghost!" continued Vera. "This old buildin' bound to 'ave a ghost or two."

"You must have other things to do rather than standing here speculating about ghosts!" said Michelle.

Vera shrugged her shoulders and stomped off down the stairs, muttering to herself.

"Can't even be bothered to say thank you. They all think I'm their bloody slave, they do. Vera, do this, Vera, do that. Bloody up and down the stairs all day."

Michelle read the note and saw that it was from Mrs Barber, the headmistress from Saint Peters, the local primary school. She wanted her to ring back and make a date for a school visit. The children in the top class, and who were due to leave in the June, always had a few computer lessons at the library. The school did not have its own computer room and it was useful for the children to have a little knowledge about computers before they went up to secondary school. Michelle enjoyed teaching and always received good feedback from the children, some even writing to thank her for the trip. She sat down at the desk and rang Mrs Barber back, arranging for seven children to visit on the following Thursday afternoon.

She then decided to log onto the Internet to see if she could find any more information on the explosion. She opened the search engine and typed in...current affairs, November 1996, explosion...

then clicked search. She was amazed at how many explosions there were in November 1996. She had forgotten to ask for U.K. only and the search engine had listed several hundred, some of which were natural phenomena. She corrected her error, included the word 'bus' in the search, and the computer came up trumps.

There were several options relating to the suicide bombing, so she decided to start at the top and work her way down the list. The first one had virtually all the information that was in the newspapers. It went into more details of the injuries, but otherwise it did not add anything new. Number two went into the group calling themselves 'The slaves of God.' The article did not have very much information about the group except that the leader was disenchanted with the human race. He believed that the world was moving too far from the real issues of why we were on the earth and he was intent on reminding everyone, by sabotaging technology and leisure pursuits.

The third reference went into the bomb itself, what it was likely to have been made of, the detonation device and the method of triggering it. The article was slightly disconcerting, there being virtually all the information one would need to make a bomb. The next reference was all about the bus route, the Bus Company and its employees.

Dawson's Excursions was a small bus company that specialised in open topped buses, showing the local sights to tourists. They did not name the bus driver of the fateful bus, but they did mention that he was the youngest bus driver they had and that he was airlifted to the Brunswick spinal injuries unit in Birmingham. He had suffered head and back injuries and had been in a coma since the accident. Michelle was very excited that she had found Colandra's body.

'That was easy,' she thought. 'Perhaps too easy!'

Colandra's voice came back, "I have to agree with you. Can you find out where the Brunswick Unit is, and then I can visit it."

Michelle typed in the Brunswick unit and then clicked on the location tab, so that Colandra could have a look at where it was. Once she was satisfied that they could get no more information from the computer, she logged out and said briskly, "One thirty, time for lunch."

Colandra told her that he was going to go to the Brunswick Unit to see what he could find there and the next moment he was gone. Michelle knew he was no longer with her, not only because she could not see the shimmer that she associated with him, but his whole presence was gone. She was left with a strange feeling of loss, as if some physical part of her body was missing.

She slowly walked down the stairs to the coffee room, got her coat and bag and went out to the car. Just up the road from the library was a snack bar, where she bought a ham salad sandwich, a packet of crisps and a cold drink. Then she drove to the local gardens and parked in the car park. She walked onto the grass and down to her favourite spot, a grassy slope overlooking a small pond, took off her coat and spread it on the ground to sit on. Slowly eating her lunch, she thought about the progress they had made. From not knowing anything yesterday, they now knew what had happened, to whom, and when, however they still had no idea who had done it and why nor did they have a name for Colandra's body. Perhaps Colandra would find the answers at the hospital.

Chapter 11

False Hope

Colandra soon found himself outside the Brunswick spinal and head injuries unit. There were large heavy doors at the entrance, and as it was not visiting time, there was no one entering. Colandra knew that he would not be able to pass through the walls of the building, so he flew around the hospital to look for an open window and spied one on the third floor. Passing through it he saw that he was in some sort of utility room. Large yellow plastic bags were piled in one corner and cleaning materials were neatly stacked on shelves on the right hand wall. Men in overalls were coming and going, either adding to the bag pile, or collecting things from the shelves. It was during one such moment that Colandra was able to escape and he made his way to the nurse's station to see if he could find out where his man might be.

Not knowing the name of the person impeded him somewhat, but he hoped that he would recognise the name when he saw it. He did not relish the thought of having to look at every patient in the building.

The nurse's station was a counter in the centre of the corridor, with bays to the right and left. Each bay accommodated one person with all the paraphernalia required to look after them. Along the side of each bay was a cupboard for all the disposable items needed to nurse the patient, and at the head of each bed was a ventilator. On the wall, above the head of the beds, was a rail running the whole length of the room, which housed the electrics and gases, oxygen, carbon dioxide etc. In the ceiling of each bay was a hoist, which could be moved all around the bed and to each side of it, so that the patient could be hoisted up or down the bed, and also out into a chair. The bays were not curtained off, but the cupboards provided an adequate division to each area. The patients were not conscious, so it was unnecessary to provide privacy, but visitors, no doubt felt better for having some sort of private area to see their loved ones in. The nurses were moving from patient to patient, monitoring and noting things down on the charts that hung above the cupboards. They talked to the patients as if they could hear and understand all that was going on, while they changed I.V. fluids or altered settings on the ventilators. Every now and then a warning beep would sound and a nurse would scurry off to see what was wrong. In all it was a busy, vibrant area, with the nurses and helpers, laughing and chatting to each other. Colandra was surprised, as he had imagined that it would be quiet and sombre like a church, the only noise being that of the patients breathing.

He moved along the bays, looking at the unconscious people, amazed at how many men and women were in this state, of being between life and death.

Above each person was a small, shimmering, light, connected by a thin pulsating thread. At first Colandra did not recognise it, and assumed it was something to do with the nursing equipment, but then one light retracted into the person below it. At that moment an alarm sounded and nurses came running to investigate what was the matter.

"He's coming round," said one of the nurses, "Call Doctor Brown. I will try switching off the machine and see if he can breathe on his own."

Colandra suddenly realised that the small light was the person's entity, waiting for its human body to recover enough for it to return, just as this one had done.

'Amazing," he thought. 'Just amazing. That's what I should be like, golden and vibrant.'

He moved back down to the reception area on the ground floor, just in time to hear one of the nurses talking on the telephone.

Colandra over-heard her saying, "I am sorry Mr. Shaw, but we can only keep your wife here for twelve weeks. You will need to look for long-term care elsewhere. I can give you a list of excellent care homes in your area when you next visit and that will help your search."

She listened to the gentleman on the other end of the line and then replied, "Yes that will be fine. What is the name of her social worker?"

Again, another pause. "He is very good. He will give you advice. I am sorry that I can't be of more help."

She listened to Mr Shaw's reply and then answered, "That will be fine. I will see you on Friday. Goodbye Mr Shaw," and with that she put the receiver down.

Colandra was stunned by this conversation, as he suddenly realised that he was looking in the wrong place. If these patients were only kept at the Brunswick unit for up to twelve weeks, then the man he sought could not possibly be still here. He must have been transferred somewhere else, but where? He must return to the library and ask Michelle if she had any ideas of where to search for the answer. He left the unit as the doors opened for visitors and wished himself at the library, entering it and returning to the computer department just as Michelle was closing up the room. He thought a hello to her, which made her jump and gasp.

"Don't do that!" she shouted. "You scared the living daylights out of me!"

"Sorry," said Colandra," But something important has happened. I have been to the hospital, and realise that we are looking in the wrong place."

Colandra explained to Michelle the experience he had had, and asked her if she had any thoughts as to how they might discover where the man could have been transferred.

"I can look on the computer again if you would like me to?" said Michelle, turning one of the machines on.

"Can you look for places where people would be cared for if they were in a coma for a long time?" asked Colandra, looking at the monitor screen.

"Yes, of course," replied Michelle and she found a site that listed all the care homes in the British Isles.

"Wow, that is a lot of care facilities," exclaimed Colandra.

"Just stick to the ones in this area please," he said.

He watched Michelle print off a list of establishments in the south and south west of England.

"Is that all you wanted?" she asked, before logging off and shutting the computer down.

Colandra followed Michelle down the stairs to the staff room. Everyone else had left the library, so after collecting her coat, she set the alarm, locked the front door and walked through the car park to her car. He thought how lucky he was to have had this young woman chosen for him to help in his search. Not only was she beautiful, but she was also intelligent and practical. He wondered if they would have any future together, once he had been re-united with his body, or whether they would each go their separate ways. 'Only time will tell,' he thought, wistfully.

Chapter 12

About Michelle

After supper Michelle sat relaxing in the sitting room, with Colandra opposite her in the guise of the thin man.

"Tell me about yourself," he said. "I have talked a lot about me, but I don't really know much about you."

Michelle was not used to talking about herself and felt a little self-conscious. She took a deep breath and started.

"I was born in April 1971in one of the houses in the village. My father was an artist, and my mother was a teacher. I never knew my mother, as she died when I was six months old. I was my father's princess and we did all sorts of things together. When I was about five, my grandfather died and left this house to my father. We moved into it a few months later and I loved it from the moment we arrived. When my father married again, I found it very difficult. I was used to having my father all to myself, and suddenly I was no longer his number one girl. I remember making my stepmother's life hell for about a year, and then I nearly fell off a horse. We were all out visiting a country park and they had horses available for riding. I told my father that I had learnt to ride at school, which was a lie. Anyway I was plonked on this horse by a girl groom, who then smacked the horse's rump, making it rear up and take off at about fifty miles an hour. Of course, I was terrified. The next thing I remember is my stepmother riding along side of me and grabbing the reins. She shouted at me to hang onto the mane and grip hard with my thighs. Then she pulled the horses head round, which made it stop.

As she pulled me off the horses back she whispered in my ear, "We won't tell Daddy that you can't ride, O.K.?"

After that day we were the best of friends. She taught me to ride properly and we would go riding every weekend. When I was older, the two of us took a riding holiday every year, and even when she was too old to ride, we would still take our holidays together. She loved the countryside and this house was her sanctuary.

My father was an artist and painted landscapes, many of which I have hanging up here in the house. He was asked to provide some paintings for an exhibition in Bristol, which were seen by the local Mayor. He commissioned my father to paint various landscapes of local interest for all the civic buildings. Many of them are still exhibited and he has ten especially good ones hanging in our local art gallery. I have been offered money for them, but I prefer many people to see them, rather than just one. When I was eighteen I went to college to sit my 'A' levels and received good passes in them all. I was offered a place at Reading University to study computer analysis and programming. I left with a degree and an offer of a teaching job at the same university, which I did for about three years.

Then I needed a break, so I worked in the Channel Islands for a few years. I loved it there, but I came home after my father suffered a stroke. My stepmother, Elizabeth, wanted to nurse him at home and it would have been impossible for her to do it alone, so I came back to help her. I started working at the local library and doing what I could for my father in the evenings and at weekends. It gave my stepmother a break, which she really needed. Unfortunately she died of a heart attack a year later and I went part-time at the library to continue caring for Dad until his death in May 2001. I couldn't have kept him at home if it weren't for my helper, Pauline, a marvellous woman who lives in the village. Even though I was expecting it, I was quite devastated when he died. Now I continue to work part-time at the library and that suits me fine. I put all Mum and Dad's stuff into the loft, as I couldn't face going through everything .I chucked out the furniture that I didn't like and bought a few new things. I've lived here ever since."

"Have you no other relatives, aunts or uncles?" asked Colandra.

"No. Not as far as I know," said Michelle. "My father was an only child, and I don't k now anything about my mother's side of the family. I put an announcement in the paper, letting people know that my father had died and how to get in touch, but no-one has made contact. When my stepmother died, I met some relatives on her side of the family, but after her funeral I never heard from them again."

"That is so sad," said Colandra. "Families are so important, especially as you get older."

"I am fine. I have always been independent, so I don't miss having relatives around me. At some stage I will go through my father and stepmother's things, but at the moment I really don't feel like it," said Michelle. She suddenly felt incredibly tired. It was always an ordeal speaking about her past. There was part of her that resented her father for not having told her more about her mother, but she knew that it was a particularly sensitive issue and had been discouraged from bringing up the subject.

Colandra must have picked up her weariness because he said, with a rueful smile, "I am keeping you up. We have a busy day tomorrow, so you had better get some sleep."

"Yes, I am tired," replied Michelle, and as she stood up, Colandra disappeared. Michelle was disappointed that she had not been able to say goodnight and a little peeved that he had disappeared so suddenly. As she mounted the stairs to her bedroom a small voice whispered in her ear, "Sorry, Michelle! Goodnight, sleep tight, don't let the bugs bite!" And Michelle smiled a quiet smile.

Chapter 13

The search begins

Michelle and Colandra studied the lists of nursing homes that they had downloaded from the Internet. The list was divided into county health authority areas and each area had dozens. They were in alphabetical order and listed the type of patient they were registered to care for. Michelle crossed through the ones that did not care for adults and also those that cared for the mentally infirm. That still left a fair number, but they both knew that it was never going to be easy. Each county had about fifty care facilities, but only a few that specialised in long term care, so they decided to start with them.

They began at the top of the country and worked their way down, highlighting the ones that looked promising. Colandra was constrained by time on Earth just like everyone else; however, he could move very much faster. Even so, neither of them wanted to waste time looking in areas that were unlikely to yield their man. So to that end they concentrated on the south west.

Michelle printed out a list of nursing homes and their addresses, so that she could show Colandra where each one was, and he set off on his quest. She meanwhile took a similar list, and set off in her car to search each one.

Her first goal was Weston super Mare and three care facilities along the beach front.

St Anne's was an imposing Victorian building with a beautiful portico. She climbed the steps, and entered the hall. On the right was a grand staircase and on the left was a sitting area. Above the door next to the stairs was a sign for reception. She went in and directly opposite the door was a desk, where a middle-aged woman sat smiling at her. "Can I help you?" she asked.

"I hope so," said Michelle. "I am looking for a place for my uncle, who is in a coma. I have been told to look for long term care and Social Services gave me your nursing home as a possibility."

"Oh," said the woman. "I am so sorry. We only care for patients in a coma for three years. After that time they are moved to a specialist unit. I can give you a list of them, if you would like me to. We do not own them, but I believe they are very good and provide excellent care."

Michelle was delighted. She would not need to trek all over the area if she had a list to consult.

"Thank you. That would be very helpful," she said to the woman, who took a booklet from one of the drawers of the desk and handed it to Michelle.

Michelle went back to the car and looked at the booklet. She cross referenced it with the list that she had printed off and noticed that most of the long term care homes were owned by a health group called Haven Health. One of the nursing homes that she had high-lighted to visit was Farrington Lodge. This home was also owned by Haven Health, so she decided to visit it. It was a large, fairly new building situated a little way from the sea front, down a wide, tree lined road. Michelle drove her mini into the front car park, only to be told by a scruffy man in overalls that the car park was for consultants only. She had to go round the back to park.

'Okay,' she thought, sarcastically. 'That's a good start. They really do want to make a good impression!'

She walked to the front door and rang the bell. A young woman, dressed in a nurse's uniform, opened the door.

"Can I help you?" she asked.

"I hope so. I would like to speak to someone about vacancies please," asked Michelle.

"Do come in. I will tell Mrs Keen that you are here and she ushered Michelle into the waiting room and disappeared. A few moments later she reappeared with a tall, slim, middle-aged woman, dressed completely in black.

"Hello. I'm Mrs Keen, the manager of this facility. How can I help?" she said, holding out her hand to Michelle.

Michelle shook hands with her and said, "My name is Sonia Jones," she lied. "I am looking for a place for my uncle."

"Let me take you through to my office," said Mrs Keen. "We can talk better in there. Colette, please bring some tea through."

Mrs Keen led the way through one of the doors into a very spacious office over-looking the grounds. She ushered Michelle to a sitting area and indicated one of two armchairs. They both sat down and Mrs Keen asked Michelle to tell her a bit about her uncle's state of health. Before Michelle had a chance to speak, Colette came in with a tray of tea and biscuits. She set the tray down on the coffee table between the two women and left the room, quietly closing the door behind her.

Mrs Keen proceeded to pour out tea for them both and Michelle said, "My uncle was involved in a traffic accident three years ago and he is in a short term, acute care facility in London. Although he is in good health, he is completely unconscious. I have been told by the doctors that he will not wake up, but you can never tell in these circumstances. You hear of people who have been in a coma for years, suddenly waking up! The manager there has told me that I need to either give them permission to withdraw his food and allow him to die, or find somewhere permanent for him. To complicate matters, I am about to immigrate to New Zealand, so it is imperative that I find somewhere that I can trust to care for him properly."

Mrs Keen sighed, "I am so sorry," she said sympathetically. "I hear of more and more stories like yours. Our health group has outstanding facilities and I believe that it gives the best care in the country. We don't cut corners or cheat our residents with hidden costs."

"I know that a lot of nursing homes have a time limit for people in a coma. Does that apply here?" ask Michelle, trying to look anxious.

"No, there is no time limit, but we don't actually cater for that group of client here," the manager replied. "We have special care facilities just for residents like your uncle. They need more nursing hours than we can give, so they are better looked after in one of our country homes, where the surroundings are more peaceful. The homes are all purpose built and they comply with all the newest regulations."

Michelle was excited by this news. It was the most promising she had heard. It would be well worth investigating further.

"Would it be possible for you to send me a brochure of the care homes? Will I need to telephone them before visiting or can I just drop in? I know the Social Services say that I should be able to visit without calling first, but I realise that you are all very busy people. Will that pose a problem?" she asked.

"There should be no problem visiting. I will let the company know. The chairman will be pleased to see you. If you can give me your address then I will make sure that Colette sends you some brochures today," said Mrs Keen.

Luckily Michelle had designed some business cards on the computer before going out and now handed one to the manager.

Mrs Keen thanked her and asked her if she would like to look around the home adding, "It is not the same as the sort of facility that your uncle will require, but it will give you an idea of the standard Haven Health works to."

"Oh, yes please. Thank you," said Michelle and followed the manager out into a back hall and up a flight of stairs. The building was modern and airy, built on the same lines as a high class hotel, rather than a typical nursing home. Michelle followed Mrs Keen into a large, comfortable lounge, with floor to ceiling windows, overlooking the well-kept garden. There were several elderly people sitting in the room, chatting to one another.

"Hello everyone," Mrs Keen called as she entered the room. "Are you all okay?"

There were murmurs around the room and one lady called out, "Will we still be going out to the art exhibition at the Town hall?"

"Of Course, Miss Rose. I believe the mini bus is coming at two thirty, so you will have plenty of time to get ready," replied Mrs Keen.

"Oh, lovely. I am so looking forward to it," said Miss Rose.

Mrs Keen led Michelle out of the room and continued their tour, looking at rooms and bathing facilities. "Do any of your patients, sorry, residents stay in bed," asked Michelle.

"Only if they are ill," replied Mrs Keen. "Most of our residents are either elderly, convalescing or need monitoring, they are not ill. People seem to think that the elderly are sick, but old age is not an illness, it is more a state of mind. If you are treated as if you are sick, you feel sick, and vice versa. If they were at home, they would be getting up, making the bed, cooking the breakfast, doing the shopping etc. So why should they suddenly be bed bound when they arrive here?" she went on.

As if to punctuate the tale, a small frail lady was walking towards them using a wheeled walking frame.

"Good morning Mrs Lawrence," said Mrs Keen. "How are you today? Did you enjoy your visit to the garden centre on Saturday?"

The lady paused and looked up at the Manager.

"I am very well, thank you, and yes it was an interesting visit. It is amazing what they can grow these days. I must have seen twenty different sorts of daffodil bulbs for sale. In my day you could buy yellow daffodils and red tulips. That was it really. Now you get all sorts of colours and sizes, some with scents, some with frills. It's quite extraordinary. I really enjoyed it. Thank you. And who is this young lady? Are you coming to stay?" she asked with a twinkle in her eye.

"Oh no. This is Miss Jones. I am showing her around," replied Mrs Keen.

"It is nice to meet you," said Michelle.

"The pleasure is all mine," said Mrs Lawrence, winking at Malinda before continuing on her way.

"She is ninety-seven, you know," said Mrs Keen, proudly. "There is hope for us all."

When they reached the front hall, Mrs Keen shook hands with Michelle and assured her that she would send her the brochures.

"Thank you for your time and showing me your beautiful home. I must say that I am very impressed," said Michelle, genuinely.

"Goodbye Miss Jones. Thank you for visiting us," said Mrs Keen.

Michelle went back to the car and visited three more homes on her list, but none were as promising as the Haven Health Group. She was looking forward to reading the brochure about the other homes and learning about the set up that Haven Health had.

She had had a very full day and when she got back home she was worn out. She kicked off her shoes and massaged her feet, before putting her slippers on. Thomas came out of the kitchen purring loudly and meowing at Michelle, so she picked him up and went into the kitchen.

"You hungry then, you soppy thing. Here you are, beef and carrots, just what you need to keep you coat sleek and glossy," she said, setting him down on the kitchen floor with his bowl.

She busied herself preparing a baked potato, with beans and cheese, and then poured herself a glass of white wine. She went into the lounge with her tray of food, pulled over a small table and set the tray down on it. Then she sat down in the armchair and moved the table over her knees. She had just taken a sip of her wine when Colandra appeared in front of her. She jumped, nearly spilling her wine down the front of her dress.

"Don't do that, for goodness sake. Arrive in the kitchen or somewhere else and call out. You scared the living daylights out of me!"

"Sorry. I will try to remember that next time. How did you get on?" said Colandra, contritely. Michelle smiled at him. "I think I got on well," she said. "I visited some of the homes on my list and at the second one I was told about Haven Health, a health care company that caters for long term coma patients. It was definitely promising. The manager there, Mrs Keen, is going to send me some brochures. What about you, any joy?"

"Well, yes and no," he said. "I did not find my man, but I did find our Jane Doe!"

"Wow. Good on you. Tell me all about it," said Michelle, excitedly.

Colandra proceeded to tell her about a conversation that he had overheard at one of the facilities that he had visited.

"Two nurses were admitting an elderly woman who had head injuries after a hit and run accident," explained Colandra. "One of the nurses mentioned another woman that they had cared for, who was in a similar condition. She had been transferred to a place called Carlton House. Apparently she had been in a coma after a bus explosion. She must be the same woman, surely!"

Michelle smiled at Colandra's enthusiasm. It would seem very probable that she was the woman injured in the same explosion as Colandra.

"I agree. It has to be worth a look," said Michelle. "Perhaps our man is in the same place."

"You forget that the man was taken to the local emergency hospital, then Brunswick spinal unit in Birmingham. Just because they were both at the scene, doesn't mean that they will end up together. It would be great if they were, but it is highly unlikely." said Colandra.

"Tomorrow I will continue my search for the man, but it would be nice to see the woman, and you never know, that may lead on to other things."

"Okay," said Michelle. "I have to go to work, but I would like to investigate the Haven Health Group. They seem too good to be true. Now I am going to bed, so I will see you tomorrow evening. We did well today. Let's hope we do as well tomorrow. Good night Colandra."

After Colandra had disappeared Michelle sat for a few moments thinking. It was strange how, just a few days ago, she would have hated sharing her home, in fact her life, with any other person, but Colandra had entered her world and turned it upside down. She enjoyed his company when he was with her and missed him when he went. Feelings that she never thought she would have!

Chapter 14

The book

    The next day it was raining, so Michelle took a packed lunch to work with her. She disliked going out in the rain at lunchtime, so, on days like this, she normally ate in the coffee room. When she reached her department, she finished her normal tasks as quickly as possible and then logged on to the Internet. She typed in Haven Health and found that they had a very professional web site, obviously well managed and updated. She read all there was on the home page and then opened all the tabs. It was a vast health group, with many, large, purpose-built hospitals and nursing homes. In addition, the group managed many smaller homes, owned by private individuals.

    Michelle went back to the home page and saw that there was the facility to search using key words, so she typed in 'Coma' and clicked search. It first gave her a medical fact sheet, which was very informative. It gave a list of all the different types of coma, including medically induced coma, reversible and irreversible coma, and brain stem coma. She had not realised just how many types of coma there were, and that a person could be dead, but still have a heartbeat. She read all there was to read and realised that a person in a coma for twelve years may not have any quality of life when they eventually awoke. Neither she nor

Colandra had considered that. They may find this man's body, but it was imperative that they carefully examine his medical condition before Colandra re-entered it, or he may be doomed to a worthless life.

Michelle moved on to the next tab, which was about the group's specialist homes for long and short-term coma patients. These were organised into counties and were either their own purpose built homes or privately owned ones. They all practised the same philosophy and embraced all the health authority guidelines. Some had an asterisk next to their name and she wondered what that meant. Perhaps they were the privately owned ones, she thought. She scanned quickly through the list of names and her heart missed a beat as she saw one she recognised, Carlton House! Colandra had mentioned the place yesterday. It was where Jane Doe had been moved to. Michelle was excited. At last she had found a connection to Haven Health. She noted that it did not have an asterisk next to the name, but was under-lined. There was another place mentioned, Hampton Green Hospital, that was also under-lined.

Just then some teenagers from the St. Mark's college came into the department. They were frequent visitors and Michelle got up, smiling.

"Hi girls. How are things?" she asked.

"Great thanks, Miss Golding," said one of the girls. "We have a new assignment, Purcell and his opera. Can we go on the Internet to have a look for some stuff about him please?"

"Of course you can," said Michelle and she showed them to one of the computers. It was already up and running, so all they had to do was sign in with their password. Once she had them settled, she went back to her desk. She printed off all the information about Haven Health and the lists of nursing homes, and then went into findaplace.com, the site she always used for travel information. She asked it how to get to Hampton Green hospital, near Bristol, and Carlton House in Honiton, Somerset, and it immediately showed her two maps, with written explanations of how to get there. She did not bother to read them, but simply printed off copies and shut down the computer.

By the time she had logged the college girls off, it was time for lunch, so she locked up the department and went down to the coffee room. Janet was the only person in there when she arrived.

"Where is everyone?" she asked.

"They have all gone to the book store. Apparently Kenneth Crow is down there signing his latest best seller. Vera is potty about him and wanted a signed copy. She reckons it will be worth millions one day," said Janet.

"Will it? Be worth millions?" asked Michelle.

"I haven't the foggiest notion," laughed Janet. "But she can always live in hope."

Michelle laughed. Vera was always collecting things in the hope that they will be worth a fortune sometime in the future.

'Her house must be full of useless junk by now,' she thought, smiling to herself. She went to her locker, took out her lunch and put the information about the Haven Health Group inside, underneath her handbag. She sat back down next to Janet, opened her packed lunch and bit into her sandwich.

After a few moments of silence Michelle turned to Janet and asked, "You've lived in Bristol all your life, haven't you?"

"Yes, pretty much," replied Janet. "I was born in Surrey, but moved to Somerset when my father was stationed at Locking. He was in the RAF. We moved to Bristol when he came out of the service, oh, twenty five years ago now, I suppose. Why do you ask?"

Michelle hesitated a moment.

"Do you remember a bus explosion in Bristol?" she asked innocently. "I think it was a suicide bomber. It must have been in the late nineties."

Janet swivelled around in her chair to face Michelle.

"Funny you should ask that," she said. "I was talking to my friend about it just the other day. I used to live almost opposite where that bus exploded. My cat was killed in the explosion. Our house, the house next door and the next one to that were actually moved three inches from their foundations. All our windows were blown out and the services to the house were severed. We had to be moved into rented accommodation while everything was fixed.

All three houses had to be knocked down and re-built. It was a terrible upheaval."

Michelle was astonished.

"I don't understand why I can't remember it," she said, puzzled.

"Well, where were you at that time? Were you away, perhaps?" asked Janet.

Of course, now she remembered! In 1996 she would still have been in Jersey! She had been acting as an advisor for the Jersey Zoo, setting up some software for their orang-utan breeding programme. Why hadn't she remembered that? 'How silly of me,' she thought. No wonder she had not heard about it.

Her thoughts were interrupted when a very excited Vera burst into the room.

"I got it! I got it!" she shouted triumphantly, holding aloft the treasured book.

"Look. 'E signed it, 'to beau'iful Vera, long may you enjoy the wonder of readin'.' Isn't that lovely," she sighed. "'E's much more 'andsome in the flesh. So nice as well. Signin' all them books. The queue went out the door, nearly as far as Woolworths," she said, plonking herself down in the chair by the window. The others followed more slowly, raising their eyes to heaven. Michelle had to stifle a giggle, lest Vera was offended.

"She is so embarrassing," said Beth, whose matronly feathers were obviously ruffled. She was the eldest member of staff, at fifty seven years of age, and wore twin sets and plaid skirts. She was a lovely person and took on the role of mother to all her colleagues.

"She pushed herself to the front of the queue, shouting that she only had ten minutes for her lunch break. I ask you, she is a liability."

Ricky and George, the other librarians, sat down on the remaining chairs.

"I don't know how you can say he is good looking," retorted Ricky, whose handsome face wore a scowl. He was Italian, and although nearly forty years old, still lived with his mother.

"He wears a toupee and has bags under his eyes big enough to fit two weeks holiday clothes in! In any case, he writes a load of drivel, if you ask me."

"You're just jealous," said Vera. "E's been voted the third most 'andsome man in England, 'e 'as," she said. "Anyways, I like 'is writin'. Is books are always excitin'. An' 'e don't write drivel. Its good stuff. Ain't that right Janet?"

"Well, It does seem to be a bit, well, politically incorrect," Janet said tactfully.

"Politically incorrect!" retorted Ricky. "Its inflammatory, that's what it is. If I didn't know any different I'd say he was deliberately trying to get people to rise up against the government. I'm surprised he gets away with it!"

And at that, he got up and flounced out of the room.

"Whatever's the matter wiv 'im? It's only a book, for goodness sake."

George got up and made some tea. "Tea Vera? Michelle do you want a refill?" he asked.

"Oh. Yeah. Great. Thanks George," replied Vera.

"I'm fine thanks George. I've got a coke'" said Michelle, raising the can in her hand.

George was a strange man. He kept himself to himself, not mixing well with the other staff. No-one knew where he lived or what he did with his spare time. At work he was pleasant enough, but he was sometimes guilty of picking fights with the younger library users. Pauline, the library manager, had given him two verbal warnings and he knew that if he didn't toe the line his next mistake would see him without a job. Michelle did not dislike him, but she found him uncomfortable to be with.

The atmosphere in the room was somewhat icy after Ricky's outburst, so Michelle finished her lunch and went back upstairs.

The rest of the day was busy with people coming and going through the department. A group of ramblers wanted access to the reference library, to look among the ordinance survey maps for footpaths and rights of way through the local farmland.

'Best of luck to you,' thought Michelle, knowing how fiercely protective the local farming community was. She was just locking up before going home, when she heard a commotion at the foot of the stairs. The stairs wound round almost in a circle and she could see a group of people below. She quickly ran down, hearing Vera's voice getting louder and louder, higher and higher.

"It's gawn I tell yer! It's gawn! It was in me locker."

Then she heard the soothing voice of Beth, saying. "Are you sure, Vera? Think, dear, could you have taken it out when you had tea, just to look at it again."

"No I never did," cried Vera. "I put it in me locker, in the bag, so's it'd keep clean. Someone took it. They've nicked it, that's what they've done, nicked it!" she glared round at everyone, just as Michelle arrived in the lobby. Vera burst into tears.

"Oh, Michelle, someone's nicked me book. Me precious book."

"There, there, Vera. We'll sort it out, don't worry." reassured Michelle.

As the longest serving member of staff, Michelle always assumed the position of authority when the manager was away and now she led Vera into the coffee room, followed closely by Beth, who said to Janet.

"Get rid of the customers and get everyone else in here. We need to resolve this before we go home. Vera may have mislaid it, but it must be found."

As Janet went out, Michelle sat Vera down and pulled up a chair opposite her.

She took Vera's hands and said gently. "Now Vera, I want you to tell me exactly what happened from the time I left the coffee room after lunch and now. Think carefully and take your time. We're none of us going home till we find your book, okay."

"Okay," gulped Vera.

All the rest of the staff had come into the room by then, so they sat down quietly and listened. Vera glanced up at them and then looked back at Michelle.

"After you'd gone, I looked at the book, mainly the back, cos there's always a bit about the writer, see, so I read what was writ' about 'im. Kenneth Crow, that is. It was intrestin' cos it said 'e was born in India. I never knew that. 'E don't look Indian. Anyways, I read it and put it back in its bag, careful like, so's not to mess the cover nor nofink'. Then I put it in me locker."

"Oh, bloody hell!" said Ricky. "Have you seen the inside of her locker? It's like a nuclear war zone!"

George sniggered. Michelle glared at them both.

"That is not helping one bit you two. If you can't contribute something useful, shut up!"

"Sorry," they both murmured. Michelle turned back to Vera. "Now Vera, after you put the book into your locker, what did you do next?"

"Well, I finished me lunch and then went back to me children's bit. I've playgroup today, so's I needed to get out some good books for the kiddies. They like them ones that pop up, you know the sort o' thing. They break 'em if yer don't keep yer eye on 'em, so I had to stay there all the time. After playgroup, I went to the coffee room for me tea."

"Was anyone else in the coffee room when you went in?" asked Michelle.

"No. But when I was making me tea, someone come in, but went out again, straight away like. I 'ad me back to the door, cos I was fillin' the ket'le, so I couldn't see 'oo it was. When I said, do yer want some tea, mate? They'd gone," she started to cry again.

"Did you look at the book during your tea break?" asked Michelle.

"No, cos I could only take a few minutes like. I 'ad te tidy up the rest of the kiddie's corner. The mums never do a thing. They let them kids make a right mess and then go 'ome. I bet their 'ouses are a right tip!" Vera replied, sniffing loudly.

"Well what happened next?" asked Michelle, trying to keep Vera focused on the problem at hand.

"It was 'ome time weren't it?" she said. "I went into the coffee room and put me coat on. It were raining when I comes in this mornin' so I brought me umbrella. It was in the sink, so I took it ou' and wiped it over wiv a tea towel."

"Oh, how gross," said Ricky. "And to think we will dry our mugs with that and you've wiped all sorts of muck on it."

"There weren't no muck on it! It was only wa'er," said Vera indignantly.

"Oh, for goodness sake Ricky, shut up. We all want to get home," shouted Beth, crossly.

"Go on Vera. What did you do next?"

"Well, after that I went to me locker and got out me bag. I thought that was odd 'cos I put me book on top of me bag, but I thought it must 'ave fallen behind it, so I felt' at the back, but there weren't no book. I looked round the room, thinkin' that perhaps I was wrong an' I 'ad left it out, but it weren't there nor nowheres. The only thin' that could of 'appened is someone nicked it!" said Vera, her voice rising higher and higher.

She sat back in her chair and glared around the room at the rest of the staff, gulping back her tears.

"Okay," said Michelle. "First, who was the person who came into the room when Vera was having her tea? It must have been a member of staff, because the public don't have access to the number on the keypad," demanded Michelle.

"That was me," said Beth. "It's no big deal. I was about to have my tea. I had just opened the door to go into the room, when I heard the phone ring. I listened for a few seconds to see if anyone would answer it and when nobody did, I went back out to get it."

"So why didn't you return to the coffee room when you had finished with the phone call?" asked Ricky.

"I did," said Beth. "It took rather longer than I thought. The person wanted to know if we had a certain book, and although the computer screen said we did, it wasn't on the shelf." She glanced at Ricky and sighed. "Someone put it back in the wrong place, so I spent half an hour searching for it. By the time I had rung the person back to tell them we had the book and then gone back for my tea break, the coffee room was empty. Why would I take her book? Has anyone searched her locker? Perhaps she has mislaid it."

"I was getting to that next," said Michelle. "Is it alright if I look in your locker, Vera? Just to make sure that it hasn't fallen behind something."

"That's okay. But only you," agreed Vera, glaring at the rest of the staff. Ricky started shuffling around on his chair.

"Oh, for goodness sake. Can we go home and finish this tomorrow. I've got to get mother's tea and if I'm late she'll have a right go at me," he said impatiently.

"Sorry Ricky, but we must resolve this tonight or we will have to get head-office involved," said Michelle, as she went to the back of the room where the lockers were lined up along the wall. Each one was approximately two foot square, stacked one on top of each other. Vera's was on top of Ricky's and his was on top of Janet's. They were only big enough for a handbag, shoes, perhaps a jacket, but not much more. None of them were locked, relying on everyone's honesty not to steal. When Michelle opened Vera's locker, a nasty smell assailed her. A mixture of banana skins and dirty socks, thought Michelle. She gingerly put her hand into the dark interior. The first thing she encountered was a pair of trainers, no doubt the reason for the smell. Then there was a packet of crisps and a bag of sweets. There were a lot of old letters and pamphlets at the bottom, but no book.

Michelle turned to her audience and said, "The book is definitely not in here. I will look in my locker next and to make sure I am not concealing anything, one of you can witness it."

Janet stepped forward, "I will and then I will open mine."

Michelle opened her locker, which was at the bottom of the next stack. Above hers was George's and on the top was Beth's. The next row had two empty ones with the manager's on the top. She was away at the moment, enjoying two weeks of Florida sun.

Inside Michelle's locker was her handbag and scarf. She took them out, and underneath was a packet of mints and the printed information about Haven Health.

Janet opened hers and it contained a pair of shoes and her handbag.

"Your turn Ricky. Open yours please," said Michelle, authoritatively. Ricky obediently stepped up to the lockers and opened his. Inside was a pile of body building magazines, a packet of digestive biscuits and a bottle of aftershave.

"I told you I didn't steal her stupid book," he said, almost relieved. "Can I go home now?"

"No, not just yet. We need to find the book," said Michelle, sighing at his impatience.

"George, yours next please."

"I think this whole thing is ridiculous," said George, angrily. "You have no right to search our personal spaces. You're not in charge here anyway."

"I am the most senior person here," said Michelle. "We can call the police, if you would prefer, but I think we would all like to try and sort it out ourselves. It's up to you."

George reluctantly stepped up to the lockers and slowly opened his. He then stepped back and moved behind the group of people, who were all straining forward to see what his locker revealed. Inside were several plastic carrier bags, obviously filled with something. Michelle pulled out the first one and gingerly put her hand inside. She pulled two leather bound reference books from inside.

"What are these?" she asked.

The others craned forward to see what she had found.

Beth gasped. "Those are the books I ordered from the Internet," she said. "They are the history of the American independence. I ordered them two weeks ago, and was promised next day delivery. I was annoyed when that they didn't arrive on time. They obviously did come, but George must have intercepted them. Why did you do that George?"

The whole group turned to stare at George, but he was nowhere to be seen.

"He must have slipped out while we were distracted," said Michelle. "Quickly Ricky, see if you can catch him!"

While Ricky sprinted off, Michelle took the second bag and opened it, not sure what she was going to find. It held Vera's book, and as Michelle took it out of the bag, it fell open at the front page. There, where just this morning Vera had proudly shown everyone the message from Kenneth Crow was red ink smeared all over the writing. Everyone gasped, stunned at what they saw.

"Me book! Me beau'iful book! Ruined, it is!" wailed Vera, rocking back and forth in her seat.

The three other women stared at her, compassion written all over their faces.

"Oh! Poor Vera," cried Beth and rushed to her, gathering her up in her arms. Meanwhile Janet turned to Michelle and said, "There's another bag in there. What's inside it?"

"I hardly dare look," said Michelle, taking the bag out of George's locker and tentatively looking inside. She took out a stack of leaflets. They were red with bold black lettering and each one said,

'Don't be a slave to humanity! Don't be a slave to technology! Be a slave to God and help change the world!'

Michelle staggered back in disbelief, dropping the leaflets on the floor. "Oh my god," she said. "This can't be real!"

The Slaves of God! Twelve years ago they were accused of planting a bomb on Colandra's bus. Could this be the same group? Were they still active, twelve years on? And how was George connected to the group?

Chapter 15

The severed thread

 Michelle was still at work when Colandra arrived back at the cottage. It gave him time to look around and get a feel for the place. Thomas greeted him in his usual bouncy way and followed behind Colandra as he explored.
 The hall was large for a cottage and made the house feel light and airy. He looked up to the ceiling which went all the way up to the eaves and admired the galleried corridors running all the way round the first floor landing. The oak stairs rose from the middle of the hall, and when it reached the half-landing with its leaded window, it divided into two, one branching to the left and the other to the right. Colandra rose up to the first floor, while Thomas padded quietly up the carpeted stairs. On the right were two bedrooms, one at the front of the house and the other at the back. The back bedroom had its door open, giving Thomas access to it. The single bed was positioned on the far side of the room, against the wall and had a blanket spread over the end, which Thomas obviously used as his sleeping place. The window, which looked out over the woods, was set into the thick walls, creating a large sill that the cat spent considerable time sitting on and observing the wildlife below. Now he invited Colandra to join him, enthusing excitedly about the many creatures that he watched.

Colandra declined the invitation and continued on with his exploration.

Because he was not a real cronkel he was unable to walk through doors and walls, but he had other means of entry. The old house had fireplaces in every room so it was easy to move up the chimney and into the room next door. This was very similar to the back bedroom, except it had a double bed and smaller window looking onto the road. All the furniture was covered in dust sheets and they didn't look as they had been disturbed for years. The walls were dark and a little oppressive and Colandra was glad to return to the back bedroom and onto the landing.

Along the left side were another two rooms, one being the bathroom and other, Colandra surmised, being Michelle's bedroom. He was unable to gain access to this room as the bathroom had no chimney and the room below, Michelle's study, had had its fireplace boarded up.

At the far end of the landing were two small doors that gave access to the two attics, one above the right side of the house and one above the left. Colandra scoured the outside of the cottage and found two small round windows at the back, one for each attic room. The one on the left had a small pane of glass missing and this gave Colandra a way in. This attic had been little used. It was dirty and house martins had made numerous nests against the eaves. Looking at the roof trusses and beams stirred a memory deep within Colandra's mind, but the more he tried to grasp it, the more elusive it became. Perhaps he had been a bird in one of his lives, he thought, making nests, just as these birds were doing.

He watched them wheeling around the attic space and then, having seen enough he made his way back into the hall. He was unable to get into the other attic so he contented himself with looking through the little window instead. This other attic room was obviously used for storage. Boxes and tea chests were piled in the corners and there were cupboards and chairs in the centre. This must be where Michelle put her parent's things, after the death of her father, thought Colandra.

The only other place he had not looked at was the garage. This was underneath the two spare bedrooms and on the left of the hall. You could not enter it from the house and it was all locked up. Colandra looked through the grubby window on the side of the garage and could just make out the shape of an old car in the dim light. It was minus a wheel, being propped up on some blocks, and looked unloved and forgotten.

Colandra heard the sound of Michelle's mini and quickly returned to the kitchen, innocently waiting for her arrival.

She told him all about the book incident, which puzzled and worried him.

When Michelle showed him one of the leaflets, he said, "Why don't you look at their web site?" directing her to the information at the very bottom of the page.

"Do you know, I never noticed that," she said. "Let's give it a go."

Colandra followed her into the dining room, which she had converted into a very smart study, and watched her turn on her computer. It was always on standby and connected to the Internet, so it only took a few seconds to log on. She typed in the web page and suddenly a most awful noise came out of the speakers. It may have been music to someone's ears, but to Michelle and Colandra it was an assault.

She quickly muted the sound and said, "Phew. That was dreadful. Whoever decided to put that on as their theme song needs their head examined."

The screen showed a man speaking, but because the sound was muted they missed most of it. Michelle quickly put the sound back on and they heard, "….for everyone, not just the few. We must all take up arms against the oppressors. God is seeking ordinary people, like you and me, men and women, young and old, to make a difference. This is our time to make a real difference. Forget about church, worship, all of that. That's not what God wants. He wants souls to carry out his work, practical work, real work, proper work. Come to our rally on Sunday, November 17th at 5pm, and see for yourself. You will not be disappointed!"

There followed a series of pictures that scrolled through so quickly that you could not see what each individual photograph represented. Then the screen went completely red and words appeared in black, bold writing, the same ones that were on the poster, and an address. Michelle copied the address onto a piece of paper and clicked on the location map. It was at a congregational hall, just outside Bristol, on the road towards the airport. Michelle printed off the page and then shut down the computer.

"What a load of rubbish," she said. "And to think, people believe this drivel. Shall we go on Sunday and have a look?"

"It would be interesting to see what it is all about," agreed Colandra.

"Oh. By the way, I have directions to Carlton House for you," said Michelle. "It is part of the Haven health group. It has a big web site and I printed off a list of their homes. There is one called Hampton Green Hospital that I would like to visit. It's near Bristol, so not too far away," and she showed Colandra the list.

"What are all these stars next to them?" he asked her. "And why is the hospital and Carlton House under-lined?"

"I don't really know," said Michelle. "Perhaps the starred ones are either not owned by the group or they are purpose built ones, but your guess is as good as mine. Why those two are under-lined is a mystery. There is no index to tell you."

Colandra looked at the directions, and said, "It is not far from one of the other homes I went to. I was going to look at Exeter tomorrow so I will visit Carlton House first."

"That sounds good," said Michelle. "I am working again tomorrow, but only a half day, so I will be finish by twelve o'clock. It will be interesting to see if George comes in. I will ring round some of the homes on the list in the afternoon."

Colandra went to Carlton House very early the next morning, hoping to enter the building when the staff arrived. It was a massive, purpose built residence, on two floors. It was surrounded by beautiful landscaped gardens, with a sweeping drive up to the entrance. Inside it smelt of fresh paint and new carpets. A lot of money had obviously been lavished on the place and it was like a showpiece. He entered the house through a large, glass covered entrance, which immediately gave a feeling of space and light. The reception area, at the back of this room, was modern and bright. On the right were two doors, one leading into the waiting room and the other to the manager's office. On the left were three doors, one to an interview room, one to a small chapel, and the last to a corridor that, in turn led to the nursing wing.

The wing consisted of six bays, each one having four beds in it with an attached bathroom and utility area. Opposite the bays was a glass fronted corridor that gave access to physiotherapy and a treatment room. Further along the corridor you reached the service area comprising of a kitchen and laundry. There was a service lift next to the kitchen, giving access to the top floor. At the end of the corridor was a small room with a single bed in it, which had direct access to the chapel. Colandra surmised that this was a viewing room for bereaved relatives.

On the top floor there were ten bays arranged in exactly the same manner as downstairs, but the glass fronted corridor gave access to the service lift, a nurse's rest room and the matron's office. At one end of the corridor was a door leading to a self-contained flat, and at the other end was another door leading out onto a terrace, which had tables and chairs arranged on it. Colandra quickly scooted round the place to get his bearings and encountered lots of nurses and domiciliary staff. He found the matrons office on the top floor and arrived just in time to hear the night nurse giving her report to the day nurses. He stayed to listen and was amazed at how many patients there were in the establishment. As far as he was able to tell, they had all been in a coma for a very long time. The nurse was reporting about turning the patients, washing them and tube feeding them.

Then she said, "Our Jane Doe, the bus explosion patient in bay twelve," and all his senses were on alert.

"She has had quite a good night," she was saying. "She was washed and turned last at six this morning. She was seen by Mr Grant yesterday evening and he is going to arrange for her to be moved to Hampton Green Hospital later this week. That's your lot, Carla. Okay? Any questions....No? Then I'm off home to bed. I'm not on duty tonight, but I haven't heard whether Karen is coming in to work. She was off sick last week, so if you want me to replace her, just leave a message on my answer machine."

"Oh1 Great! Thanks Pat. Have a good day," said Carla, and Pat left the room. Carla turned to the rest of the staff and said, "The mobile scanner is coming tomorrow at nine thirty for the children's brain scans. Caroline Connor, Sylvia Turner and Frances Donovan are booked in and the parents want to be telephoned only if there is any change."

She looked at one of the nurses and said, "Mandy, I will leave you in charge of getting the children prepared tomorrow morning. Also you will need to explain to the new parents what happens during the scan. It will be the first follow up scans for Frances and Sylvia, so go carefully, especially with Frances' mother, who looks very frail. Right, the rest of you know what to do. Key workers, I will want a meeting at about two pm so find me if I'm not in the office. Okay everyone, let's get on."

At that, they all got up and went off in different directions. Colandra followed the nurses out of the office and made his way to bay twelve.

As he moved through the bays looking at the beds, he could see hovering just above each patient's head, a small orb, bright and golden, that Colandra now recognised as the person's entity. The entities were attached by a thin pulsating thread, just as Colandra had seen at the Brunswick spinal unit. These entities were bright and almost dancing. They appeared to be communicating with each other, and just waiting for their human body to heal.

When he reached bay twelve he looked at the occupant of each bed. Two were young men, the third a woman of about thirty years old and the fourth was an elderly woman with dark grey hair. She seemed to be just sleeping, her chest rising and falling rhythmically, as she breathed. Her skin was pallid and her eyes sunken. There was something about her that he recognised, but he could not think why. The chart at the foot of her bed told him that her name was Jane Doe, the nomination for any unknown female, and that her temperature, pulse and respirations were steady. Startled, Colandra saw that there was something very wrong with this female. Her entity was missing; the golden thread, to which it should be attached, was frayed. The thread was still pulsating, but each time it did, a tiny drop of energy spilt out into the air. Where was the entity and why had it been so viciously torn from its thread? It was no wonder that this woman had been in a coma so long. Although she was being tube fed by the nurses, the energy that this generated and that she so desperately needed, was slowly seeping away, killing her just as surely as if she had been stabbed through the heart. Colandra wept for this woman, who had had her essence so cruelly ripped away. But who would do such a thing? Colandra knew that only someone evil could do such a terrible deed.

As he looked at the woman one of the nurses entered the bay with an impeccably dressed gentleman following behind her.

"This is Jane Doe, Sir," she said, indicating the elderly woman. The man, a middle aged, rather portly gentleman, walked up to the bed and looked down at the woman.

His brow furrowed as he stared at her and he said under his breath, "She looks older than she is," then added loudly, "You are sure that she has no relatives? Nobody comes to visit her?" The nurse shook her head.

"No, Sir, she has never had a visitor except for the general manager. He visited once or twice when she was first admitted, but not anymore. Now she just continues to go downhill."

The man turned to the nurse and said, "How sad. Have her ready by ten o'clock tomorrow and I will arrange for Batemans to transport her to Hampton Green Hospital."

Colandra watched him turn away and saw him quietly smiling to himself. He certainly did not portray a man who was moved at the plight of this woman, a woman whose life had been so cruelly stolen from her.

Chapter 16

The Demon

On Sunday, the 17th November, Michelle went to the meeting of the Slaves of God. It was a cold, wet evening and she was well wrapped up against the weather.

Colandra, who could neither feel the cold or the rain, couldn't understand what she was complaining about.

"It's just weather, you wimp," he said, as Michelle parked the car and prepared to leave the warm interior.

"Just because you can't feel anything," she teased back.

Her coat did not have a hood, so she wound a fluffy scarf around her head and neck, turned up the collar of her coat and got out of the mini. She locked the car and walked briskly up the road to the congregational hall. There were already about one hundred people in the hall, but she managed to find a seat at the back. She was amazed at the number of people who had turned up. She sat down next to a youth in a duffle coat, who smelt of cigarettes and booze. Just the sort of character who would be interested in this sort of meeting, she thought.

"You're right," she heard in her head and smiled quietly to herself. In the front of the hall was a raised stage and several men were sat on chairs in front of a long table, a microphone placed in the middle. She studied the men and then gave a jump.

"That's George," she thought to Colandra. "Second from the left, in the blue jersey."

"Are you sure?" said Colandra.

"Of course I'm sure. I see him nearly every day," said Michelle, impatiently. "although he hasn't been in since the book incident," she added.

"Sorry, man. What did you say?" said the youth, breathing a mixture of cigarette and garlic fumes in her direction.

"Oh. Nothing. Just talking to myself, sorry," said Michelle, embarrassed that she had forgotten to think. She was shocked that George was up on the stage, but then he had had the leaflets, so he must have something more to do with this than being just a casual bystander. He was looking gaunt and pale, not his usual self, she thought.

There were three other men at the table. One was thin and had a sallow complexion, another was black with dreadlocks and the third was much older than the other two, with grey hair and a beard.

Suddenly a door to the right of the stage opened and a man walked in. He was about thirty, with dark hair, and was handsome in a rugged sort of way. He walked purposely towards the stage as the ripple of conversation slowly died away. The room was silent as the man climbed the steps of the stage and walked over to the table. He stood behind the table between the four men and looked out over the assembled audience.

Although he was not a big man, he had a charisma that commanded attention and Michelle found herself strangely drawn to him. Everybody craned forward in their seats and waited expectantly for him to speak. The silence was almost tangible.

The moment was suddenly broken by the slamming of the big doors at the back of the hall.

The man at the centre of the table tapped the microphone and said, "Good afternoon, ladies and gentlemen. My name is Lars. Thank you all very much for coming, especially as the weather is not conducive to coming out of your nice warm houses."

A ripple of laughter followed and someone at the back clapped.

"We have the heating on, so it should warm up pretty quickly," he went on. "You are all here because, like us, you are fed up with the way things are developing on our planet. The world is being stifled by countries that do not care about our environment. All they are interested in is having the latest technology, the richest economy and the most powerful forces. The strongest nations of the world have technologies way in advance of any of the poorer ones. All their most important areas are controlled by computer, but only a handful of people have the knowledge to control this technological wizardry."

'What a load of drivel,' thought Michelle.

"Did you know that computers control ninety-five percent of all the services in the world?" continued Lars. "If a hacker was to hack into these systems, he could wipe humanity out in one week? That is a very frightening thought. No one human being should have that much power. We do not want to move back into the middle ages, far from it, but we do want to protect our right to choose. We want control of the world to be outside the realms of humanity itself, thus saving it from destruction. This way it would not be governed by rich, fat cats who only want more and more for themselves. Then we all would be free from worry, free from poverty and free to do whatever we wished, safe in the knowledge that our universe will still be there for generations to come."

The room exploded with enthusiastic cheering and clapping. People stood up to stamp on the floor. It was bizarre.

"Did I hear right?" said Colandra. "Did he just tell all these, perfectly normal and presumably, intelligent people a whole pack of lies, and then suggest a computer control the universe?"

The youth next to Michelle had stood up with a group of others and was shouting. Michelle was worried about what she had heard, but she did not think that Colandra had it right, although she could not quite figure out where he was wrong.

"Hm. I'm not sure," she said. "It sounded like that and it may be what he wants them to believe, but I'm not sure. I personally think he was actually saying something quite different. If that is the case, I think we should be very afraid."

"I'm not sure that I understand you," said Colandra.

"Think about what he said. 'We want control to be outside the realms of humanity itself.' Computers are only as good as the programmer that programs them and then, only so long as changes are compatible with the programs ability to learn. They will always require human imput to update and upgrade them," explained Michelle. "What if he was not suggesting that everything was controlled by computers, but by something or someone else? Now that would make more sense, don't you think?"

Colandra agreed. "I see why you think we should be afraid," he thought back.

The audience was sitting down once more and Lars was saying, "All these politicians make us turn away from the lord. We all need to be strong and change our way of thinking. Force the governments of the world to listen to us. Only then can we influence our environment." As he spoke the man's eyes swept the room. Michelle heard Colandra gasp.

"What is it?" she asked him.

"He sensed me, I'm sure of it. But how could he? Nobody from this material world can sense me. Unless, of course, he is not of this world," added Colandra.

"What do you mean 'not of this world.' Surely he is just a man. You can see who he is," Michelle replied, suddenly feeling afraid.

The hall was silent. The man had stepped off the stage and had started to walk down the middle aisle, staring in Michelle's direction. She tried to shrink down into her seat.

"You are all needed by the lord to do important tasks," he said quietly, scanning everyone as he walked. "Those who are chosen will be honoured to take part in this exciting adventure. You will become more, much more than you ever hoped to be. The lord wants souls to renounce the evil path that our leaders are asking us to follow. We want to make a new world, a world where we can do what we wish without so called leaders making us follow their bidding. What makes them an authority on our futures?"

"The lord he talks of cannot be The Lord," Colandra said to Michelle. "He would never promise anything like this. The lord he speaks of must be another. This man is evil. We must leave, Michelle, now. You life is in danger. We must go!"

Michelle could sense the panic and terror in Colandra's thoughts. As his words echoed around her head, she gasped. Lars stopped and looked over in her direction once more. As he did so Michelle felt a probing of her mind, like an inside itch. She recognised the feeling, as Colandra invoked it sometimes when he searched for her, but this was different, this was uncomfortable. She instinctively closed her mind to the probing, but not before she realised that she had met this being before. When and where she could not recall, but she knew that this was not the first time this entity had tried to enter her mind.

He was halfway down the aisle now. He had stopped talking to stare at her, and then he looked behind her as if seeing another person beyond. The whole hall had exploded with cheering and clapping when Lars paused and Michelle took advantage of this to stand up. She turned toward the double doors and walked purposely to the back of the hall.

One of the men, with a long, black beard, stepped in front of her and asked, "You going already. He's not finished yet. You need to stay to understand it properly."

"It's not quite what I thought it was going to be," she said. "I thought it was going to be all about meditation, that sort of thing. You know…. How to reach your inner self."

The bearded man looked over her head at Lars, who had started to walk towards them. The rest of the audience swivelled round to get a better look.

Then she heard Colandra urgently saying, "You need to leave. Now! Get out! Go! Michelle, Go!"

She made to move around the man, but he stood in her way.

"Get out of my way, please," she said, panic starting to rise. "I would like to leave. You have no right to prevent me from leaving."

Then Lars walked up behind her and said quietly, "You came here of your own free will. We did not force you to attend. The lord picked you to be here, to receive his blessing. You were chosen, just as all these people were chosen."

Michelle was getting frightened now. She tried to reach Colandra's mind, but he was fighting his own battle.

Then a strained voice in her mind said, "Get out Michelle. This is no man. He is evil. He is trying to find me. I cannot hold him off much longer."

Michelle felt his despair and knew that if she did not do something quickly, his energy would be spent and he would be lost. The man was menacing, but he had been unable to enter Michelle. She had felt him on the edge of her consciousness, probing, searching for a way in. Then he was gone.

In that moment she knew, that for some unknown reason, he was unable to penetrate her mind and she shouted to Colandra, "Come to me. I will protect you. Let my spirit surround you."

Michelle welcomed him into her soul and her spirit enfolded him, wrapping him in her goodness and purity. He was like a ship in a storm that had suddenly found a safe haven.

Chapter 17

Sanctuary

Lars may have lost Colandra, but he still had Michelle. She ran towards the double doors, but the bearded man pushed the heavy bolt across the lock and turned to her, saying. "You're not going anywhere, young lady," he grinned, showing yellowed, uneven teeth.

She screamed at the man, "Get out of my way. I want to get out. Leave me alone. You have no right to hold me here!"

People in the last few rows had started to get concerned. They had stood up and were spilling out into the aisle. Some were making their way to the back of the hall, each trying to see what was going on. They soon reached Lars, who was slowly advancing towards Michelle, impeding his progress.

Michelle, meanwhile, was still battling with the bearded man, who was temporarily distracted by the surge of people moving towards him. Michelle saw her chance. To the right of the door was a staircase that led up to the choir loft. She quickly ran up the steps which wound in a spiral.

Then she heard Colandra. "At the top, turn left and left again."

She followed his instructions, but she could hear heavy footsteps behind her.

"You can't get away. There's nowhere to run," the bearded man hissed. She was so frightened, she thought she might stumble and lose her footing. Following Colandra's directions, she turned left and was confronted by a thick, red curtain from floor to ceiling.

"It's a dead end," she wailed.

"No. Behind the curtain there's a doorway," said Colandra, who had spent several minutes when they had first arrived, exploring the building. Michelle fumbled behind the curtain and almost fell through the open door.

"Close it, quickly. There's a key in the lock. Quickly, he is nearly upon us," she heard Colandra shout. Michelle slammed the door shut and locked it, just as the man reached her. She could hear him turning the handle, and pushing on the door.

Then she heard another voice.

It was Lars, "Break it down, you fool," he shouted at the bearded man.

Then he let out a roar, the like Michelle had never heard before, while the bearded man pounded on the door.

"There is no time to rest," said Colandra. "We must get to hallowed ground. He is not of this world."

They had reached a large window that opened out onto a balcony.

"This is a congregational hall. Surely this is hallowed ground?" said Michelle, breathing heavily and staring out of the window.

"It may have been once, but it is certainly not anymore," retorted Colandra.

Michelle stepped out onto the balcony, which was slippery from the rain.

"Come on, down the fire escape. You should be able to get to your car from there," said Colandra.

Michelle half fell, half ran down the fire escape to the street below and ran round the corner where she quickly found her mini. It was at times like this that she was glad that she favoured a shoulder bag, which she always wore across her chest. Finding her keys, she quickly unlocked the car, got in and drove away as fast as she dared. Looking in her rear view mirror she saw Lars and the bearded man standing in the road shaking their fists in the air at the departing car.

She was panting and her heart was beating so fast that she was sure it would burst from her chest, she was so frightened. She continued driving and then saw a sign which read, 'Saint Mary's church of the Evangeline'.

Thank God, she thought and made for that direction. She turned into the car park of a beautiful Saxon church, wedged between a newsagents and a shoe shop. Still, it was hallowed ground and that was all that mattered. She got out of the car and rushed into the church. She was immediately aware of the peace and holiness of the place. Once they had entered the church, Colandra left her and she was suddenly aware of a great feeling of loss.

There was no one else in the church and Michelle sat down on one of the benches near the back. As she relaxed, she put her head into her hands and cried. What had she got herself into? She only wanted to help, but now things were different. They had been mysterious, yes, even exciting, but now things had become dark and dangerous. She was afraid, very afraid for herself, but also for Colandra. She was also angry. This Zoth person, whoever he was, was he aware of what was going on? Did he realise that Colandra was in danger? Did he care? And who was this evil man? What did he want? Her thoughts were interrupted by Colandra's voice in her mind.

"Michelle, are you alright?" he asked gently.

"Oh, Colandra, I was so frightened. I thought he was going to catch us. How did he know you were there?" she said. "If Lars was indeed an evil spirit why didn't he leave his hosts body and chase us in his spirit form?"

"That's a question that I was asking myself," said Colandra. "If he had done, he would have easily defeated me. He was much stronger than me. When he touched my thoughts I was able to sense a lot about him. He is pure evil. He obeys no laws but his own, neither mortal laws nor God's laws. We must only hope that he respects the laws of nature, but I have my doubts on that too."

Michelle stood up and walked quietly towards the front of the church. "I recognised him when he was trying to probe my mind. I am sure I have met him before," she said quietly.

"That is impossible," retorted Colandra. "When would you have had contact with an evil being? Or was it the man. Did you recognise the man?"

"No, I have definitely never met the man before. I would not have forgotten. He has a certain charisma about him that is unforgettable," said Michelle.

"Yes he is quite good looking, if you like the rugged type," Colandra agreed, reluctantly.

"But now we must decide what to do next. We can't have this evil man finding us, but, at the same time, we can't spend the rest of our lives living in a church."

Michelle thought for a few moments and then said, "If you are safe when merged with me, then you must do that. If he has to stay inside his host's body all the time, then he can only find me by following me. He does not know where I live, work or anything else about me."

"Hmm. You forget one thing. George knows all about you and he has no reason to like you, after you found the stolen book in his locker? And George is a friend of Lars."

"George doesn't know where I live, only where I work and he hasn't been back to the library since the book incidence. I shall ring in sick tomorrow, with a chest infection. If you stay merged with me he will never find you."

"It is very tempting, but I can't stay merged with you for long, because you would slowly lose your individuality. We would eventually be unable to function without each other," said Colandra, looking at Michelle seriously.

"Well, if that's the case, we need to see if he is outside. Look through the window and see if he is anywhere around. If Lars has not followed us here, then we have a very good chance of making it back to my house without being detected," said Michelle, firmly.

Colandra looked through the church windows into the gathering gloom.

"There is only your mini under the trees in the side car park as far as I can see, and there is nothing at the front of the church.

There are a couple of people walking down the street, but none of them seem to be loitering about," Colandra said.

There were no windows at the back of the church, so he could not say for certain that there was nobody out there. They would just have to try their luck.

Michelle slowly opened the door, looked left and right, then walked briskly to her car. It had started raining again and it was getting late. She got into the car turned on the headlights and slowly drove out of the car park towards the city centre. She passed the first set of lights and could see the next church on the corner. Nothing untoward had happened so far. She indicated for the car park and drove in. She parked the mini, got out, locked it and walked quickly up to the church porch. She tried the door. To her dismay it was locked! She felt trapped!

'Calm down. Don't panic,' she thought. The porch was large and she surmised that it was still hallowed ground. The porch was large and deep, plenty of room to stand well back in the shadows. She backed as far as she could into one of the corners, trying desperately to keep calm. The street lights had come on and even though there was one right outside the church, she hoped that she could not be seen by anyone in the road. But where was Colandra? She had assumed that he would accompany her in the car, but he hadn't. Perhaps he had sensed something after she had left St Mary's. She peered round the edge of the porch and looked around. There were only a few people walking down the street and Michelle noticed through the rain, a man walking purposefully toward the church, his head bent forward and his coat collar pulled up around his neck. Her heart was thudding so hard; she thought it would jump out of her chest. The man started to walk across the car park, but Michelle was sure that he could not see her in the porch.

'Oh Please God, help me. Don't let it be Lars,' she thought.

When the man reached the porch he called out softly, "Michelle where are you. It is I, Colandra."

Michelle almost fell out of the porch, so great was her relief. "Oh, thank God!" she cried. "I thought you were Lars, come to get me."

"No. He was nowhere near the church. I returned to the congregational hall to test a theory. He can only sense me if I am very close to him as an entity, but if I take a solid form he cannot sense me at all," he said laughing.

"It's not funny!" shouted Michelle. "You could have been killed! I was scared stiff!"

"I am sorry! And you are right. I should have been more thoughtful," said Colandra, contritely.

"Can we go home now, please? I've had enough excitement for one day," said Michelle.

"Yes, let's go home," said Colandra, thinking how lovely that sounded. They both got into the car and Michelle drove back to the sanctuary of her house.

Chapter 18

The hospital visit

The following morning the brochures arrived. Michelle had rung Beth and told her that she was taking the day off, so now she would visit one of the Haven Health care facilities. The brochure showed glossy photographs of all the homes, except the ones underlined or marked with a star. These just had the name of the home, the address and a message, stating that you needed an appointment to view. She hoped that Mrs Keen had informed the group about her previous visit, so that it would be easy to make appointments.

Most of the homes with the asterisk were in the South West, but there were a few in Yorkshire and Scotland which she ignored as she thought it unlikely that Colandra's body would be moved up north. There were two in Bristol, three at Exeter, another three in Yeovil and several in Devon and Cornwall. There was Carlton House in Honiton that Lysander had visited, and Hampton Green hospital in Bristol. Before going anywhere she decided to telephone and introduce herself, so she began with Yeovil.

The gentleman who answered her first call seemed pleasant enough, but told her, "You need to speak to head office, if you want to visit," and Michelle had the same response to each home she tried. Just out of interest, she telephoned one home from the brochure that was not marked, only to find that they were the complete opposite, very happy for her to visit at a time that would suit her. Michelle found this most odd and decided that, if she was not welcome without an appointment, she would have to devise a plan. She logged on to the Internet and went into findaplace.com. She added each home that was marked with an asterisk into the search slot and clicked 'go'. Once all the sites had been located she displayed them in small windows on the monitor. There must be some mistake, she thought, because each one was a government property of some sort. One was a disused airfield, another was an old fever sanatorium and the third was a closed isolation hospital. Hardly the location for a private nursing home, she thought, so she refreshed the search. Once again the computer displayed the locations and once again it appeared that each site was on a disused government property. The addresses were either old military sites or disused health establishments. Even Hampton Green Hospital was on a government site; that of an old army fever hospital. She had not given it much of a look before she had printed it out, but now she thought that it was becoming more and more bizarre. She was determined to visit one of them, so since it was nearest, she picked the Hampton Green Hospital near Bristol.

    She set off in the car, armed with the map, and arrived at the address. It was an old, single storey, block built building, with paint peeling off the walls and windows painted with whitewash. It was completely deserted and locked up. She wandered around looking through the grimy windows for some signs of habitation, but could find nothing. She was about to leave when she saw a man climbing up some steps from an underground area.

    "Excuse me!" she shouted and the man turned. "Can you help me please?"

    She walked briskly towards him and he stood still, just staring at her.

    "What are you doing here?" he asked gruffly. "You have no right to be here."

    "Sorry," she said, "But I have an appointment to see the manager of the hospital. This is the address that I was given. I have driven round and round, but I can't find an entrance."

The man looked at her most suspiciously. He was a big man, over six feet tall. She didn't want to get on the wrong side of him.

"Mr Grant doesn't see people. Where did you get the address from?" he said, crossly.

"I was sent a brochure," said Michelle, innocently. "I rang up and made an appointment to see Mr Grant's secretary at five o'clock," she lied, keeping her fingers crossed behind her back.

"That woman's too big for her boots," he muttered. "Making appointments, for goodness sake. As if Mr Grant hasn't enough to worry about. Well, I suppose it's not your fault. Go back out of this gate and follow the road round to the left. Turn right and you will see the hospital drive ahead of you. It's easy to miss, what with all the trees."

Michelle thanked the man and walked back to her car. She could still see him watching her as she drove out onto the main road.

Michelle drove down the road and turned right. Sure enough, there ahead of her was the entrance to Hampton Green Hospital.

'Why didn't I noticed it before?' she thought. She parked in the car park and walked up to the front entrance. A young woman with red hair and abominable fashion sense was standing in front of the reception desk.

"Come to see Miss Florence, have you?" she asked.

"I believe that is her name. She did not say, just that she was Mr Grant's secretary," said Michelle, wondering how the young lady knew. Perhaps her basement friend had telephoned her.

"That's her," said the girl. "I'm Muriel. I run errands." Muriel did not elaborate, but asked Michelle to follow her. She led Michelle down a short corridor off the reception area. Everywhere was bright and clean. The carpet was thick and luxurious. Michelle was impressed. Muriel stopped outside a room and knocked, paused a moment and walked in.

"Miss Florence, your visitor." she announced, and ushered Michelle into the room. "Do you want me to bring some tea or coffee?" she added.

"No. That will be all. Thank you," said Miss Florence, as she came forward to greet Michelle. Miss Florence was an elderly lady with grey hair, scrapped back into a bun, giving her the appearance of severity. She appeared to be frail, but when she stretched out her hand in greeting, her hand shake belied her frailty.

Miss Florence turned towards Muriel and said impatiently, "I said that was all, Muriel. You can go. I am sure you have lots to do."

Muriel stared belligerently at Miss Florence, then whirled around and flounced out of the room.

"Young people these days have no manners," said Miss Florence. "Please, do sit down," she continued, indicating one of two armchairs that were arranged next to a small side table. They both sat down and the elderly lady looked Michelle over.

"I am so sorry, but I don't remember your name and I had completely forgotten our meeting," she said apologetically.

"That's okay," said Michelle. "You must be very busy and sometimes priorities take precedent. I called you about my uncle. He had a car accident three years ago. I have been told that he cannot stay where he is and the manager of a home near me suggested I get in touch with you."

Miss Florence looked at her intently and then said. "I am sorry, but we only take patients who have very precise needs."

Michelle thought for a moment and then stood up, saying, "I am sorry to have wasted your time. I am moving to New Zealand in a few months and I wanted this all sorted out before I went. There will be no one here to deal with this once I have gone," she sighed. "Can you recommend somewhere else?"

"Don't let's be too hasty?" said Miss Florence. "Perhaps we can help. How long has he been in a coma? Three years was it?" and Michelle nodded. "That may be all right," continued Miss Florence. "Let me speak to my colleague a moment. I will be straight back."

Michelle sat back down. Miss Florence had definitely changed her mind once she knew that her uncle would have no relatives to worry about him. Why was that important? She had tried to disguise it with the length of time that he had been in a coma, but Michelle had seen through that.

Miss Florence returned with a portly gentleman whom she introduced as Mr Grant, the manager. He reassured her that there would be no problem with the admittance of her uncle. There would be a few formalities to sort out, but that should not pose a problem.

"Miss Florence will give you all the forms and a letter for the home in which he is staying at present," said Mr Grant, wheezing a little. "You will have to arrange all the transport, but we can recommend Batemans as the most reliable and efficient ambulance service. We use it fairly frequently and have never had cause to complain. You need to read through the terms and conditions carefully, sign them if you are happy and return them with the other forms as soon as possible. Well it is very nice to meet you, good bye." And with that Mr Grant left. Miss Florence looked after him and turned to Malinda, saying, "He is a wonderful man, but he is so busy. He runs all our long stay facilities, you know. Yes, very busy, but he doesn't have any people skills," she sighed.

'What a strange thing to say about a person who was the manager of a hospital,' thought Michelle.

"We like to be paid by standing order, one month ahead," Miss Florence was saying. "You will find all the information in this envelope, including the telephone number of Batemans and the letter for his current care home. Give me a ring at least two weeks before transfer, so that we can make all the necessary arrangements. We want to make everything as easy as possible. Is there anything else that you would like to ask?"

"Just to be reassured that my uncle will be able to stay here for life. I don't want to have to return to England and start looking all over again. And that no decisions be made about terminating his life without consulting me," said Michelle, firmly.

"There are no problems with either of those conditions. In fact, you will find something similar in our terms and conditions," Miss Florence reassured her. "If you were a lot older, we would insist that you make provision for his fees in your will, but as it is, that will not be necessary. Would you like to look around at the accommodation?"

"Oh yes please," said Michelle.

Miss Florence took Michelle to the lift that was located at the back of the reception hall. They stopped on the first floor and Miss Florence led Michelle down a corridor, similar to the one downstairs, and into one of the rooms. It was large and the windows looked out onto a lawn surrounded by trees.

"That's probably why I missed your drive; all the trees. I ended up at a disused army barracks or something. It's a good thing a man came up from the basement or I would never have found you," said Michelle.

Miss Florence looked at Michelle and for an instant there was panic on her face, but she quickly recovered and said, "A man. Did you speak to him?"

"Well yes. He kindly gave me directions. I would probably still be wandering around there if he hadn't," said Michelle.

Miss Florence abruptly took Michelle's arm and led her out of the room.

"If that is all, I will call Muriel to escort you back to your car," she said, taking a telephone out of her pocket.

As Michelle walked back to reception with Muriel she said, "It looks like my uncle will come here. It was kind of Miss Florence to show me round. Are there a lot of patients here? In a coma?"

"Hundreds," said Muriel, an odd expression flitting across her face. "She showed you round, did she? That's not like her. I never go down there. It's too depressing. All those people with no lives. It's too awful to think about. How they work down there I'll never know."

'Hundreds. Down there. What was she saying?' thought Michelle. There was more to this building than she was being made to believe. Michelle looked at Muriel, who was staring straight ahead of her.

"Is there no chance of them ever coming round?" she asked.

"Oh, no! Never! They never will!" said Muriel, with a shiver. Alarm bells were ringing in Michelle's ears and she knew in that moment that it was imperative that Colandra visit this hospital.

As they reached the reception area, Michelle bade Muriel goodbye and walked out into the sunshine, taking a great lungful of fresh air.

As she drove home she thanked God that she was alive and well. 'At least people in a coma are not aware of what was happening to them,' she thought. 'Or were they?'

She did not arrive home until it was getting dark. She hated the winter; the weather, the dark evenings, nothing to look forward to. Christmas was always lonely and reminded her of how it used to be, when the family was all-together. She made herself some pasta, fed Thomas, and waited for Colandra to return, eager to see him and hear his news. When he had not arrived by the time she had finished her supper, she switched on the television and turned to the news. It continued to rain in most parts of Africa and Asia. Heavy rainfall had washed away towns and villages in many parts of South East Africa and there were moving pictures of families clinging to the roofs of their huts, babies in their arms. The death toll was rising every day and hundreds were fleeing to higher ground to escape the floods. It was the same story in India and parts of Southern China.

Welsh rugby was doing well and was on track to win the cup, Scotland lying second. There was an old movie after the news and still Colandra was not back. Michelle started to worry.

'Perhaps I can find him with my mind,' she thought. She sat back in the chair and tried to relax, blocking out all the extraneous thoughts. She visualized Colandra standing in front of her. Nothing.

'Colandra is energy so I must think of him as the feelings that he evokes in me,' she thought. So once again she relaxed and emptied her mind, then thought of him, how he made her feel when he merged with her and suddenly he was there, right inside her mind. She could feel his warmth, his humour, his vulnerability. She had forgotten how wonderful the feeling was and it nearly overpowered her. She opened herself up to him, allowing him to fill her very being. She felt a complete oneness with him, a feeling that she had never felt with another being before.

"Hi, Michelle," he whispered. "How are you?"

"I'm fine now," she said. "I was worried about you."

"You don't need to be. You would know if I was in danger," he replied. "I was just saying to myself, how much I was missing you. I guess you were feeling the same."

Then, just as suddenly, he broke away from her and was standing in front of her, as the thin man. She was saddened at the disconnection, but very relieved to see him.

"When you weren't back, I thought that Lars must have found you. I was very worried." Colandra smiled and it was like the sun coming out after a rainstorm.

"We have a connection now, so I think we would know if either of us was in danger. How was your trip to Bristol?"

"It was very unnerving," Michelle said and related her experience at the hospital, adding that it should be one of the places that he checks up on.

"There was something about it that was definitely spooky," she said. "I was shown a room on the first floor and I didn't see a single patient. The girl, Muriel, said there were hundreds of them and that she never went down there to see them. Why did she say down? I felt that she was talking about a completely different place. It was really strange. Miss Florence made a strange comment about the manager, Mr Grant. She said that he had no people skills, which seemed an odd thing to say about a man that managed care homes. They gave me all these documents and the terms and conditions are very strange."

Michelle spread the leaflets out on the coffee table so that Colandra could read them.

Colandra looked at them.

"You can't move him once he is there, and you have no say in his treatment. They add that they are free to treat him as they see fit. If he dies in their care then they will arrange for the disposal of his body. It all sounds rather odd," said Colandra. "I hope that is not where I have ended up."

Michelle looked at him, alarmed at the suggestion.

"If you are, it may be very difficult to get you out. Muriel said that no one gets out of the hospital. Or rather, no one wakes up from their coma."

"Come on, they can't keep me there if I am awake and I am determined to wake up. I just hope I find my body quickly enough. This Mr Grant, can you describe him to me?" asked Colandra.

"He is about forty-five years old, fat and balding. He smells of stale tobacco and wheezes a lot. Very smartly dressed though. Nice suit, tie, the usual manager type uniform. Why, do you think you know him?"

Hmm. He sounds like the same man who runs Carlton House, where the woman is a patient. I forgot to tell you that I recognised her. I don't know where from, but I definitely know her from somewhere. She is being moved to Hampton Green Hospital tomorrow," he said.

"That's interesting," said Michelle. "I am working tomorrow, so I will see if I can find out anything about Mr Grant. Will you be able to find the hospital on your own?"

"Oh yes. When we merged you had the place very firmly in your mind, so it was easy to see your concern. I won't have any problem. I will talk to you when I get back, but no merging," he said sternly, and with that he was gone. Michelle felt a profound sense of loss. She had become used to him being there.

'What will happen once he is reunited with his body?' she thought. 'I hope that will not mean the end of our friendship.'

Chapter 19

The contract

Colandra had no problems either finding the hospital or getting into it. He entered with a group of people, and once in the reception hall, he found that he could travel anywhere within the building. He knew that Michelle had seen Miss Florence on the ground floor, but on examination there appeared to be another level under that one. Colandra found the office that Michelle had had her interview in and the room Miss Florence had shown her, but he could not find any other rooms in the building at all that were habitable. He searched out the lift and slipped down the shaft to the lower ground floor. In front of the lift doors was a very long corridor that seemed to go on forever. At the end it opened out into a round hall, a bit like a roundabout, with more corridors running to the right, left and straight ahead. There was no natural light; everything was illuminated by neon lights set into the ceilings. There were rooms along each side of the passageways, evident by the doors that opened on to it, and Colandra was just wondering how he was going to get into them when one of the doors to his right began to open. A group of women came out of the room and Colandra quickly moved through the open door before it swung closed. He found himself in a ladies toilet and luckily there was a ventilation shaft directly over the washbasin area. He loved ventilation shafts, as they gave easy access to virtually all areas of a building. He moved through the grill into the air duct and explored the first room. He emerged into an enormous space with subdued artificial lighting. On both sides of the room, and as far as he could see, were beds with men, women and children in them. They were all breathing on their own, but totally asleep. There was no other furniture in the room save the beds, and the walls and floors were clad in pale green tiles. At one end of the room was a set of double doors and at the other end, covering the entire wall, was a floor to ceiling curtain. Each body was attached to an intravenous infusion, but otherwise there did not seem to be any artificial intervention. Above each body, and seeming to come from the heads of the sleeping people, was a golden thread. Most of the threads had a golden entity attached to it, while some disappeared through the ceiling and walls. Others, like Jane Doe, had a golden thread that ended in a ragged tear where an entity had once been.

'What is happening here,' he thought, and as he was thinking, the entities around him looked up and moved towards him. He could feel their anguish, and if that was the case, perhaps he could communicate with them. He approached one of them and sent an emotion of love toward it. It immediately responded by returning the feeling.

"Can I converse with you?" he asked.

"Oh yes. Please do. It's such a long time since any one talked with us," it replied.

"My name is Colandra. I am like you, but I have become detached from my body, so I have come back to earth to seek it out and rejoin with it," explained Colandra. "But tell me what has happened here? Why are some of you missing and why do some of the golden threads disappear above?" asked Colandra.

They all started talking at once. There was such a flood of noise that Colandra could not understand any of it.

"Wait, wait," he said. "Don't all talk at once or I won't be able to understand you."

They all stopped talking and there was a silence until one spoke.

"I am Roger. We will answer the easy questions first, and get on to the difficult ones afterwards. The threads, which seem to finish in the walls and ceiling, are still attached to their entity, but the entity is travelling."

"Travelling?" asked Colandra. "What do you mean?"

Another entity replied, "Hi. I'm Lucy. We have been here a long time and have learnt that we are able to travel quite a distance from our bodies without losing the connection. The thread is extremely tough and very elastic. Our entity is snapped back by the thread if we travel too far or are bodies are disturbed. Our travels are our only distraction, and before we learnt how to do this, we had only ourselves to entertain us. We know everything there is to know about each other, so we turned our attention to other things."

The other entities were totally attentive and one said, "To begin with we went on short journeys, but as we got more confident, we went further and further. Now we can leave the earth without breaking our threads. All of us have visited our loved ones, and some of us have tried to contact them, but to no avail. You are the first visitor to actually talk to us."

"You say that you are one of us, but that you have become detached from your body. Were you taken by the evil ones too? Did you manage to escape?" asked one of the entities, moving closer to Colandra.

"Be careful Paul, he may be one of **them**!" said a scared voice.

"No he isn't. He is certainly not evil," said the one called Paul.

"What did you mean when you said, 'taken by the evil ones'?" asked Colandra. "Why should you think me evil?"

"It is the reason that some of our entities are missing," said Roger, his voice becoming quiet.

"Beings come. Dark evil beings. They come in a whirlwind and steal our entities. They take us back to some evil place."

"I was not taken by the evil ones. I was injured and my entity was jolted from my body. Now I must find my body in order that I might reclaim it," explained Colandra, "but if these bodies have no entities why don't they die?"

"Because our bodies are strong and we are well cared for," replied Roger. "There is nothing physically wrong with us. There may have been once, but not anymore. We have explored our bodies and we can find no damage. The nurses attach us to a machine to keep our muscles toned, but we are prevented from waking up by drugs given to us through the intravenous infusions."

Colandra looked at their bodies lying asleep and said, "That would imply that the nurses and doctors know what is going on. They must be in league with these evil beings if they are keeping you alive and asleep," said Colandra.

"That is what I keep saying to the others," said Roger. "But they won't listen. They argue that the nurses look after us, that they care for us. If it were not for them we would die. But I say, if they did not drug us we would wake up naturally and then we could go back to leading normal lives again. But they won't listen."

"We do listen, we do," clamoured the others. "But we are scared, so scared."

"What do the evil beings want with your entities?" asked Colandra.

"We don't know. None have returned to say," said Lucy sadly. "My twin brother is one. They took him just yesterday. We both had the measles when we were two and ended up here. We have been here for ten years."

"Ten years!" exclaimed Colandra, horrified. "That is dreadful! Do you have any warning that the evil beings are coming?"

"No we don't. All we do know is that it happens every day. This room is number two and there are many more rooms just like this one. The evil beings can appear in any one of them," answered Roger.

"Many rooms," repeated Colandra, puzzled. "How many rooms?"

"On this floor alone there are ten," replied Roger. "Then there are more on the floor below us and the two above."

"That can't be right!" said Colandra, confused. "The floor above us is just a reception area, manager's offices, that sort of thing and the first floor has only one usable bedroom. The rest of the rooms are storage areas. There is only this floor below the ground floor, so I think you must have that wrong."

"I do not mean to contradict you, but we have been here for many years and have explored all there is to see. I assure you that these floors exist. When I first arrived here there was only this floor, but they have expanded as the need has arisen. The building you describe is next to this. It is only a façade for visitors. This building is connected to the other by an underground corridor. Above us is a disused fever hospital, but the building hides another within it," explained Roger.

Colandra looked astonished.

"I must return to the ventilation shaft and explore further. I will come back to you as soon as I can."

Colandra entered the shaft and this time he went straight up. He came out through a duct in the roof and immediately realised that the corridor in the basement of Carlton House travelled underground all the way to the run-down fever hospital that Michelle had described earlier. The entities were right. To anyone visiting the site, it would appear deserted and derelict. You would never know that, hidden behind the façade, was a hospital full of comatose patients. Colandra re-entered the shaft and this time went down, all the way to the bottom. Again the entities were right. There were four floors all together and each floor had ten rooms exactly the same as the one Colandra had visited. He had seen enough. He returned to room two and looked at all the little beings that were gathered around him.

"You were right," said Colandra. "I cannot believe that there are so many of you. Why are you here? It is obviously not to recover or why would the staff be keeping you sedated. And why don't your families visit you?" he asked.

Before anyone had a chance to answer him Lucy gasped.

"Oh no! I think it's our turn today," she said and shot off to disappear inside her body.

"We have discovered that we can hide from the evil beings inside our bodies. They can only take us by ripping our entities from the golden threads. You must hide too or they will take you as well," explained Roger, disappearing from Colandra's sight.

Now all the entities had gone and Colandra was alone in a room full of unconscious people. As he moved slowly along the beds, it suddenly became very cold. He could see the vapour in the cold air as the people exhaled. He moved quickly into the air duct and waited and watched. As he did so a wind started up in the centre of the room, swirling round and round. Colandra had a strange feeling that he had experienced this before. He remembered hiding and watching a similar scene, but when and where eluded him.

Although Colandra had been in the cronkel pot and had learnt a vast amount, he was not a true cronkel. If he had been he would have known that this wind was the forerunner of a strange phenomenon and that it was the appearance of this that had caused him to start to evolve. His life had started ordinarily enough. A tiny drop of energy from the primordial pot had been placed inside a spider's egg sac while the female spider attached it carefully under the eaves of a building. When the eggs hatched and the hundreds of tiny spiders emerged, they ran in all directions in order to find a safe hiding place. Even so, many of them were eaten within the first few seconds of life. The ones that survived grew fast and soon were making their own webs and producing their own young. One spider had taken up residence in an old building next to a bakers shop. He had built a web inside the house and was very successful at catching prey. The first time the wind had come it had destroyed the web and blown away the spider's store of food. It had taken three more nights and three more winds for the spider to learn that it must move the web somewhere more secure. During those three nights the spider had evolved, not enough for the spider to realise, but enough to earn it a name and a place in the cronkel pot when it died. But Colandra was not a cronkel and thus he did not know that when the great fire of London consumed everything in its path, it took the life of this same spider and that spider became a cronkel named Colandra.

Now as he watched from the grill covering the duct, he became more and more disturbed. He recognised the wind and knew what would happen next. He watched the vortex build and he saw the black shadows emerge, knowing that they were there for some evil purpose. The shadows moved from one sleeping being to another.

"You think you can hide from us, but you will be caught eventually, all of you will be caught," snarled one of them, hissing as he slunk from bed to bed. Colandra scanned the beds and gave a start. Two entities were still travelling; their threads stretching up and disappearing through the ceiling. Would the black shadows notice? Colandra hoped they would not, but it was not to be. With a guttural shout they all pounced on the two golden threads and began to pull. The two entities snapped back into the room, but they were unable to rejoin their bodies. The evil beings had hold of their threads and the fear emanating from the entities was palpable in the room. They were screaming and sobbing.

"Please, please let us go," they begged, but the evil beings just laughed at their misery.

"You are needed for greater things than this puny existence," said one, biting into the thread. Each time he bit, the entity screamed in pain, and the evil being delighted in tearing the entity away from its anchor. A similar fate had befallen the other, and the evil beings went back into the vortex carrying the sobbing entities and laughing at their misery. The vortex closed up behind them with an ear-splitting explosion, which was replaced by a wailing noise, that at first, Colandra did not recognise. Then he realised that it was an alarm.

The entities slowly ventured out of their bodies, as a voice boomed over the intercom system,

"Code blue! Code blue! Crash team to room three!"

That could only mean one thing, thought Colandra, someone was dying!

"Where is room three?" asked Colandra, urgently. "I have to go there, but I must use the ventilation shafts?"

"Follow me, its right next door," said Lucy, whose bed was closest to the grill covering the shaft. The other entities dove through the wall and all Colandra could see were dozens of golden threads streaking across the room and terminating at the left hand wall.

"Will you be okay in the shaft?" asked Colandra, anxiously.

"I'll be fine. I can move freely through solid, liquid or gas," she reassured him. "I will have to move through the walls every now and again, to get my bearings, but it's no problem." Colandra followed her through the grill and into the ventilation system. She sped ahead of him, a little glow in the darkness, until they came to another grill. They both popped out into room three, which was a replica of the room they had come from, just in time to see a team of doctors and nurses trying to resuscitate the unconscious person. Two men were arguing in the centre of the room and Colandra immediately recognised one of them as being Mr Grant.

"I want a complete investigation as to what happened," said Mr Grant, his face red and sweaty. It was obvious to Colandra that this man was in charge and that he was also very annoyed.

"Of course, Sir. That goes without saying. I can't understand what went wrong. The sedation is made up by one nurse and checked by another before it is administered. It should be impossible to deliver incorrectly."

"Well, Anthony, I will want to speak to the nurse who administered it. Obviously someone has messed up, and messed up big time. Find out who it was, and send them to me," shouted Mr Grant.

"Yes, sir. Consider it done," replied Anthony.

At that Mr Grant nodded, and strode from the room, slamming the door behind him. Colandra turned his attention to the bed. The team was still trying to save the man, but as Colandra watched, two figures approached the bed. They shimmered and exuded a feeling of peace and pure joy. Colandra knew what this meant. They had come from the spirit world to escort the newly released being up to the Celestial Hall. All the entities from the other bodies, including the ones from the other room, watched in awe. They saw the golden thread break from the man's body and watched the released entity rise up to meet the spirits. As they joined they glowed, brighter and brighter, until the whole room was flooded with their joy. Then they disappeared and the room was cold and bare once again. The entities were silent, awed by the beauty of what they had just witnessed. Colandra was the first to break the silence.

"I should have said something, told the spirits about the vortex. I have missed a golden opportunity. Oh, I am so stupid," he chided himself.

The team of nurses were wheeling the bed to the end of the room that was curtained off.

"I must see what will become of him," he told the others. "I will return straight away," he promised and quickly followed the group of people. Anthony pulled back the curtain, revealing a double door similar to the one at the other end of the room. He opened the doors and the attendants wheeled the bed out into a wide corridor and turned right. This corridor had five doors on the right hand side, but only two on the left. The bed was wheeled up to the first of these doors which Anthony opened to allow the nurses to wheel the bed into the room. They transferred the body onto a trolley and wheeled the bed back to the ward. Colandra was just wondering what was to become of the body, when a big man walked in.

'He must be the man that Michelle saw. He is certainly big,' thought Colandra. 'You would not want to get the wrong side of him!'

The man wheeled the trolley out into the corridor to a large lift. He pressed the button and almost immediately the lift doors opened and the man pushed the trolley into it. He pressed the top floor button, and when it reached its destination, the man pushed the trolley out into the corridor. A short way down the corridor was a door to the right, and after unlocking it, the man wheeled the trolley into the room. He pushed the trolley down to the far end and up to a great iron door set into the end wall. He pulled the door open revealing that it was an enormous furnace. He moved the trolley so that the end was against the opening and raised the head of the trolley, causing the body to slide down straight into the cavity. He closed the door with a loud clang and wheeled the trolley back against the wall. The man fiddled with some dials and a great roar told Colandra that the furnace was lit. He had seen enough. He went back through the door that stood ajar and down to room three, where Anthony was talking to one of the nurses.

"James is dealing with it now, Nurse Johnson, so when he has finished get him to sign this sheet for me," he said, passing a chart to the nurse, who went out through the double doors to the incineration room.

"You others can go for lunch, but think carefully about your statements. Mr Grant will expect a report about this incident, so get your stories straight. I don't want any slip ups. I need something solid for the manager, a reason why it happened or our jobs are for the chop. Do I make myself clear?"

They all murmured quietly and left the room, taking the emergency equipment with them. Anthony stood in the centre of the room and slowly looked around him.

He sighed and said, quietly, "What a mess. How did I get myself into this dreadful situation? I always prided myself on caring for people. Now look at me."

He shook his head sadly and walked slowly from the room in the same direction as the other staff.

All the entities had either returned to their bodies or were travelling, so Colandra went back into the ventilation shaft to make his way to room two. As he moved, he could hear raised voices coming from somewhere above him. He followed the voices up to the top floor where the incineration room was located. The sound was coming from one of the offices, so Colandra moved along the duct until he located the room that the sound originated from. He found himself looking down into Mr Grant's office. A shudder ran through him, as he recognised one of the occupants as Lars. Colandra could see Mr Grant standing behind his desk with the demon in front of him, leaning on the desk with his face thrust forward.

"I don't want excuses," shouted Lars. "We had a contract, and you have not delivered. Every soul, we said. Not every soul, bar one. All you have to do is keep them alive. How difficult is that? My Lord is not happy. One of his workers was terminated by your ineptitude. Perhaps you would like to replace him?" suggested Lars.

"No, no! That won't be necessary," spluttered Mr Grant, "Remember, we have your woman arriving this morning and I have a man coming soon. I interviewed a lady who wants her uncle to come here. He will be strong, once we have healed him and made him well. He could last many years," he said, whining.

"Very well," growled Lars, leaning back. "I shall return when the new one is here. I am disappointed, Mr Grant. One more error on your part and it will be your last. If you do not deliver, I shall be forced to make an example of you so that others do not presume that they can make mistakes. After all, a contract is a contract."

The demon turned sharply, pulling open the door so violently that it slammed against the wall, making Colandra jump back in surprise. Lars stopped and looked up. Colandra was transfixed by fright. Had the demon sensed him? Colandra was sure that he had. Lars stared through the grill for a moment, then looked away and marched out of the room.

Once Lars left the room, Colandra moved back to his observation position, watching Mr Grant as he slumped in his chair. Sweat was pouring down the sides of his face, his skin pale, his breath laboured. He took a handkerchief from his pocket and wiped his forehead, his hand shaking uncontrollably. Then he opened the top drawer of his desk and took out a small bottle of whiskey. After unscrewing the lid, he put the bottle to his lips and took a long swig of the amber liquid. He pressed the bottle to his right temple, closed his eyes and groaned.

"What have I done?" he said aloud. "Keep them alive, he said. Then you can have immortality. Everyone thinks they're dead anyway. It's simple, simple. But if they die, I'm doomed, doomed. He'll take me to Hell! I only wanted immortality. But not like this! It's too late, too late!"

Mr Grant was wringing his hands and rocking in his chair. Colandra watched this wretched man as he muttered to himself, realising that Mr Grant had made a pact with the devil. Colandra could see that it was only a matter of time before Lars would no longer need this man and then his suffering would really begin and continue for all eternity.

Chapter 20

Difficult choices

Colandra made his way back to room two and found the entities gathered together discussing what had happened in the other room. Colandra knew that he must tell them what was going on, as he would need their help if he was to overthrow Lars. One way or another, the demon was going to have his contract terminated!

"Oh, we are so pleased to see you! We thought you had been taken, you were such a long time." Roger said. *He sounds just like Michelle*, he thought, smiling. Michelle had become more important to him than he had anticipated.

"I need you to gather all the entities together. We know that the evil beings will not visit again today, so everyone is quite safe. Can you get them all to come here?" asked Colandra.

"We have never gathered together in the same place before, but it should be possible," replied Roger. "We will each go to a different room and explain to the others what is happening. It may take a little while, as some of them might need persuading."

With that they all went off in different directions and Colandra was alone. He went back into the ventilation shaft and moved rapidly to room three. When he arrived he looked around it, noticing that it was different from room two only in that there were many more bodies without entities. Probably three quarters had frayed golden threads, their entities bitten off by the evil beings. Colandra wondered how many other rooms were similar. His thoughts were interrupted by the noise of the doors opening and a group of nurses entering the room pushing trolleys laden with bowls, towels and other washing paraphernalia. They filled the bowls with water from a wash basin at the far end of the room and moved quietly from bed to bed, washing the patients, turning them and massaging their limbs. One nurse was pushing a tall, metal trolley which she pushed from bed to bed. She was obviously in charge of the drug administration, as Colandra watched her take down the empty infusion bags and replace them with new ones. Before reconnecting them to the unconscious person, however, she took a vial of medication from the trolley and checked them against a chart. She called to another nurse to watch her draw up the required amount and inject it into the bag of fluid, before attaching it to the infusion pump. They both checked the rate at which the pump was running and, satisfied that all was done correctly, they moved on to the next person. Colandra watched as the procedure was repeated all the way down the ward and an idea started to form in his mind.

"I thought Monica was our drug queen today," said one of the nurses.

"She was, until today. She has been suspended over the death of number 632. Didn't you hear what happened?" asked the other nurse.

"No. I've only just come on. I couldn't find Anthony for a report. What happened?" the first nurse said.

"Well, the drug company sent double dose packs of the sedation and Monica didn't notice. She gave 632 his normal amount, presuming it was the single strength, but of course we now know that she gave him double what he should have had. It's the first death we have had here since I've worked at the hospital, and that is almost nine years." explained the second nurse.

Colandra had seen and heard enough. He knew what he should do. He now had a plan, but could he convince the entities that it would work?

He moved into the ventilation shaft and quickly made his way back to room two, where he was met by a blinding light and a cacophony of noise. There were so many entities in the room that their energy transformed the space, making Colandra feel as if he had stepped onto the surface of the sun. They were all talking at once, wanting to know why they had been asked to gather together. They all knew that the summons was significant, but few realised just how significant it was. Colandra rose up and hovered in the centre of the room, waiting for them to settle down. Slowly they quietened until there was silence. Colandra looked at them all. So many of them, he thought.

"Hi. My name is Colandra and I am like you, but without a body," he said and proceeded to explain to them what had happened to him. They were all very attentive and seemed to understand what he was saying. He told them what he had seen in the incinerator room and what he had overheard between Lars and Mr Grant.

"I believe that Lars is the servant of Lucifer and the evil beings are his slaves. The vortex is obviously a means for these evil beings to enter this world and snatch souls from their living bodies."

He then went on to tell them about, the cronkel pot and the Celestial Hall.

He explained about the escorts that they had seen in room three, adding, "I believe that the souls the evil beings have stolen, can be saved if the body is allowed to die. The soul will return to its body from wherever it is being held and will be escorted to the Celestial Hall by the spirits. Once there, it will await assignment to the cronkel pot," he said. "We cannot continue to allow Lucifer to take souls for his own means. They do not belong to him. They have lives to live, aims to pursue, and destinies to fulfil."

The entities all murmured their agreement. Then there was a general clamour as they reacted to what he had said.

"Can you choose someone to be your spokes person?" he asked. "I am having a great deal of difficulty understanding you, when you all talk at once."

One of the entities moved forward.

"I am Vincent from room one," he said calmly. "I was one of the first humans to be brought here, so I suppose I am the oldest among us. They want to know how we can save our friends."

Colandra thought for a moment.

"Your bodies are maintained in an unconscious state through the use of drugs. I was thinking that I might be able to influence the nurse into giving the wrong amount of sedation. Apparently some double strength bottles of the drug were sent here in error and I could make the nurse pick up one of those bottles, thinking it is the correct one and thus give double the dosage. It must be restricted to a room where all the entities have been taken, as it will be too difficult for me to give the nurse individual messages. If my theory is correct, and all goes well, the entities should return to their bodies and they will be escorted up to the Celestial Hall. We can continue doing this with all the stolen entities and then Lars will have to think again."

"We understand," said Vincent. "We will need a little time to look for a room where all the entities are missing. I am sure there must be some rooms that fit the bill. We tend to travel together and fewer and fewer of us meet up. The other thing that you must understand is that we have made friends while we have been here and some of us, like Lucy, have relatives here. They will have to make a decision about those friends and relatives that will be very painful and difficult. I need to convince them that you are right and that the only way to save them is as you describe. They need to believe that the souls that have been taken can never be reunited with their golden threads. I will try to make sure that they have understood what you have told us, so that they are able to make an informed decision. It is not something to be taken lightly."

Colandra could not agree more. It would be the most difficult decision that they would ever have to make. It would be a leap of faith and one which he could not help them with. He hoped that they had all felt the sincerity in his voice and would make the right choice.

Colandra told them that he would return the following day to hear what they had to say, then bid them farewell.

Colandra was very glad to get back into the open air, as he was finding it very claustrophobic in the underground hospital. As he was about to return to Michelle's side, an ambulance pulled up in front of the hospital and Colandra was immediately reminded that Mr Grant had arranged for Jane Doe to be transferred that morning.

He watched the orderlies pull the stretcher out of the back of the ambulance just as Mr Grant and a nurse came out of the building. They all disappeared into the hospital and Colandra was tempted to follow them, but he had had enough of the depressing place and was eager to get back to Michelle, besides, he knew that he would have to return tomorrow to see what decision the entities had come to so he would visit the woman then.

When he returned to Hazelwood cottage, he settled down in his thin man's body and told Michelle all about his day.

"So the 'Slaves of God' have definitely got some connection to the comatose people," said Michelle. "I wonder who Lars is. Or what he is? He is obviously human, but again he isn't. Do you think it is possible that he is in a possessed body? Perhaps he has taken someone's soul and then used the body by possessing it himself? Perhaps someone from the hospital." she continued.

Suddenly Colandra let out a piercing cry as realisation tore through his mind.

Michelle jumped up from her chair in alarm, making her cry out, "What is it? What's wrong? Tell me!" she shouted.

Colandra was rocking in the chair, wringing his hands and crying, "Oh, No! Please no! Not that!"

He dropped his head in his hands sobbing, as he knew he must be right.

Michelle ran to him, but as she put out her arms to embrace him, he disappeared and was once again a shimmering entity.

"What's wrong? What's going on?" said Michelle, her voice strained and agitated. "What is it? Please tell me. I only want to help."

Colandra could not at first put his thoughts into words, so terrible was the suggestion, but he could see no other alternative. Lars had stolen his body! That was why the spirits could not trace it! That was why Lars sensed him. Lars must have recognised Colandra as the rightful owner of the body that he possessed!

"Oh Michelle, I have been so stupid," he said, at last. "Lars has taken my body! Somehow he must have merged with it when I was catapulted from it. He may have been living in it ever since the explosion. I don't know, but I am sure that he is in it now. He has somehow healed it and is now using it for his evil purposes.

Oh! What will become of me? I cannot take it back, not from a demon. He is much too powerful for me alone. I must inform Zoth about all the things that are happening. This is far too serious a development for me to deal with."

By this time Colandra had calmed down sufficiently to allow him to appear as the thin man again and now he was looking at Michelle with such sadness that he was sure she must know what he had decided to do.

"No Colandra, you can't. You can't leave me now. I need you. If your body dies you may never be able to return and if you do we may never meet up again. If you die then I will die with you, then we can speak to Zoth together."

Colandra looked horrified. "No! Never say that. You will be doomed for ever if you kill yourself. It proves to the Great Lord that you have no regard for life, no wish to learn, improve, and ultimately gain immortality. You will go into the primordial pot and be lost forever," he said in a shocked voice.

"Why will I go into primordial pot? They will see that I am not flawed!" Michelle said indignantly.

"If you kill yourself it is deemed that you have no regard for life, you do not respect it and you judge your life as meaningless and worthless. The Great Lord of all has given all beings a regard for life that is so pure that they will try to survive even when survival is untenable. If you kill yourself it is deemed that that instinct is missing and therefore you are flawed. If you are flawed you cannot grow and develop, and therefore you are returned to the primordial pot to be mixed with the energy within it and cleansed. Any being that acts against the laws of nature are deemed flawed. For instance a being should only kill for food, to protect another or for self-preservation. If it kills for pleasure then it is acting against the natural way of things and doomed. The primordial pot is constantly being fed with energy from Celestina and this keeps the pot pure, but you would be lost forever."

"I understand that, but I would be giving up my life for a purpose, not because I am flawed," objected Michelle.

Colandra sighed, "It depends on your state of mind and what you believe at the time of death. If you truly believed that you were taking your life for a noble cause then you would not be doomed, but that can only be ascertained when you enter the Celestial Hall and are judged in the Hall of Judgement. In your case you would be taking your life for purely selfish reasons, because you do not want to continue life on your own, and there is nothing noble in that," continued Colandra.

Michelle was crying now. She looked at Colandra so tenderly through her tears that it tore at his heart. He knew that he did not want to lose her, but he also realised that there was no future for them as they were. If he wanted more he must seek help from Zoth. He needed to return to the Celestial Hall in order to see the spirit and the only way he could do that was to die. The future of mankind was depending on him to make the right decision.

But could there be another way, apart from dying?

"I have assumed that my body must die in order for me to rise up to the Celestial Hall, but what if I was to hide among the entities at the hospital when they are escorted up. After all, I am already an entity, so perhaps the spirit escorts will not notice me. It would be worth a try, don't you think?"

Michelle stopped crying to listen to Colandra.

"Do you think that could work?" she asked, tentatively.

"I do not know, but it must be worth a try. I will rise with them, enter the Celestial Hall and talk with Zoth," continued Colandra. "Once he has decided what we must do, I will return here to tell you what is to happen. It will be okay. What we have together is too strong to just disappear. We are now connected, you and I. You know that. But if I don't do this the whole human race will be in danger. Well, what do you think?"

He looked at her so tenderly that she smiled and said, "It may work, but if it doesn't, promise me that you will return here, before you make any new decisions."

"I promise. Now you need to sleep," Colandra reassured her.

Michelle was reluctant to go to bed lest Colandra leave without her knowledge, but he understood her concern and said, "Do not worry. I will not leave until you have rested. Lie down and sleep. I shall still be here in the morning, I promise."

Michelle lay down on the bed, but despite her assertion that she would not sleep, within seconds of her head touching the pillow she was gone. Colandra watched her sleeping, her face relaxed and her breath softly sighing through her partly opened mouth. He knew that he had been changed forever by her sweetness and he could not imagine life without her by his side. But now he must fulfil his destiny and play his part in the saving of mankind.

Chapter 21

Trego's big mistake

Unbeknown to Colandra and Michelle, Zoth was having problems of his own. He was getting reports that animals on Earth were suddenly becoming self-aware. He began to doubt that the problem with Colandra was an isolated one. Had Trego messed up again? His training had been meticulous. He had passed all the tests that had been set him and he had, in fact, scored better at some of them than Zoth had himself. Perhaps that was the problem. Perhaps Trego thought he was better than Zoth and was making up his own rules. But the rules had been laid down by the Great Lord of All. The whole of nature interlocked. Mess around with one small part and you mess up the whole thing. The very fabric of existence could be destabilised. Zoth took a big proverbial breath and calmed himself down.

'I won't be any use to anyone if I get into lather,' he thought, 'I must investigate this properly before jumping to the wrong conclusions.'

Zoth decided to question Trego and try to establish where he had made changes to the system, if indeed he had made any. He summoned Trego and asked him, if he could improve the system of cronkel assignment, how he would do it.

"Well," said Trego. "I am glad you have asked me that, as I have some ideas that I think would make the system run more efficiently and also save suffering on earth."

'Oh no,' thought Zoth. 'Please don't say that you have actually put your thoughts into reality.'

Trego went on to elaborate on his ideas. He suggested that when a person or animal was going to die, the Cronkel Master Assignor could delegate a person to be in charge of releasing the life's entity before the being started to suffer. This would obviously prevent pain, but also save hours of futile effort on the part of other beings trying to help them.

Trego was most enthusiastic while he explained his theory to Zoth and was crestfallen at Zoth's obvious displeasure.

"The changes cannot work," said Zoth. "You are naïve if you think they can."

"Ah. You are wrong," said Trego. "I know that they can work, because I have tried them!" he said triumphantly. "Alright, there have been one or two little problems, but nothing that cannot be sorted out."

Zoth groaned. Oh No! It was worse, far worse!

"You will have to tell me exactly what you have done and when. We need to correct these 'little problems' as soon as possible or the Great Lord of All will discover the mistakes and your life as well as mine, will be in jeopardy!" said Zoth, giving Trego a hard stare.

Trego did not understand the gravity of the situation.

"Why can't we carry on with my changes? You think you are better than everyone else. You think that nobody, but you, can think up good ideas," he said crossly.

"That is not the point at all," said Zoth. "I do not make changes without thorough discussions with the Great Lord of All. We are his creation and he knows all there is to know. We are like ants compared to Him. Nobody makes changes without His say so and certainly not a young upstart such as yourself!" Zoth was getting angry. It was one thing to suggest new ways of doing things, it was quite a different story if one changes a system that has been in place since time began, and also expects a pat on the back for doing it!

"So, why won't my changes work?" said Trego, looking deflated.

"You have to understand the whole picture, which you obviously don't," said Zoth patiently.

"Everything that happens on Earth has a purpose or reason. You say that you want to relieve suffering, but that very state may be what draws that being up to a higher level of consciousness. It may be the very catalyst that brings about change, not just in the being that is suffering, but also in the beings around them. Also, you cannot be sure that they are destined to die. The suffering may initiate a growth in knowledge, which results in saving that being. The whole of your changes are built upon an unsound foundation. I am not blaming you. You are young and want to make a difference, which is commendable, but you are going around it in the wrong way. You have become so identified with your wish to help mankind, that you have forgotten many of the basics. "

Zoth watched Trego's expression go from one of indignation to one of profound devastation. It was obvious to Zoth that Trego had genuinely wanted to help the beings on Earth, but by changing the course of nature he had actually done the opposite. Zoth realised that it was going to be an enormous task to put right everything that had been affected by these changes.

Up in Heaven, The Great Lord of All sat back on his cloudy throne and closed his eyes. He knew everything, of course; after all he was omnipotent, omniscient and omnipresent. He had been aware the moment Trego had changed the rules and now he was curious as to how it was all going to be resolved. He had noted that many animals had not been raised to human status and some humans had not climbed up to the appropriate stage of their evolution. Had Trego inadvertently caused lives to swerve down the wrong path? If so, did this mean that they may never move up to the next phase of existence? Now that would be a tragedy and then the Great Lord of All would have to perform one of his spectacular feats.

He smiled to himself and said, "Ah! Another one for the history books, I think. Perhaps even more spectacular than the parting of the Red Sea!"

Meanwhile Zoth was trying to ascertain how long ago it was that Trego had started changing the system. He knew that it was at least twelve earth years ago, because of the situation involving Colandra, but Trego was suggesting that it may be as long ago as twenty!

'There are a lot of births and deaths in twenty years,' he thought.

He went over to the ledge along the wall and looked intently at the Scrier. Its mirrored surface rippled slightly and colours started to flit across it. Slowly figures began to appear and Zoth noted down to memory those facts that were of interest to him. The problem did not seem to affect the lesser beings such as insects, viruses, bacteria, plants and trees, as they did not end up in the cronkel pot, but certainly animals, birds and humans were affected. Animals that should have evolved up to humans had not done so. During the time between Trego removing their essence early and the real time of their death, some important event did not occur that would have enabled them to move on. Some of them had lived the same life over and over again, affecting those animals that were ready to move up a stage. Of course they would not be aware of that fact, but still it was not right, and the humans may well have had heightened feelings of déjà vu. Others were moved up a stage too early and that may result in the person feeling inadequate, even unworthy, perhaps resulting in suicide.

"What a mess!" said Zoth to himself. "This is going to be a mammoth task to sort out! If only he had come to me first!"

While Zoth knew that a cronkel could be moved up into a more advanced group, it was impossible to quicken their ability to learn. Every being developed at their own pace. Some learnt lessons from their various experiences and applied that knowledge to new circumstances, while others continued to make the same mistakes over and over again.

Some beings were reliant on other beings to progress, living out their lives side by side for many years. A change in the rules may have caused these 'soul mates' to become disconnected and the loss of contact could result in them becoming stuck in the system.

Zoth shivered. 'It doesn't bear thinking about,' he thought.

Once he had obtain all he wanted from the Scrier, he went to Trego's office and told him to record every birth and death of all the mammals, birds, reptiles and humans for the last twenty years.

"You must leave nothing out," he said sternly. "Use the Scrier if you need to, but it must be your most accurate work. The only way we can rectify this catastrophe is to know exactly what we are dealing with. Once we have the list we will be able to ascertain which lives have been affected, however small, and see whether we need to change anything. We will then decide what needs to be done to repair the situation."

It sounded really simple, but Zoth knew that it was going to be far from that.

The Great Lord of All also knew this to be true, and he also knew that it was just a matter of time before Zoth would need to ask for his help.

Zoth read through the lists that Trego kept depositing on the desk. There were millions of them, not just humans, but mammals, birds, reptiles and fish. In fact all life that had made even the smallest evolutionary step was potentially involved. He had known that this task was going to be difficult, but he was beginning to doubt his own ability to solve this one. He hoped that they were going back far enough, because if this was the result of just twenty years, he dare not even think about what it would be like if, in fact, they should be going back further. He recruited four more helpers to collate the entities into categories and then into length of existence. He knew that he could forget about those that had too short an existence to be affected by the mix-up. The others were still going to be a problem and he would need to decide whether to get the Great Lord of All involved or whether he could resolve it himself, as he knew that part of his personal development was wrapped up in the decisions he made and the way he participated in the development of others. One mistake he had made was not anticipating problems with Trego's identification with his role as Assistant Cronkel Assignor. He had left him alone too early. He knew that now, but he had been distracted by a personal situation that he had regarded as more important and that was his other fear; that the Great Lord of All would find out what it was. He must not think about it or the Great Lord would hear his thoughts and know.

He was brought out of his revelry by the entrance of Trego with yet another sheath of papers.

"Sorry sir," said Trego. "But I have another set of lists. I have completed twelve years, with another eight to do. Sorcell from weather would like to know if he can be of any help to you. Also Bellure, in the landscaping department, wants you to know that you have her support."

"Tell them, thanks very much, but I want to try to keep this within the cronkel department if I can. If that's not possible then I may well call on them both. I have recruited Verda from the first level to help, and as she cannot come up to this level, I have placed her in an antechamber next to the Celestial Hall. She is scanning reptiles and amphibians on the Scrier for me," said Zoth, softly.

He was tired and he knew that he needed energy from the heart of Celestina, so he moved to the edge of the Cronkel Department and into the Spirox. As he floated in the vertical corridor, he looked up towards the Heavenly kingdom and relaxed into pure ecstasy. Soon he was surrounded in colour and his spirit soared. Higher and higher he rose; the feeling of power and energy completely enveloping him. Although this feeling was familiar, it always felt as if it was the first time. Every part of him throbbed, until he thought he would burst. Every sense was heightened and he could hear musical sounds that were pure and sweet. He knew that all his senses were being fed in this one instance.

And then he saw the Great Lord of All. The magnificence of him was both awesome and terrible. Zoth bathed in his beauty and radiance, feeling completely at peace, all his problems melting away in those moments. Oh! If only he could remain in this state forever, what sheer bliss it would be! He knew that he had a long way to go and many efforts to make, before that would happen. For now he could only enjoy the small tastes that were afforded to the lower level beings and marvel at the sheer joy of being part of something so magnificent and glorious.

Chapter 22

Down to Earth

Trego had finished the last list and taken it to Zoth. He was very contrite and realised that he had caused his boss much misery. And all because he thought he was better at organising things. He knew that now. He thought that Zoth was too easy going and not bold enough to change a system that had been in place for eons. Now he knew that it had been in place that long because it worked!

He took the last lists to Zoth and placed them on his desk.

"That's the lot," he said with a huge sigh. "What else can I do to help?"

"Well, I have made a list of all those beings that I think may be having problems. I want you to take the list and physically check on each one. Report back to me if you observe anything that looks suspicious," said Zoth.

"What! Go down to Earth and have contact with the material world?" said Trego, suddenly afraid.

"Yes," said Zoth. "They will not be able to see you. And if they are aware of you they will only think you are a ghost."

"What if I get stuck there? What if I can't get back? Then what will happen to me? It was hard enough being a human when I was evolving without getting stuck there," said Trego, his voice quivering with emotion.

"Don't be daft! Of course you will be able to get back. You just have to think of here and whoosh! Here you are! And remember, although you can manipulate and change things on Earth, you are forbidden to interfere in any way!" said Zoth impatiently. "Now take the list and get started."

Before he knew what was happening, Trego was standing in the middle of Meadow hall shopping centre in Sheffield. He had a moment of alarm as he hovered above the market and immediately wanted to go back to Celestina.

"Get a grip, Trego, for goodness sake," he said to himself.

The centre was crowded with people, pushing and shoving. The noise was intolerable and Trego felt absolutely terrified. He could see birds flying about, high above the crowds and wished he was up there among the steel roofing girders. Then, just as he was thinking how much better that would be, he was hovering amongst the metal beams, way above the people below. He imagined that he was a bird flying through the air and suddenly he was doing just that. He zoomed through the shopping mall, just skimming the heads of the shoppers hurrying about their business.

'Wow,' he thought. 'This is great. If they could see me they would think that I was superman. This is much better than assigning.'

Suddenly a voice in his head shouted. "You are supposed to be working, not flying about all over the place. If you can't do the job then I will get someone else to do it instead! I have plenty of other things that I can give you to do!"

Trego was so shocked that he almost flew right through the shoppers heads below him.

"No sir," he stammered. "I was just getting my bearings. I'm on the case."

Suddenly he sensed something behind him, just out of his vision. He turned and saw a shimmer, like a heat haze, over to his right. As he focused on it, it disappeared, however he recognised it instantly. He had been a cronkel assignor for a long time and knew a cronkel when he saw one, but what was it doing on Earth? It should have been safely ensconced in the pot, not wandering around a shopping centre. How could it have escaped, surely that would be impossible? He decided to keep tabs on this little cronkel while he was carrying out his job.

He thought about his task and started mentally running through the beings on his list. Among the places he needed to visit were London and Oxford as well as this shopping centre. The reason that he was here was to check up on a group of mammals living on the lower floors of the building. He thought of the target area and found himself in the basement. The rats that were living there immediately sensed his presence and that in itself was odd. They should be totally unaware that he was there, but that was obviously not the case. The family group in front of him looked up and stared in his direction, chattering excitedly to each other. Trego felt very disquieted by this and noted it down to report to Zoth when he returned to the spirit world. He had seen enough, so he moved on to Oxford University, the site for his next check up. He hovered above a triangle of grass. Around the three sides were tall buildings, with large leaded windows and built of warm, yellow, oxford stone. Trego could hear singing coming from one of the buildings, which he assumed was the chapel, and headed towards the roof-tops. He wanted to reach the bell tower to check on some doves that were on Zoth's list.

As he approached the tower the air suddenly exploded with white feathers, as dozens of birds flew out of the slatted apertures around the top of the tower. Trego was shocked that the birds had detected him from so far away and that they had reacted so dramatically to his presence. Then a deafening noise pierced his mind and a sonic wave catapulted him up into the air. At first he could not work out what had happened, then he realised that it was the bells ringing out the hour. The doves had not known he was there at all, they had merely learnt to leave the tower when the bells were about to ring. That was a relief and he was pleased that these animals could be left to their own devices.

His next stop was London, so he thought of Piccadilly Circus and suddenly he was being mobbed by thousands of pigeons, screaming and diving at him.

'This can't be happening.' He thought. 'They really seem to be able to see me. What on earth is going on?'

He soared high above the square, hoping to rise too high for the pigeons to reach him, but they followed him up, up and still up. Now he was above the clouds, too high for a bird to fly, but still they kept going. Soon the pigeons started to suffer from oxygen deprivation and one by one they dropped back down to earth until Trego was alone. He was unsure what to do next, as it would be impossible to observe the bird life if they were able to see him. Certainly something was not right. Birds do not communicate intelligently with each other. It is true that they fly together when migrating and will collectively take off when frightened, but that is instinctive, rather than intelligent behaviour. What Trego had seen was a group of birds, intent on persuading him to leave their territory and working together to achieve that goal. Like the rats, they also knew he was there. They could actually see him.

He now understood Zoth's explanation of how all laws are connected. Change a small part and everything is affected. He began to feel afraid. Had his misguided zeal changed things beyond repair? Was the universe about to end because of his meddling? Certainly things were very wrong, but would Zoth be able to put everything right again?

His next stop was London Zoo, where he was to look at some reptiles in the reptile house. Trego thought of the area that he wanted to visit and he was instantly standing in the corner of a small room. The tanks and cages that housed the reptiles backed onto this room, for ease of cleaning and the feeding of the specimens. A man in overalls was talking to another man, who was in some sort of uniform. The first man was explaining to the officer that the snakes had somehow told the lizards how to open the cages.

"Were they specially trained lizards?" asked the officer, completely missing the point about the snakes.

"No, of course not!" exclaimed the man, impatiently, "they are just ordinary lizards. They were imported from Africa. They weren't even tame. Not only that, they also climbed to that skylight up there."

"How? There doesn't seem to be any way up to it," said the officer, staring up at the window in the roof.

"The snakes reared up in the air forming a ladder and the lizards climbed up them. Then the snakes climbed up each other. Only the last one was not able to get out and he committed suicide rather than stay in captivity," explained the man.

"Don't be stupid." exclaimed the officer, crossly, "Snakes don't commit suicide."

"Then how do you explain the CCTV footage then?" said the man, annoyance plain to hear in his voice. "It clearly shows the snake climbing down from the table, sliding over to the plug socket and pushing its tail into the live pin hole electrocuting itself. It didn't do that by accident. It had three choices of hole and it chose the live. It knew which one would kill it. That is suicide!"

There was silence in the room. Trego was absolutely shocked.

He had heard enough, so he moved out of the zoo, and although his next call was in India, he decided to check up on the cronkel that he had seen in Sheffield.

He thought about the sky and immediately he was flying through the air, above the earth. As he was approaching the city he saw the unmistakable energy signature. It was moving around inside a large building, going from room to room as if searching for something or someone. Trego did not want to get too close and frighten it off, so he hovered high above the building watching the entity. As he watched, he became aware of another cronkel to his far right. It joined the one in the building and the two of them moved off together into Sheffield. Trego followed at a discrete distance, astonished at their sense of purpose. The two cronkels moved on into a residential area of the suburbs and into a tree lined street. The houses were well kept and the front gardens were neatly manicured. They made their way into the back garden of one of the houses, and Trego saw at once that there were six more entities. They surrounded a man and a woman, who were slowly walking along the path towards the end of the garden. The woman was sobbing and clutching a large wooden box. The man was obviously trying to comfort her, but to no avail.

"Why?" she wailed. "The vet said it was a small infection. He said the antibiotics would work. How could he have been so wrong? Oh, my poor darling."

She was inconsolable. Tears streamed down her face as her husband put his arms around her.

"These things happen, my love. There is no explanation. It was her time to die."

"No! No!" shouted the cronkels, so loudly that it hurt Trego's senses, but the humans could not hear them. They were all agitated. Trego could sense their despair as they tried to communicate with the humans.

'What are they doing here and what do they hope to achieve?' thought Trego.

The couple had reached their destination, a large hole in the ground, beneath a weeping cherry tree, at the bottom of the garden. The woman knelt down and gently placed the box on the ground beside her.

The man knelt down next to her and said gently, "Do you want a last look before we bury her?"

The cronkels were all shouting and clamouring.

Trego could make out, "Open the box, please open the box."

And "She's not dead. Just open the box and look."

The woman looked up at the man and shook her head.

"No. I couldn't bear to see her like that. She was so precious."

"I know," said the man. He picked up the box, and as he did so the cronkels became hysterical.

"Please do something, someone. She's not dead. Make him open the box."

They shouted as one. Their anguish was almost tangible.

Trego knew that they were unable to interact with the material world, but he was different. As a spirit he could intervene in this world and manipulate things within it. However it was strictly forbidden to do so, a law that had been broken by one of the spirits with dire consequences. Trego remembered Zoth's last words before sending him down to earth, but no-one was here to see him. There was no-one about and it was such a small thing to do, to right a wrong that he had clearly caused.

As the man held the box, Trego made it shake, just enough to notice.

The man shouted, "The box moved! I felt it!"

He put it back down on the ground.

"What do you mean? Are you saying she is not dead?" said the woman.

"No, I am not saying that, I am just saying that the box moved. I think we should look inside, just to make sure," said the man.

"You look, you open it," said the woman, her voice quivering.

The cronkels all strained forward.

"Yes. Yes. You open it. Please, please open it now," they urged.

The man gingerly opened the box and lying inside was a small, brown and white spaniel. He gently lifted her out and handed her to the woman, who held her close to her chest, sobbing quietly and smoothing the dog's coat. As she stroked the little dog, the cronkels moved as one and melted into the dog's body. As they disappeared from Trego's sight, the little dog shuddered.

The woman screamed. "She's alive! She's alive! She's not dead! I felt her move!"

Her husband said, "Let me see. You are imagining it. She can't be alive," but the woman interrupted him.

"She is. She really is. Quickly, help me up. We must take her indoors and get her warm." The man helped his wife onto her feet and the pair of them walked quickly up the garden path and disappeared into the house. Trego followed the couple, and saw, to his amazement, the little dog moving in the woman's arms and licking her face.

At that moment he realised how wrong he had been, believing that he could predict when a life was about to end. He knew that he had assumed that this dog was to die, but in doing so he had not only ended a life prematurely, he had ended eight lives. At least, in this instance, he had been able to put right his wrong. He would not be able to stay however; to find out how this much loved dog would cope with her seven little puppies.

Chapter 23

India

    Trego knew that all these happenings were not normal, and he also realised that they were a result of his meddling. He thought about Colandra and wondered how he was getting on locating his body, and suddenly felt a great sense of remorse at how he had caused so much grief to him and so many others.
    "Well, dwelling of these things will not help me complete this assignment," he thought, and shook himself out of his revelry.
    He consulted the list that Zoth had given him and thought of India, where the next strange occurrence had manifested itself.
    Here, something had impressed itself on Zoth. Trego only had a reference to a woman who had been healed, seemingly miraculously, and a small girl who had been brought back from the dead. However Trego did not put a great deal of credence on this. Small children can seem dead one moment and be as right as rain the next. Still, he had better check on it or Zoth would be annoyed. He already had so many examples of bizarre behaviour that he was undoubtedly responsible for, that it would be nice to find something that was not his fault. The woman lived in a village on the outskirts of Delhi. Trego was immediately struck by how poor these people seemed. They lived in houses made from mud bricks, with open windows. However, they were adorned in

colourful fabrics and tapestries. The children ran about laughing and shouting at each other, while the women prepared food outside the homes. They sang and chanted while they worked, kneading bread dough and putting rice into large pans.

Trego moved slowly through the village, but nobody sensed he was there. He felt relieved that everything was as it should be. He turned the corner of the path that he was walking down and a small child, about five or six years of age, stepped in front of him. The child looked straight at Trego and asked him who he was. Trego was startled by the question. He looked around; assuming that the child was talking to someone in the street, but the child was looking directly at him.

"You can see me?" he said.

"Of course," said the child. "Why shouldn't I? "

"Can you see me clearly?" asked Trego.

"Not as clearly as the people of the village, but as clearly as I see the others," said the child.

"Others! You see others like me?" said Trego, startled.

"Oh Yes," said the child, nodding enthusiastically. "Except the others shimmer and they don't answer me, they just run away. I think they are frightened of me."

"What is your name?" asked Trego.

"Malati. That means flower," said the child, proudly. "I am named after my great-grand mother. She lived to be 104 years old, so I hope I will be like her. Would you like to visit my home? It is only a short walk from here."

"Thank you, but no. I have come to see Kusami. Can you show me where she is?" asked Trego.

"Oh. You mean the Goddess," said Malati. "She is this way. Come, follow me," and she beckoned to Trego.

Trego followed Malati to the end of the village, where a small house was set back from the others. There, sitting on a wooden bench, was a beautiful woman dressed in a rich, red and orange sari.

She stood up as Malati approached and said, "Who is this spirit, come to visit me?"

Trego was shocked that the woman was aware of him. It was one thing for a child to see him, but quite another for an adult.

"Come closer so that I might see you more clearly. Have you come to give me what you promised?" she said.

Her voice was soft and musical, but as Trego moved towards her, her attitude suddenly changed.

"Who are you? Who has sent you to me? Answer me now! I must know," she exclaimed loudly.

"I am here from the spirit world, because it is thought that you healed a woman and brought a child back to life. Is that true?" asked Trego.

"First you must answer my questions and then I will answer yours," said Kusami, suspiciously.

"Very well. What are your questions?" agreed Trego.

"I have done all that was asked of me and more. When am I to be given that which I was promised?" said Kusami.

"What do you mean?" said Trego, puzzled, "What were you promised and by whom?"

Kusami stepped back and stared at Trego.

"I took over this body as instructed and I have been in it for twenty years. The body was old and diseased, so I healed it and made it whole again, but I do not wish to be here. I have been here too long. Now I want to return to where I was," she said.

"And where was that?" asked Trego, already knowing what she would answer.

"I was with my God," she said. "It is where I should be. I don't want to be here, on earth. I gain nothing from being here."

"Why have you taken the body of this woman?" Trego asked.

Kusami hesitated, "Who are you and where are you from?" Kusami asked Trego.

"I am Trego of the Cronkel Department, in Celestina," he replied.

As he spoke, Kusami's whole demeanour changed.

"I was forced to enter this body," she whined. "I had no choice. Please take me back to Celestina with you. I cannot stay here."

"Who forced you to enter this body?" asked Trego.

"I do not know. It matters not who it was. Just take me back and I will tell you all that I know," said Kusami, giving nothing away.

Trego was suspicious. He feared that there was more to this than Kusami was prepared to tell, so he thought of Celestina, promising to return to India when he had some answers.

Zoth was not in his office when Trego arrived back in the Cronkel Assignment Department. On Zoth's desk were even more lists, but when Trego looked more closely, he saw that they were lists of dates not names. Some went way back in the past while others were in the future. He knew that, although the Earth had a linear time line, time was, in fact, not linear at all. The past, present and future were inter-connected. If Trego wanted to access Earth he merely had to think of when and where he wanted to be and he was there. And furthermore, time was a phenomena exclusively associated with the material world. It did not exist in Celestina. As he waited for Zoth to return he thought about the situation in India. If Kusami was a spirit as she claimed, it would be impossible for her to be trapped inside a human body. All she had to do was to think of the spirit world and she would be there. No, something was not quite right with Kusami. Either she was involved in something voluntarily or she was somehow being held in this body by force. He had been unable to establish who had forced her to merge with the old woman, but this situation did not seem to have a bearing on his meddling. He went up to the Scrier and looked into its surface, asking for the name of the woman that Kusami was possessing. Her name had been Brianna and she had indeed died, but only three Earth years ago, not the twenty years that Kusami claimed. If the woman was dead, how was it that her body was still living on Earth? Trego decided to return to India and visit Kusami again. There were some unanswered questions he needed to ask her.

In the blinking of an eye he was outside the house of Kusami. He knew at once that she was not there. He was moving above the people of the village trying to sense where she might be, when he saw Malati sitting cross-legged, outside one of the huts. She immediately sensed him as he approached her.

"Malati, where is Kusami?" asked Trego.

"I do not know. Several other spirits came, dark spirits and took her. She told me that she was going on a journey. She has gone. I was frightened for her so I followed them to the edge of the forest between our village and the town. She has not returned," she replied.

"Thank you. I will search for her, as I have some information that I need to share with her," said Trego, disturbed by Malati's description of the dark spirits.

Trego thought of the area that Malati had described and at once he was surrounded by trees. Because he was a fourth level being, his senses were perfect. He could smell the mould in the undergrowth and hear the soft rustle as leaves fell through the canopy above. The birds sang high among the branches and small creatures scurried about below. He could hear earth worms tunnelling through the rich soil and even see the water coursing through the veins in the leaves of the woodland plants.

He moved through the trees searching cautiously for Kusami, with all his senses tuned. He could not understand why he was not instantly able to sense her as he moved through the trees, but he was aware of a feeling of dread, a cold shudder surging through him.

He moved hesitantly forward and reached the edge of a clearing. There was a large stone, like an altar, in the centre, and an eerie light illuminated it, like a spotlight on a stage.

Kusami stood in front of the stone wearing a long, purple robe. She had her arms stretched out above her head and she was chanting something. Her voice was even more musical and the chanting was more like singing. Trego had never heard anything like this before and he was suddenly afraid. What was she doing and why?

As he went to step forward, he noticed five dark, solid shadows standing on the opposite side of the altar. They too began to chant, but in a deep, throaty tone. He knew at once that they were demons and that they were here for some evil purpose. While he watched, he saw small lights swirling above the altar, which became larger and brighter as Kusami and the demons sang. Soon the lights were identifiable as figures, suspended in the air above Kusami. They were beautiful, swaying and dancing to the singing. It was hypnotic to watch and Trego was almost lost in the experience. He was so engrossed watching the figures that he did not notice what was happening to Kusami. She had slowly ascended into the air and now, hovered above the altar. The figures surrounded her, whirling and dancing to the rhythm, while the dark demons watched intently, just outside the circle of light. Then the singing started to change. It became guttural and sinister. The light around the altar slowly darkened, until it become deep red. The earth started to tremble and there was a throbbing in the air. High above the altar a dark cloud appeared that crackled and spat lightning bolts down to earth. Then, with a loud shriek, a vortex formed and dark shadows floated down from it to join the other beings around the altar. They all began to engulf Kusami, who suddenly woke from her trance. She cried out loudly for help, but it was too late. She was lost. She screamed and writhed about as the demons slowly dragged her up into the mouth of the great hole above the altar. The shadows followed her and soon they were all swallowed up in the vortex. A high keening noise followed them, and the vortex closed behind them with an ear-splitting explosion. Once the vortex had gone, the light disappeared and the forest became black, blacker than night itself.

Trego was very afraid. He needed to return to Zoth, and tell him of this occurrence, but when he thought of the spirit world, nothing happened. He remained where he was. He gasped. This can't be, he thought. What is happening? Why could he not return to his world? The very thing that he was most afraid of was happening. He would be trapped forever on Earth, a wandering spirit, unable to return to where he was meant to be.

However, now that the vortex had gone, the darkened sky began to lighten. The forest returned to normal. The birds started to sing and Trego could hear the rustle of the leaves in the refreshing breeze. It was as if nothing of the past event had happened. He tentatively thought of his own world, and to his great relief, he was back. He quickly went to the Cronkel Assignor's office, only to find it empty once more. He asked the other assistants for Zoth's whereabouts, but no one knew where he was. Trego was beside himself. He had vital information for Zoth and the Cronkel Assignor was nowhere to be found!

Chapter 24

Zoth's secret

Zoth was having problems of his own. He had been the Cronkel Assignor for a very long time. He was about to enter the fifth stage of his journey, and knew that once he entered the higher spirit level he would no longer be able nor want to interact with the lower levels. If he was to make a difference, then he needed to act now.

He was at a crossroads. One way led to glory, the other to doom, but the road to glory seemed selfish to him, whereas the one to doom led to the safety of another being. He was tormented by this decision and had been for some time. There was no way that he could take this path without the Great Lord knowing of his actions, but he also knew that someone else was relying on him to save their soul. What he contemplated was not evil, but it was forbidden. If he had been a second or third level being, he could be forgiven, but as a being of his experience, there was no escaping the consequences of his actions.

While Trego waited impatiently in the Cronkel Assignors office, the Cronkel Assignor was visiting the Hall of Judgement, presided over by Michelus, a sixth level spirit and one of the wisest.

The Hall of Judgement was where all cronkels ended their material existence. When they had learnt all they could from living their lives in the material world they entered the Celestial Hall for the last time, and instead of being put into the cronkel pot, they entered the Hall of Judgement to be tested as to whether they were ready to start their spiritual journey. In the Hall of Judgement, their lives were assessed by Michelus, under the watchful eye of the Great Lord, and a decision was made as to which route they would take, the six steps to heaven or the six steps to hell.

The room had two doors; one opening into the corridor that led to the Celestial Portal, allowing spirits into the first level of Celestina, and the other opening into a short passageway, at the end of which was Hades Gateway, giving access to Hades, the city of the dammed. Down in Hades the doomed souls became fiends, learnt their trade and plied their evil wares, until Lucifer decided they were worthy to visit him in Hell. A one-way spiritual lock protected the latter, so that nothing from the world of evil could escape.

Zoth wandered around the room and mentally noted how the cronkels were judged. Michelus merged with their thoughts and encouraged them to part with their deepest emotions. It was an ordeal that Zoth had never forgotten. Your whole life was scrutinised and every action and thought was examined, to ascertain whether it was deemed possible for you to eventually attain immortality. Most cronkels were accepted and became spirits, having gained completeness through hard work, great efforts and persistence; however, there were beings that were evil. Michelus would know the moment he merged with them that they were evil, but some were devious, able to disguise their true personality and these were more difficult to detect.

Zoth noted that Michelus only asked for the help of the Great Lord if he had difficulties. Most of the time he took complete charge, making the decision as to which portal the cronkel was to pass through. Zoth had seen enough. It was now or never.

Zoth thought of his soul mate, Jessica, and he was immediately by her side. They had journeyed through life together many times. Each new life had been different, but they had always managed to find each other. Zoth had lived his last life with Jessica, many years ago and he had started his spiritual journey ahead of her. He had been assured that she was ready to continue her journey on Earth without his help and that it would only be a matter of time before she would join him in Celestina. She should have lived at least two more life times since he had left her, but the fact that she had not returned to the Celestial Hall had bothered him and this had prompted him to act.

As he joined her, he was immediately overwhelmed by her situation. He knew that she had not developed any further than when he had died, those many years ago. She was still living in the same place that they had shared at that time, and her age was all wrong. She should have been over one hundred, but it was obvious that she was a young woman. She had been eighty when Zoth had died and left her behind, so he knew that something awful must have occurred to cause this dilemma.

Zoth agonised over his soul-mates distress. Why she was still living the same life? Something dreadful had gone wrong.

'Was it something to do with Trego's changes?' thought Zoth. Had his meddling ruined his beloved Jessica's life?

He looked round the kitchen; the same kitchen that he had shared with her. It was very homely, with a large pine table in the centre of the room. An old range was centrally positioned in the recess that once was the big fireplace, and logs filled the spaces on either side of it. Outside the recess were two soft armchairs, one to the right and one to the left of the range, and Jessica sat knitting in the right hand one. Two dogs sat at her feet and a cat was curled up on the chair opposite.

'My chair,' thought Zoth, as he watched her. He thought how different she seemed from the last time he had seen her. Then she was old, but now she was young. Her red hair framed her face, but it was drawn and pale. She had a worried expression and frequently glanced at the clock above the range.

Suddenly she stood up, put her knitting on the chair and walked briskly through the kitchen and into the hall. She stood there, looking anxiously at the front door. Zoth heard a car pull up outside and he glanced out of the window to see a blue estate car stop on the drive. A large, surly looking man got out, pulled a sack from the passenger seat and strode to the porch. He fumbled for his keys and unlocked the door. Jessica stood transfixed as he came into the house.

He threw the sack on the floor in front of her and said, "There, Sarah! Deal with them!"

Zoth gasped. He was right; she was still living the same life, as if caught in a loop. She dutifully picked up the sack and took it into the kitchen. She opened the sack and took out two dead rabbits. She gasped and gave a little moan, gently stroking their soft fur.

"You poor dears," she murmured softly, as tears ran down her face. "He found you then."

"Thought yer could hide 'em from me didn't yer? Stupid bitch. They're not in this world for lovin', they're 'ere for eatin'," the man said roughly, following her into the kitchen. "Now you can skin 'em and gut 'em. We'll have 'em for dinner."

"I can't," she sobbed, childlike. "They were my pets and you've killed them."

"Pets! Pets! There ain't no place for pets on a farm. If they ain't feedin' us, then they go. Do you understand woman. If yer don't like it you can go an' all," and he pushed his face close up to Jessica's and spat at her.

Jessica shrank back in horror.

"This is my home. I will stay as long as I like," she said.

"Your home! Your home!" he shouted. "Who pays for everythin' in this place, eh, eh? I do. So that makes it my place. See! And don't yer forget it, Miss high and mighty."

Jessica sat at the table and wept. Zoth listened despairingly to her sobs, knowing that he could do nothing to console her in her desolation.

"Bloody woman. You do nothin' 'cept cry. All the bloody time. Anyone would think I ill treated yer. Well do I, do I? No I bloody don't."

He grabbed hold of Jessica's face with his right hand and squeezed her thin cheeks together, pushing his face up to hers and shouting, "Shut up, you moron, shut up!"

He let her go and she gasped with pain, two big bruises already showing on either side of her mouth.

"After dinner yer can clean out the pigs," he continued. "I didn't 'ave time this mornin' cos I were too busy chasin' after yer precious pets. I need te rest cos I'm knackered. Dinner in one hour, yer hear me, one hour!"

He lumbered off upstairs to shower and she quickly hid the rabbits under the sink. She took some meat out of the fridge and put it into a large pan. After adding salt and pepper, she placed the pan onto the range and then started peeling potatoes. Zoth noticed that she lacked any enthusiasm and shuffled around the room. Her actions were almost automatic, hardly registering in her mind. So different from the vibrant woman that he had known so well.

Zoth sighed, long and deep.

'This is so sad, so sad,' he thought.

She was living a life of hell with this monster. Something would have to be done. He should have had the courage to visit her long ago, when he suspected that there was a problem, but he had been afraid, afraid for himself and of the consequences of his actions. Now he must do something to put things right. The first thing he needed to do was to find out why she was caught in this time warp, and in order to do that, he must return to the spirit world and ask some pertinent questions of the Scrier!

Just at that moment, the man reappeared, walked through the kitchen and into the sitting room. He sat down in one of the chairs, put his feet up on the footstool and turned on the television. He tuned into the football and shouted to Jessica to bring him a beer. She dutifully took a bottle out of the fridge, opened it and brought it through to him. He took it without a word of thanks or even an acknowledgement. Jessica returned to the kitchen and tested the meat. Zoth knew that there would be no way that Jessica could pass this stew as rabbit. She would have to cook the meat for two or three hours to make it tender enough.

The man came into the kitchen and sat down at the top of the table.

"Yer hours up," he said. "Is it ready?"

Jessica quickly stirred the meat and prodded the vegetables. He started to tap the tabletop with his knife.

"It's nearly done," she said quietly.

She took as much time as possible laying the table, slowly placing a knife and fork in front of the man and bringing out the salt and pepper.

All the time the man continued to tap the table and then started to chant, "Dinner, dinner, dinner."

Jessica slowly drained the vegetables and mashed the potatoes. She took a plate out of the warming oven and put a quantity of meat, carrots and potato onto it, adding gravy, which she poured liberally all over the food. She put the plate in front of the man and took out the tomato sauce.

"Where's yours?" he demanded, "Lost yer appetite? Don't fancy eatin' yer pets, then?" and he laughed loudly at her, sneering at her discomfort.

"No, I ate earlier," she said. "I will go and clean out the pigs before it gets too dark," and she quickly scuttled out of the kitchen.

She went into the porch and changed into her wellington boots and anorak. It was cold and windy outside and she pulled her coat around her as she made her way across the front yard to the large barn. Zoth stayed for a bit, watching the man eating his food. The man put a large piece of meat into his mouth and started to chew.

He let out a yell, "This ain't rabbit!" he screamed. "Sarah! What yer done with 'em? You bloody bitch. Thought yer could fool me did yer. You wait till I git yer. Yer life ain't worth zilch. I'm goin' te kill yer!"

He leapt to his feet and ran to the front door. Zoth immediately joined Jessica out in the barn. He wanted to warn her that he was coming, but he was too late. She had heard the man's shout, even from this far away. She had already thrown a strong rope around the beam above her head when Zoth materialised in the barn. She was positioning the stepladder under it and was getting ready to climb to the top, the noose in her hand.

"No!" shouted Zoth, who knew she would be doomed if she carried out her plan. "No! Don't do it. Please."

She stopped and turned, peering into the gloom. Could she see him, he thought, or perhaps sense him? Suddenly the door of the barn was flung open and Jessica backed away as the man started to advance.

"What yer doin' in 'ere, Sarah baby?" he wheedled, slowly walking towards her. "Papa's come to kill yer baby," he said softly. "I'm goin' to squeeze the life out of yer body, just like I done to yer pets. Come to Papa. Yer know yer can't get away."

He lunged at her and grabbed her arm. She was no match against the big man. Her slight frame was like a child's compared to his muscular body.

"Stop, stop! You're hurting me!" she cried.

"I don't care if I'm hurtin' yer. Yer wanted to kill yerself," hissed the man. "Well, now yer can."

The man dragged her to the rope, knocking over the stepladder as he went. Jessica was shouting and kicking. The man punched her in the face, temporarily stunning her. He went into the barn next door and fetched his leather gloves. Jessica was starting to stir, so he quickly reached up for the end of the rope that Jessica had thrown over the beam. Zoth watched the man place the noose around Jessica's neck. The man grabbed the other end and threaded it through one of the rings that was used to tether the animals. As he pulled the rope, taking up the slack, Jessica awoke. She immediately started to scream. Everything seemed to go into slow motion. Zoth tuned himself to her mind and tried to reach her.

"Sarah, it's okay. Sarah!" he said. She slowly looked round,

"David? Is that you?" she whispered.

"Yes. Yes. It's me. Everything will be alright," said Zoth.

She stretched out her arms towards him.

"Have you come for me? I've missed you so much. Why did you leave me?"

"Hush. Hush, my love. You are safe now." Zoth said soothingly.

The man had started to pull the rope, tighter and tighter until Jessica's feet only just touched the ground. She started to choke and gasp for breath, her face taking on a blue tinge.

"Just concentrate on my voice," continued Zoth.

"David, David, help me. I don't want to die." but now she was not speaking the words. Her spirit, glowing warmly, was already leaving her body. Sarah, the human ceased to exist and Jessica, the cronkel rose up and saw Zoth. He opened his arms and held her close, murmuring soothingly to her.

"Hush, my love, hush. All is well. You are safe now."

As they joined together, their light grew stronger and stronger, brighter and brighter, but unseen by any human eye. They soared up into a sky that had turned pink by the setting sun, and together they left the material world for the start of Jessica's new challenge.

Zoth escorted Jessica to the Celestial Hall and left her in the care of his assistants, reassuring her that he would return as soon as he had tidied up a few loose ends down on Earth.

When he arrived back in the barn he watched the man tie the rope to the ring and stare at Jessica's body, slowly rotating at the end of the noose. It was quite dark in the barn now, so he went to the door and turned on the light. He smoothed over the straw beneath Jessica's body, picked up the stepladder and placed it underneath. Then he knocked it over to look as if Jessica had kicked it after placing the noose around her neck. He surveyed the scene, and then smiled smugly. He went to the door, turned out the light and went back to the house.

Zoth followed him into the porch and watched the man take off his gloves and boots and put on his slippers. He placed his boots under the bench and put his leather gloves on the shelf above the coat hooks. Then he went into the kitchen and rang the police and ambulance, explaining that his wife had committed suicide.

Zoth returned to the barn just as the ambulance and police car drove up the drive.

The man took them over to the barn, saying "I won't go in, if yer don't mind. 'Er hanging there an' all."

Zoth listened to the conversation between the man and the policemen.

"She's bin depressed fer weeks," continued the man. "It's obvious what she done, ain't it? She come over 'ere and tied up the rope. Climbed the ladder, put the rope round 'er neck and kicked the ladder from under 'er. Yer can see fer yourself."

One of the paramedics came out of the barn and went over to the other policeman. He said something to him and they went back into the barn together.

The police man was gone for only a few moments, and when he came out he asked the man,

"Have you touched anything in there, Sir?"

"No. I ain't touched nothin'. Nothin' at all. It's just as she left it," said the man, adamantly.

"Has anyone else been here? Perhaps entered the barn, tidied up, anything like that, Sir?" asked the policeman writing furiously in his notebook.

"Definitely not," said the man, shaking his head violently. "No one comes 'ere. No one comes 'ere without me knowin'. We don't 'ave no visitors. I rang you, soon as I saw what she done. I ain't touched nothin'. No one's touched nothin'."

"In that case, she could not have committed suicide, Sir. I will have to arrest you for her murder," said the policeman, taking hold of the man's arm.

"No! That ain't possible," shouted the man loudly, shrugging the policeman's hand away and pushing through the door to the barn. Zoth followed and watched the man as he stood transfixed, staring at the scene in front of him. Jessica still hung from the rope, just as he had left her, but the straw under her showed that there had been a massive struggle; a struggle for life. At the far end of the barn, neatly stacked against the wall, was the stepladder, the man's leather gloves carefully placed on the top rung.

Zoth stayed just long enough to see the man being led away by the police, satisfied that his little bit of housework had had the right result.

When he returned to the Celestial Hall he found Jessica gone. Where was she, he wanted to know? She was taken by Michelus who said that she did not belong here, he was told.

He went to the Great Hall and approached Michelus.

"You took a cronkel from my care," he said.

"Yes. She is in one of the ante-chambers," said Michelus. "She does not belong with you. She is flawed. She will be added to the primordial pot in the next release."

"No! She is not flawed. She did not kill herself. She was killed by another human," said Zoth. He was trying hard to appear unattached to this cronkel, but it was very difficult.

"Her intention was to kill herself," said Michelus. "The fact that she did not was only due to the intervention of another. If her attention had not been swayed from her task, she would have succeeded."

"But she admitted, before being killed, that she did not want to die," argued Zoth.

"This is true," said Michelus. "But, if she had been allowed to carry out her intended task, she would have been dead already. Anything after the intervention cannot count towards her redemption. Just because she stated that she did not want to die while she was being killed, does not mean that she would have felt the same way when she was about to kill herself. We cannot assume that, can we? After she was distracted, her state of mind was altered. Before that time she was very clear about what she wanted to do. She wanted to die. Her life had no value, no meaning to her and therefore she wanted to end it."

Zoth was beside himself. What had he done? Had his very action to save her actually doomed her? She would be placed in the primordial pot and mixed with the raw energy, lost to him forever.

"Why are you so concerned with this particular cronkel, Zoth?" asked Michelus gently.

"I feel that we have not been fair to her. She was living the same life, over and over again. She had, somehow, become stuck in the system. She could not evolve, because we did not give her the means to do so. It was not her fault, it was ours," explained Zoth.

"Stuck in the system, is that possible?" asked Michelus. He did not know about Trego's mistake, so Zoth had to choose his words very carefully.

"Yes. It happens once in a while, but not usually with such devastating consequences. I have some very young, second and third level spirits, working in the Cronkel Department and sometimes they can be a little over-enthusiastic."

Michelus thought about what Zoth had said and then replied, "In view of what you have told me, I will allow this particular cronkel to have a hearing. There will be only one hearing and the decision will be final. Please amass all the information you have that will help me decide what course to take, anything at all that you think will be relevant to this case. If you are not able to convince me that there were mitigating circumstances, then this entity will be placed into the primordial pot. When you are ready, call me and I will come down to your level," and Zoth was dismissed.

Chapter 25

The meeting

By the time Zoth returned to his office, Trego was beside himself. Zoth could see immediately that Trego was acutely upset. In fact he was in such a state that the only way that Zoth could get him to relate his information was to make him replay the experience in his mind. Zoth was horrified. He recognised the vortex immediately. The Great Lord of All had talked of this phenomenon before. Lucifer had created the vortex in order to move freely about the universe. He had sought to rule the earth, but after a great battle, he had been banished to Hell with his minions. The vortex had been sealed, and now the only way to Lucifer's kingdom was through the Grand Portal. Lucifer knew that any attempt to leave Hell would result in the destruction of the very fabric of existence, so why was he using the vortex again. He must know that this would result in his own annihilation.

Zoth could not understand why he would want to destroy everything.

'It does not make sense,' thought Zoth.

"Perhaps he does not wish to destroy," said Trego, reading Zoth's thoughts. "Perhaps he seeks something else. After all, power is all consuming in the wrong beings hands."

"You may be right," said Zoth. "Perhaps he wants more than he has. I think I need a meeting with the other administrators. Will you set up a secret place that is protected from any outside interference? Once you have done that, summon us all so that we can discuss this event in private."

"Very well sir," said Trego, and he left to prepare an area, calling on mystical protectors and energy fields to provide a secure meeting place.

Meanwhile Zoth entered the Spirox and went up to the fourth floor where Sorcell, the weather controller, had his office. Sorcell was a fifth level spirit, who would move up to the sixth level imminently. When Zoth had first taken over the Cronkel Department, Sorcell had been his mentor and Zoth had always found him to be fair and considerate. He had a great deal of respect for the spirit and would never hesitate to ask for his advice if the need arose.

Zoth explained that he had something of a delicate nature to discuss with him and the other administrators, Bellure, the world landscaper, Dorias, the solar system guru and Roxall, the evolutionary wizard. All Zoth would say was that he had some disturbing information that he needed to share with them all. Zoth used the Scrier in Sorcell's office to communicate with the others and asked them to meet with him as soon as a secure area had been made.

Zoth returned to the Cronkel Department and waited for Trego to call. He was very worried about this newest twist to their problem. Perhaps Trego was not as to blame as he had first thought. Trego had nothing to do with the vortex, of that Zoth was certain, but what was Lucifer up to?

Suddenly he heard Trego quietly calling. All was ready, so he went to the Scrier and summoned the others and they joined Trego at a remote area of the universe. Zoth could see that Trego had excelled himself. He had prepared a meeting place behind two force fields. Between the two fields he had placed mystic protectors who swirled around, patrolling the area. Trego opened a doorway through the energy fields to allow the spirits to pass into the centre area and quickly sealed it behind them.

Zoth explained to all his colleagues why he had summoned them and what had happened, from the first discovery of Trego's mistake, to his viewing of the vortex in India.

"He has been naive and misguided, but whatever he did was done for the good not for the evil. This event in India is certainly nothing to do with him," said Zoth.

Once again Trego was asked to play back his visit to the Earth, from the animals who displayed strange behaviours, to his experience in India.

"There are so many different episodes here. What about these cronkels? I did not think it possible for them to escape from the cronkel pot!" said Sorcell. He was the spirit in charge of weather and he had looked after this area of the universe seemingly forever. He had held that position when Zoth had first arrived in Celestina and he had a great deal of respect for him. He was wise and fair, always trying to see the best in a person.

"I understand Trego's enthusiasm, but he cannot be held responsible for missing cronkels, surely?" he continued.

"The only way that a cronkel could be roaming Earth is if they escaped the cronkel pot," surmised Roxall. He was particularly interested in the cronkels because he was responsible for their evolutionary journey. Roxall was strong and reliable. He was only a third level spirit, but he was already in a position ahead of Trego. His mentor and predecessor had moved up to the sixth level just a short while ago, so Roxall was anxious to make sure that his department carried on working well.

"Escaped the cronkel pot!" exclaimed Zoth, defensively. "That's impossible! In all the time that I have been in charge of the cronkel division, I have never had any cronkel escape from the pot."

"I know that it is difficult to believe, but it is the only plausible explanation, sir," said Trego, and re-iterated the event that took place in the back garden. "They were knew exactly where they had to go and they knew that the dog was not dead. If their belief was strong enough, perhaps it gave them enough power to escape."

"So, assuming they are escaping, do they have anything to do with the vortex?" asked Bellure. She and Roxall were soul-mates and had arrived in Celestina virtually together. It was unusual for soul-mates to stay together for such a long time, but they were as close as any two spirits could be. Bellure was the complete opposite of Roxall. She was gentle and considerate, helping other younger spirits to become more confident. She was Verda's mentor and these two spirits were very alike in many ways. She could never imagine evil in anyone. Although she was in charge of the landscaping department, she still accepted help from Sorcell when necessary.

"I don't think cronkels could have anything to do with the vortex," said Zoth. "The vortex was a device created by Lucifer many eons ago. He used it to move from Hell to other parts of the universe. When The Great Lord discovered what Lucifer was up to, the vortex was programmed to always return to Hell itself and as it originated from there, all it did was follow a circular path. Lucifer and his minions assumed that it no longer worked, because they never went anywhere!"

"Oh! Clever," said Trego, admiringly.

"Could Lucifer have found out that it was not broken, merely sabotaged?" asked Bellure.

"I suppose it is possible. Though the only way he would have found that out is if someone with that knowledge told him," said Zoth, "and to be perfectly honest, I can't see anyone doing that."

"Could he have made another vortex in Hades instead of Hell?" asked Dorias, the solar system supervisor. He was a fourth level spirit, at the same stage of development as Zoth. He ran his department, on the first floor, like a well oiled machine. He used many first and second level spirits in his department and because of this his department was most like the material world. These young spirits had only just left their material existence behind them and needed a more grounded area in which to grow and develop. Dorias instilled discipline and rules that the young spirits could identify with and this made them feel safe and secure.

"Lucifer couldn't make a vortex in Hades, because he is trapped in Hell. The other demons have no power to create. After Lucifer's fall from grace, it was decreed that creation is only possible through love and I don't think there is much of that in Hades!" said Zoth, laughing with the other spirits.

Dorias suddenly shouted. "Look! Out there! What is that?"

They all looked in the direction that he was indicating, but too late. Whatever had been there was gone, leaving only haziness in its place. Two of the mystical protectors were fully drained of power and hung in space like wrung out cloths. It was evident that another was in difficulties. Trego opened a doorway in the force field and brought the three injured protectors inside, replacing them with four more and enhancing their powers.

Meanwhile Zoth and Roxall were questioning the third protector as to what had attacked them. It was very weak, but was able to tell them that it had never encountered anything like it before. It was something evil, but with real purpose, the protector said. It had seemed desperate to enter the field, even to the point of injuring itself in the process. It was driven, the protector said, as if it had no mind of its own, as if someone or something was controlling it.

"So why did it stop?" said Sorcell, "when it was so clearly winning."

"Perhaps it wanted to see how powerful we were, testing the water so to speak," said Roxall.

"No. I think its master knew, that if we were to see it, we would recognise it and so called it off when Dorias shouted," said Zoth.

"I wonder," said Trego.

"What?" said Bellure.

"It may be nothing," said Trego, "but when I was making the list for Zoth, I saw Alvienne. She was outside my room and disappeared when I opened the door. She may have had a legitimate reason for being on our level, but if that were the case someone would have had to escort her, so why run away? She seemed to be snooping, but why, and for what?"

"Hmm," said Zoth." I think we need to have a word with that little being, don't you think so Sorcell?" Sorcell agreed, so they both decided to go down to the first level to see what she had to say.

"When we return, we must decide whether to inform the higher beings of these matters," said Zoth. "Trego, while we are busy with Alvienne, examine the cronkel pot to see if there are any rifts in it. You may need to ask one of the first level spirits to enter it to get a better look. Verda will be the best one to ask. She will not scare them and will be more attentive than some of the others."

Trego left at once to start on his task and Zoth sighed. It was all getting more and more complicated. The problems seemed to be escalating out of control. He turned to Roxall and Bellure.

"Can you both look at the records in the Cronkel Assignment office for the entries that Trego has described, in particular Kusami? The records are easy to look through; you only need to ask the Scrier for the information."

"Very well," said Bellure. "If we find that Kusami is a fourth or fifth level being do you want us to speak with Petra or Gabriel? As you know, they are the higher spirits assigned to us by The Great Lord."

The Great Lord of all was not accessible to the lower spirits and so he assigned two sixth level spirits to act as a liaison between them and Himself. This task was only given to spirits who were about to enter Heaven itself and they were as close to the Great Lord as any spirit could be.

"No, not at this time. I want to try to keep these problems down here if I can!" said Zoth, dispiritedly. "I didn't want to say this within Trego's hearing, but I think his meddling is only a small part of a much bigger and wider-ranging problem that has nothing whatsoever to do with him."

The other spirits agreed with him and Zoth secretly knew that the whole of Celestina would have to become involved in dealing with this threat if it was to be resolved successfully.

Chapter 26

Alvienne's confession

Zoth and Sorcell stepped into the Spirox and moved down to the first floor, where they convened in the large central hall. Because it was frequented by newly ascended beings, it appeared much more solid than the rest of the spirit world. It still had the soft, calm atmosphere that was apparent all over Celestina, but the floor was divided up into rooms and each room had windows and doors. New spirits had to learn how to manipulate the energy within Celestina and until they had mastered this art, they could enter the rooms using a more conventional method.

The two spirits were met by Sevenath, the administrator on the first floor. He was typical of a first level spirit, albeit one who was at the top of the level. These spirits were more solid than higher level ones and had fewer abilities than those at a more advanced stage. They were not able to communicate telepathically, for instance, nor could they use the Spirox. They had to use the Scrier to communicate with the other spirits, unless those spirits came down to their floor, as in that case of Zoth and Sorcell. Sevenath was a quiet and serious individual, completely devoted to his role as administrator. Any task given him was performed with enthusiasm and dedication.

Sevenath appeared flustered, but not unduly worried. It was an honour and somewhat rare to find higher level beings in his domain, but he knew Zoth well, as they worked very closely together. Zoth was Sevenath's mentor and guide, and their relationship was one of mutual respect. He was obviously curious as to why Zoth and Sorcell were on his floor, but he knew it must be serious.

"We need to speak to you in private," said Zoth.

"Follow me," said Sevenath and led them through one of the doors into a large room with enormous windows, looking out into the space. Sevenath opened one of the windows and stepped out onto a narrow platform. Zoth and Sorcell followed Sevenath up a flight of steps leading upwards, seemingly to nothing. The steps twisted and turned, rising ever higher and higher until they reached a flat area, much like a dais. The space surrounding them had a soft pink glow and Zoth could smell vanilla in the air around them. He felt as if he was in the middle of a flower surrounded by its petals. Sevenath stopped on the dais and turned to Zoth.

"We will not be disturbed here and no-one can overhear our conversation. The air around us is impervious to sound and feelings, so everything that is said or felt here will never go any further. Even if someone were just outside the area they would be unable to hear or sense anything. I found it by accident and knew that it would come in useful one day."

Zoth had been to the first floor many times, but had never heard of this place before. He was most impressed. He explained that he and Sorcell wanted some information about Alvienne. He said nothing about why or about her trip to the upper levels, in case it influenced Sevenath or made him cautious.

"Well," he said. "She is very strange. You know that she is, in fact, a third level being and that she was banished to this level for conducting herself improperly?"

Zoth and Sorcell nodded.

"Yes. I was at her trial," said Zoth solemnly.

"She is not comfortable here and does not mix well with the others. She is secretive and spends a lot of time daydreaming. She will never ascend to the next level if she continues as she is. I have spoken to her many times, but she does not respect me, even though I am the administrator. She feels that I am inferior and her reply is always, what is the point. Well, that is, up until the visitor." Sevenath sighed and Zoth looked at him curiously.

"A being came to see her," he continued. "This being was strange, and made me feel uneasy. It was neither male nor female, which was strange, nor could I say what level it was at, almost as if it deliberately hiding its feelings. Alvienne did not share any information with us nor did she make any introductions. The being communicated with her telepathically and Alvienne did not show any emotion during their communication. After the being left, Alvienne stood looking into space for some considerable time. Now she is different, always busy doing something. When I enquire what she is doing, all she says is that she is preparing for the next level."

"Preparing for the next level! She is far from ready for that!" exclaimed Sorcell.

"I know," said Sevenath. "When I ask her to explain, she just smiles. I have heard her talking, and when I ask her to whom she is talking, she says she is talking to herself. It is all very odd. I don't entirely trust her. Some of the others complain that she snoops on them, using her telepathic abilities to eaves-drop on their thoughts. There is something different about her. It is as if she is driven by something or someone." Zoth looked at Sorcell. He had heard something similar just a short time ago.

'This cannot be a coincidence,' he thought.

"What feelings did you get when this being was visiting? Did any of the others say anything to you about it?" asked Sorcell.

"I felt cold and so did some of the others, particularly those who were in close proximity with it. On an emotional level, I felt depressed. If I were still human I would say almost suicidal. Some of the others said they felt uneasy, as if something awful was going to happen. After it left they all felt light and dizzy as if they had had too much alcohol to drink, but of course, that's not possible. It was all very strange and disturbing," said Sevenath.

Zoth looked at Sevenath, and said, "I think it is time to see Alvienne. Bring her here by a non-direct route so that she will not be able to find this place again," said Zoth.

"It does not matter which route I use as the place changes its access every time someone uses it," said Sevenath. "I am the only one here that is in tune with it. Each administrator on this level inherits this knowledge, but only knows this if they have need of it."

After Sevenath left, Zoth looked at Sorcell, and he knew that he was having the same thoughts as himself. Who was this being that had come to visit Alvienne and more to the point, if it was evil as Sevenath had said what was it doing in Celestina? The first level may be only a small step from the material world, but it should be impregnable from anything evil, even thoughts. The beings within it were all vetted most carefully by Michelus and everyone was intent on rising to the sixth level and Heaven, not plotting to overthrow the universe!

His thoughts were interrupted by the appearance of Sevenath, who was leading Alvienne to the room. She was arguing with Sevenath and had obviously been doing so all the way up the steps.

"I don't know why some spirits want to see me. What on earth can they want? Why can't you talk to me about it?" she was saying. "Oh! It's you," she said as she arrived on the dais and saw Zoth.

"Thank you Sevenath," said Zoth, and Sevenath walked back down the steps, disappearing in the pink mist.

Zoth looked at Alvienne and was immediately reminded of the trial that he had had to give evidence at. Zoth had not seen Alvienne since that time and she had changed little. She was still a bold spirit, almost manly. She always seemed to be scowling, which took away her spiritual beauty, making her seem petulant and hard. During the trial, Zoth could not recall her being anything but bad tempered and irritable, not good traits for a third level spirit.

Now he turned to her and said, "I have asked Sorcell to accompany us so that everything is clear and above board."

Alvienne recognised him and said, "Oh. It's to do with that error I made when I was working in the weather control department." She sounded relieved. "I was tired and was not concentrating. We all have lapses. None of us are perfect," she added defiantly. "Well, what do you want? I am very busy. I have places to go, people to see. You are interrupting my schedule."

"What schedule is that?" asked Zoth. "What places, which people?"

"Just people. No-one you would know." she said, guardedly.

"You told Sevenath that you were going to move up a level shortly. Is that right?" asked Zoth.

"Right that I told him, or right that I am going to go up a level shortly?" she replied, suspiciously. Zoth could see that she was puzzled by his questions. He also realised that they were getting no-where very fast.

"I know that you were unhappy about your punishment, being sent back to the first level, but you needed to understand that we must abide by the rules. There are always consequences for our actions," said Zoth, calmly.

"I was unhappy, but not anymore. I have found a way of moving up, painlessly and effortlessly," Alvienne said smugly. "You teach us to become one with all the centres of our being in order to be whole and enable us to reach immortality. I struggled for eons to achieve that and when I make one small mistake, all that effort is for nothing. Here I am back where I started. Well, now I don't care. Do you know why? I will tell you why, because I have found a way of moving up without effort, without pain and without suffering."

Zoth and Sorcell stared at her. What had Alvienne done? Who had this stranger been that had obviously offered her something that could not be delivered?

"Alvienne, tell me what you want to ultimately achieve, what all beings want to achieve?" said Zoth, gently.

"Immortal life in complete harmony with all things." she said without hesitation.

"And how can that be achieved Alvienne?" asked Sorcell.

"Normally, by knowledge, truth, experience and practise, but I have learnt of a better way, an easier way," said Alvienne, defiantly.

"It is impossible to gain immortality without pure knowledge and truth. It is impossible to gain pure knowledge and truth without experience, and it is impossible to gain experience without practise," said Sorcell. "If you were to gain immortality without these things, it would be false. You could not sustain it and therefore it would not be immortality. If you put a snake in a room with two cages, one full of male mice and the other full of female mice, it would soon die, because it would not have the experience and knowledge to let them breed, thus supplying him with meals for ever. It would eat its way through one cage of mice and then the second. Once they were all eaten the snake would starve to death. And so it is with us. If we gain immortality without knowledge or truth we do not have the means to exist forever."

"No, that is not so," cried Alvienne. "I have been promised. It is all arranged. Once I have finished my tasks, I will be transported to the highest level and become an immortal."

"Who has promised you these things? Who will transport you?" asked Zoth, gently.

"I cannot say, I must not say or I will be destroyed. I will be doomed to Hades," she cried in terror. She was moaning now and wringing her hands in a dreadful way.

Zoth looked at her sympathetically.

"It's alright. No one can hear us in this place, no one, not even the Great Lord. You must tell us all you know. It is the only way that we can help you. No-one will know that you have told us. We can make everything right for you," said Zoth. "But we cannot help you if you don't tell us everything."

"Oh no. Oh no," she cried. "If I tell, I will be doomed by the being for breaking our pact and by The Great Lord for what I have done in the beings name."

"I believe that you were forced to do all the things you have done," replied Zoth. "I shall advocate for you on your behalf when we speak to The Great Lord and I am sure he will understand and see your anguish. I believe that he will look kindly on your predicament and make an acceptable offer," continued Zoth. "I will implore Petra and Gabriel to intercede for you also and they will do so, as long as you are honest."

Alvienne looked from Zoth to Sorcell and let out a piercing scream.

"Oh! You have ruined everything. I wanted so much to have immortality, but I knew I never would attain it. He saw that. He felt my frustration. He feeds on negative emotions and I was full of them, so he came to me. What he asked was easy. He said he would give me immortality in exchange for her. She would have been doomed anyway, so what was the harm? She came willingly. I did not force her!

He said that his way was forbidden, because it gave you immortality without knowledge. But he said he knew a way of getting knowledge directly from immortals and that once I was on the highest level, he would show me what to do."

"Did he say why this way to immortality is forbidden?" asked Zoth, puzzled as to whom Alvienne was referring to when she spoke of 'her'.

"Did he explain that the only way that you can get knowledge from an immortal is to steal it? Did he explain that if you steal knowledge from an immortal they die? That is why it is forbidden. Did he tell you these things?"

Alvienne looked shocked. She was stunned. This was not how it was supposed to be. The being had made it seem so easy. Alvienne just had to carry out his instructions and then he would make her immortal.

"As I said before, there are always consequences to our actions. Nothing worthwhile is easy to attain. We must take you to see Petra and Gabriel. They will know what to say to the Great Lord," said Zoth. "Come, we will take you to the Celestial Hall while we talk to the others." Alvienne merely nodded numbly and followed Zoth down the steps, with Sorcell taking up the rear. Once on the first floor it was an easy journey to the Celestial Hall, and Sorcell and Zoth left Alvienne being cared for by Zoth's assistants. Moments later Zoth and Sorcell had returned to Trego's secure area, facing the other three administrators and Trego.

Zoth quickly explained to Roxall and Bellure, Dorias and Trego all that had taken place with Alvienne, and they agreed that the time had come to involve the higher beings.

"Do you think she will tell us who this stranger was?" asked Bellure, "And who was the female that she alluded to? What did she do with her?"

"I do not know the answer to any of these questions, but perhaps Petra will be able to get her to divulge the answers," said Zoth.

He asked Trego if he had resolved the issue with the cronkel pot.

"There is a hole," he said, excitedly.

He had gone to the Celestial Hall and looked all around the cronkel pot, even looking underneath it, he explained.

"I could see nothing amiss," he told Zoth, who nodded smugly at the others. "Everything looked exactly as it should," he continued. "I asked Verda to search the bottom of each room, paying particular attention to the walls. She entered the pot and went into each compartment, moving slowly down to the centre, where the walls all join. At first she couldn't find anything untoward, but just as she was about to leave the mammal compartment she noticed a strange roughness right at the very bottom. We took all the cronkels out of the room and put them back into the celestial Hall so that I could go down and take a look. She was right. I could see the hole. It was like a split in the fabric of the pot. Each side of the split overlapped each other, like a valve, so it was very difficult to see. You could only see it if you were facing the edges of the split. I asked her to go outside the pot and I would step through the hole so that she could see where the hole was from the outside. When I stepped through the hole I found myself next to Verda, but she did not see me emerging from a tear or split. She said I just appeared from nowhere. When we examined the base of the pot there was no evidence of a split. I asked Verda to repeat my test and it was as she said. One minute she was not there and the next she was by my side. We examined the tear again from the inside and it is partly in the mammal room and partly in the human room. It is where the walls meet at the very bottom of the pot, but there is nothing to see on the outside."

"So what have you done to protect the cronkels?" asked Zoth, visibly shaken by this turn of events. He was so sure that it was not possible, but now, not only was there a deliberate tear, there was also some magic performed on it to prevent anyone from seeing it. Why would someone do that, and for what purpose?

"I have divided the bird room in two and put the humans in one half and done the same in the reptile room to give some space for the mammals. It is not very satisfactory, but will do until Gabriel can sort out the hole for us," said Trego.

"Can you not change the spell?" asked Zoth, who was aware of Trego's skills in magic.

"No. It is completely out of my league," he said sadly. "Whoever set it up is very clever."

Zoth found it most unnerving to think that a higher level being must be behind this piece of sabotage and this was the deciding factor in persuading him to talk to Petra and Gabriel.

The information that Roxall and Bellure had learned regarding Kusami was worse, far worse. She had indeed taken the body of a cronkel, but according to the records the cronkel, Brianna, died and arrived in the Celestial Hall about three years ago. The cronkel had been put into the human compartment of the cronkel pot and from there, had been re-born as a baby in Hungary. If Kusami was still in possession of the body of the same cronkel, she must have healed it and be using it as a host for her own spirit. Dorias told Zoth that Kusami was a fifth level spirit, due to move up to the sixth and final step to Heaven. She should not have wanted to leave Celestina, so what was so important, of such magnitude, that it could entice her away from her goal? What was she doing on Earth and why was she in the presence of evil demons?

Zoth's companions were in total agreement with his decision to speak to Petra and Gabriel. Petra had only just attained the sixth level and had been an advisor for the Cronkel Department ever since he had risen to the fifth level. He had a vast amount of experience dealing with problems associated with non-spirit issues as well as the usual problems that come hand in hand with dealing with confused cronkels. However, Zoth knew that he would never have had to deal with anything of this magnitude before.

Gabriel was also a sixth level being, but he resided just outside Heaven and acted as a liaison for lower beings. He was in charge of portal security, but spent much of his time teaching. He would soon attain his goal of immortality and enter the inner sanctum of Heaven itself. He was disappointed that he had not managed to take Trego as his assistant and future successor, but he had been too slow and Zoth had got to him first.

The task ahead would probably be the last that he would have to carry out before his ascension and Zoth hoped that it would not be his undoing.

Both Petra and Gabriel listened to Zoth's story and asked many questions.

"You have done well to have found out as much as you have," said Petra. "And I agree that this is no small Cronkel Department problem."

"I think my first task must be to seal the cronkel pot and then I think we had better speak to Alvienne," said Gabriel, sadly.

Zoth was glad that the two higher beings understood the gravity of the situation.

Colandra's revelation had opened a whole can of worms that threatened to destroy everything that the Great Lord of All had created. Not just mankind, but the whole universe was in danger and Zoth knew that everyone would have to work together to prevent disaster.

Chapter 27

The big decision

    Down on Earth Colandra had bade Michelle a very difficult farewell and returned to the hospital. He hoped that he would be able to return to her as soon as he had seen Zoth.

    Once at the hospital, he gained entry in the same manner as he had before. He made his way to room one and spoke to Vincent, who was in the company of three other entities.

    "Well, what have you decided to do?" asked Colandra.

    Vincent hesitated. "Many of my friends have found it very difficult. They still believe that these souls will somehow return unharmed, even though I have tried to explain that that is impossible. I tried to tell them that it was not what they wanted, but rather what was the right thing to do, but I don't think they understood. Some of them are very young, both in human terms and in soul terms," he answered sadly. "It is different in this room. It was the first room to be used for comatose patients. Now there are only the four of us left. All the others have been taken by the evil ones. We are all old souls, as well as mature men. We have decided to ask you to terminate our lives. We have all agreed that by dying in this way we will be saving others and therefore we are laying down our lives for our friends. Does that make sense to you?" asked Vincent.

"Yes, I understand," said Colandra, "but I do not want you to die, nor is there any need for that. You may be needed in the future to help save the lives of the others. How many rooms are there where all the entities have been stolen? " asked Colandra.

Vincent knew of only one, room forty. As he entered the room Colandra looked at all the young men and women lying in their beds. All their threads ended in a ragged tear, and drop by drop their energy was ebbing away.

"Why do the other entities not want to save these souls," asked Colandra, clearly at a loss. It all seemed patently obvious what must be done, but somehow he had not been able to convince all the other entities. Vincent was plainly upset.

"One of these men is the husband of a woman in room twenty three. They were both attacked by muggers and shot. They arrived here about six years ago, and this man's entity was taken two years after his arrival. I could not convince his wife, Ellen that she would be releasing him from a terrible fate, but perhaps you could talk with her."

As they were speaking a small entity slid into the room and hovered above one of the beds. Colandra knew that this was the woman, Ellen, and moved to her side. He could feel her despair and could not help reacting with sympathy towards her.

"I know that you love him," he said, "but you are not helping him by refusing to let him go. He has to rely on you to do the right thing because he is helpless. You know that the evil beings have not stolen his entity for any good purpose, but now you have the opportunity to save his life. I do not know in what sort of hell he is being kept, but believe me it will not be pleasant. You can save his life, not his life on Earth, but his true life, his soul, so that he can continue to grow and progress."

As Colandra spoke, Ellen was clearly affected by his words.

"I am afraid that I shall be banishing him from the only life he has," she said. "What if you are wrong? What if his entity comes back on its own and can re-attach itself. I will be killing him!"

Colandra could understand how torn she was.

"Did you not see the escort spirits that came for the young man who died in room three?" he asked gently.

"No!" she said. "I was not there. If you can show me someone, other than yourself, that can honestly say that they saw this, then I will gladly let my husband go," she said.

Colandra turned to Vincent and said, "Please ask Lucy to come here."

Lucy entered the room and went up to Colandra.

"You asked to speak with me," she said quietly.

"Yes I did. Can you describe to Ellen what happened in room three? She was not there and would like to know."

Lucy immediately told Ellen how the nurses tried to save the man's life, but to no avail. Then she described the entity rising from his body and the escort spirit meeting him. She explained how all the watching entities could feel his love and warmth rising up with him and how his radiance glowed all around them.

"It was beautiful to see," she went on. "We were transfixed at the wonder of it. I am no longer afraid to die, because I know that I will be welcomed into the next life by someone kind and gentle, and that my soul will live on."

Ellen had listened attentively throughout Lucy's story and now she turned to Colandra and said, "Let us release my husband from these evil monsters. We cannot let them win and certainly not with my husband's soul!"

"When he returns to his body, and before he is escorted to the Celestial Hall, you will be able to see him and say goodbye to him, I promise," reassured Colandra, hoping not to let her down.

Now that Colandra had her consent, he explained to Vincent and the others that he was going to ascend with the other souls when the escort arrived.

Vincent gasped, "You will ascend with them? Is that not dangerous?" he said.

"I do not know, but it is necessary. Once I have ascended I will explain to the spirits what is happening down here," he said, "and then hopefully things will change for you all."

Vincent stared at him.

"Will you be able to return to Earth?" he asked, obviously worried.

Colandra sighed. "I do not know. I hope so, but that is not important. What is important is that the spirits are told what is going on, not just here at the hospital, but in other places too."

By now room forty was full of all the entities at the hospital. They all wanted to witness this event and bid farewell to their friends. Colandra explained that he needed to find the pharmacy so that he could put the first part of his plan into action and Lucy volunteered to show him where this room was. Colandra followed her through the ventilation system until she emerged into a small room with shelves all along its walls, filled with bottles and boxes. The two entities waited for a while in the empty room until two nurses unlocked the door and entered. Colandra watched as they went to a desk and opened a book that was lying on top.

"Room ten," said one nurse, running her finger down a list on the left hand side of the page.

"There are three of them on antibiotics and Anthony wants us to tell him when we have given the last dose. Hmm, they need to have one now and another at six o'clock. Then they will have had the full course. They have all had their sedation, so if we give out the antibiotics, we will still have time to do the sedation round in room forty before our lunch break. You okay with that?"

She looked over at the other nurse, who nodded and said, "It's a bit early, but it shouldn't make that much difference," and she opened a small fridge by the door and took out three vials of liquid. She took them over to the first nurse and they both checked them with the entry in the book. She drew up the doses into three syringes, placed sticky markers around their shafts and placed each one onto individual plastic trays. Both nurses left the room locking the door behind them.

"When they come back they will be checking the sedative for the patients in room forty," said Colandra. "I must look for the bottles so that I can persuade the nurses that they have the right ones. Unfortunately I do not have a clue as to what I am looking for!"

Lucy chuckled, "It's just as well I came too then, as I see the bottles every day,"

Lucy scanned the shelves until she found what she was looking for. The bottles held two hundred and fifty millilitres of the sedation and there were about twenty bottles on the shelf. Colandra could see that they all looked very similar. It was easy to see how Monica could get it wrong, especially as she would not have expected some of them to be double strength ones. The only noticeable difference was that the single strength one had a red cap covering its top and the double one had a blue one. Colandra could see that the writing was different, but that was not difficult to change in a person's mind. You just had to suggest that it was the right one and the person assumed that it was. Colandra needed to change the nurse's perception of the coloured caps and it should all go like clockwork. He hoped! A short while later, the two nurses returned to the pharmacy and consulted the book once more. One of the nurses, walked over to the shelf that held the bottles of sedative. Colandra was hovering above and did his magic! She picked up the double strength bottle and took it over to the desk.

"Is that the right one? We don't want to make the same mistake as Monica," said the other nurse, but Colandra was instantly there making sure that both of the nurses saw the bottle as single strength sedation. Satisfied that all was as it should be, the nurses left the room. Colandra and Lucy entered the ventilation shaft and made their way back to room forty.

They arrived ahead of the nurses and told the entities that everything was set up and the nurses were on their way.

After a short while the big double doors opened with a bang and the team of nurses entered the room. Colandra watched the nurses washing one of the bodies. They were not aware, of course, that these patients had no souls and washed, turned and massaged each one carefully. One nurse started to add a dose of sedation to a new bag of dextrose saline, the salt and sugar solution which was feeding the patients. All the entities watched closely as she repeated this action all along the room, each patient being given a double dose. The second nurse followed along behind her checking that the right amount was added and restarting the pumps that delivered the fluid. Colandra watched her adjusting the rate, and as she did so he confused her, so that she set each one faster than before. Now, not only were the patients getting a double dose, they were getting it at a quicker rate. The nurses finished their tasks and left the room, totally unaware that their actions would cause mayhem in a just few moments.

The room was quiet now, apart from the sound of the patients breathing, and Colandra broke the silence by saying, "They should just go into a deeper and deeper sleep and eventually stop breathing. That should signal their entities to return and alert the spirit escorts to come for them."

As he was speaking, it was evident that the patients were slipping away, as one by one their entities arrived. They were pale and dull, unlike their companions around the room, but everyone was jubilant that the plan was working. The new souls were surrounded by their friends, who tried to give them some of their energy. Colandra saw, to his joy, that his promise to Ellen was fulfilled as she met her husband and the two merged for a few blissful moments. Then the bleeps started to sound, one after the other, until the room was reverberating with sound.

Over the intercom came an urgent voice: "Code blue! Code blue! Room forty! Crash team to room forty! This is not a drill, I repeat, this is not a drill!"

The double doors suddenly opened and a large group of nurses rushed into the room. Anthony came in behind them, pushing a red trolley. Then they all stopped and stared, totally shocked. There were thirty patients in the room and all the intravenous pumps were lit up like Christmas trees. Where should they start and who should they try to save? Just then Mr Grant entered the room.

"What the hell is going on?" he shouted. "Don't just stand there, do something, you useless twits!" he continued. But everyone knew it was too late. There were too many needing help and too few people to give it.

Colandra and the entities watched, fascinated, as the new souls slowly rose up into the air to be met by two spirit guides. They would escort these souls to the Celestial Hall where they would be able to draw strength and energy, enough to be able to recount their ordeal at the hands of the evil beings.

Colandra quickly joined the new souls and rose up with them, pleased that his theory was correct. He hoped to be able to help Zoth deal with the awful events that were very quickly escalating out of control.

Chapter 28

Closing a contract

    Vincent had watched Colandra and the souls that had been stolen by the evil beings disappear with the spirit escort. He was glad that his friends had had the courage to let them go, for now there was hope where, before, there had only been despair. He would have to trust that Colandra would be able to help rescue him and his friends from their living death.

    Mr Grant was saying to Anthony, "Close this room until I decide what to do. If we are not very careful, we will end up in a massive enquiry, which I cannot afford. There is too much at stake for that."

    Anthony stared at him and said, "You can't be serious. There is no way we can hide thirty bodies, no way. We can deal with one or even two people dying, but thirty. For goodness sake, we can't make thirty bodies disappear."

    "According to the authorities, these people don't exist. Leave me to deal with it, you just follow my orders and then everything will be fine. Talk to the nurse who administered the sedation and see if it is related to the other day. Now dismiss the team and give everyone a tea break while I make a few phone calls," and with that he marched out of the ward. Anthony spoke to the team and they all left the room together. Vincent pondered on what

Mr Grant had inferred. It would seem that no one was concerned whether he and his friends were alive or dead. In fact it seemed that their families thought they were already dead. It was time for the entities to visit their loved ones and see if they could provide them with some answers.

Vincent spoke to them all saying, "You all heard what Mr Grant said. According to the authorities we are already dead. I think it would be a good idea if we each check up on our families and see if that is the case. It will be easy to see whether they believe we are dead or alive. We will have to wait until the evil beings have visited, then we will know that we have until the following day to travel, find out what we can, and report back. Is everyone in agreement?"

All the entities agreed, and fled to their respective rooms, to hide within their bodies, waiting for the right time.

Vincent knew that Colandra needed all the information that was possible to get, so he followed Colandra's trail through the ventilation shaft until he found Mr Grant's office.

Mr Grant was sitting at his desk with the telephone receiver to his ear, when Vincent emerged.

"Thirty persons, dead! Yes dead!" he was saying. "The General Manager will come! No! I have not told him. I don't need to. He will know. He is a demon! He knows everything!"

He listened for a moment, the sweat pouring down his cheeks, as the person on the other end of the telephone spoke back to Mr Grant.

"Yes, but not thirty! He told me he would kill me after the other one! What do I tell him? How can I defend this? I am doomed, doomed!"

He listened again.

"What sort of compensation? He will expect another thirty souls! I can't find thirty people. Don't be ridiculous!"

Again he paused, but now he appeared calm.

He slumped back in his chair and said, "Well, if I suddenly disappear, don't presume that I have gone on holiday! He will have killed me, I know it. Be careful or you will be next. Just don't let them die or the demon will want revenge and his revenge will not be sweet!"

He was interrupted by a knock on the door and Anthony came in.

Mr Grant nodded at Anthony and said into the telephone, "I must go and sort out this business. Goodbye." And he put the telephone down.

"Sorry, I didn't realise you were on the phone," said Anthony. "I have spoken to the nurse who administered the sedation and she is absolutely certain that she gave the correct amount. The nurse who checked it with her is also adamant that the correct amount was dispensed. Sorry but I can't shake either of their stories."

Mr Grant sat with his head in his hands and sighed deeply.

He looked up and said, "Very well. Get them to write statements in case we need them, and also ask James to come and see me please."

Anthony looked at Mr Grant and Vincent could see the look of pity that passed over his face. As one of the first patients to arrive at the hospital, Vincent had seen the staff come and go. He knew that Anthony had worked at the hospital for eight years and at first, had been diligent and caring. Now, he obeyed orders.

Managers had come and stayed for a few years, but always left abruptly. One minute they were there and the next they were gone. This manager, Mr Grant, had arrived three years ago. Then, he was full of vigour and enthusiasm, but now he was a shadow of that man. Vincent presumed that the pressure was too much.

"Can I do anything to help?" Anthony was asking. "You know that we had a call from Carlton House yesterday, don't you? We will be admitting two children from there later this week, and we have that woman's uncle coming soon."

Mr Grant looked up and said, "Yes, but unfortunately I need thirty by today."

He stood up and walked over to Anthony. He grasped his hand and said, "Thanks for all your support. If you hear of my demise, be suspicious, be very suspicious."

He opened the door of his office and said, "Please ask James to come and see me," and then ushered Anthony out, shutting the door firmly behind him.

Mr Grant went back to his desk, sat down and leaned back in his chair.

James opened the door after tapping on it.

"You wanted to see me guv'nor?" he said.

Mr Grant stood up, "Yes, James. I need you for an unpleasant task. We have had a tragedy in room forty. I need you to dispose of the bodies. You will need Tim to help you, but be discreet. You will have to reset the incinerators, as they went wrong after yesterday's tragedy, and Arotech had to come out to fix it. Check them through first. You know how temperamental they are. We don't want any more problems."

James tipped his cap and said, "Very well Mr Grant. One day they will blow up, you know and I just hope I am on my hols when they do! Can I promise young Tim the same payment as usual?"

"Yes, of course. Offer him a bonus too. You'll understand when you go down there."

James walked to the door saying, "Very well sir. I'll report back when the job's done." and he left.

Just as Vincent was about to go, the telephone rang. Mr Grant slowly walked over to the desk and picked up the receiver. Vincent surmised the call was unpleasant, as Mr Grant closed his eyes and took a deep breath, saying "Yes, please Miss Florence. Send the General Manager down, thank you," and replaced the receiver.

Vincent heard Lars striding down the corridor, as Mr Grant moved to the front of his desk. The door opened with a crash and Lars stood in the doorway. He roared like a wild animal at Mr Grant and strode over to him. He grabbed him by the throat, looking deep into his eyes.

"Give me a good reason why I should not squeeze the breath from your body?" he snarled, making Vincent cringe back into the ventilation duct.

"Nothing to say? Can't find a good reason? Perhaps you think that would be too good a death for you. You deserve excruciating pain, I hear you say. You are right of course. You deserve a long, painful death, so that you have time to reflect on your misdemeanour. Thirty workers I lost today, thirty. How can you be so stupid as to let this happen?"

As he squeezed, he lifted Mr Grant up off his feet. Mr Grant grabbed both of Lars's arms and worked his mouth, desperately trying to take a breath.

Lars released his throat for a few seconds, enough for Mr Grant to say, "Wait, I have more. They will be arriving tomorrow. Anthony has it all in hand. The nurse will be punished. She's the one who should be punished, not me."

The beast listened to Mr Grant's ramblings and laughed. "You have disappointed me one last time, Mr Grant. You are finished here. My Lord's wrath is too terrible to describe. Your death will tell all the other miserable humans that he will not be wronged. I didn't set this whole business up just to have one ignorant twit ruin it all."

As he spoke he raised his left hand and grabbed Mr Grant by his hair, lifting him off the ground.

"Consider your contract closed Mr Grant. Now you shall have immortality, serving my Lord, just as I promised," he said, gruffly.

He suddenly plunged his right index finger up under the man's left ear and into the base of his skull.

"Not enough to kill you, just enough to be useful," he said laughing, as his finger severed Mr Grant's spinal cord and mashed up his medulla oblongata. He dropped the paralysed man on the office carpet and rang the reception.

"Code blue, Mr Grant's office," he said calmly into the receiver and left the room.

Vincent looked aghast at the crumpled body of Mr Grant lying on the floor, a twisted grimace on his face. He could see that the man was paralysed, his eyes being the only part of his body working. They flicked back and forth in their sockets, trying desperately to make sense of all that had happened. Vincent watched the crash team arrive. After a stunned silence their professionalism took over. The placed him carefully onto a trolley and wheeled him out into the corridor. Vincent followed behind them as they took him into the emergency room. He watched as they connected him to a ventilator and attached an infusion pump to a vein in his arm.

"It is ironic," he thought. "That the only real patient to arrive at the hospital is the Manager!"

As he looked at Mr Grant, he saw a single tear run from his left eye and trickle down the side of his face, wetting the pillow under his head.

Chapter 29

Loose ends

As Vincent left the emergency room to return to his body, Lucy came to him. It was obvious that she was scared. She told him that a man was visiting room fifteen.

When Vincent arrived in room, Lars was already there. He was looking at the woman that Vincent knew had been admitted yesterday.

"Oh Christina, just look at you," said Lars. "What a state you are in, but it was your own fault. You were given a choice. If you had let my Lord Vorce merge with you, he would have healed you with his goodness and you would be here, by my side, reigning supreme over the universe. As it is, you are doomed to a life of servitude, pain and humiliation."

He paused and looked around the room, as if sensing the entities watching him.

"But, no matter. I still have your daughter! Michelle will be everything that you were not: young, vibrant and available. She will be persuaded to merge with my Lord and the two of us will follow our dream together."

He turned away and strode from the room. Vincent followed behind him, careful not to lose sight of him. He knew that it was most unusual for the General Manager to visit the sleeping patients. Never in all the time since Vincent had been at the hospital had he known such a thing to happen. He followed Lars down the corridor and into room forty. He stood in the middle of the room watching James and Tim moving the bodies of the dead patients onto trolleys and pushing the trolleys to the other end of the room. The floor to ceiling curtain was drawn back revealing double doors, which were now wide open to allow the passage of the trolleys.

Lars walked towards the doors and James looked over to him.

"Hey Mr," he said. "You shouldn't be in here. What do you want?"

Lars put his head on one side and said, "I don't want anything. I just want to watch. I am interested in your work. I am the general manager. Mr Grant knows I am here."

James stood looking at the man, then he shrugged his shoulders and went back to his job. Vincent and Lars followed the two men through the doors and into the corridor. It was obvious that all the rooms on this floor had similar hidden exits which opened onto this corridor, as there were several doors on the right hand side of it. Lars and Vincent followed the men into the back room and watched as James opened the hatch of the incinerator. The two men pushed the body from the trolley straight into the oven and James closed the hatch. He pushed a button next to the hatch and immediately a roar told the three men that the gas-fed fire inside was at full blast.

"The system seems to work well," commented Lars.

"Well it is today," said James. "It can be a bit temperamental. The furnace is very old and sometimes backfires. One day the whole thing will blow up. I just hope it's on my day off." Lars walked back into the corridor, but instead of turning into room forty, he went past the double doors, continuing down the corridor. At the end of the passageway he went into the next room, quietly opening the door and stepping out from behind the curtain. Vincent wondered what he was doing. He could understand why he had gone to room forty. After all, it was the scene of his wrath, but he had no reason to visit this one. Lars walked up the room and stopped in the middle, slowly turning and looking at all the sleeping bodies.

Vincent watched him suspiciously and whispered to the other entities, "Stay in your bodies. Don't leave them. This man is evil. He is responsible for all our lost souls. He has control of the evil beings!"

Lars slowly walked up and down the rows of beds as he said, "I know you are here. You think you can hide, but you can't! I know you had something to do with the thirty lost souls and you think you have won a point, don't you? Well you haven't. I will get you all eventually. Not one of you miserable souls will escape me. My minions will take you for my Lord and none will be spared. You make sure that you tell all your friends that their time will come, maybe not today, maybe not tomorrow, but soon. We have waited many eons for this, and when we are strong enough we will march on this earth and take what is ours."

At that the demon turned and marched down the room to the double doors. Flinging aside the curtain, he left the room, slamming the doors behind him. The entities were safe inside their bodies, but Vincent knew that they had heard everything that Lars had said. Now he was more afraid than ever and wondered what the demons next diabolical act was to be!

The following day the evil ones chose to visit Vincent's room and they were met by the demon. He had marched into the room very early that morning and when the evil beings appeared through the vortex, Lars told them that they must step-up their visits and make them more often and less predictable.

"We need more souls if our projected schedule is to be met," he growled.

The beings bowed low and said, "We are doing our best, Master, but the blasted things constantly hide from us. We are sure that they are having help from someone. The death of the thirty was no accident. Perhaps we should visit another hospital for a while and catch these ones when they become more unwary."

"I don't care where they come from as long as the cavern is serviced. We need their souls to gain our strength and we need their bodies for later. You have my permission to move on. Just get on with it or my Lord will be angry," and he stepped up to the vortex.

"Is it ready? Can I step through?" he asked.

One of the evil beings looked at Lars and said, "Yes, Master. Hax has sent a messenger. All has been prepared for you."

Lars glared at him, saying, and "It better be so. I don't want to find myself crushed to death," and he stepped into the vortex and was gone. The evil beings looked around the room, then turned and followed the demon back to their unsavoury kingdom.

As soon as the vortex closed, the entities rushed out of their bodies.

"Who was that man? He went through the vortex. I thought only the evil beings could go through," said one of them to Vincent.

"I didn't like his comments about our bodies. He said that he was going to use them for some evil purpose?" asked another.

"He is Lars, the general manager, but he is also a demon," said Vincent. "He is responsible for all the evil beings."

Vincent agreed that it all sounded very ominous, but he did not understand the implications of it all. He sincerely wished that Colandra would return so that he could talk to him, as he felt out of his depth. He agreed with the others that it was good news that the evil beings had said that they were going to another hospital, but that meant that they would never know when the evil beings would return.

Vincent decided that everyone was safe for now and sent word to all the other entities.

"It should be safe to travel to our loved ones now. Find out all you can about how you were sent here and try to ascertain whether your families believe you to be alive or dead. If they presume that you are dead as the General Manager has said, explore where you are supposed to be buried and anything else that you think will help Colandra overthrow this demon. Our very existence depends on what we find. Now go, my friends and safe journey."

When Vincent fell silent, the entities paused for just a moment to say farewell to each other, before hundreds of golden threads streamed out of the hospital, each bearing a golden entity at its head. Vincent was the last to leave, turning before he did so to offer a silent prayer for all those wretched souls that were still labouring away in torment in the demons cavern.

Chapter 30

Lucy's worst nightmare

Lucy had been two years old when she and her twin brother, Patrick, contracted measles. They had both been admitted to Hampton Green Hospital and been there for the last ten years. Poor Patrick had been taken by the evil ones just a year ago. Now Lucy sought answers, just as all the other entities did, so she searched for her mother. She found her walking down the high street in Peckham.

When Lucy and her brother were first in the hospital they had visited their mother frequently, but once they realised that it was not possible to communicate with her they had stopped. Now Lucy watched her walking down the road, laden with shopping bags and shouting at a teenage boy, who was trailing along behind her.

"Come on Robert, will you. Take one of these bags for me, there's a good lad."

But the boy just made a face at her.

"I must pay a visit before we go home and if we don't hurry it'll be closed," his mother continued.

The boy stopped, shut his eyes and said, "Oh for God's sake mother. They've been gone ten years and we still have to go through this ritual."

"Don't you say that! Don't ever say that!" shouted the woman, angrily. She turned to look the boy straight in the face.

"You go on. I'll catch you up. Here take these bags and get home."

She thrust the bags at the boy and walked quickly away. Lucy followed her down the road to the traffic lights and into the underpass. When she emerged at the other end, she watched her mother walk through some wrought iron gates into a park. After walking for a few minutes her mother entered a long low building made of yellow brick. She went up to the reception desk and showed a pass to the woman sitting in front of a computer screen. The woman pressed a button and doors opened to the right of the desk. Lucy followed her mother into a long room and immediately turned right. All along the walls were brass plaques with names and dates on them. Lucy read the plaque that her mother was looking at and it read: 'Lucy and Patrick Page. Born 16th September 1996. Died 21st January 1998.'

"No!" shouted Lucy. "No! We are not dead!"

Her mother looked round as if she could see her. She stretched out her hand and gently touched the plaque.

"I'm so sorry my darlings. Every day I wish I had not given permission to turn off your life support. I miss you both so much."

Tears were streaming down her face and she leant against the wall for support.

Just then the door opened and the receptionist popped her head around the doorframe, saying,

"I'm sorry Mrs Page, but we are about to close."

Lucy's mother gulped back the tears and wiped her face on a tissue.

She walked out of the room and the receptionist said, "Same time tomorrow?"

Mrs Page nodded and walked back out into the fresh air. Lucy was astounded. No wonder no-one visited her, everyone thought she was dead. Surely her mother would have seen her and her twin brother after they had died. There must have been a body to have a funeral or a cremation. Lucy went back through the walls of the building and investigated the plaques. There were about two hundred of them, but there was nothing behind any of them, just bricks. Perhaps it was just a memorial to loved ones, somewhere to come after the ashes were scattered, she thought. She went back to the reception hall and looked at the notices that were pinned to a notice board. They clearly stated that this was a building whose sole purpose was to store a person's cremated remains. But where were the ashes? Lucy searched through the building, but there was nothing other than the wall of plaques and the reception hall. Lucy left and quickly caught up with her mother, who was turning down a side road.

"I'm not dead," she shouted. "Look at me, please," she begged, but there was no response. Along the road were rows of neat terraced houses and Mrs Page turned into one of them.

Robert was already sitting in the lounge, his eyes glued to the T.V.

"Alright, Mum?" he called. "Want a cup of tea?" and he got up and walked into the kitchen.

"Thanks, love. That would be nice," she said sitting on one of the kitchen stools. Robert boiled the kettle and made them both a mug of tea.

"I've put the stuff away," said Robert. "I'm sorry I got grumpy. It's just that I think you have to accept that they've gone. I know it's hard, particularly when you blame yourself all the time. It wasn't your fault. It was no-one's fault. They got sick and died."

"Oh Robert," sighed Lucy's mother. "I just wish I had seen them, so that I would know for certain. They wouldn't let me see them. I wanted a burial, but they insisted that they were cremated. They said that they had contracted a contagious disease and they had to be in a sealed coffin. At least they were together, that was something, but I will never be totally convinced. There is always that little doubt in the back of my mind."

Lucy was shocked. Why would someone do that? Why pretend that she and her brother were dead? It was incredible!

She watched her mother take a sip of tea.

"If only your dad was still around. He could always perk me up. Still there's no point carrying on about it. What would you like for your tea, son?"

Lucy did not know what to think. It was all too fantastic. The authorities must have known that she was not dead and the people who transported her and her brother to the hospital must have known that they were not dead. So what was going on? She had had seen all she needed to see. It was time to go back and report to Vincent.

When Lucy returned to the hospital all the entities had returned. They all had similar stories to tell and she cried in pain when she recalled her experience to them. She was distraught and realised that neither her mother nor her brother was going to come to the hospital, batter down the doors and rescue her. At the back of her mind there had always been a faint hope that someone cared enough to search for her, but she now knew that that was not the case, and that was a dreadful conclusion to have to come to, even more so when you were only a twelve year old child!

Chapter 31

The attic's secrets

Back at Hazelwood Cottage, Michelle was already missing Colandra and was finding it difficult to concentrate on anything. She was worried that she would never see him again and that thought was too terrible to bear.

In order to take her mind of everything she had decided that the time was right to go through her father and step-mothers things up in the attic. She shut Thomas in the kitchen before climbing the stairs, as he had a habit of following her up and getting lost. She walked down the right hand hallway to the small door to the attic above the spare room. Adults had to bend their heads in order not to crack them on the door jam, but she remembered as a child playing up there all the time. When she opened the door there was a slight musty smell that wafted down towards her and she gingerly climbed up the narrow stairs. This attic was the only one that was used; the other one was too small to be of any real use. Michelle stepped into the room and found the light switch. Immediately the room was flooded with light and Michelle was able to get a good look at what the task ahead entailed. It was a large attic, being above the spare bedrooms and the garage, and there were two round windows, one at the front and one at the back, overlooking the woods. Michelle could easily stand upright in the room, even where the ceiling sloped down above the garage on the right. Along this wall was a range of built in cupboards where Michelle had kept her toys and she remembered playing up here in her own little world.

Now there were lots of pieces of furniture taking up the space, including two chairs, a chest of drawers and lots of black bags of clothes, all of which needed sorting. On top of the chest of drawers were two large boxes that held all her parent's papers and legal documents and she decided to leave these until last.

She pulled the black bags down the stairs and piled them up in the front hall, ready for her to take to one of the charity shops in the village. She went back upstairs and found some empty boxes, which she would use for any books that she found. The boxes were small and strong, which would be easy to carry downstairs. The chest of drawers was full of books and she quickly emptied them into three of the boxes, carrying them down to the hall to join the black bags. Once all the drawers were empty, she put the boxes on the floor and pushed the chest against the wall, opposite the built in cupboard. The room was already looking clearer and now she was able to move the chairs to the back wall on either side of the window.

The next job was to sort out the cupboard. When she opened it up, she was amazed to find that it was still full of all her childhood toys and mementoes. Her step-mother must have kept everything she had made and all the work that she had done. There were drawings, cards and weird things made from yoghurt pots and toilet rolls. There were all her old school reports and photos and in one cupboard she even found her old school uniforms. She decided not to clear them out as they were all neatly stacked away on the shelves.

Now the one job that she had been dreading; the boxes. She dragged them to the back of the room, by the window, so that she could sit on one of the chairs while she went through them. She had not been relishing this and that was why she had left this job till last. She would make three piles, she decided, one for keeping, one for shredding and one for throwing away. She had a black bag for the rubbish and had kept one of the strong boxes for the keeping pile. The shredding would go onto the other chair.

Now that she was organised, nothing was preventing her from plunging in! She took a deep breath and opened the first box.

The first few things were bank statements and used cheque books. These would be shredded before they were binned so she put them on the chair. There were lots of photographs, some very old, but she did not recognise anyone in them, so they went into the black bag. She was nearly at the bottom of the first box when she came across some photograph albums. The first album was full of photographs of her father's wedding to Elizabeth. She remembered the day, but not happily. She had been rude and churlish, causing her dad a lot of pain, she remembered. Now she looked at them and could see how much her dad had loved Elizabeth. She was beautiful in her cream wedding dress and her bouquet of peach and cream coloured roses. The photographs were definitely for the keeping box. The second album was older than the first. There were photographs of Michelle as a baby and as a young girl, playing in the garden, in her school uniform, on horseback. This was also for keeping.

Having emptied the first box, she turned to the other one. This had a lot of legal documents in it, house sales and that type of thing. She found the deeds of Hazelwood cottage and attached to it was a legal document in very old English. It was dated 1898 and she could not understand it very well. It seemed to be a covenant giving the cottage and a parcel of land to Arthur Golding as a wedding gift.

'That would be my Grandfather,' thought Michelle. She knew that her father was born in 1924 because he would tease her about how he was an old man of forty seven when she was born. There was an ordinance survey map with the two documents highlighting the house and gardens. She studied it, noticing something odd. The highlighted area was in red, but there was also a green line that overlapped the red one, which included Burtell woods and the house that was owned by Mrs Mosley. She knew that Burwalls woods was part of Leigh woods, most of which was now owned by the National Trust, having been given to them in 1909, and she had just presumed that Burtell Wood was too. She put all the documents to one side and decided to investigate it later.

There were some old newspapers that looked interesting and a large brown envelope. The envelope was sealed and looked as if it had not been touched for years. Michelle took it out and carefully opened the top. She pulled out several pages and some old photographs. The top page was a divorce certificate naming her father and a woman called Christina Ford. It was dated September 21st, eight months after Michelle was born.

'She must have been my mother,' thought Michelle. 'So why did my father tell me she was dead? Unless, of course, she died after the divorce.' The paper had her parent's dates of birth and she realised with a start that her mother was just twenty three when Michelle was born. That made her twenty four years younger than her father.

'If she is alive, she will be sixty now,' thought Michelle. She also wondered what was so terrible in her mother's life that would cause her to leave her eight month old baby.

'Perhaps she hated me,' she thought. 'Perhaps I was such a terrible child that she couldn't bear being with me.'

Michelle looked further into the brown envelope and found a letter dated 1971 and addressed to her father.

Dear Michael,

The cat is driving me bonkers. He is trying to possess me. I have to get out. The baby senses there is something wrong. I look at her, but feel nothing. It has all gone wrong. It was meant to be so perfect, but now it will never be the same again. When she is older, tell her that I love her,

Christina.

Michelle did not understand the letter. It seemed to be the ramblings of a mad person. She unclipped the photo and looked at it. It was a picture of a beautiful young woman holding a very small baby. The woman was smiling down at the baby and a man, whom Michelle recognised as her father, stood behind them with his arms protectively round both the mother and the child. It was a lovely picture and Michelle gazed at it, tears welling up in her eyes. She wiped her tears away with the back of her sleeve and put all the papers back into the envelope. She would make an appointment with her solicitor tomorrow and show him all the things she had found, about the house and about her mother.

There was nothing else of much interest left so Michelle put the empty boxes in one corner, put the brown envelope and the house maps into the keeping box, and gathered up the stuff for shredding. She carried the shredding, the bag of rubbish and the keeping box down to her study and then went back up to the attic. As she open the window overlooking the woods she thought how strange it was that so much in her life was changing. Colandra had opened her mind to so many new ideas and now the attic had revealed a part of her life that she had never known existed. She gazed out at the trees and remembered how, so long ago it seemed, she had wished for a new direction in her life and now it was so different that it was unrecognisable.

Chapter 32

Rescued Souls

In the Cronkel Department, Zoth was busy thinking out his defence for Jessica. He knew that he would have only this one chance to save her, so it had to be good. He was interrupted by Trego, who told him that a cronkel wished to speak with him.

"What are you talking about?" he said, holding back his irritation.

"A cronkel says he must speak with you," repeated Trego. "He says that it is a matter of life or death for the human race."

Zoth stared at him. "Who is this cronkel?" he asked, suddenly suspicious.

"It is Colandra," said Trego.

"Well, why didn't you say so," said Zoth, hurrying down to the Celestial Hall. The Hall was full of cronkels and the emotional turmoil coming from these newly released souls was almost physical. One of them immediately broke from the group and approached Zoth.

"I must speak with you privately," said Colandra, urgently. "I have important information

For you and these entities must be guarded until you have had a chance to talk with them."

Zoth looked at Colandra, knowing immediately that he was speaking the truth and that this information was somehow connected to the other problems that were unfolding. He could see that the cronkel was almost spent of energy and very frightened.

"Trego, I am taking Colandra to one of the antechambers. We will be with Sorcell. Only interrupt us if it is absolutely necessary," said Zoth, "In the mean time place some mystic protectors around the Hall and keep all these entities inside. Try to reassure them until I return."

With these words, Zoth merged with Colandra and took him to one of the antechambers. These rooms were located between the Celestial Hall and the Hall of Judgement. They could be used by either the Cronkel Department or Michelus and his staff. They afforded protection to any vulnerable cronkel and its walls exuded energy, allowing cronkels to rest and recuperate in a calm and peaceful environment. Zoth gently encouraged Colandra to relax and draw sustenance from the energy within the antechamber.

"I shall be asking another spirit called Sorcell to join us, so that you can give your account to us both. Is that alright?" asked Zoth.

Colandra nodded and Zoth continued, "You will not see him as clearly as you see me, because he is of a higher level, but be assured that he has your best interest at heart. He is fair and understanding, but he will need to ask questions that you may find a little disquieting. It is important that he understands fully everything that you have to tell us."

When he thought that Colandra was recovered, he telepathically called Sorcell to the ante-chamber and introduced him to Colandra. Zoth could see that Colandra was awed and reassured by the presence of the spirit Sorcell.

"I sympathise with your predicament," Sorcell said to Colandra, "and I appreciate how difficult this must be for you. Now take your time and explain as fully as possible everything that has happen."

As Colandra talked, Zoth became more and more bothered by what he was saying. Zoth asked him to repeat the description of the vortex, as he realised that this was the same phenomenon that had occurred in India. He also knew that this same wind had initiated Colandra's evolutionary journey and he suspected that Colandra had recognised it, even though he would not have understood its significance. Zoth took Sorcell to one side, and to prevent Colandra from listening in on his conversation, telepathically conversed with him. He explained who Colandra was and his connection to the event that took place in 1666.

"Yes it is definitely the same vortex," whispered Sorcell. "It is as we feared; the same vortex as in 1666. We had to burn the city. Nearly everyone was killed. Lucifer had to be stopped and it was the only way. It definitely sounds as if he has found a way of making another vortex and he is up to something just as nasty, by the sound of things."

Zoth looked at him and then at Colandra.

"So Colandra was right, that the only way to save a soul taken by Lucifer is for the body to die?"

"Oh yes. Quite right," said Sorcell. "All the souls of the persons who had supposedly died during the plague were, in fact, taken by Lucifer. It is thought that he introduced the plague for just that purpose. When London burned, millions of souls were released from Lucifer's grasp and saved from the torment of a living hell. While he keeps the bodies alive, he can use the souls as he likes. That is why all those souls, stolen at the hospital, have returned to us. It was the same all those years ago. This Lars is no doubt a servant of Lucifer who has somehow made a pact with the Managers of the hospitals. It is the only way that something of this magnitude could be kept secret. Don't be fooled into thinking that this is only happening in Colandra's hospital. I suspect the same thing is happening all over the world." he continued.

Sorcell turned to Colandra and asked, "This demon, Lars that has taken your body, can you visualise him for me, not his physical body, but his voice and any psychological impressions he may have given you?"

Colandra replayed the evening when he and Michelle first met Lars and the subsequent meeting in Mr Grant's office.

"You did well to escape from his clutches. From the feelings that he evoked in you, this creature will be one of Lucifer's demons rather than a fiend."

"What is a fiend?" asked Colandra.

"A fiend is a cronkel that has gone bad," explained Zoth. "When cronkels enter the Hall of Judgement they will either be deemed good and become a spirit, or they are deemed bad, in which case they become a fiend and are banished to Hades."

"Is it always that simple; either good or bad?" asked Colandra innocently.

"No it is not," said Sorcell. "Sometimes a cronkel must return to the material world to relearn some of the lessons. But tell me Colandra, this woman that you were fleeing with, she is important to you?"

"Oh, Yes," replied Colandra. "She has been helping me to find my body, but now she has done far more. She wants to help and knows that the human race is in danger."

"But tell me, what does she mean to you?" he asked gently. "She is obviously very important to you and yet you have jeopardised this relationship to come back to us."

Zoth watched Colandra and saw that he was having difficulties answering the question.

"I suspect that she means more to you than as a mere helper," he said gently.

"Yes, she does," Colandra replied. "I think I love her. She means everything to me. But what use is that, if the human race is dead. It seemed a simple enough task, to find my body and rejoin it, but now that I know that this monster has it, I realise that I cannot get it back on my own. Michelle has been tremendous, putting her life in danger for me, but now it is not safe for her. We need help."

"Is there anything else that we need to know, anything at all?" asked Zoth. Colandra was silent for a moment.

"I have told you about the vortex, the ripped golden threads, the evil beings and Lars. I have told you about the hospital and the comatose patients, and I have told you about Michelle. The only other thing is that when I was listening to Lars speaking to Mr Grant, he spoke of a contract that Mr Grant had broken. He gave the impression that he had contracts with many other people, which implies that there are other hospitals with more people in them."

Zoth looked at Sorcell and nodded sagely. It was just as the higher spirit had surmised.

"I think that is all," continued Colandra. "but I urge you to speak with the entities that accompanied me here. They will have more information about the hospital and of course the life they were being forced to live."

Zoth told him not to worry; they would certainly speak with them. As Zoth went to take Colandra back to the Celestial Hall, Colandra turned with a cry, "Wait, I have forgotten Sirtis," he said. "He was the green lizard in the cronkel pot with me, in the human compartment, but he is Michelle's cat, Thomas. He should not be a cat, he should be a human and he knows that. He told me that he has lived his nine lives and is most upset to discover that he has returned to Earth as a cat."

"He knows this?" asked Zoth in surprise, remembering watching the fire-breathing dragon and the green lizard cavorting about in the cronkel pot.

"Yes, most definitely. He immediately recognised me and spoke to me telepathically. He is very upset and feels that he has been wronged," added Colandra.

Again Zoth reassured him that he would look into the matter and took Colandra back to the Celestial Hall, where he told him to rest and recuperate. Then he took the other entities into the antechamber, for a discussion with himself and Sorcell.

Zoth and Sorcell listened to the entities who had escaped the clutches of Lucifer. They had all been taken while they were travelling outside their bodies, they said. Some of them had only just arrived at the hospital when they were taken by the evil beings, while others had been at the hospital for several years. They described the pain of separation and the journey through the vortex. They had been taken to a great cavern, where many more entities were being held. Once there, an evil being probed their minds and used their thoughts against them, creating alternative futures that they were forced to enact, again and again. Each time the nightmare would become more and more agonising, bringing into play emotions too painful to recall, but the evil beings would laugh at their torment, feeding off these emotions and became more and more powerful.

Zoth asked them how many evil beings there were and they told him that in the beginning there were few, but as the number of entities grew, so the number of evil beings grew. Zoth asked them if there was a leader among the beings and if so, could they describe him. They all agreed that there was one being, more powerful than all the rest. He came and went fairly frequently, sometimes through a doorway in the cavern, but also through the vortex. The other beings seemed afraid of him, bowing low, addressing him as My Lord. He encouraged the other evil beings to be more and more inventive with their mind games. If the beings were not aggressive enough or did not enter into the games with enough enthusiasm, My Lord would punish them, but they could not explain what he did. All they knew was that it must have been very painful, as the beings would scream and writhe about. It was terrible to see, they said, but they could not help feeling a little gleeful, however, their glee would soon change when My Lord left, as the beings would take their anger out on the entities.

One thing they all agreed was that the evil beings had grown in strength since they had first arrived in the cavern.

"Do you think 'My Lord' is the same being as Lars the demon?" Sorcell asked Zoth.

"I do not know. Colandra never mentioned Lars going through the vortex. If he has the body of Colandra then I think it highly unlikely that he could take the body down to Hades, that's assuming the cavern is in Hades, of course. The other alternative is that he leaves the body so that he can travel. According to Colandra's story, Lars did not leave his host when he was chasing Michelle from the congregational hall. That would imply that he could not do so, because why else would he miss an opportunity to eliminate a threat?" replied Zoth.

Zoth looked at his colleague, knowing that these newest cronkels were becoming exhausted and that they needed to recuperate. He did not want to put them into the cronkel pot yet, as they may be needed again, so he summoned Trego and asked him to cordon off a part of the Celestial Hall and place the cronkels there, where they would be able to rest, but would be easily accessible.

Trego took the cronkels away and Zoth sighed deeply. Sorcell went back to up to the fourth floor to talk to Petra and Gabriel leaving Zoth to his thoughts. Zoth knew that, a problem that started as an innocent mistake made by an over enthusiastic Cronkel Assignor Assistant, was in fact one small symptom of an Earth changing catastrophe. It was no longer a case of trying to hide the problem from the Great Lord of All, but a matter of convening a meeting of all the spirits to work out a way of defeating a cunning and vicious adversary.

Chapter 33

Preparations

Gabriel would soon ascend into Heaven and become immortal, but he was not so far advanced that he was unable to appreciate the problems that afflicted younger spirits. He was charged with advising the administrators and in particular sorting problems arising within the Cronkel Department. He had listened attentively to all that Colandra, Zoth and Sorcell had to say and decided that it was time for him to inform the Great Lord.

He had a meeting with Felicia, who was the liaison between all spirits and the Great Lord. Felicia resided in Heaven and sat at the feet of the Great Lord. She was His most beloved spirit. She agreed with Gabriel that this was a most serious threat to both the spirit world and the material world and therefore it must be investigated by both worlds if a satisfactory solution was to be found. Felicia had instructed Gabriel to arrange a meeting in Celestina, but set up in such a way so that all parties could contribute.

Gabriel was now deep in thought as to how this could be achieved. The meeting place would need to span all the levels and include the cronkel division, which was just outside the spirit world. He did not want to create a whole new place for the meeting, but he must create a system that would allow everyone to hear what was going on regardless as to what floor they were on and at what level they belonged. He could not rely on the Scrier as that would be too time consuming.

He went down to the cronkel Department and asked Zoth if he might borrow Trego. He knew how keen Trego was with regard to magic and he thought that the two of them should be able to come up with a working hypothesis. After some deliberation Gabriel was satisfied with his and Trego's system.

He went to the Scrier and told Felicia that he had finalised the meeting place.

"Where will the meeting take place?" she asked him.

"Here, in Celestina. I wanted everyone to feel relaxed and in a familiar place. They may be required to make difficult decisions and I thought that would be easier here than anywhere else."

Felicia told him that she would chair the meeting, Petra would be in charge of bringing forward the witnesses, and Zoth was to chaperone Colandra and the cronkels when they were called to give their accounts.

Gabriel generated an orb of energy within the Spirox and created a platform within the orb. This platform was called the Cassell and was a living entity. It would slide up or down the Spirox giving access to any spirit who wished to use it. When a spirit was standing on it, his or her thoughts were transmitted to the Cassell which in turn radiated these feelings to everyone within Celestina. Normally it was impossible for lower beings to be able to see or hear higher level beings, but it was imperative that during this meeting everyone could see and hear what was going on.

Gabriel needed to make sure that not only the spirits could be seen and heard, but also the cronkels and Colandra. They did not need to take part in the meeting, but they needed to tell their stories. So Gabriel created a gap under the Celestial Portal to allow the Cassell to extend under the Portal when it was on the first floor. This meant that when a being stood on the Cassell behind the Celestial Portal, it had the same effect as when a spirit stood on it in the Spirox and everyone within Celestina would hear and feel the beings thoughts. Normally the Cassell worked both ways, radiating out the feelings of the spirit using the platform and absorbing the feelings of the other spirits within Celestina.

This gave the spirit on the platform a burst of energy that fortified them during this difficult time. Gabriel knew that this would be a unique experience for the beings waiting in the Celestial Hall. Spirits were well used to this, and learnt how to cope with it, but some of the cronkels may be overawed.

"It may be too much for the cronkels and Colandra," said Gabriel to Felicia. "There will be so much energy being transmitted to them that they may not be unable to function properly. In order to limit the amount of thoughts and feelings being absorbed by the Cassell, I have put a binding spell on the platform, so that the questioner must enter the Spirox in order to communicate with the witness. This way the beings will only absorb one spirits energy, rather than thousands. They may still find it difficult, however."

"I shall ask Zoth to prepare them for this," said Felicia. "If he explains it to them and demonstrates what it will be like, it will alleviate some of their stress. I realise that they have been through a great deal, but if we are to overthrow this tyrant, it must be done."

Gabriel went to the third floor to speak with Zoth and Trego.

"Felicia has asked that you talk to Colandra and the cronkels and prepare them for their ordeal," said Gabriel to Zoth.

"Yes, he has communicated with me. I understand what must be done," replied Zoth.

"The beings need to be kept in the Celestial Hall until they are needed, but we will need your statement before that time," said Gabriel. "The binding spell on the Cassell will only apply to the cronkels and Colandra. It will not affect spirits who are telepathically aware. Where are Alvienne and Jessica being held?"

"Jessica is in an ante-chamber off the Hall of Judgement and Alvienne is in the care of Sevenath on the first floor," answered Zoth.

"Felicia has decided to try Jessica's case at the end of our meeting. Have you compiled all your evidence?"

"Yes I am quite ready. I shall be glad to have it sorted out."

Gabriel dismissed Zoth to carry out his duties with Colandra and the cronkels, and turned to Trego.

"Trego I need you to ensure that Alvienne is safe. We cannot risk her escaping without her telling us all she knows. I feel sure that she is a key player in this hideous drama!"

"Very well, sir. I will set up some mystical protectors around the room that Sevenath is keeping her," and with that he entered the Spirox and was gone.

Gabriel was left in the Cronkel Department by himself. He stepped up to the edge of the floor and looked out into the Spirox.

'What a tragedy it would be if all this was destroyed,' he thought, looking all around. 'We cannot let that happen. And if it means that we must fight, so be it.'

Gabriel knew that he had done all he could to provide a safe and fair environment in which to learn about this dreadful situation. Now they just had to hear the evidence and decide on the right course of action. He knew that many spirits were totally unaware of what was happening and for them it would be a frightful shock, but these were dangerous times and they all had to become involved.

Chapter 34

Investigations

    A hush descended on Celestina as Felicia called upon the entire spirit world to take heed, and attend a most important and serious event. The Great Lord of All was evident above, but He would only interfere if Felicia needed Him. Zoth and Petra hovered in the Spirox, just outside the orb of energy where the Cassell silently waited. Every spirit in the kingdom of Celestina moved to the edge of their floors and looked out, some of them mystified as to reason for the summons. The last time a meeting of this magnitude had been held was when Lucifer had tried to conquer the spirit world and now Felicia hoped that they would they be able to stop him permanently this time?

    Felicia entered the Cassell, called the spirits to order, and to bear reverence to the Great Lord of All.

    Every spirit within the place looked up at the Great Lord with exultation and excitement. Every spirit saw him differently. For each one, he was their own personal God. He was their reason for living, their fortitude and strength. He radiated his warmth and pure goodness down into each one, giving them sustenance. As he gazed down at them his presence flowed through them, right down to the lowest level where Colandra and the cronkels waited. A feeling of joy and exhilaration burst throughout the kingdom, and each being, from the highest to the lowest, felt uplifted and ecstatic.

Felicia asked Petra to explain to everyone why the meeting had been called and what threat hung over the entire universe. Petra entered the Cassell, and told the assembly all there was to tell, starting from when Zoth realised that a mistake had occurred, to the arrival of the thirty cronkels in the Celestial Hall. Felicia knew that for many spirits it was a shocking story.

Felicia asked Zoth what he had done to rectify the mistakes made by his apprentice, and what conclusions he had come to. Zoth entered the Cassell, and explained that he had compiled a list of all the beings that he surmised had been affected by this error, and that he had sent Trego to Earth to examine various phenomena that worried him. Felicia asked Trego to step forward. Trego entered the Cassell with great trepidation. He told the spirits all about his journey to Earth, what he had seen and what he had done.

Felicia made no comment when Trego told him about the cronkels and the little dog, although he could feel the emotions of the other spirits. He told them of the man who had lost his soul-mate and the cronkels in India. He explained what had happened in the woods with Kusami, describing the vortex, and how he was unable to get back to the spirit world. Felicia could feel a ripple of fear pass through the spirits at this point of Trego's narrative, and she knew he needed to rest. She asked Zoth to escort Colandra to the Cassell so that she could ask him about the vortex.

Colandra and the cronkels had been listening attentively to all that was taking place. Felicia could feel the fear rising in Colandra when Zoth showed him how to use the Cassell and she stepped into the Spirox and said, "Do not be afraid, Colandra. This is your chance to make a difference, to stop Lars and rescue all the other souls on Earth."

Colandra spoke confidently and explained about Lars and the vortex, the hospital and the evil beings. Felicia could feel the spirits concern and thanked Colandra for his bravery.

Next it was the turn of the cronkels, and they were asked to describe in great detail what the evil beings looked like, the cavern, and the one that the evil beings called My Lord.

Each one was called, and each one gave their account of their ordeal at the hands of the evil beings. Once they had all given their evidence, Felicia instructed Trego to place them into the appropriate compartment in the cronkel pot for re-assignment. She had heard enough about the hospital, and knew that something must be done sooner rather than later, if they were to stop this demon of Hades from carrying out his objective.

Once the cronkels had been safely deposited in the cronkel pot, Felicia asked Zoth what had been done about the tear in the pot.

"The tear was done by someone who is aware of mystic fields and magically repairs," explained Zoth. "It is difficult to see from inside the pot, and almost invisible from outside. Trego has put a temporary patch on it, but Gabriel will need to look at it for me. I believe that it must have been made by a spirit not an evil being and it must have been done from inside the pot, not outside. The only beings that can enter the pot are cronkels and spirits, but the door can only be opened by either Trego or I, which poses a problem. Neither of us is capable of creating the hole!"

At those words a ripple of fear ran through the whole of Celestina.

"We will leave that question for the time being and move on," said Felicia. "What has been done to trace Kusami?"

"She is apparently a fifth or sixth level being. That is all I know," replied Zoth, and stepped off the Cassell, vacating it for Petra.

"I have found out that she is, in fact, a sixth level being, but she is no longer here," he said.

"She claimed that she was forced into the body of this elderly woman, but we all know that a higher being is not constrained in that way. She must have left Celestina of her own free will for it is impossible for her to have been stolen from here!" he continued. "The only conclusion I can come to is that she was on Earth, having taken over the body of this old woman, and was approached by the demon, perhaps offered something that she wanted more than to stay here."

Sorcell stepped onto the Cassell, and asked, "Why would she want to take over the body of this woman, and what can the demon have offered her that was preferable to eternal life in Heaven?"

All the spirits murmured their agreement.

"Perhaps she wanted power and a God-like status, and she gained that on Earth in this body," suggested Petra, taking Sorcell's place, "She had all the power of a fifth level being. She could pretty much do what she wanted within a material world. She would have known, however that she could never return to Celestina after what she had done. Perhaps she grew bored or tired, and when the demon came, he deceived her into believing he was from Celestina rather than from Hades and offered her forgiveness. Please will Trego re-tell his experience in the forest and in particular the change in Kusami when she realised that it was an evil demon, not a spirit that was aiding her."

Felicia called Trego once more and asked him to re-tell his tale. It was plain from his story that the beings at the altar had started singing musically, and that it was not until Kusami was in a deep trance that the beings had shown themselves as truly evil. It was then that Kusami had been afraid, and realised that she did not wish to accompany them.

"We have to assume that she has been taken by the evil beings, but where, remains a mystery. She cannot survive as a human being in Hades, so perhaps the demons have worked out a way of using the vortex between different places on Earth," said Felicia.

Once the spirits had heard all there was to hear, Felicia called for a rest period while she discussed the findings with the Great Lord. They still had to hear about Jessica and make a decision as to whether she should go into the primordial pot or the cronkel pot, and also speak to Alvienne and hear her part in all this, but for now Felicia sensed that many of the spirits needed to recuperate, so a rest would revitalise them for the next stage in the proceedings.

Chapter 35

Alvienne's admission

Felicia re-convened the investigation and asked Trego to return to the Cassell.

"The situations that you witnessed with the reptiles and pigeons, do you realise the significance of these unusual events?" she asked him.

"Yes," he replied in a shame-face voice. "I realise that these animals should have been assigned to a higher level, one of greater intelligence. It was my fault for taking their souls too early."

"You are right," replied Felicia. "If you had left them to die naturally, they would have achieved something that would have signalled to you and Zoth that they were ready to rise up a level, but you did not allow them that chance. They should have gone into the mammal compartment to begin that stage of their development."

"I am glad that Zoth gave me the opportunity to witness the effects of my stupidity," he said contritely, "And I would like everyone to know that I shall never change anything again without first consulting a higher being."

He was so sincere that all the spirits were impressed with his remorse. Felicia told the hushed assembly that in light of Trego's obvious regret, the Great Lord had chosen to dismiss Trego's interference.

"He feels that Trego had been over-enthusiastic," she said, "but now that he is aware of how catastrophic changes can be, he will be more circumspect! He also knows that Trego's changes have nothing to do with the circumstances that we find ourselves in now."

Trego bowed low and accepted his admonishment. Felicia knew that he would never change the rules again without consultation with his advisors.

"I would like to start the next proceedings by talking with Alvienne," continued Felicia and she asked Petra to call the spirit to the Cassell.

When Alvienne arrived the spirits waited expectantly for her to enter the Cassell.

She hesitated and Felicia said, sharply, "We cannot help you if you are not willing to divulge your part in this ghastly scheme. This is your only chance at redemption. We will only protect you if you are honest and frank."

As Alvienne stepped onto the Cassell, all the spirits could feel her anguish and inner turmoil. The Cassell plainly told them the story of her unhappiness, and hopelessness she had felt when she was relegated back to the first level.

Felicia said softly, "We feel your pain and sorrow. You can redeem yourself, but it is up to you."

Alvienne took a deep breath and said, "I know that I am doomed and that the demon will find me eventually, but I cannot allow this world to be doomed along with me. I will tell you all I know, but in return you must protect me from the demon. Be warned, however, that he is very powerful and has many other demons at his disposal."

"He came to me in disguise," she continued. "At first I thought he was a spirit, for he has managed to create a cloak that makes you see what you think you should see. I expected a spirit to visit me and so he appeared as a spirit. I do not know how he does it, but it is very effective. He promised me immortality if I was to recruit a sixth level being to help him. He knew that there was a spirit who had delusions of grandeur. He had watched her on

Earth possessing bodies and pretending that she was a god. He said that it was obvious that she enjoyed it. I knew that it would only be a matter of time before you or Michelus would sense it in her and banish her to the first level. I used the cloak to enter the third floor and spoke with her through the Scrier in the Cronkel Department while everyone was busy. She agreed to visit me and I passed on the demon's message. That's all I did. What she did in the demons name I do not know."

"I think we can all guess what she did," said Felicia. "I am convinced that it was she who made the hole in the cronkel pot. It would have been easy to merge with the dying Brianna and enter the cronkel pot with her, particularly if she used this cloak that Alvienne speaks of. The Cronkel Department staff would expect to see a cronkel and so would fail to notice that Brianna had a parasite with her. Once in the pot it would have been simple for her to make the hole and escape back to Earth. The question now is why it was important for her to make the hole? What was it required for?"

The whole of Celestina was silent and Felicia could tell that the information that Alvienne had disclosed and the conclusion that Felicia had come to, shocked everyone, but the question still remained, who was 'she'?

"Thank you for telling us what happened to you," said Felicia, gently. "Can you tell us the name of the spirit that you recruited?"

"Her name is Kusami," said Alvienne, quietly. "The demon wanted a woman. It had to be a woman. Whether that is important or not I do not know, but maybe it is."

"I think it is important," said Felicia. "Thank you. Is there anything else that you wish to tell us?"

"No," answered Alvienne. "That is all."

"Very well," said Felicia. "Gabriel, please take Alvienne to the Hall of Judgement and place her into one of the security ante-chambers. Place a seal on the door so that no-one can enter bar you. She must be protected at all costs. We cannot allow this demon to take any more souls from us."

Once Alvienne and Gabriel had left Celestina, Felicia told the meeting that they must not judge Alvienne too harshly. She was in a deep depression and had been for some while. Every spirit should think carefully as to whether they could have helped her deal with her problems before she had sunk so low as to attract the attention of this evil being. Several spirits hung their heads in shame and Felicia guessed that they avoided her rather than get involved in a difficult situation. She would have to deal with Alvienne later, but for now she had several other matters to sort out.

Chapter 36

Reinforcements

Colandra was called back to the meeting by Zoth. He had been in the Celestial Hall by himself since the cronkels had been taken to the cronkel pot. Now he was nervous, as he knew that the spirits were about to decide his fate. He stepped onto the Cassell and Felicia asked him what he would like to do.

"Well, I would like to return to earth to finish what I feel I started. In order to do that I will need help. The demon who has stolen my body is much too powerful for me to fight on my own, I am not strong enough. If I could recruit all the patients in the hospital and I had the powers of a spirit, then between us we may be able to do something to stop him, but I cannot do it on my own."

The Great Lord of All gazed down at Colandra. He loved all his cronkels, but he had a soft spot for this rather endearing little soul, and after all, impossible things were his forte!

All the spirits had been told how the Cronkel Department had failed Colandra, and this was the opportunity for Celestina to make amends.

Felicia stepped forward into the Spirox and said, "It is my decision that Colandra should return to Earth to complete his task with all the qualities any true cronkel has. He is to be accompanied by Trego and Zoth, who are to use whatever powers are appropriate to bring about the demise of this demon without putting themselves or any humans in danger. There will be two objectives, the first is to defeat Lars and the second is to reclaim the body of Colandra."

There was a murmur of agreement from everyone. Felicia looked at Zoth and Trego and the pair nodded their acceptance.

"Colandra are you content with this decision?" she asked.

Colandra was more than content. The decision was a far better one than he had hoped, and now he felt that at last something was going right for a change.

"Thank you, yes. I am more than happy."

Zoth took Colandra back to the Celestial Hall and said, "Trego and I are still needed at the meeting, so you must wait here until we are ready to return to earth."

While Colandra waited for their return, he thought about his situation. It had changed dramatically since before the meeting. Now he was as a true cronkel would be. He knew all there was to know, but he also had the wisdom to guard it well. He now knew why the vortex was so familiar to him and realised how important it had been to his development.

'Even evil things can work for the good,' he thought.

He knew that now he had the best chance to succeed with the two spirits to help him, and although he was anxious to start on his quest to reclaim his body, he was also excited and scared at the same time.

Zoth returned to Colandra's side and told him that he was needed for an important task and could not accompany him to Earth.

"I shall come to you later. In the mean time visit Michelle. But be discrete about what you say to your friend," he warned. "She cannot help in this matter, even though she may want to. We cannot risk putting her in danger unnecessarily."

Colandra reassured him that he would be guarded in what he said to her and asked, "Felicia said that I would have the true qualities of a cronkel. I have already discovered that I have the knowledge of a cronkel, but was there anything else that I should be aware of?"

"You can travel in the same way as a cronkel, in that you are not constrained by any solid object, but you can only communicate with us and Michelle. Do you have any questions?"

"When I was here before, I could influence others to do things that they would not necessarily do. Can I still do that?" asked Colandra.

"No. You are on a completely different plane of existence," answered Zoth "You are only being permitted to communicate with Michelle because the Great Lord has deemed it so. It is a gift given to you by the Great Lord, to help you in your quest. If you need to interact with others you must do so through Trego or me, unless you ask Michelle of course. Go now and enjoy the time you have with her. You will soon be embroiled in a fight the like of which you have never encountered before. I will call for you as soon as you are needed."

At that Zoth disappeared and Colandra found himself in the crisp December air outside Michelle's cottage. He was thrilled to be back and excited that very soon he would be by the side of the woman he loved.

Chapter 37

Jessica's trial

Now it was Jessica's turn and Zoth had returned to the Spirox to wait for Felicia to speak. Felicia knew that Zoth had recorded his testament, and that this would be the only chance for her salvation. Without any more delay she called him to the Cassell, and asked him to put forward his plea.

Zoth told everyone what had happened when he had gone down to Earth and explained his part in her moment of death.

"I realise that my intervention may have changed her emotional state, but I was her soul mate and as such I felt responsible for her."

As he said those words, all the spirits gasped.

"I had not intended to interfere; I had only intended to observe her situation, just as I would any other soul that I was concerned about. But what I discovered changed everything. Please let me explain," he said.

There was a murmur from all the other spirits and Felicia said, "Continue, we are listening."

Zoth looked at her thankfully.

"When I finished my journey and entered the spirit world as a second level being, Jessica was only two or three life-times away from reaching the same goal. Someone robbed her of that.

Whoever was the Cronkel Assignor at the time took everything that she had worked for away from her. She was misplaced, and because of that she lived the same life as Sarah four, maybe five times more with no hope of growing. The same life! Over and over again! That is criminal. Anything she learnt during the next five lives was dismissed, and she would still be doing that if I had not intervened. I have been unable to ascertain who the Cronkel Assignor was at that time, but that is the spirit who should be called to the Cassell."

Zoth was emotionally depleted. He stood in the Cassell and all the spirits could feel his anguish.

The Great Lord called for a rest period, and then spoke privately to Felicia. "I have seen within Zoth's heart and his heart is true," he said to Felicia. "You must investigate these claims more thoroughly before making any decision."

During the rest period Felicia focused on when Zoth had died for the last time as Jessica's soul mate, David. Jessica was indeed ready to continue her journey without him. Admittedly she had not reached the same level of consciousness that Zoth had, but she was not far behind. Felicia called upon her powers and returned to earth just before Zoth died. He was an old man well into his nineties, and sitting on the edge of his bed, was his lovely wife Jessica. She was only a little younger than him, seventy or eighty perhaps, but they were so obviously a couple. Zoth's aura was bright and shining, almost white, while Jessica's was orange and yellow. She was saddened at the thought of losing him, but she had accepted that it was his time.

"Oh, David. You have been so much to me. I hate to lose you, but I know that you go to a better place. I will never stop loving you, even in death and I know you feel the same."

David looked up into her blue eyes and smiled.

"Sarah, I love you more than you will ever know," he said. "My life has been so enriched by your presence. I would have been only half the man I am without you by my side. You are the air I breathe and the food I eat. I have been truly blessed to have been part of your life. You must promise me that you will not lose heart once I have gone. Now promise me," and he held her hand, and brought it to his lips.

"I promise David," she said tenderly. "I will tend the garden and feed the cat, waiting for the time when I too die, and return to your arms."

She bent over, kissing him gently on the forehead. At that, his entity rose on its golden thread and the escort arrived to take him to the Celestial Hall.

"She will be alright, won't she?" Felicia heard him say anxiously, as his thread broke from his body and his entity rose with the escort.

But the escort did not answer. Felicia followed them up to the Celestial Hall, from where Zoth was taken to the Hall of Judgement. Felicia watched as Michelus determined whether Zoth was ready to start his next journey on the first step to Heaven, and again she heard him ask whether Jessica would be alright. "It will be the first time that she has had to continue life without me," he said, concern in his voice.

"She will be fine. You must not concern yourself with her now. It is time for you to move on alone to continue your personal development," he was told.

Felicia returned to earth at the appointed time of Jessica's death. She was not alone nor was she dying. A man was with her who was about forty years old. She appeared to be about thirty and Felicia immediately thought that she had appeared at the wrong time. She knew that Jessica died three years after Zoth, so she thought again of Jessica at that time. Again she found her as a young woman, very far from death. Something had happened between Zoth's death and now, so she decided to go back in six monthly increments. The first six months showed no change, but a year earlier she was a frail woman and Felicia moved forward in time, month by month. Four months later Felicia watched Jessica moving slowly towards the seat in the garden, her back bent, her body frail. Just as she reached the seat a great wind came out of nowhere. It knocked Jessica over and as she struggled to stand, a vortex appeared right on the spot where she was crouching. Felicia was a sixth level being and should not be afraid of anything within this material world, but she was certainly feeling fear now. She watched as dark beings moved out of the vortex, and the one who seemed to be in charge, looked down at Jessica lying on the ground.

"Who are you and what are you doing here?" he asked, in a guttural voice.

Jessica was so stunned, that when she opened her mouth, nothing came out, just a low moan.

"You!" he shouted at one of the beings. "Keep an eye on her while I go back down and tell the Master that we are in the wrong place again."

The other being stood over Jessica, and said, "Yes, Sir. We await your return."

Once the others were alone with Jessica they all crowded round her and one tried to grab hold of her arm, but his hand moved through her body.

"Oh, can no-one get this thing right," he said, evidently annoyed.

"Well, it is only a trial. No-one said we could touch anything," said another.

"Perhaps we can enter her body instead," said a third. "That might be interesting."

"How gross! You can if you like, but I'm not going to. You might get stuck in there!" said the first, with a shudder.

One of the dark beings moved toward Jessica, who tried to crawl away from him. He hovered for a few moments just above her head and then dived down. In a split second he was gone. Felicia watched these dreadful creatures as they huddled around Jessica.

One of the dark beings peered into her face and asked, "Are you in there?"

"Yes I'm here. This is great," came the answer.

The being inside Jessica made her stand up and walk about.

"She's really old though. All her joints are ceased up and her circulation is dreadful. I will see if I can repair her body and then I might keep it."

"Now remember what the Master said. We are only to observe and try out the vortex to see if it works. We are not here to steal bodies, well not yet anyhow," said one of them, jeering.

While he was talking, Jessica's body was undertaking a transformation. Her stooped back straightened and her legs became well muscled and strong. Her arms were now lithe and tanned and her face was that of a woman sixty years younger. The evil being within her made her dance and cavort about.

Suddenly there was a shrieking noise from the mouth of the vortex and one of the evil beings said, urgently, "Quick, he's coming back. You had best get out of her body."

Just at that point, the one in charge returned.

"Usual thing," he said. "Someone made a mistake. Hax says we should be on the other side of the world; India I believe. We are to return to Hades and try again. Hey! What's going on?" he added, as he suddenly became aware that one of the beings was missing.

The being inside Jessica made her body move toward the vortex and said, "I'm here, in this body. It's great," and he made Jessica dance about the garden, albeit in an uncoordinated way.

The dark being turned angrily and shouted "Get out of there, you stupid oaf! You will alert the spirits! We will have plenty of time to steal bodies later!"

Jessica collapsed in a heap on the grass, sobbing piteously.

The evil beings followed their boss through the vortex, screaming with laughter, and with an ear splitting shriek, it closed up behind them.

Felicia looked at Jessica and realised why she had not developed. She had never grown older from that moment on. The evil being had permanently altered her, so that her body would never progress. Although he had made her whole again, he had done so through evil, not good, and by doing so, he had destroyed her ability to grow and mature. She would stay exactly as she was at this moment. The evil stored within her body would wear her down, eating into her very heart, making life an ordeal rather than a pleasure. No wonder she had become depressed, living like that day after day, year after year, knowing that there was no escape. Even death eluded her. Felicia knew that the evil would prevent her from dying naturally, because she was no longer governed by nature. The only way that Jessica could die was if she died at her own hand!

Felicia had seen enough. She returned to the spirit world and summoned everyone to the meeting, where she explained what she had seen and what it meant.

"Zoth was right," she said. "But it was not the fault of the Cronkel Assignor. It was a demon who had stolen her soul, as surely as the evil beings had taken the souls of the people at the hospital."

Felicia found it incredibly difficult to imagine anyone so evil, as to take the life of a soul and destroy it so wantonly. She could feel the emotion of the other spirits, and even before she took a vote on Jessica's fate, she knew what their answer would be.

Jessica must be given back to the Master Cronkel Assignor and re-assigned. Zoth would be forgiven for his interference, for without it the trial would never have happened and no-one would have known about the evil dance that poor Jessica had been made to perform.

Felicia closed the meeting and thanked the assembled company for attending. Just as he was about to ask Gabriel to dismantle the Cassell, Zoth arrived back from the Hall of Judgement.

"She has gone!" he cried. "Jessica has gone!"

"Calm yourself," said Felicia. "She cannot be far. What did the attending spirits have to say?"

Zoth was distraught and answered, "They told me that she was at the meeting giving evidence and when I told them that the meeting was over, they could not tell me where she was."

Felicia called Michelus to the Cassell and asked him what had occurred.

"I was waiting for Petra to call for Jessica, so when Alvienne appeared and said that she had been asked to escort Jessica to the meeting; I presumed that she had been sent by Petra. It never occurred to me that she had any malicious intent."

"But Alvienne was in an ante-chamber being guarded! How come she managed to get out? Did no-one see her?" asked Felicia.

"I had gone onto the first floor to use the Scrier to try to locate Kusami, but I had left perfectly capable spirits in charge," said Michelus.

"Ask them to come to the Cassell. I would like to question them," said Felicia.

She was disappointed in Michelus, particularly as he knew how important these two beings were.

Two spirits entered the Spirox, looking nervous and contrite.

"Please will one of you step onto the Cassell," said Felicia.

One of the spirits, a tall, graceful female, stepped forward and the Cassell rose silently to meet her. As she stepped onto the platform everyone could sense her nervousness.

"Do not be afraid," reassured Felicia. "Just answer the questions as truthfully as you can. You were left in charge in the Hall of Judgement while Michelus was busy, is that right?"

"Yes, I was. I am left in charge quite often," she said.

"Tell us what happened while he was gone."

"Well, to begin with nothing untoward happened. We had suspended all the tests while the meeting was in progress, so I was meditating. The door from the corridor opened and a spirit entered. I did not recognise him, but then I rarely leave the Hall of Judgement to see any spirits other than those I work with. He said he needed to ask Alvienne a question about the meeting. He said that you had forgotten to ask her and it was most important. He said that I need not release her as he could ask her telepathically. I could see no harm in that. I was charged with preventing a demon from stealing her, so as long as she remained in the ante-chamber he could ask as many questions as he liked."

"So then what happened?" asked Felicia.

"After some moments, the spirit thanked me and left, again through the same door."

"Could you hear what he said to Alvienne?" asked Felicia.

"I could have done if I had wanted to, but I saw no reason to eaves drop. Alvienne did not seem afraid, nor did she cry out or ask for help. After the spirit left, Alvienne came out of the chamber and told me that she had remembered something important to tell you and rushed out of the Hall."

"Did you not try to stop her?" asked Felicia, amazed that it could be that simple.

"No! I had not been told that she could not leave. I was to stop anyone entering the ante-chamber, not the other way round. I was not told that she was a prisoner!" said the spirit, shocked.

"No. no!" reassured Felicia. "She was not a prisoner. But tell me what happened next?"

"Alvienne re-appeared some moments later and went up to the other ante-chamber, where Jessica was being held, and spoke to my colleague."

"Very well, thank you. You may step down from the Cassell."

Felicia asked the other spirit to take the first ones place and she said, "You were looking after Jessica, were you not?"

"Yes," said the spirit. "I was conversing with her. She was a little fearful as she did not understand what was happening and wanted to know when she would be released. She is a beautiful being, quiet and gentle."

"Please tell us what happened when Alvienne arrived," said Felicia.

"Alvienne said that the trial had started and it did not appear to be going very well. There were lots of accusations being made about Jessica. She said that it was not fair that Jessica could not answer them. I said that it was a dreadful shame and could Alvienne do something to help her. She said she would try. Then she left. She was gone quite a while, but when she returned she was all excited. She said that she had spoken to Petra and he wanted Jessica to come into the meeting and answer some questions. To be honest, I was delighted. Alvienne asked me if I would like to come with them, but I declined as I had several hundred cronkels to care for. She left with Jessica and I went back to my other duties. It all seemed so normal, that I never imagined anything was amiss."

Felicia sighed. 'That everything could seem so normal and yet be so dreadfully wrong was stupefying,' she thought.

"Can you say in what direction they went?" asked Felicia.

"They seemed to be heading for the Cassell as they went out through the corridor between the Hall of Judgement and the Celestial Hall. That was another reason to presume everything was as it should be," said the spirit.

"You may both return to your duties," said Felicia. "Michelus, have you been able to trace any of these spirits yet?"

"All three of them went through the tear in the cronkel pot, but none of them are on Earth or any other place within the material world, as far as I can make out. I have to reluctantly conclude that Jessica and Alvienne are in Hades, but as to Kusami I do not know."

Everyone in Celestina was aghast. So that was why the tear in the cronkel pot was necessary; it allowed an easy route in and out of Celestina!

The Great Lord sighed, a long heartfelt sigh. He had no powers in Hades and to lose two souls in this way was beyond words. He could feel the others anguish and their desire to help, but he did not want to risk losing more.

"We must rescue her!" they cried. "If Alvienne and Jessica can go to Hades, so can we!"

The Great Lord of All looked down at the spirits and smiled sadly at their enthusiasm. He knew that they meant what they said, but he also knew that he had no powers in Hades. He could no more go there, than Lucifer could go to Celestina. This would need a great deal of discussion before a decision could be made. He hushed the spirits, saying, "Quiet now. I must have a private discussion with the higher level beings. This does not mean that nothing will be done, nor does it mean that we will march down to Hades with all guns blazing. We must work out a plan that will have the highest level of success. When we have finished our discussion, you will all be told what our decision is and you will be given a chance to vote. That is all for now. You may all return to your duties," and with that they were dismissed.

Felicia led all the sixth level beings onto the Cassel and they rose silently up into the higher levels of Celestina and on into Heaven itself. He would discuss all their findings with the higher level beings and they would hopefully work out a suitable plan that would put paid, for all time, the threat that Lucifer and his demons posed upon their very existence.

Chapter 38

The letter

Colandra was not aware of the new revelations being made in Celestina, nor did he know when Zoth and Trego would join him on Earth, so he would make the most of his visit to Michelle.

It was December and the garden of Hazelwood cottage was white with frost. Colandra could see that Michelle was at home by the lights that shone through the downstairs windows. He was a bit sceptical about whether Zoth had been right about the new mode of travel, but when he thought of Michelle he was immediately by her side.

'Amazing,' he thought.

It felt as if he had been away a life time, but she was just as he remembered her. She was sat in her study, her head bent over a letter that she was reading. Her long fair hair fell around her shoulders and rippled in the pale December sunlight, as it shone through the leaded window.

The letter was several pages long and Colandra decided to let her read it through before announcing his arrival. Colandra watched her reading and saw many emotions flitting across her face as she read the letter.

As she came to the last page she looked up and tears started welling up in her eyes. By the time she had finished reading tears were streaming down her face. She put the letter down on the desk, dropped her face into her hands and cried like a baby. Colandra could bear it no longer. He merged with her and felt her anguish. She was aware of him immediately and opened her soul up to his sweet love. He was immediately aware that the letter had been from her dead father and in sharing her grief, it was a little diminished. Colandra knew that she had never grieved properly when her father had died and that she needed to express her emotions.

As the sobs subsided Colandra put one word in her mind, TEA, and now she was sat in her favourite armchair sipping a cup of sweet tea, while Colandra shimmered in front of her.

"Tell me about the letter," he said gently.

"I decided to clear out the attic, while you were away," she said. "I found some interesting papers and took them to my father's solicitor to have him explain them to me. Apparently, my father had had a mini-stroke before his main one and he was worried that he would die. He had things in his past that he couldn't talk to me about, so he put it all down in a letter and asked his solicitor to give it to me when the time was right.

When my father first met my mother he was putty in her hands. He was thirty nine and she was just fifteen. He had been presenting some paintings at the Bristol Art gallery, and she was part of a group of school girls being taken round to view his work.

They got married when she was eighteen and I was born, they were both over the moon. My mother developed post-natal depression and found it difficult to bond with me.

Then there had been an accident. We apparently had a cat, Rocky, that loved sleeping in my bedroom and one night he slept over my face. It was only the quick thinking of my father that saved me. My mother had dreadful mood swings after that, one moment stroking my face the next screaming at me. Her whole personality changed and she saw danger everywhere. She never went out and at times would lock herself in the bedroom. She even feared the cat, saying it was possessed! One day my father found the cat dead. It had been brutally slashed to pieces. My father was sure it was my mother. He tried to get her to visit the doctor, but she would accuse him of wanting to have her committed to an asylum!

Eventually she left and refused to say where she was going. That was the last my father ever saw of her. The last paragraph of the letter was an apology for her mother. He wrote, 'She was not the same as the young girl that I met all those years ago," said Michelle, reading from the letter. 'I kept telling myself that it was the post-natal depression and she was just unhappy that she could not care for you properly. But something happened to her after the cat incident. She was withdrawn, unpredictable and aggressive. She definitely changed the day the cat tried to kill you.'"

"All this time I thought my mother was dead," she went on, "but she would only be sixty now, so there is every possibility that she is alive. I shall ask Peter, my father's solicitor, to try and trace her. If she is alive I might be able to meet her. Wouldn't that be wonderful?" She turned to Colandra, smiling through her tears. He listened to Michelle and smiled at her enthusiasm. 'And she said that she doesn't need relatives!' he thought.

"So what else has happened?" he asked.

Michelle went into her study and came back with the envelope that contained the papers about her house.

"I found these when I was sorting out the attic," she said and took out the papers and spread them on the floor for Colandra to read.

"This is a map of my house and Elm tree Cottage, the house down the road," she said.

"I took these to my father's solicitor and he told me that I own both houses and the woods behind them. See where the line is drawn," she pointed to the map, but Colandra was not looking at the map at all. He was staring at the photograph attached to a birth certificate that was lying on the floor on top of some of the other papers.

"Who is this woman in the photograph," he whispered, dreading the answer.

"That's Christina Ford," said Michelle. "She's my mother."

Suddenly everything fell into place. The woman at the hospital, that Colandra thought he recognised, was Christina Ford, Michelle's mother! The resemblance was uncanny, but age had blurred the likeness, which was why Colandra had not immediately recognised her. How could he tell the woman he loved, that she was never going to meet her mother? Yes, she was still alive, but she would not be able to see her beautiful daughter, nor touch her, hold her or kiss her, for she was laying in a hospital bed, totally unaware of the passing of time, a victim of Lars, that unspeakable demon.

Chapter 39

The plan

It was not the right time to disclose to Michelle the information about her mother. Colandra would hold it close to his heart until he felt she needed to know. For now they both relaxed in each other's company while Colandra told her all about his journey to Celestina, the meeting and its outcome. He told her all she needed to know, nothing more, nothing less and they both waited for the arrival of Zoth and Trego.

"So what is the plan?" she asked, impatiently.

"I won't know that until the spirits arrive," he said for the tenth time.

"What will be my role?" she said. "I won't stand by and not be part of it; after all I was present at the beginning!"

Colandra looked at her, admiringly. She was certainly feisty!

"You will have a part to play. Zoth will give you something to do, something important, I promise."

It was at that moment that Colandra felt the presence of the two Spirits. Michelle sat back in her armchair, aware that Colandra was conversing with them but unable to see or hear them.

"I am sorry that we have been so long," said Zoth. "We have been given a plan. Come we must hasten to the hospital."

"Wait!" said Colandra. "Michelle wants to know what her role is in all this. She is anxious to help and it is important that she has a part in the plan."

"She cannot help. She is human and too vulnerable," said Zoth, abruptly.

"She can help!" objected Colandra. "If it were not for her we would not have discovered all the things that have been going on down here. You cannot dismiss her like that!"

Trego moved forward and said, "There are plenty of things that she can do. She would be most helpful at the hospital after the demon has been overthrown. There will be many people to care for and they will be confused and scared."

"Oh, very well," said Zoth reluctantly. "Tell her that she is to go to the hospital, but she must wait until you give her a signal before she enters the grounds."

Colandra told Michelle what she must do, but he was not sure that she thought it was an important enough role to play. He was worried that she would take matters into her own hands and get into all sorts of trouble.

"Come, we must get to the hospital and relay our plan to the entities," said Zoth, gruffly.

Colandra could not understand why Zoth was so changed. He had always been kind and considerate to him, but now he seemed rough and impatient.

"What is wrong," he asked, "Are you unwell?" He had never heard of a spirit being ill, but it was the only way he knew how to convey his concern.

Zoth turned and stared at him as if he were looking at an alien.

Then Trego said, gently, "He was not there, remember? He was not at the trial, and he will have no knowledge of how the meeting finished."

Trego took Colandra to one side and said, "Zoth is in terrible pain. His beloved soul-mate, Jessica, has been taken down to Hades by the demon. We do not know if it is possible to rescue her. Please be patient with him."

"Oh, no!" shouted Colandra. "That is dreadful. We must find her. We must go to Hades and get her back!"

"I thank you for your consideration," said Zoth. "And I apologise for my bad humour, but it may not be possible. We can only trust the Great Lord and the spirits to do all they can to rescue her. They mount a fight in Hades, as we mount our fight down here. Hopefully we will all be successful."

"Let us go!" said Trego, and in the blinking of an eye they were in room two at Hampton Green Hospital.

They were immediately surrounded by entities that were anxious to tell him their news.

"The evil beings have stopped coming," one said excitedly.

"Did you hear what happened to Mr Grant?" said another. Then one of them became aware that Colandra was not alone. They could not see Zoth and Trego clearly, but they could see the light that radiated from the two spirits.

"Who are they?" said one in a scared voice.

All the entities had backed off, and some had retracted into their bodies.

"It is alright, you don't need to be afraid. These are two of the spirits from Celestina. They have come to help us defeat the evil beings," reassured Colandra. Slowly the entities moved forward, and those that had hidden came back to Colandra side.

"Where is Vincent?" asked Colandra. "Will someone fetch him?"

Within moments Vincent had arrived, together with most of the other entities. Colandra introduced Zoth and Trego to them all, and explained how they would be able to help them. Vincent told Colandra and the spirits about the last visit of the evil ones, Mr Grant's fate, the new woman and the man who could walk through the vortex.

Colandra expected the entities to be able to hear Zoth and Trego and he was disappointed that they could not.

"It will be very difficult if I have to translate everything that you say," said Colandra. "What about signals and stuff like that. It may be the difference between life and death."

Zoth agreed, so he and Trego lowered the pitch of their voices to allow the entities to hear them.

"We know of this demon's schemes, but we think that we can stop him with you help," said Zoth. "It is important that no more of you are taken, so when we have told you of our plans, you must return to your bodies and stay there, until you get the signal to fight."

The entities were glad that at last they would get the opportunity to do something constructive, and listened eagerly to Zoth's instructions.

"Before I explain what our plans are, we would like to see Mr Grant and the woman. Can someone take us to him?" asked Zoth.

"Follow me," answered Vincent. "He is the only one of us that is truly in a coma."

Vincent took them to the top floor and into one of the rooms. In all the rooms that Colandra had visited, the only sound had been the soft breathing of the patients, as they inhaled and exhaled. In this room, however, he was immediately aware of the rhythmic sound of a machine. He looked over to where the noise was coming from and could see one of the bodies attached to a ventilator. Colandra went up to the bed, and saw with a shock that it was indeed Mr Grant. His eyes were open, and he stared up at the ceiling without blinking. His eyes were red, and tears had formed a crusty residue around his eye lashes. He was certainly in a very sorry state. No-one could look at him and not be moved by his plight. Whatever Lars had done, he had made certain that Mr Grant was never going to recover. Colandra notice that there was no broken thread, so his entity must be intact, but where was it?

Zoth went to the foot of the bed and said, "Mr Grant, come forth from your body. We are here to help you."

Everyone waited and watched. Very slowly the entity of Mr Grant emerged from his body, and trembled on the end of his golden thread.

"He is certainly a miserable soul," said Zoth, "but at least he has not yet succumbed to the fiends."

The entity hovered anxiously, ready to dive back into his body should he perceive any danger.

"Who are you?" he asked timidly.

"We are spirits from Celestina, the place you know as Heaven. We have come to right a wrong made by the evil one that is called Lars, and you call the Master," said Zoth.

"If you are spirits, can you kill me?" asked Mr Grant.

"Only if there is no other alternative. Why do you seek death?" ask Zoth.

"I have no useful existence. The one you call Lars, has punished me for failing him. As you can see, I am no longer able to function as a human being and my Master only waits for me to emerge from my body so that he can tear me from the thread. He has promised me eternal life as a slave to his Lord. I was tempted by his offer of immortality, but now that I have seen exactly what he is doing I no longer want any part of it. If I could do something constructive to defeat him, I would do so, but I do not think that I am capable of aiding anyone, as I am weak and helpless. I want to die, but I am afraid that when I do the Master will take me down to Hell."

Mr Grant's entity had become duller and duller as he spoke. Zoth told him to return to his body while he pondered on his predicament.

Zoth, Trego and Colandra return to room two with Vincent.

"I don't think he is strong enough to help us," said Trego, "He is likely to change sides as his survival dictates, so I really don't think we can trust him."

"I will reserve my judgement," said Zoth. "For now we will continue with our plans and deal with Mr Grant at a later date."

Zoth was aware that Lysander was anxiously trying to get his attention. "What is wrong, Colandra?" he asked.

"The woman that Vincent spoke about, I would like to see her. I think that she is the one who was involved in the explosion that destroyed my bus. I saw her being admitted when I was here last, but never had a chance to see her," he said.

Zoth looked at Vincent and asked him if he knew of the whereabouts of this woman.

"I do not personally, but someone will," he said.

An entity moved forward, "A woman was admitted to my room yesterday morning. That is room fifteen. I don't know if she is the one, but I can show you."

Colandra looked at Zoth who indicated for him to go with the entity.

When Colandra entered room fifteen many of the other entities followed and soon the room was filled with their light. Colandra moved slowly along the ward looking at the occupants of the beds.

Then he saw her. She was lying so still he thought that she must be dead, but then he saw her chest rising and falling as she breathed. He read the chart at the foot of the bed, 'Christina Ford. DOB: 26.7.1948.' Colandra was stricken. She was indeed Michelle's mother. She was only sixty years old, yet she looked far older.

Just then Colandra felt Trego's next to his own.

"Do you know this woman?" he asked.

"Yes. It is Michelle's mother. I saw her some time ago, when we were searching for my body. They had named her Jane Doe because her identity was unknown. Although her face was familiar to me, I did not establish the connection until Michelle showed me a photograph of her," replied Colandra.

"Is Michelle aware of her mother's state?" asked Trego.

"No. I decided that it would not serve any useful purpose to tell her. She knows that I found Jane Doe and that the demon had stolen her soul, but nothing else. She was so excited about the fact that her mother may be alive, after believing all her life that her mother was dead, that I could not destroy that belief. There will be plenty of time to tell her, after we defeat the demon."

Trego and Colandra looked down at the woman for several moments and then Trego said, "Come Colandra, we have more souls to safe. Take me to the incinerator room and show me this monster incinerator."

Colandra took him to the incineration room and went through the procedure that would fire up the furnace. He was glad that he had followed the body that had died, as now he could describe accurately what James had done to make the furnace work. Trego listened attentively, looking carefully at the machine as Colandra spoke. Then it was Colandra's turn to watch Trego. As Trego stared at the incinerator, the dials slowly started to turn and the gas burners fired up.

"It is definitively alight," said Trego. "But I cannot open the door while it is alight."

"Perhaps there is a safety switch on it," suggested Colandra. "It would be pretty dangerous if it was possible to open the door when it was a light, don't you think?"

"Hmm. You are probably right. I will get into the furnace and take a look." Said Trego.

"Won't that de dangerous," said Colandra, alarmed.

"I am a spirit, don't forget," said Trego, laughing softly.

He entered the furnace to have a look for the safety switch. Colandra would have kept his fingers crossed if he had some. If Trego could find the switch then he could fool the machine into thinking it was not alight and then it should be possible to open the door.

"Yes, you are right," he said when he re-emerged. "There is a switch, but unfortunately it will be impossible to do both things at the same time, cool the switch and open the door. You cannot interact with this world, so I will need Zoth to help."

"How about Michelle or one of the staff," suggested Colandra.

"No, that won't do," said Trego, firmly. "A human being would surely die when he opened the door, because when he does the fire from the furnace will roar out into the room. No, it will need to be Zoth."

He turned the furnace off and the two of them returned to the room as Zoth was telling the entities what they were hoping to do. He was explaining that they were going to wake up the patients in this hospital first and then do the same wherever Lars had control. Once everyone was safe, they would destroy the places in whatever manner was possible. The entities wanted to know what they could do to defeat Lars and get Colandra's body back.

"Your time will come," said Zoth. "I am hoping that the evil beings will re-establish contact here and I am banking on them choosing a room that they know has many souls to take. Lars will want to watch them harvesting more souls. It is crucial that he has as many as possible if his plan is to work. I believe that he has demons waiting in his cavern to take over your bodies, but you will not be asleep, as he assumes. You will be feigning sleep! When I give you the signal you must rise up and attack Lars, helping Colandra defeat him and take his body back. The most important thing is that Lars must not be allowed to return to the cavern through the vortex. Trego and I will help in that matter by placing a mystical lock over the entrance, but we will only be able to keep it up for a short while."

The entities set up a great cry of joy.

"Yes! Yes!" they shouted. "We can do this. We can jump on him and force him from Colandra's body!"

Zoth smiled at them. "They are certainly enthusiastic!" he said to Trego and Colandra.

"Indeed," said Trego. "I have a problem in the incinerator room that will require your help." And he proceeded to explain what needed to be done.

"If we can make the furnace malfunction then we can burn the hospital down, thus releasing the stolen souls, but we must be careful that we do not begin until everyone else is safe. There is only one set of stairs in the building and there are many people to evacuate."

Colandra had taken no part in the decisions. The plan had been worked out very carefully by Felicia before Zoth and Trego had returned to Earth, but now he voiced his concern, "What about the staff?" he said. "They must be saved as well. It is not their fault that Lars chose this hospital as the birth place of his evil army."

Zoth and Trego turned to look at Colandra.

"You are right," agreed Zoth. "We will not harm them."

He turned to Vincent and said, "You will set off the fire alarm as soon as you see the signal to rise from your beds, then all of you must help each other to safety. You should have plenty of time to get out if Trego and I don't rig the furnace until we hear the alarm."

"Now, is everyone clear as to what they have to do?" he asked, looking around the room at the shining entities.

"I shall neutralise the sedative so any drugs that are given from now on will not have any effect on you. You will find that over the next few days you will wake up. Bear in mind that once you are awake, you will not be able to see or hear us anymore nor the evil beings; however you will see the vortex and Lars. The nurses will continue to feed you with the infusions so do not be afraid. Stay calm, but when you have the opportunity, exercise your muscles, as they may be weak. When you see the lights flash that will be your signal to rise up and take on the demon."

Colandra looked admiringly at Zoth. It seemed that everything had been worked out and if it all went according to the plan it should have a good outcome, but Colandra was a pessimist, he knew that if it could go wrong, it probably would!

Chapter 40

Lars

Lars was a demon created by the great Lord of All as a companion to Lucifer. He was part of the conditions that were agreed upon by the two supernatural giants when Lucifer first resided in Hell. Everything in nature has an opposite, it cannot exist without one. Black and white, hot and cold, life and death, and in this case, good and evil. It was such, at the beginning of the world, when Adam and Eve sinned in the Garden of Eden.

Lucifer did not have direct access to Earth, but he could influence human life. He vied with the Great Lord, trying to persuade the humans to follow his path rather than the path to Heaven. In the main, good conquered evil, but Lucifer harvested his fair share of the corrupt and evil people of the material world.

But Lucifer became greedy. He wanted more than his entitlement. He wanted direct access to Earth, so he created a vortex, a passage in time and space, which allowed his minions to enter the material world and articulate it. He encouraged them to shower the humans with all sorts of abominations, plagues, viruses, floods, to name but a few.

Lucifer discovered that he could project the vortex to a place on Earth and watch his demons, while they possessed the bodies of the humans, or tore their souls from their human bodies, causing these souls to wander the Earth forever searching for a resting place. Some demons would bring these souls back through the vortex to entertain Lucifer in hell.

Lucifer enjoyed these interludes. He found the human souls more entertaining than his servants. They were unpredictable and vulnerable. He liked that, as he could watch while his demons inflicted unspeakable atrocities on them. He found it quite intoxicating and addictive. He wanted more and more.

He realised that there was much to be gained from direct access to these humans and he devised a plan to get just that. He instructed Lars, his favourite demon, to journey through the vortex to steal the souls of the dying plague victims. Lars brought them back to Hell to be held as hostages.

The next step in Lucifer's abominable plot was for Lars and some other demons to possess the priests of the cities church, in order to attract the Great Lord's attention. Lucifer knew that the Great Lord would get this message and he hoped that his little hostages would give him enough leverage for a good outcome. Once he had the Great Lord's attention, he would put his demands forward. It was not a big request, after all the Great Lord had a whole universe to play with! He could well afford to give Lucifer just a small part of it.

He had decided on London as the arena for his demands, as the plague was rife there and many people were dying. Lars set off on his mission with the other demons, sending the vortex into a building that was used for the containment of bodies before burial. They made their way to the churches, but the priests were visiting the sick and dying, because of the demands made upon them by the people.

Lars turned to his companions, "Come, we will go to the market place and search for the ones we seek. Follow me."

They moved quickly towards the market place and Lars saw one of the priests talking to a stall holder. He merged with the man, expecting some challenge, but the priest collapsed to the ground. Lars realised that this man was as weak as the plague victims themselves. He had not eaten for days and was exhausted. As the priest lay on the ground, Lars saw a great crowd of people surging into the square, shouting and yelling, "Fire! Fire!"

Lars could smell smoke through the old priest's nostrils and he could feel the ground tremble, but he could not get the priest to rise up. A mass of people swarmed through the market place, knocking stalls over in their panic. Children fell under the crowds and still more came. The body of the priest was carried along in the crush, being too weak to withstand the power of the people. Now Lars could see the red sky behind him and hear the crashing as buildings fell under the flames. The smoke became more and more intense and people were scrambling over each other in their panic to escape death. Soon the flames were right behind the crowds and Lars could feel the heat. He knew that it was only a matter of time before the priest would fall and be consumed by the fire. Nothing was going the way Lucifer and he had schemed. He would have to abandon the plan if he was to escape. He looked above the crowds and started with fear. He could see small lights darting backwards and forwards above the houses. Every now and then a beam of white light would burst from them and ignite another part of the city. Lars knew at once what this meant. The Great Lord of all must have found out Lucifer's plot and he had sent spirits to reclaim the souls that the demons had been stealing by destroying their bodies. Lars dare not leave the body of this man, as he knew that as soon as he took on his real identity, the spirits would see him and destroy him, but he also knew that if he did not find another body to enter he would be trapped.

Then he saw the rats; thousands and thousands of them, fleeing the city.

He knew that his companions were close by and now he shouted, "Enter the bodies of the rats! Quickly! It is our only hope!"

The rats were leaving in droves; streaming out into the countryside and safety. Lars left the sick priest and quickly merged with a large rat and ran for his life. He did not stop until he had left the city behind him. Then he turned and watched in horror as the houses burnt down to the ground, knowing that all the entities that they had so carefully harvested and taken to Hades were now re-united with their bodies, and no doubt would soon be making their way to the Celestial hall.

He looked around him, and saw that a small group of rats had stopped with him, and they were now looking at him expectantly, hoping that he would have a solution to their predicament. He knew that a rat has a very small brain and that it would only be a short while before they would be unable to remember anything, let alone put a plan into action. He must try to make them focus and help him call the vortex into being. Before he had a chance to call to them a sudden wind came up, swirling faster and faster, at first in the air then swooping down to the ground. Lars recognised it immediately and was so relieved to see it. He started to run towards it, shouting at the other rats as he ran. They took off towards the mouth of the vortex and reached it before him, but as he approached, lights appeared from the centre and he immediately knew that this vortex was not of Lucifer's making. He cowered down into the undergrowth, trying to hide from the spirits that emerged from the vortex. The other rats were not aware of the danger and continued to run towards it lulled into a false sense of security by the familiar sight. But the spirits showed no mercy. The beam of white light hit the rats as they ran; obliterating them as easily as the great fire was obliterating London.

Lars could hear a voice in his head, "All you demons, you are not welcome in this world. The passage between here and Hades will be closed for ever and you will be forced to wander this Earth for all eternity until we have destroyed you all. Know this; that we will seek you out, wherever you try to hide and we will destroy you as surely as night follows day!"

Then, with an ear splitting shriek, the vortex closed and all that Lars could hear was the screaming of the people and the roar of the fire. He knew that he must merge with a higher animal before his rats brain no longer remembered who he was, so he walked purposely towards the city.

Chapter 41

The black puma

    Lars spent most of the following three hundred years in the bodies of various cats. He found them most satisfactory. They were agile, independent and intelligent. The only drawback to this existence was that he was restricted as to where he could go. Travel was not easy in these early years, nor was it terribly reliable, but by the time Queen Victoria was on the throne, travel abroad was commonplace. The aristocracy would take safari holidays, bringing back all manner of dead animals to hang up in their great halls.

    Lars managed to hide away on one of the great ships and travelled to Africa. Once there he merged with the great cats until by chance, he was caught by a hunter and transported back to London. The hunter was collecting specimens for the new Zoological Gardens which were soon to open to the public. Everyone was excited about the promise that a black puma would be exhibited as no-one had seen one before. The great day arrived and people were queuing up to get entry tickets. Soon there was a thick crowd in front of the iron cage that housed the black beast. The small hut at the back of the cage clanged open and the crowd hushed, straining forward for a better view.

Lars strode out of the hut in the body of the puma and stood on the concrete stage in front of the people. He raised his magnificent black head and sniffed, looking first to the right and then to the left, taking in the crowd in front of him, and then he let out a horrendous roar.

The people panicked and turned to run, but the zoo keeper shouted, "It is alright. He can't hurt you. The cage is very strong. He is just saying, 'hello'."

The crowd tittered nervously, but looked back at the puma. Lars, meanwhile, had turned and climbed onto the hut. He looked all around the cage searching for weak spots that might give him a way out, but it all looked impenetrable. He would have to wait for a chance when his keeper was caught off guard.

Unfortunately for Lars that was never to happen. He lived through three generations of black pumas, until he was part of a breeding program involved in television films. Lars entered the body of a young puma cub and was sold to a private collector in Surrey. This collector trained big cats for films and advertising, and Lars was raised with two other cats in a spacious cage in the back garden of a house in Sutton. He was well cared for and soon grew into a well muscled healthy animal, just waiting for a chance to run!

In 1970 he managed to escape from his cage and lost no time disappearing from the public eye. He ended up in Bodmin Moor, becoming the Beast of Bodmin. The public would get tantalising views of him every now and then, but in the main, he kept himself well hidden, growing in strength until he felt ready to try merging with a human. Lars and the puma were comfortable with each other, the demon having merged with the cub before its eyes had opened. Lars left the body of the puma very rarely, as he was always aware that a spirit could easily find him if he was unprotected. The puma had become quite a celebrity and hunters came to the moors occasionally to try and trap it, but it was not an ordinary puma. It had its demon, and Lars protected the animal, just as the animal protected Lars.

On one occasion a group of men came with a television crew in the hope of catching a glimpse of the black cat. One of the men fell behind the rest of the group and rather than catch up, he sat down to rest under a group of trees. Lars saw his opportunity and made the puma pad silently towards a large oak. He bade the puma drop into the undergrowth, and once he was satisfied that its body was completely hidden, Lars emerged from its body and entered the body of the man.

The man immediately reacted violently to the intrusion. He began screaming and writhing about, rolling on the ground. Lars was aghast! The other men heard the noise and ran back, staring at the man as he flailed with his arms and legs. Two of them jumped on the man's body, while a third tried to push a branch between his teeth. This was not going too well for Lars. He was unsure as to what to do, having never been in a situation such as this before.

'I'll try talking to him, perhaps that will placate him,' he thought.

"It is alright. I am not going to hurt you. Calm down! Just relax."

That made it worse. The man let out a roar and started punching the two men that were sitting astride his chest. He managed to punch one of his assailants on the face, who rolled off him shrieking and holding his bleeding nose.

The man who had been trying to force the branch into the man's mouth suddenly dropped the stick and slowly raised his hand, pointing towards a bush, his mouth hanging open and his eyes bulging. The rest of the group, who had been watching the fight, turned and stared at what their friend was pointing at. Lars, merged with the man, saw the group staring and turned to see what it was that had got their attention. There standing quietly watching the furore was the black puma, froth starting to form around its mouth as its tongue slowly licked its upper lip. The possessed man became aware of the puma at the same time as Lars. He was now faced with three enemies; his three friends, Lars and an enormous black cat. He became rigid, then slowly raised one knee and tried to crawl backwards away from the puma. Lars was aware of the danger, as he knew that the puma had not eaten properly for several months, however, he could not permit the big cat to attack the men, however much he would enjoy watching it. It would attract too much attention. He had to leave the man and remerge with the puma.

As he merged with the big cat once more, he realised just how close these humans had come to being the main course of the puma's first proper meal in many months. Now, once more in the body of the puma, he slipped quietly away back among the trees, realising just how difficult getting himself a human body was going to be. He would have to work out another plan of action. He needed an ally, someone just as evil as he, that he could confide in and who could help him attain his goal.

He needed to get back into contact with humans, if his aim was to join with one, so that he could learn what their weaknesses were and how to merge with one so that they did not immediately reject him. He knew that domestic cats were very close to their human masters, so perhaps he should try merging with one of them. He had only ever merged with wild cats, so it was with some trepidation that he wandered closer to human habitation.

Around the moors there were many small farms. They always had several cats roaming around to keep the vermin down. Lars walked to the edge of the tree line and lay down to watch these cats, looking for one that stood out from the rest. There was a large ginger tomcat that was obviously the leader of his little pack, but what would he be like as a solitary item. Lars crawled forward on his stomach, eying the cat with his puma eyes. He wanted to isolate him so that he could jump him and merge with him before he realised what was happening. Suddenly he got his chance. The farmer's wife came out of the kitchen and called the cats for their supper. They all sprung off, except the ginger tom. He stood tall and gazed over to the farmhouse, but did not move towards it. Lars tried projecting thoughts towards the cat and the ginger tom immediately turned in Lars direction.

"What do you want?" he asked gruffly.

Lars was astonished. He could always project thoughts to animals, but they had never before spoken to him.

"You can speak!" he said.

"Well of course I can speak! Stupid fool!" retorted the tom cat. "What do you want? I am frightfully busy. You are making me miss my supper, and nobody is allowed to do that!"

Lars stood up and stared at the cat.

"Don't you realise that I could eat you for my lunch." he said, licking his lips. The tom cat just turned around and looked in the opposite direction.

"I don't really care!" he said. "I am so fed up being in this ghastly body that it would be a real relief!"

Lars walked around the cat so that he was facing him once more.

"What do you mean?" he said.

The tom cat started to wash his right paw.

"I mean that I should not be in this cat at all. I suppose, in a way, I am lucky, but things could be a lot better."

Lars was amazed. This cat knew things that he should not know. 'What was going on?' he thought.

"Tell me all about it, I am fascinated," he said,

"I used to be a human many years ago, but I committed the one great sin; I killed a man. There was no excuse, there was no reason and I have to admit that I enjoyed it. When I was hanged at the prison, another man died of natural causes at the same time and both of us went up to the Celestial Hall together. Some idiot messed up big time and put the other poor sod in the primordial pot instead of me. They decided that I had more lessons to learn, so stuck me in the body of a cat. You wait till I get back there! Fur will fly, I'm telling you! Excuse the pun!"

Lars sat down to digest all this and eventually said, "Not happy then," threw back his head and roared with laughter.

Once he had controlled himself he said, "My name is Lars. I am a demon from Hell. I have been trapped on Earth for four hundred years and now I wait for Lucifer to sort out how he is going to get me back to Hades."

The cat put his head on one side and said, "Hmm. That might be difficult. I'm Vorce, by the way. You know that Lucifer has been banished to Hell, don't you. I don't think he is able to come to Earth to rescue you. Perhaps another of his demons might be able to, but it would need some sort of passage to connect you to it."

Lars looked stricken, "Banished! What about the vortex, can't he make one so that I can get back?"

"No, I don't believe so. I understand that the vortex has been sealed and Lucifer has had the powers of creation taken away from him."

Lars could not control his anger. He raced around the field roaring like a banshee. Suddenly a light went on outside the farmhouse kitchen and the door opened. The farmer emerged with a shot gun. Vorce and Lars decided that now would be a good time to make a hasty retreat and they both ran into the woods and safety.

Lars could not believe how fortunate he was. If he had been able to choose a companion he could not have chosen better. Vorce and he became firm friends from that day on and would cause mayhem in abundance together!

Chapter 42

Allies

Lars and Vorce were very alike in many ways, both having the same sadistic streak and evil temperament. Lars was soon able to convince Vorce that great things were possible if one only applied one's mind in the right way. Vorce enthusiastically joined Lars in plotting to get even on the Great Lord for all the suffering that they felt they had had to bear. Lars explained what Lucifer and he had tried to do in 1666.

"My biggest problem at the moment," said Lars "is trying to merge with a human. Whenever I try, the person panics and I have to leave them in a hurry. I don't know what I am doing wrong."

The cat looked at him and asked, "Have you ever been a human?"

"No. I was created a demon. I was never intended to evolve, just keep Lucifer company." Lars replied.

"That is your problem then," said Vorce. "Humans are very insular animals. They tend to keep themselves to themselves. Their minds are their own and they consider their thoughts private. Humans don't have collective brains so they are not used to sharing. If you try to possess one you have to eject the owner or subdue it so much that it no longer is able to think. However if you do that you will have to control the whole body and you will need experience if you are to pull that off convincingly," explained the cat.

He looked at Lars and shook his head, saying, "Let's face it; you are not a very successful puma, are you?"

Lars stared back at the cat, obviously annoyed. "What do you mean? I have been in this puma for twenty three years."

"Yes," said Vorce. "You can tell. Look at yourself! You are dirty, mangy and covered in fleas. You never wash yourself nor do you eat those things that a cat needs to keep its coat sleek and its system working properly. Look at my coat, see how it shines. That's because I eat grass and herbs as well as meat. I spend at least half a day, every day, washing and grooming my coat. I don't think that I have ever seen you groom yourself, not even once."

"Well I don't want to be a cat, I want to be a human," said Lars.

"Then it's even more important that you understand about being human. You can't just go about in a human body. You think that you are being a puma just because you are in its body. Merge with me for a few moments and watch the puma," suggested Vorce.

Lars left the puma and joined Vorce in his cat's body. The two of them watched the puma. For a few moments it just sat where Lars had left it, blinking its huge orange eyes, then it shook itself and rolled over and over in the grass. Then it started a mammoth wash. It started with its paws, then its legs and then its body. It washed its face, its ears and its underbelly. Lars watched fascinated. When the puma had finished it got up and walked through the trees towards a stream that ran through the forest. The puma followed the stream until it joined a large lake and then it plunged into the water, splashing and thrashing about.

"What's it doing," said Lars, alarmed at the puma's antics. "It will drown!"

"No! No!" said Vorce. "It is washing the fleas away. They do not like being immersed in water and will swim out of the puma's coat."

Lars was fascinated by the antics of the puma and had not realised how complicated its life should have been. The puma was pulling itself out of the lake and once on dry land it gave an almighty shake, spraying water all over Vorce and Lars. When Lars re-merged with the big cat he was careful to allow its own entity to take some control, but still retained his own superiority.

"If you want to merge with humans why don't you start with sick people?" suggested Vorce.

"So to that end, the pair set off for Bodmin Hospital. Lars realised that he could not continue to live in the body of the puma if he wanted to live more closely with humans, but he also knew that it was too dangerous to roam the Earth in his natural state as he would easily be detected by the spirits that still sought to kill him, so he shared the cat's body until they came up with a more long-term solution.

The cat reached the town perimeters and saw the signs for the local hospital. Once there the cat sniffed the air and followed his nose to the kitchens. He walked to the door and started to cry.

"Whatever are you doing, making that dreadful noise?" asked Lars.

"Just watch," answered Vorce.

The door opened and a woman in a green pinafore came out of the kitchen and said over her shoulder, "I told you I could hear a cat. Oh poor thing, it looks half starved."

Another woman poked her head out and said, "Starved, my foot! It looks fat enough to me. It's probably got fleas. Don't let it in here!" and retreated back into the kitchen.

The other woman, on the other hand, said, "Don't you worry about a thing, Kitty. I'll get you a bowl of something. Just you wait there."

She went back into the kitchen to get Vorce a bowl of food, leaving the door just ajar. Vorce pushed at the door and it opened enough for him to get into the building. He slunk along the floor to the safety of some large boxes that were stacked along the wall.

When the woman returned she called the cat, "You must have frightened it off," she scolded her friend. "Poor little mite. I'll leave the bowl outside the door in case it comes back."

She put the bowl on the step and closed the door, muttering to herself before resuming her chores.

Vorce quietly made his way to the wards, hiding every time someone came into sight. Once the cat arrived at the chronic care ward he stopped and waited.

"I'll be okay here," said Lars. "Go and hide yourself while I put your theory into practise. Give me a few hours and then come back for me."

"You'll need more than a few hours," said Vorce sceptically, as Lars left the cats body and entered the ward. Vorce turned and padded quietly off down the corridor.

Lars wandered down the ward looking at the people sleeping in their beds. One or two were obviously unconscious, as they were connected to life support machines. Lars saw the golden threads with the entities attached to the end and remembered taking similar ones to Hell for Lucifer many eons before. He could not resist a little tormenting. He went up close to one of these souls and hissed at it.

"I could tear you from your thread as easily as bursting a bubble. Then where would you be?"

The little soul shrank back in fear. It had never encountered a demon before.

"You thought you were safe in here, didn't you? After all it is a hospital, one should be safe in a hospital, shouldn't one? Well you're not. The only reason I don't destroy you now is because I choose not to. I have other plans. You never know, we may meet again."

The little entities quivered with fear, piteously crying. Lars suddenly remembered why he was there and set about picking patients out that were sick, but not so sick that they were unable to move about. And so he began the serious task of learning how to be human.

Chapter 43

The demon pet

Lars first attempts at manipulating humans were a disaster. Instead of merging and just experiencing being inside a human, he immediately started to try and move the body about. This bizarre behaviour drew the attention of the doctors and nurses, which resulted in the patient being sedated. After three of four tries Lars relaxed and slowly he allowed his hosts to have more control. He understood what Vorce had been saying about the insular nature of human beings and began to realise that he needed a lot more practise if he was to pass as human and be accepted by other human beings. He spent the next hour just residing in his human hosts and experiencing how their bodies worked.

His hour was up and he moved out of the ward into the corridor to meet up with the cat. As he merged with Vorce there was a shout.

"Who let that cat in here?" said one of the nurses.

Pandemonium was let loose in the corridor. The ward doors slammed closed and the passageway suddenly filled with people, all intent on catching the cat. Vorce slunk along the corridor close up to the left hand wall, his back arched and his tail erect. He began to spit and hiss at the people, as they moved towards him. Lars looked around, searching for an escape route. He saw a small flap at the bottom of the opposite wall, some sort of ventilation unit. It opened and closed as the air went in and out.

"Over there. Can you see the hole? Do you think you could fit through it?" he asked Vorce. The cat eyed the flap.

"I don't know, but I can have a jolly good try."

In one bound the cat leapt across the corridor and threw itself into the hole. Its head went in so the rest must follow, so with a tremendous squeeze, the cat forced itself through the flap and emerged into a small shaft going straight down! As the cat fell, Vorce and Lars could hear voices that were getting louder and louder. They were sure that the humans were tracking them and dreaded reaching their destination, not just because it was going to hurt, but also because they feared that they would be caught.

It was just as they predicted; it hurt and they were caught!

The cat was unceremoniously bundled into a pillow case and the RSPCA took him to their animal shelter. Now he was sitting in a glass cage wondering what was to become of him. The door at the front of the cage opened and a white coated arm pushed a bowl of meat into the cage. It retracted just as quickly and the door was closed. Vorce walked over to the bowl and sniffed at the meat suspiciously. It smelt alright and he was ravenous, so he ate it, licking the bowl clean when he had finished.

"So, what now?" asked Lars.

"I don't know!" said Vorce, irritated. "I've never been in this predicament before. In fact I wouldn't have been caught if it wasn't for you!"

Lars kept quiet. He knew his friend was right. He left the cats body and wandered around the shelter. It was very big and catered for all sorts of animals, even wild ones. Lars moved along the corridor and into the reception area. There were people sitting on benches, some with boxes and others with small cages. Lars was intrigued as to what these people were waiting for. As he watched, a woman in green overalls came into the room. She called for one of the women to follow her and Lars went with them, a silent shadow, unseen by either of them.

On the table in the centre of the room was a white cage and inside it was a grey tabby cat.

"Here she is, Mrs Thompson," said the woman.

Mrs Thompson stepped forward and put her box on the floor. She stretched out her hand and put her fingers through the bars of the white cage. The cat licked the fingers and started to purr.

"Oh, she is just divine!" enthused Mrs Thompson. "It will be so nice to have a cat again."

"Now don't forget to keep her inside the house for the first week. She has had her second lot of injections, but you need to bring her back in six weeks time for the last ones."

The woman opened the white cage and gently lifted the cat out, while Mrs Thompson opened her box. The cat was put into the box, which the woman closed with string, and Mrs Thompson walked out of the room with the box in her arms and a pleased smile on her face.

Lars rushed back to Vorce.

"This is a place where people pick up cats. They are given to someone and taken back to their home. This couldn't be better. We need to be picked up by someone who would be receptive to me merging with them, perhaps with children. Children can't be difficult to merge with, surely."

Vorce stared at Lars as if he had gone mad.

"Who, in their right mind, is going to want to take me home? You're living in cloud cuckoo land! I am a wild cat!" retorted Vorce.

"Well, you will have to pretend that you are the most docile, loving cat in the whole world," said Lars. "If we are to carry out our plan we need to be given to a family, and if that means you need to be the perfect family pet, so be it. Start practising, here comes our supper!"

The door of the cage opened and again an arm appeared. As the bowl was put down, Vorce sidled over to the arm and started to purr very loudly. The arm hesitated. Vorce gingerly rubbed his head against the hand and pulled away. The hand turned palm upwards and extended just a few more inches. Vorce put his head into the hand and the hand petted him. Vorce allowed the hand to rub around his ears and he had to admit to Lars later, that he found the sensation very pleasant. Then the hand was gone and the door was closed.

"See, that wasn't that bad, was it?" asked Lars.

Vorce made a gruff noise and wolfed down the bowl of meat.

"At least the foods okay, I suppose," he said reluctantly.

The next day one of the humans took Vorce out of his cage and placed him on the floor of the corridor.

His first instinct was to run, but Lars steadied him, "its okay. Just keep calm and sit down," he said. Vorce forced himself to sit down on the floor and wash his paws.

"Oh, look. He's lovely. Those people at the hospital said he was vicious," one of the humans said.

"He was probably scared stiff, all those people shouting at him, poor thing. I reckon he will make someone a lovely pet," said another.

The first human went up to Vorce and picked him up. Vorce tensed, ready to spit and scratch, but Lars said, "Relax. Go completely limp. Now close your eyes and purr."

Vorce followed the instructions to the letter and the magic worked.

"I know just the family for you, Ginger. You'll make them a wonderful pet," and she placed him carefully back into his cage.

"You did it!" shouted Lars. "See, just a little bit of acting and we can do anything, even fool those idiots!" and he laughed a long, deep laugh.

Chapter 44

Possession

Michael and Christina Golding came to pick Vorce up the next afternoon. He cried all the way in the car, but the humans seemed to expect that. They carried his box carefully into the kitchen and set it down on the floor. When they opened the box he lifted his head, blinking in the bright light, leapt out of the box and shot under one of the kitchen units.

Vorce stayed under the unit for three days, only coming out at night to eat and use the litter tray. The humans called him Rocky and eventually won his confidence, allowing them to entice him out of his hiding place. Meanwhile, Lars wandered around the house and became familiar with the humans routine. Michael, tall and fair haired, spent most of his time in the little bedroom, painting, and Christina, small and slim, was out during the daytime, returning home in the evening. Lars had tried to merge with the man, but found it impossible to even penetrate the outer recesses of his mind, so he had abandoned any further attempts. The woman was another matter. He had merged with her during the night, while she was asleep. She believed that she had had a nightmare, but found it difficult to explain her experience to her husband, as he never remembered his dreams and didn't understand.

Lars continued to merge with the woman, until one night he discovered that her body was occupied by another entity, a younger, stronger entity. Lars did not understand that the woman was pregnant, but avoided merging with her while there were two entities to contend with.

The baby was born on the 4th of April, 1971 and she was the most precious thing to enter the household. Both Michael and Christina were completely bowled over by this tiny little being, and even Rocky found her fascinating, spending hours staring at her while she slept. She only had to make the smallest noise and both parents would come running to see what the matter was.

Lars saw this as an opportunity to try to merge with someone different, but a new being has the strongest entity of all. They have only just left the cronkel pot and are still filled with the strength that they have gained from the spirit world. Lars found it impossible to join with her, so went back to the woman, even daring to merge with her during the daytime as well as at night. Christina found this very confusing and did not understand what was happening to her. She would be doing one thing and then suddenly find herself doing something completely different with no memory of what happened in between. At first she thought that she must have dropped off to sleep, but when she questioned her husband he denied that this was the case, saying, "You put down your cup, walked up to the baby's room and just stood staring at her," or "One moment you were folding the washing and then you started ripping the pillowcase into tiny shreds."

She became withdrawn and depressed. She started to lose weight, neglecting herself and her baby, to the point that her husband was now looking after both his wife and his daughter.

She told her husband that she was being possessed, but she could not make her husband understand. All he kept telling her was that it was post natal depression, that it happened to a lot of women and she should make an appointment to see her doctor.

She told him that the cat was also possessed, as his personality changed frequently. When Lars was sharing the cat's body with Vorce he would continuously remind Vorce that he was supposed to be a family pet.

"If you go on behaving so badly, the family will send you back to the cat's home and our plan will be ruined," he admonished him. Christina tried to keep the cat out of the baby's room, but he had learnt how to open the door and she would enter the nursery to find him sitting in the cot watching the baby.

Lars knew that he could eventually take over the woman's body completely, but he still hankered after this young, fresh being. One evening he was watching the baby with Vorce and said, "Do you think I could take over this small being if its entity was removed or weakened somehow?"

"How would you remove its entity? I thought you said it was too strong for you," replied Vorce, stretching out on the baby's coverlet.

"Yes, it is too strong if I wanted to co-habit its body," agreed Lars, "but I was thinking that if I was to tear its entity from the thread, as we did during the plague, then I could take over its body completely."

The cat put its head on one side and stared at the baby, who had started to stir. This usually brought her mother into the room and Vorce knew that that signalled the end of his visit, as she did not like him lying in the baby's cot.

"I want you to sneak into the room tonight so that I can see if the baby's entity leaves its body. I have not seen it do so during the day when it sleeps, but perhaps at night it is different," instructed Lars.

At that moment the mother came into the nursery, "Shoo, Rocky! Bad cat! You know you are not allowed in here," she said, picking him up and depositing him in the hall.

That night Vorce waited until the house was quiet and all the humans were asleep. He stretched up to the latch of the baby's room and opened the door. The baby was softly snoring as she breathed and Vorce jumped onto the rail of the cot and looked down at the baby. Lars could see that her entity was well ensconced within her body. He would not be able to attack her this way.

"I wonder if her entity would leave her body if she were dying," mused Lars, "Then I could grab her soul, rip it away from its thread and then enter the body."

"It may be possible," asked Vorce. "I suppose you want me to almost kill her."

Lars thought for a while.

"Yes. Don't kill her exactly; just suffocate her sufficiently to make her panic. That should make her entity leave her body for an instant. What do you think?"

"I can give it a try, but I've never almost killed before. If I kill her don't shout at me," he said. The cat crawled carefully over to the baby, trying hard not to wake her. He spread himself over the baby's face and waited.

Something woke the man and he lay in bed listening, wondering what had disturbed his sleep. He could hear nothing, but he had an uneasy feeling that something was amiss.

The man got up and padded over to the door. He went out into the hall and walked over to the baby's room. When he entered he saw nothing untoward at first, but when he approached the baby's crib he saw the cat apparently asleep across the baby's face. He rushed to the cot and grabbed the cat, throwing it off the baby. The baby made a gulping noise and the man lifted her up and placed her over his shoulder, gently patting her back to stimulate her. There was a second of silence and then the baby began to wail. This brought the woman running to the room, asking the man what was wrong.

"She is fine now. The cat was sleeping on her and I had to shoo him off," he said, trying to play down the incident, but the woman would have nothing of it.

"It is trying to kill her!" she screamed. "It wants to possess her!"

The man was still soothing the baby and now he said, "Don't be silly! Cats don't try possessing babies. They often sleep on them. I have heard of it before."

The woman was sobbing, which made the baby start to wail once more.

"You go down to the kitchen and make us a cup of tea while I settle Michelle. We must make sure that the cat is put out at night so that this can't happen again," reassured the man.

The woman turned and left the room and the man crooned softly to the baby.

As he turned from the room, having settled the baby back into her cot, he scooped up the cat and firmly shut the door behind him.

The man went into the kitchen, opened the back door and dropped the cat unceremoniously on the door mat.

He locked the back door and said to his wife, "Come now, Christina, you are being paranoid. Cats don't think, let alone try to take over babies."

Christina slowly turned her head towards him.

"Don't tell me I'm paranoid Michael," she said very quietly. "This house is evil. Something in it is evil. I know that the cat has a demon in it and that demon wants Michelle. That cat must go. We must take it back to the centre. I will not have it living in this house!" She got up from the table, strode out of the room and marched upstairs.

Lars listened and watched as the man stared after her retreating body.

Christina stayed in the baby's bedroom for the rest of the night, sitting bolt upright in the

nursery chair; watching Michelle as if her life depended on it.

Lars also watched the baby, but he decided that it was too difficult to merge with it. He would concentrate on the woman. Her husband thought she was so unhinged that any strange behaviour would be blamed on that. Now that he had made a definite decision, Lars felt wonderful. 'I will put my plan into action tomorrow,' he thought, excitedly.

Chapter 45

Self-sacrifice

From that day onward Christina became more and more protective of her baby. Lars was glad that he had decided not to pursue her, but now it was much more difficult to merge with Christina, as the woman rarely slept and she was constantly in an agitated state. There was only one solution for Lars; he would have to force Christina to allow him to merge with her. He knew that she would do anything to protect her daughter, so he proposed to use this as a means of getting her to cooperate with him.

One night, when Michelle was barely three months old, Lars entered the baby's bedroom to find Christina dozing in the armchair. This was his best opportunity to date, so quickly he entered her and merged with her mind. She was immediately aware of him and awoke, trying desperately to push him away.

"You cannot expel me," said Lars. "I have entered your conscious and sub-conscious mind. You must listen or I will harm your child."

Christina sat upright in the chair and held her breath.

"You have a simple choice; save your child or yourself" said Lars. "If you choose to save yourself, I will make the cat take the life of your child and I shall consume her soul and take her body for myself. Her life will be mine to do with as I please. If, however, you choose to save your child, I shall live in harmony with you, residing in the deep recesses of your mind. When I have no need of you I shall leave you to continue your life unhindered, with the understanding that you surrender your body to me as and when I need it. Think deeply as once a decision has been made, it cannot be changed. I shall return tomorrow night to learn what you have chosen."

Lars left her and returned to Vorce, who was loitering outside in the garden, waiting to hear what had happened.

"I think that I have frightened her sufficiently," said Lars. "I am convinced that she will choose to save her daughter, and tomorrow I should be in possession of a body, at last."

Lars quickly returned to the baby's room to find her standing up and looking at her daughter sleeping in her cot. The woman began to cry, quietly at first, getting louder and louder. Her husband woke up and came into the room, approaching her hesitantly.

"What's the matter? Why are you crying? Is the baby alright?"

He rushed over to the cot, but the baby was sleeping peacefully. Christina looked at him and walked out of the room. She went downstairs and into the kitchen, followed by her husband. She wrung her hands and made a keening noise, a sound that her husband had never heard her utter before. Lars looked on, gloating at the reaction his ultimatum had caused.

"I have to choose, but either way one soul is doomed," she cried. "Oh, Michael, what should I do?"

Her husband went to her and gathered her in his arms.

"What are you talking about, choosing. Choosing what?"

"They are evil, pure evil! He tried to kill her. I must kill him first. Yes! Yes! That is the thing to do! Then we will be safe!"

Christina got up, shrugging Michaels arms from her slight frame.

"Who are you talking about killing?" he said, urgently, following her out of the kitchen.

"I have a whole day before he is back," she replied. "Don't worry; I know what to do now." And she went back upstairs and for the first time in many nights went into their bedroom and lay down on the bed. By the time Michael had reached the bedroom, Christina was in a deep sleep. Lars left her to rest as he wanted her body to be fresh and ready for him. He and Vorce went on a hunting spree, returning to the house in the early hours of the morning.

The next morning, Christina was woken by Michelle's cries. Michael was still asleep, so she carefully rose from the bed and went into the nursery. She looked at the baby, who had stopped crying and was smiling up at her mother, expectantly.

"Daddy will be in to see you in just a moment, my princess," she said, stroking the baby's face. "I have a task to attend to that is vital to our continued existence."

Christina went out into the garden and called softly, "Rocky, Rocky, where are you kitty. I've got your breakfast."

Lars had left him momentarily and the cat slunk suspiciously out from behind the hedge, his ginger coat shining golden in the early morning sunlight. Christina stroked the cat and rubbed him behind his ears. He purred contentedly and followed her into the garden shed. She closed the door and picked the cat up, placing him on the table under the window where she had previously placed a large bowl of minced lamb. The cat started to eat the meat, eagerly.

At that moment Lars returned and missed the cat.

"Vorce, Vorce, where are you?" he called.

"I'm eating. Go away," said the cat, his mouth full of minced lamb. "I can never enjoy my food when you are watching me."

Lars looked through the window of the shed just as Christina raised her hand. There was a glint of metal as her hand flew down towards the cats back, and a spray of red covered the window pane.

"No! No!" screamed Lars. "Vorce, Vorce answer me!" But Vorce could not answer.

Over and over again she stabbed at the cat, his coat no longer ginger and his body no longer recognisable as a cat. She did not pause in her task until the cats body fell from the table, leaving a pool of blood spreading rapidly over the Formica top.

Lars was distraught. His friend was dying. He could see his soul as it emerged from his body.

"Quickly. We have only a short time before the escort spirits come. What do you want me to do?" said Vorce, urgently.

"Speak to Lucifer, or one of his servants. Tell them that I still wait to be rescued. I don't care how, just make them get me out of here," replied Lars.

Christina did not see Vorce leaving the body of the cat nor could she hear the conversation between him and Lars or see Lars hiding in the dead cat when the escort spirit came down to collect Vorce.

She walked out of the shed, leaving the door open, and went into the kitchen. She took off her clothes and put them into the washing machine, put soap powder into the soap dispenser and turned it on. She walked back upstairs to the bathroom and had a hot shower, putting on one of the bath robes that hung on the back of the door. When she came out of the bathroom, Michelle had started to cry again. Christina went into her bedroom just as Michael was getting out of bed.

"I'm on it," he said. "You go back to bed and I'll bring you a cup of tea."

Michael went out to the baby's room as Christina got back into bed. Lars knew that she thought she was safe. He would convince her otherwise! As she slipped between the sheets a shudder ran through her body.

The now familiar voice spoke deep inside her mind. "You thought you could win by killing the cat, didn't you? Well you can't! I can still kill your daughter, but the cat's way would have been kinder. Me, I have no finesse. All you have done is doom your child to a slow, painful death, instead of a quick, painless one. Make your decision. What is it to be, you or your daughter?"

Christina knew that she had no option. She could not let her daughter die, but her husband and child would never know the sacrifice she was forced to make in order to keep them safe.

Chapter 46

Rescue at last

By now Lars was well established in the body of Christina. She would alternate from being the loving wife and mother, to being a tyrant and a bully. Her mood swings became impossible for Michael to cope with and he hid himself away in the spare bedroom whenever Lars took over. Lars hoped that Christina's mood swings would not drive Michael and the baby away as he intended to merge with Michelle as soon as he was strong enough. He also knew that if that were to happen he would be unable to find them as he could only leave Christina for short periods of time.

But in the event, it was Christina who left. Lars had been so confident that she would never leave her baby that when it happened he was shocked. Her desire to protect her daughter was stronger than her maternal needs. One night, when the house was quiet, he watched her write a letter to Michael, prop it up on the kitchen table and silently leave the house for the last time.

Lars spent another twenty years living within the confines of Christina's body. Why it was taking Vorce so long to rescue him he could not say, only that perhaps Vorce had been re-born into another body and was having to live that life to its conclusion before he was able to get Lars message to someone in Hades.

Lars did not waste his time while he waited, however. He slowly took over control of Christina's mind so that she rarely surfaced at all, her bodily functions working on auto pilot. He learnt how to operate her body faultlessly, so that no-one would have known that she was possessed by a strange demon. He perfected the art of suggestion and slowly gathered together men and women whom he could manipulate. He had bought an old congregational church hall that he used as a meeting place for his disciples and there he plotted his revenge on the world and waited for Vorce to join him. He had already started on Lucifer's plan, but he was becoming more and more annoyed at why it was taking them so long to find him.

One evening he had just finished a recruitment drive. The hall was empty and he was about to turn off the lights and head for home, a terraced house just outside the city centre, when the ground began to tremble and the walls shake. He stood still for a moment, unsure of what was happening then he remembered the vortex! He dashed to one of the side recesses and hid behind a column. Even though it had happened hundreds of years ago, he recognised the signs. It was a vortex, of that he was sure; but was it a good vortex or a bad one? He waited as the wind grew and the tornado appeared. The mouth of the vortex slowly lowered down to the ground and there was a pause. Lars watched suspiciously as something emerged from the centre. It was a dark shadow and a relieved Lars stepped out from the pillar as he recognised his old friend.

"You took your time!" he exclaimed. "I have been stuck here on this miserable planet while you have been messing about enjoying yourself! Still, it's good to see you Vorce."

By now other demons had appeared and Vorce said, contritely, "I am sorry that we have been so long Master, but we have only now perfected the Vortex. I have demons and fiends who want to join you."

"Fiends as well," exclaimed Lars. "You have done well. Mind you, it's easy to persuade fiends when you are one yourself." And he laughed loudly.

"Well, I see you merged with her then?" said Vorce looking at Lars' host. "I still think you look better as a cat though."

"Well, she was the only human I had available, but that's a long story," said Lars.

"So how is Lucifer?" he added.

"Lucifer thinks you are dead and does not want to get embroiled in fights and schemes," admitted Vorce quietly.

"He thinks I'm dead!" shouted Lars. "So how come you are here? How did you make a vortex, if Lucifer is not involved?"

"Don't get so angry. Everything is fine; in fact it's more than fine. I have spoken with many demons and fiends about your idea of taking control of a part of the universe and they are very enthusiastic. They all think Lucifer has become soft and does not feel inclined to contemplate new ideas. They are looking for a new leader. The time is right. It is our time now, yours and mine. Together we can make a world of our own. But let me tell you what I have done."

Lars relaxed and looked at his friend, surrounded by anxious fiends and demons. Some of the fiends were young, probably having just been banished from the Hall of Judgement, fresh and eager to take on the whole universe. And Lars was ready. He had planned for this day for a very long time and now that time was here. He was invincible. He let out a great roar, happy to rejoin his friend on their new adventure together.

Chapter 47

Vorce

When Vorce had been killed by Christina, he had entered the Celestial hall and deemed evil by Michelus. He was sent through Hades Gateway as a fiend, to start on the first step to Hell.

He found himself in the Arrivals Hall, a huge tall room with great pillars that rose up from the floor and met the ceiling some thirty meters above his head. The room was thick with a heavy perfume that Vorce found almost suffocating. A dark smoke hung in the air like a huge cobweb and he could hear moaning interspersed by guttural laughter.

Hax, the Gateway Guardian, met him and explained the rules, or to be more precise, the lack of rules. He was a huge brute, with heavy set face and long, black straggly hair. He walked with a gorilla-like gait, with his arms swinging from side to side. He carried a great, thick stick that he used to great effect when a demon or fiend got in his way.

"You may not leave this hall until I deem you worthy of the next step, so in the meantime entertain yourself in any way you like," he said gruffly. "If you cause any bother, expect to be punished," and he jabbed his stick into Vorce making him cry out in pain. Hax laughed and shuffled off.

"First, I must speak to someone most urgently," said Vorce, determined not to let this great oaf get the better of him.

Hax threw back his head and laughed.

"Speak to someone! Why would anyone want to speak to you, you snivelling wretch?"

Vorce made to attack Hax, but he had more important things to do. Hax could wait.

"I have an urgent message from my master, Lars."

Hax stopped dead in his tracks and stared at Vorce as if he had seen Lucifer himself.

"Lars, Lars! Did you say Lars?"

"Yes, you stupid fool. Are you deaf or something?" shouted Vorce.

"Why didn't you say so before? Lars was my master too. But he is dead, killed by the spirits many eons ago," said Hax, adamantly.

"Who told you he was dead?" cried Vorce. "He is not! He is very much alive and living on Earth. I was killed and had to leave him, but I promised him that I would find a way to get him back here."

"There is no way to get him back. Lucifer has abandoned him. He has forbidden anyone from uttering his name. He sent me here as a punishment for letting him be killed by the spirits, but I was not even there at the time! I am certain that Lucifer has forgotten all about us! There is no way out of this place and certainly no way to get to Earth!"

Vorce could sense a difference in Hax, a slight reverence in his voice as he looked at Vorce.

"There must be a way!" declared Vorce. "I will find a way!"

He looked around the room. It was hot and fetid, stinking and noisy. All he could hear was the constant moaning of other fiends and demons. Although the hall was enormous it was over crowded, groups of fiends huddled together doing all manner of cruel and sadistic things to each other, while demons stomped about shouting orders to anyone who listened. Vorce wandered about looking for a space that would allow him to observe the comings and goings of the lives of these beings. He was determined to find a way of rescuing Lars no matter what Hax said.

He watched the new fiends arrive in the hall from the Hall of Judgement and he noticed that each time the Gateway opened to allow a fiend to enter, a small drop of light appeared and floated to the bottom of the hall. Vorce moved to the bottom to look at the drops of light. He tentatively touched the drop and pain instantly shot through him, causing him to scream in agony. The demons surged over to him, laughing and shouting derisively at him.

"He touched the 'goodness'! The idiot!" shouted one.

"Doesn't he know anything?" snarled another.

Vorce turned to them and said, "'Goodness'! What are you talking about?"

One of the demons stepped up to him and said, "That little thing there is a drop of pure 'goodness'. It can kill you as surely as the Lucifer himself could kill you. You touch enough of it and you will shrivel up and disappear through the walls, just like the 'goodness' does."

Vorce looked at the 'goodness' and it was as the demon said, it slowly drained away into the fabric of the walls. He looked carefully at the wall where the 'goodness' seeped through and noticed that it was thin and spongy. Surely he could use these drops of 'goodness' and take advantage of the thinness of the wall.

He spent considerable time watching the drops and seeing how long they took to disappear. If there was a large amount of it, the drops seeped very slowly, but when there were only one or two drops they disappeared very quickly.

A demon was staring at him, "What are you watching that stuff for?" he asked, gruffly.

"Why do you only glance at it when there are a few drops, but stare at it intently when there are piles of the stuff?"

Vorce had not thought that he looked at it differently. He then realised that, when there were many drops together, he was willing the drops to slow down in order to count them. Perhaps the demon had hit on something. Perhaps he was inadvertently influencing the drops in some way. He looked at a fresh drop as it started to fall from the portal. As it fell Vorce visualised it stopping in mid flight and it did! It actually stopped! He tried moving the drop to the right and then to the left and it followed his directions. After many attempts Vorce found that he could collect the drops up and leave them in a big ball suspended in the room. They did not disappear nor did they move until Vorce commanded them. The hall was very crowded now and his ball of 'goodness' was using up valuable space. The fiends and demons could not go near it and many of them were complaining to Hax.

'I just need more room,' Vorce thought and suddenly a doorway appeared in the wall where the drops of 'goodness' used to disappear and Vorce could see a cavernous room beyond it. He cautiously moved through the doorway into the cavern. He turned around and could see back into the hall and his ball of 'goodness' slowly spinning by the doorway. He commanded the goodness to enter the cavern and suddenly the darkness disappeared and the room was filled with light, as the ball of 'goodness' obeyed Vorce's command.

"Wow!" said Vorce completely astonished at his find.

Demons and fiends were straining to see what Vorce had created. They were all pushing and shoving, anxious to look into the room.

Vorce roared at them, "Stay back!"

As he spoke, he moved the ball of 'goodness' towards them, making them move away rapidly. Hax come over to see what everyone was staring at and could not believe his eyes.

"How have you done this?" he exclaimed in awe. "You must indeed be a powerful Lord!" and he bowed low to Vorce.

"Come," said Vorce. "We have much work to do if we are to find our master and return him to our side."

"Of course, my lord, just tell me what must be done and I shall do it," said Hax.

"I need followers who will be faithful to Lars. You know these beings well. Talk to them and recruit those that you deem trustworthy. They will be richly rewarded for their loyalty."

Vorce sent Hax back into the hall while he collected more 'goodness' and took it through to the cavern.

He wanted to see if he could create other things with the 'goodness' and his first task was to create a vortex. It was not as difficult as he expected it to be, however what was difficult, was getting it to go somewhere. He only had a rudimentary concept of what a vortex was like, having never seen one nor travelled in one. He could create a phenomenon that looked as Lars had described, but because he did not know how it linked one place with another, it was just a mouth with no tunnel. After many fruitless tries he decided to abandon the image that Lars had given him and use logic instead. He visualised a passage between the cavern and the hall and suddenly there was a great wind and a roar and the vortex appeared. Vorce approached it tentatively. He looked through the mouth and could see Hax talking to some demons. Vorce called a demon over to him. It was suspicious at first, but after some encouragement he came into the cavern and moved up to the vortex.

"Step through there and tell Hax to join me," he said.

The demon looked at Vorce as if he was mad.

"What do you take me for?" he said.

As quick as lightening, Vorce spun a tint drop of goodness out of his ball and flung it at the being, which screamed in agony and writhed about.

"Now, step through the vortex!" he snarled. "Or perhaps you want another dose!"

The demon growled, but said nothing. He approached the mouth of the vortex and was suddenly swallowed up in it. A few seconds later Hax appeared through the vortex and stood reverently in front of Vorce.

"My Lord, what can I do for you?"

Vorce was ecstatic. He jumped about shouting and laughing.

"I've done it! I've done it! Now we can rescue Lars!"

He closed down the vortex and looked at Hax.

"How is your recruitment drive going? Have you selected any fiends and demons that you feel are worthy of our new adventure?"

"Yes, my lord, several," said Hax, enthusiastically. "Many demons are interested in following you and Lars. Most are fed up with Lucifer's leadership. They think that he is only interested in beings in Hell. He has no time for those in Hades, even though they have been loyal to him. The fiends are new evil beings, but they are just as enthusiastic."

"I must practise with the vortex and when I am satisfied that it works perfectly, I will inform you. I shall need some fiends and demons to send down the vortex to make sure it is safe, before I use it," said Vorce.

"Very well my lord. I shall select the most worthy and you need only say and they will be ready," said Hax, bowing low.

Vorce spent some time trying out the vortex. He visualised it creating a passage to an unoccupied part of Earth, and after watching the animal occupants scurrying about for a while, ordered one of the demons to pass through it. After some painful encouragement, the demon rushed through the vortex and rushed back, terrified that he would be trapped.

Vorce eventually plucked up the courage to pass through it himself. He was then terrified, just as his minion had been, that the phenomenon would close down, leaving him trapped, just as Lars was, but this never happened. He realised that the only way that the passage would cease to exist was if he visualised it closing, so he was in complete control of it. Back in Hades he collected more 'goodness' and placed it behind a protective cage, which was only penetrable by him, and now at last he was ready.

He called to Hax and told him that he was going to create the vortex at the last known place that Lars had occupied and hoped that he was still there. He summoned the Vortex and sent it to the garden, just outside the shed that Christina had slaughtered him in. He looked through the mouth and could see that it was evening, but there was no-one about. Vorce stepped through and into the garden. It was all overgrown and the house beyond was in darkness. He moved swiftly through the house, but it was clear that there was no-one living there. He stepped back into the cavern and explained to the disappointed Hax that Lars had vanished. Vorce would have to think again. How could he find Lars?

He thought about what he did when he created the vortex; 'I visualise the place and then I am there!' he thought.

"Of course!" he shouted, as he suddenly realised what he needed to do.

"Hax, go back into the hall, but don't show me where you are," he commanded.

Hax followed the instructions and Vorce summoned the Vortex. It appeared at the feet of Hax, making him jump quickly out of the way. Vorce realised that he had merely to visualise the vortex opening in the vicinity of the person that he sought and it would do as he commanded. He closed the vortex and called to Hax.

"This is it. This is the real thing. Do you wish to accompany me or remain here?"

There was no way that Hax was going to stay. He wanted to be part of this momentous occasion, so he stepped forward, together with half a dozen or so demons and fiends.

"Okay then! Is everyone ready? Then here we go!" shouted Vorce.

In a blink of an eye the wind came up, and with a great roar the vortex appeared. Vorce stepped through the mouth of the vortex to be confronted by a very angry Lars.

Chapter 48

Revenge and pacts

Lars was still angry, though not with Vorce. He was angry with Lucifer; that his lord and master, whom he had served faithfully for eons, could dismiss him so easily. He was amazed at Vorce's progress and started to relax as he realised that they did not need Lucifer in order to put his and Vorce's plan into action.

He looked around at the demons and fiends that had accompanied Vorce through the vortex and suddenly shouted, "Hax, you old scoundrel! Is that you? I never thought that I would see you again."

Hax bowed low, "Oh master! You recognised me. I am so glad to see you. When my lord Vorce told me that you were still alive, I could hardly believe him!"

Lars laughed, "Well we have much to do. Vorce, how big is this cavern of yours?"

"It is as big as you want it. I have created it so that it expands, depending on the size of the room required. When it becomes full, it grows bigger. Why, what have you in mind?" asked Vorce.

Lars had made many friends while Vorce was away, influential friends, friends who could help his cause.

"I am going to continue with the plan that Lucifer and I thought up many years ago, but with a slight variation!" said Lars. "We will steal the souls of humans and place them in the cavern. Then, when we have recruited sufficient numbers of demons and fiends ready to follow us, we will take over the bodies of the stolen souls and march on the Earth. It should have been ours many years ago if Lucifer's plan had not gone wrong."

The demons and fiends gasped. Lars could read their minds as they envisaged all the pain and suffering that they could mount on the beings that inhabited this world.

"That is exquisitely beautiful Master!" said Hax.

"Come, we have much work to do before we achieve that," he continued. "Hax, you will be in charge of all the stolen souls that are brought to the cavern. Use them to strengthen the fiends that you recruit for our new world. They must be completely trust worthy. We cannot risk someone informing Lucifer of our intentions. Vorce, you need to remain here with me to help complete the system that will guarantee us as many souls as possible. Once we have achieved that you can return to Hades to help Hax."

The hall was suddenly empty with only Lars and Vorce standing beside the Vortex.

"Will it be safe here?" Vorce asked indicating the phenomena.

"Oh, yes," replied Lars. "Nobody has access except me, and the windows are so high up that you can't see into the place without a ladder!" He laughed. "This is where I hold meetings for my followers," he said, waving his arm out expansively. Vorce was impressed. He took a tour of the church and returned to Lars' side.

"This is great! It's ironic really, when you think what the hall used to be used for. Now I can feel the evil in the walls. What do you intend to do next?"

"I have control over many of the ministers working in the health authorities and I have manipulated them into believing that they should centralise the care for people who are in irreversible comas. They are setting up hospitals for these people up and down the country and I have persuaded them that I should manage these facilities. I need you to help me make these facilities difficult to find."

"You mean use the 'goodness' to create some sort of a mirage, so that the average person sees one thing rather than the real thing, something like that perhaps?" suggested Vorce.

"That would be perfect," exclaimed Lars excitedly. "Can you do that?"

"Hmm, I don't know. I have never tried bringing the 'goodness' through the vortex, but if I put some kind of field around it, it might work," agreed Vorce, "And it would be useful to have a ball of 'goodness' that I can move around with me."

"Come, I will show you the main facility," said Lars. "I cannot leave this body, so I use a car to get about. I feel most encumbered, but needs must."

Vorce merged with Lars and within a few moments they were in the car park of a derelict building.

They entered the building through a double steel door, the paint was peeling from the metal and the frame looked as if it would collapse at any moment. Vorce emerged for Lars and followed him as he descended some stairs to the basement. When Lars stepped through the doors at the bottom of the stairs it was suddenly like being in a totally different building. It was all bright and clean. The floors and walls were tiled in pastel green. Lars walked down the corridor and opened a door on the right. This revealed a large room with beds all along the sides. In each bed was a body being fed via an intravenous infusion pump. The only sound in the room was the gentle breathing of the occupants.

"Well, isn't this wonderful?" said Lars, proudly. "Soon this whole building will be full of bodies just like these, waiting for a new life in our service," said Lars, laughing quietly.

"How do we do it? You know; get the souls?" asked Vorce in a whisper.

Lars laughed again.

"I have come down here as a demon and seen the entities attached to their golden threads. It is just how I remember it. The entities are timid now, but soon they will be more courageous, even learning how to leave their bodies and travel to other places. Once they habitually leave their bodies it will be easy to grab them and tear them from their threads. I am just biding my time until we have a few more," said Lars. "This is just one facility.

We have many more, all over the country. Soon I will have set up similar places in other countries, and then when we are strong enough, we can take over the world!"

"But if these people are in a coma what use are they to us?" asked Vorce.

"The ministers think that these people's comas are irreversible, but that is not the case," said Lars. "Each person is sedated, not enough to kill them or require artificial breathing apparatus, but just enough to prevent them from waking up. When we are ready and our servants have entered them, we will cease the sedation and they will rise up to carry out our bidding."

Lars kept his word and three years later the hospital was full. The health authority had expanded the building so that it now had two floors with the proviso that it could eventually expand to four. Lars was supervising ten different hospitals all over the UK and now there were other facilities in India, America and China.

During this time, after a few false starts, Vorce had perfected the vortex. To begin with, because of his limited knowledge of the Earth, he had sent the vortex to the wrong location, causing slight problems for humans around the world. Now he was able to summon it with hardly a thought and would get it right every time.

The fiends and demons visited all the facilities on a rotational basis, so that the entities did not know when they would receive a visit. Vorce would open a vortex and the demons would surge through catching the entities off guard. Many of them would still be travelling away from their bodies and the demons would grab hold of their threads, gnawing away at the golden anchor until they were left with a sobbing, writhing entity, pleading for its life.

Once the entities were in the cavern, they were submitted to a series of imaginative mind games which made them believe all manner of dreadful things. Vorce would encourage the fiends to be as imaginative as possible in order to get as much emotive energy from the entities. This energy fed the fiends, making them stronger and stronger. Vorce would punish the fiends and demons if they were not enthusiastic enough in their pursuit of new ways of causing pain and suffering to the entities, by stabbing them with shards of 'goodness', making them scream in agony, until they begged for forgiveness.

The plan was proceeding well. Lars, in the body of Christina, had arranged to meet Vorce at the congregational hall for an update. He drove through the town centre, and as he overtook a scenic tour bus, his car was hit by a wave of energy so powerful that it lifted the vehicle up into the air and catapulted it some fifty yards down the road. As it smashed onto the tarmac, Christina was hurled through the windscreen and ended up across the bonnet of the car. Lars immediately knew that she was seriously hurt. There was blood pouring from a wound on her forehead and her lower body was lying at a crazy angle. Lars left his host and looked around. There was carnage everywhere. The dead and dying lay all around him. The bus was unrecognisable, as the driver's compartment had been sheared off from the main part and was now lying upside down, imbedded in one of the shop windows.

Lars cautiously moved over towards the bus, hoping for a body to merge with, but as he neared the bus drivers cab, spirit escorts began to arrive to help the souls that were leaving the dead bodies. Lars panicked. He knew that they would kill him should they see him, so he leapt into the nearest body to escape detection. To his surprise he found it unoccupied, but he knew that it was not dead. He searched the body, only to discover that the thread that connected the body to the soul was missing. It was not torn or broken, it was completely missing.

'What a stroke of luck,' he thought.

He realised that the body had been damaged, but it was certainly not as badly damaged as Christina's was. He decided to stay put and wait to see if it would heal sufficiently for him to use it.

Soon the emergency services were swarming all over the explosion site. Firemen were cutting people from their vehicles and ambulances were ferrying the injured to hospital.

Lars was taken to Frenchay Hospital for emergency care and once he had been stabilised he was moved to the Brunswick spinal unit for assessment on his back injury.

Lars was lying in his hospital bed hoping that Vorce would find him. He would arrive at the congregational hall to find it empty. It should not take him long to surmise that there was a problem, he mused, and as he was thinking that very thought, a vortex appeared right next to his bed and Vorce stepped through from Hades. Lars laughed at the surprised expression on Vorce's face, when he found himself in the middle of a hospital ward.

Lars explained to Vorce what had happened and asked Vorce to find out who his host was and what was wrong with his body.

"According to these charts you are a bus driver and you have a broken back, fractured skull and left leg. If you ask me you are in a right state, certainly not in the prime of life!" Vorce said.

"Well, I didn't ask you. All I wanted was a diagnosis, not the doom and gloom of the situation!" Lars said, gruffly. "Go away, if you can't come up with any helpful comments!"

"I could bring some 'goodness' here and mend your body, but only if you ask me nicely!" said Vorce, coquettishly.

Lars glared at the fiend, realising that he would have to be nice to him if he wanted to be whole again.

"Okay, please," said Lars reluctantly.

"That's not nicely enough!" said Vorce, bravely.

Lars knew that Vorce had the upper hand now. Their roles had suddenly changed and he needed Vorce more than Vorce needed him. Their plan could easily be carried out without Lars and Lars knew that. The demon waited anxiously for Vorce's next move.

"I will strike a deal," said Vorce. "I will heal you, but I will be The Lord; The Lord of all fiends and demons in our new world. You will still be the Master and have the right to command, to make new rules and plan new ideas, but I shall be your Lord as well as theirs . Do we have a deal?"

Lars was quiet. He said nothing while he thought. He was not losing what he already had; his place in the order of things would not change. The difference would be that he would have to acknowledge a rise in Vorce's position and accept him as his Lord.

'Would that be very difficult?' he thought. Vorce had rescued him, found a way to make his plan work and now would heal this body so that he could survive; surely he deserved recognition for that?

"Very well, I agree. You shall be My Lord. I will serve you just as loyally as I served my Lord Lucifer and together we will conquer the world," said Lars emphatically. The pact was made, the order of things set out and their friendship sealed forever.

Chapter 49

Neo-Lunar

    The fiends and demons grew in strength as the stolen souls within the cavern grew in number. Vorce knew that soon the evil beings would be strong enough to occupy the bodies that the souls had vacated. He had planned with Lars to create simultaneous vortex to all the strongholds that had been set up on Earth and that now had many thousands of vacant bodies, just waiting for his word.

    All seemed to be going well until some of the stolen souls were sucked out of the cavern by some unknown force. Vorce demanded a meeting with Lars and an explanation as to the reason for this occurrence.

    "The manager of one of the facilities has allowed bodies to die," Lars said. "I have warned him that this cannot happen again."

    Vorce was furious. "We have not spent all this energy planning our glory, for some stupid human to sabotage it," he shouted. "We are so close to fulfilling our dream, an empire of our own. He must be punished. I will not have this! What have you done to him to show our anger?"

    "I have given him one last chance," said Lars.

"You mean to say that you have let him off! What's the matter with you? Are you getting soft?" shouted Vorce. He thought that he would explode, he was so angry. Nothing, but nothing was going to stand in his way.

"I am sorry, my Lord, but I do not think it was of his doing. I have a feeling that there has been some intervention that is not of Earthly origin. However, I have warned him that he will not be spared if it is to happen again. He has got our message, loud and clear."

"What do you mean; intervention? Do you think that the spirits have found out what we are doing?" said Vorce with alarm. "This has the whiff of the first time you tried this, does it not?" said Vorce.

"Yes, my lord, during the plague. I cannot see how the spirits could have discovered our plan? I have been most careful," said Lars. "Do you think it would be worthwhile giving some thought as to how we can create a bolthole, should the Great Lord find out what we are doing?"

"Perhaps," murmured Vorce, already thinking the same thing. He turned towards the mouth of the Vortex.

"Keep a close eye on things down here. We are so close now. Don't let anything jeopardise our future!" and he returned through the vortex, back to his cavern.

Once back in Hades he mulled over what had happened on Earth.

'There must be other planets in the solar system that we could hide in,' he thought and summoned one of the fiends whom he knew to have been a learned human before being banished to Hades.

"Tell me about the solar system," he demanded, and spent the next few hours being educated about the planets, their composition and their moons.

Vorce chose a small moon that orbited Uranus as the birthplace of his new world. He knew that humans would be unable to exist on the surface and to create a whole ecosystem around this moon would be too difficult and too obvious to anyone using a telescope. He summoned a vortex to the centre of the moon of Uranus and before stepping through it, he created a space beyond, very like the cavern. He took a small ball of 'goodness' through the vortex, into this new cavern. It was quite small to begin with, but with the help of the 'goodness', he started to make the cavern bigger and bigger by compacting the material within the centre of the moon. Soon the cavern was the size of a small town, but it was just a vast hole. He realised that while he and the other inhabitants of Hades could easily move about in a great space, humans would need solid ground on which to live. He would need to create a habitat that the humans could not only exist on, but grow and multiply.

His germ of an idea was becoming more and more exciting. If his plan to capture Earth was thwarted, he could move everyone into this new world and wait until his army was strong enough and big enough to completely overthrow the Great Lord. How to make it habitable for both the demons and the humans was still eluding him, but he was confident that somehow he would achieve it.

He watched the ball of 'goodness', slowly rolling around in the space in front of him and considered how he was to accomplish this difficult task.

'Of course, the ball of 'goodness'! It revolves in the space' he thought. 'Why not create a planet inside the moon to revolve, just as the ball of 'goodness' does! Instead of compacting the substance inside the moon, why not remove it and place it in the centre. If I set it spinning like the ball of 'goodness' it will become compacted just like a planet!'

He was elated. He set to and made the cavernous space as big as the moon would allow, without compromising its structure. The rocks and soil were stored in the centre, just floating there, like a massive slumbering beast. Once he was satisfied with his new planets size, he set it in motion in the centre. He suspended the ball of goodness in the space around the new planet to provide light and now all he needed was an atmosphere, so he summoned a vortex to Earth and opened the two ends. With a roar, air rushed through the vortex into the moons centre, taking with it microbes and germs, seeds and spores that embedded themselves into the dirt of the new planet. Vorce was very pleased with his work and decided to call it Neo-lunar. No-one could be able to see his work, the moon orbiting Uranus looked exactly as it always did, but hidden inside was an outer world for his fiends and demons, and an inner world for his humans. Perfect! The outer world of evil would shield it from the prying eyes of the Great Lord and protect it from spirits who would seek to destroy it. All he had to do now was see if the atmosphere was able to sustain life, so he returned to Hades to talk to Hax.

Hax had been very busy with his recruitment drive.

"I have even been down to Earth," he told Vorce, proudly. "I used the vortex. It was great. I found several lost souls while I was there and it was easy to persuade them that I was the answer to all their problems!"

"Well done Hax! You used your charm, did you?" said Vorce, roaring with laughter. "Now all I need to do is find a body to try out my new planet."

He knew that to find a human who he could persuade to join him would not be possible, but if he could somehow recruit a spirit then the spirit could take a body as a host and bring it to Neo-Lunar. He also knew that there were some disgruntled spirits who might be duped into believing that Vorce had something irresistible to offer them.

"I need to be able to enter Celestina," he said.

"Enter Celestina!" shouted Hax. "But My Lord, you will be caught and banished to the primordial pot!"

"Yes, I know. But what if the spirits think that I am one of them, what then?" asked Vorce.

Hax was silent and Vorce laughed at his discomfort.

"While I was protecting the hospitals down on Earth with the 'goodness' I thought, if I can disguise a building then I should be able to disguise a person, so I experimented with it. I have created a mist that I can hide in and the mist will take on any appearance that I describe to it. Any being that looks at me will see what I want them to see," explained Vorce.

"With respect, my lord, but it sounds a load of rubbish to me," said Hax, gruffly.

Vorce went to the cage at the back of the cavern, where his ball of 'goodness' slowly rotated, and took a small piece from it. Hax watched as Vorce slowly disappeared behind a thick fog, then suddenly Lars stood in his place.

"Master," said Hax, surprised. "I did not know that you were here! How did you get in to Hades? You are human! Humans can't exist in Hades!"

"It is alright Hax. It is I, Vorce. You only see me as your Master because I have made it so."

Hax was embarrassed by his mistake and started shouting and cursing, while hitting demons with his stick.

"Stop!" commanded Vorce. "Do you deny that it works?"

Hax calmed down and rushed back to Vorce, bowing low and mumbling to himself.

"I will not be able to send a vortex to Celestina," said Vorce. "But I may be able to send one to the cronkel pot or to the corridor between the Celestial Hall and the Hall of Judgement."

As it turned out, Vorce could not send a vortex to either of these places. They were too well protected. He had to go to Earth and wait for an escort spirit to attend a death, before he could ascend with them, disguised as a cronkel.

The Celestial Hall was always very busy and it was easy for Vorce to change his appearance to that of a spirit. Although he managed to enter the Spirox with a spirit, he found that he could not rise any further than the first floor. He would have to find what he wanted here. He needed a spirit who was discontented and to his joy he found Alvienne. She wanted immortality at any cost, so it was easy to persuade her that he could deliver what she sought. By the time she realised that he was not as he seemed, it was too late; she was his!

"You must find me a higher level spirit, a female" he said. "When you are ready to deliver her, go down to Earth and wait for me. Once you have done that, I will tell you how to attain what you seek."

He gave Alvienne the location in the Evangelical Hall and instructed her on how to send a message through the vortex, and then he returned to Hades.

Eventually the message came through the vortex.

"My Lord, the spirit waits on Earth for you," said Hax. "Do you want some protection?" he continued, raising his stick and whirling it above his head.

"No, thanks Hax," said Vorce, "And be careful with that stick or you'll kill someone!"

Hax laughed and brought the stick down on some poor demons head with a mighty crack.

Vorce travelled through the vortex to the hall, having disguised himself as before and found Alvienne waiting for him.

"Where's the spirit, then?" he asked impatiently.

"She is here, beside me," she answered. "Can you not see her?"

When Vorce looked carefully, he could just make out a shimmer and when he tried to touch her he could feel warmth radiating from her. Then he heard her voice. It was musical and pure. Vorce had never experienced anything like it before.

"What is it you want of me?" asked the spirit.

"If you do not need me further, I shall go and return later for your 'gift'," interrupted Alvienne.

When she had left Vorce asked the spirit what her name was and what it was that she sought.

"My name is Kusami," she said. "I want to be a god, with my own kingdom and my own subjects."

"Do you believe that I can give you these things?" asked Vorce.

"Alvienne tells me that you can and I believe her," replied Kusami.

"Very well," said Vorce. "But in order for you to have these things you must do something for me."

"Tell me what I must do and I will decide whether I can do it," said Kusami.

"I must be able to recruit subjects that are willing to serve you. There are many cronkels who are unhappy with the assignment process and these will be more than willing to serve you. I need you to enter the cronkel pot and create a hole in the bottom that will allow them to escape. Those that do not wish to be with you will be returned, but those that do will be given new lives in you kingdom."

"How will I enter the pot? Only spirits from the Cronkel Department can do that," said Kusami.

"I have thought of that," said Vorce. "If you enter the body of a dying person, then you can merge with her and enter the Celestial hall with her and then on into the pot. Once in the pot, it will be easy for you to make the tear, disguise it so that it is not easily discovered, and return to Earth through the hole."

Vorce waited for the spirit to make up her mind.

"When I return to Earth, will I get what you have promised?" she asked.

"Yes, indeed," said Vorce. "It may not be straight away, as I will be very busy recruiting suitable cronkels, so return to the woman and stay hidden within her body until I seek you out."

"Very well, I shall do as you have asked. It is not such a dreadful thing, after all. But you will only recruit willing cronkels. You will not force them."

The bargain was made and Vorce returned to Hades, leaving Kusami to do what she had to do. She had no idea that Vorce had just chosen the mother of his master race and that soon she would be residing in Neo-Lunar. She may not become a god, but she would certainly have her own kingdom and her subjects would be her own children, born of the seed of a demon.

Chapter 50

The Goddess

    Vorce returned to Hades and explained the next step in his plans for Neo-Lunar to Hax. Hax listened intently to Vorce, but Vorce knew that his intellectual capacity was not great. Give him a spirit to beat up or an entity to torture and he was your man, but plans and subtleties were not his forte, still, he was all Vorce had so he patiently went over and over the plan until he was satisfied that Hax had understood it all.

    "We must disguise all the demons and fiends that are taking part in this operation, or we will be lost. If Kusami thinks for one moment that we are not spirits, we will not convince her to accompany us," said Vorce.

    "Very well, my lord Vorce," said Hax, meekly. "What will be my role in this plan?"

    "Yours is most important," said Vorce. "You will be the one who must co-ordinate all the demons. I shall take some fiends with me to bring Kusami to the designated spot, but you must make sure that all the demons, disguised as spirits are floating above the altar. I shall have left the vortex suspended in the air, so it will only require me to open it when we have Kusami in the right position."

"It sounds very complicated, my lord," said Hax, warily. "Are you sure it will work."

Vorce was getting impatient with the demon.

"Of course it will work if you do as I say. It will only go wrong if you mess it up!" said Vorce angrily. "I shall convince Kusami that we need to perform a ceremony in order to cleanse her of all her wrong-doings. By the time she realises that we are not going where she expects, it will be too late; she will be ours!"

Hax and Vorce spent considerable time choosing the right demons and fiends to carry out their plan. Vorce created the vortex a short distance away from Kusami and went in search of her. Once he had located her he returned to the others.

"Scout about and find a suitable place for our plan," he told some of the demons. "It must be such that Kusami will believe it is special, where she would expect a ceremony to take place," instructed Vorce.

They found exactly what they wanted. Just outside the village was a forest that had many small glades deep among the trees. They picked one that had a convenient flat stone in its centre and Vorce summoned the vortex to appear above it, using his small ball of 'goodness'. He watched Hax as he positioned demons around the edge and placed the carefully chosen fiends in the air above the altar. All of them were disguised as spirits and Vorce had to admit that Hax had done well.

"Do you think Kusami will see this as a suitable place for a ceremony, my lord?" Hax asked Vorce, anxiously.

"This is perfect, just perfect," said Vorce. "You have done very well! She will be completely fooled. She will believe that we have created the whole thing for her special ceremony!"

"It will be a very special ceremony!" laughed Hax.

"Once we have brought her here, I shall use the 'goodness' to place her in a trance-like state. Once she is completely in our power the fiends can lift her up and force her through the vortex."

"What if she awakens?" asked Hax.

"It will be too late by then," said Vorce. "There will be enough demons and fiends to carry her through if she resists. Is everyone ready?"

Kusami was in her house when Vorce and his companions arrived. He was unaware that Malati stood in the shadows watching. Kusami went with Vorce and Hax readily enough. She was eager to start the ceremony that would give her dream. She went up to the altar and started singing with the 'spirits.' Once Vorce was satisfied that she was completely in his power, he placed her in a trance. The singing became deeper and deeper until it was more chanting than singing. Now the 'spirits' changed. Their brightness became darker and more sombre until they had become malicious and evil. They moved towards her and together with the fiends started to lift her up towards the mouth of the vortex that hovered above them. Vorce opened the vortex and with a roar it connected with Neo-Lunar.

As Kusami neared the vortex, she awoke and realised the danger that she was in. She could see Neo-Lunar through the tunnel that the demons and fiends were slowly taking her towards and was terrified. These beings had deceived her. She was betrayed. She knew that she was lost, but could not fail to scream out in pain and anguish.

"No, No!" she wailed. "You have tricked me. That is not what I asked for. That is not my kingdom!"

Vorce laughed a deep throaty laugh.

"You are right, it is not your kingdom, but it is your destiny. You are to be the matriarch of a new race of humans and in doing so will bring my dreams to fruition!"

With that she was sucked up into the vortex and the next moment she was spewed out of its mouth together with the fiends and demons, Hax and Vorce onto Neo-lunar. Vorce quickly closed the vortex, least Kusami try to escape.

All the beings watched her as she lay where she had fallen, her body shaking with sobs. They could all hear her anguish and feel her distress, but they laughed and called her names.

"Come, we must not torment the Goddess, mother of our new race," said Vorce, smiling indulgently at his servants. "It is all a bit strange for her at the moment. Leave her be for a while," and he dismissed the beings and sent them back to Hades.

When they had gone Vorce watched Kusami anxiously. She was the first human to enter his new world and he needed to be sure that she would be able to survive.

Kusami slowly stopped crying and looked up from her position on the ground. She looked at the trees and plants near where she lay, the like of which had never existed before. The trees had black trunks and were twisted and gnarled. They had leaves, but they were not green as one expected them to be. Some were dark purple, while others were brown and dry as if all the goodness had been sucked out of them. Some had fruits suspended from their branches, like gourds, while others had cone like structures that sprang out from the trunks.

Kusami stood up and looked towards a light in the distance. She slowly walked towards it, until she was directly beneath it. Vorce watched her raise her head to look up at the light; squinting against the brightness. Hanging in the sky above her was the ball of 'goodness', trapped in a cage and revolving slowly. Standing under the 'goodness', was like being in an oasis. The grass was lush and green, the trees were tall and covered in fruit, and the plants and bushes were thriving. There was a pool in the centre of the oasis where fresh clean water bubbled up from underground. Kusami tentatively bent down and cupped her hand under the spurting water, sniffing it before putting it to her lips. The water was good. It came from the 'goodness' and did not know how else to be. Only the area directly underneath the ball of 'goodness' was pure and fertile. The rest of the planet was warped and loathsome, like its creator. He had no idea how a planets ecosystem should be, so it was created like him; hideous, foul and abhorrent, but for all that, he now knew that it could sustain life and he had his first human being!

Chapter 51

Hospital in crisis

Down on Earth, Zoth called quietly to Colandra, "All is ready! The battle begins! Let's go!"

Colandra said goodbye to Michelle and disappeared with Zoth to the hospital. Michelle was determined to go too, so she got into her Mini and drove quickly to Hampton Green Hospital, parking her car some distance from the hospital and walking the rest of the way.

Meanwhile the patients in the hospital beds were all awake, but feigning sleep. They had been making themselves fit throughout the quiet periods when the nurses had left the room and now they lay still in their beds, waiting for the signal to spring up and attack Lars when he emerged from the vortex.

Lars had been to Neo-lunar to inspect the planet and meet Kusami. He was most impressed with his lord Vorce's creation, however, Kusami was not really who he wanted to mother their new race. His heart was set on Michelle, he reluctantly accepted Kusami as a second choice. He hoped that they would have no need to use Neo-lunar, as he still believed that they would be successful in their fight for the Earth. Vorce had assured him that all the fiends and demons were more than ready to take over the stolen soul's bodies and all they waited for was the order from

Lars, But Lars wanted more souls. There were still more to be harvested at Hampton green Hospital, and as his first conquest, it had become a matter of pride, to take them all! It was becoming a private vendetta against the entities and he would not let even one fail to be caught by the evil reapers!

As Lars stepped through the vortex into room four of Hampton Green hospital, he did not notice the lights flashing on and off. He had barely taken a couple of steps forward when the ward burst into noise. Naked patients leapt from their beds, screaming and shouting. He was so surprised that he had no time to defend himself. He fell to the ground under the onslaught as the patients jumped on his back, punching and biting. He tried to crawl to the double doors behind the curtain, but there were too many of them. He had no time to wonder why they had woken from their sedated sleep, nor how they had hidden the fact from their carers. He was being battered and gouged by a furious pack of very angry human beings!

As he lay on the floor he looked over to the vortex. It was still open, if he could only just get to it. He took a deep breath and roared with all his might. The walls trembled at the sound and the patients hesitated, just long enough for him to stand up and sprint towards the vortex. He would leave Colandra's body and join his Lord Vorce in Hades.

As he looked up, ready to leave his host, Zoth and Trego appeared. He jumped back, unable to pass. He was faced with a dilemma; if he left his host he would be safe from the patient's wrath, but he would be killed by the spirits. If he stayed with his host, the spirits would be unable to harm him, but the patients would beat him to death. He decided that he had a better chance with the humans than with the spirits.

Just at that moment the vortex closed with an ear-splitting screech. He took advantage of the distraction, imitating a rugby tackled and diving along the tiled floor towards the curtained wall. Disappearing behind it, he flattened himself against the door and quietly turned the handle. He opened the door just wide enough to allow him to squeeze out and shut it quickly behind him. Once in the corridor he took a deep breath and sighed. He was free!

Then a wailing noise started!

'Oh, now what?' he thought, as James went rushing past him towards the incinerator room, shouting, "'The furnace has gone wrong!"

He followed the running figure and entered the room. The lights above the door were flashing red and Lars turned to James and said, "What's happening?"

"Oh, Lordy, lord," James said. "She's going to blow! I knew it would one of these days."

"Can't you do something?" shouted Lars above the din of the alarm.

James went up to the panel and fiddled with the knobs, but shook his head.

"No, sir! We need to get out of here before it explodes. We have perhaps five minutes; that is all."

Lars took off like a bat out of hell, reaching the door to the stairs seconds later. James followed, hitting the fire alarm button as he went and shouting into his mobile phone, "Fire service. Hampton Green Hospital. We have an emergency."

Lars turned as an enormous blast came from the incinerator room. A ball of fire burst out through the doorway, hit the opposite wall and was diverted down the corridor in each direction. Lars watched with his mouth open as James was engulfed in white hot flames, his body reduced to ashes within seconds. Lars jumped through to the stairwell and slammed the door closed. He took the stairs, two steps at a time, just as the fireball hit the door.

The fire-doors into the rooms were no match for the flames. The fire completely destroyed the first five rooms, just as the occupants reached the safety of the stairwell. Suddenly there was a horrendous noise as the incinerator fell through the floor down into the room below. As it did so, it exploded, flinging white hot metal in all directions. Patients and staff were all panicking and running for the fire escape, as the fire raged out of control. It had now reached every floor and the temperature within the building was intolerable.

The spirits had not had to do anything to the furnace. It had chosen the opportune moment to blow up, just as James had predicted, however, he had not been on holiday when it happened, unfortunately!

Lars rushed up the stairs as fast as possible. Smoke had started to seep into the stairway making his eyes water and his chest uncomfortable. Soon panic stricken people were surging onto the stairwell from every floor, intent on escaping the fire that raged in the building. Lars needed to keep ahead of them or he would be engulfed in the panicking throng. He could hear them screaming and crying down below and almost flew up the stairs, bursting through the door to the car park.

He stood for a moment in the crisp, cold air and took huge lungful to cleanse the smoke from his chest. As he did so he saw a figure running towards him. Incredibly it was Michelle!

As soon as she saw him, she tried to swerve away, but he grabbed her saying, "My, my! What have we here? If it isn't little Michelle?"

As he held her close to his body he thought he saw something, something that he recognised. It was a being from the spirit world he was sure, but not actually a spirit.

"So, you've found yourself a little friend!" he hissed in her ear. "Well no-one can help you now, not even the spirits."

He forced her into his car, pushing her across the passenger seat into the driving position.

"Drive to your home or I shall kill you!" he snarled.

As the car moved out of the car park Lars looked back at the hospital as the flames started to flare out of the roof of the building. The car passed the fire brigade, ambulance and police as they rushed to the scene, sirens blaring out.

'Everything is going wrong!' he thought. 'But at least I have Michelle. I shall have my queen on Neo-Lunar, after all!'

Chapter 52

Getting ready

In Celestina, the Great Lord had finished his discussion with the higher spirits and now everyone waited for his decision. He looked down at all his loyal followers and nodded gravely. He hoped that they were ready to cast their votes.

"I give you two choices," he said, quietly. "The first is easy, the second is hard. Before you make your minds up you must know that if you choose the second option I cannot help you, only arm you for your ordeal and hope that your own steadfastness will suffice and you will be ultimately successful."

He paused to look into each spirits soul and knew which course they would choose. Sadly he also knew which spirits would survive and which would not.

At last he said, "As you know Zoth and Trego have gone down to Earth to help Colandra fight with the demon, Lars and rescue his body. Lars is one of our adversaries, but there are others in Hades who seek to destroy our very existence. We have two options; we can do nothing, but wait to see where the demons strike. The problem with this is that by the time the demons are attacking Celestina it may be too late to repair the damage that they have already done. The second option is to fight the demons in Hades itself. The surprise will be to our advantage and they will not have sufficient time to form a defence. If you choose the second option you will have to rely on your own integrity and cunning, as I am unable to enter Hades and fight at your side. I can give you weapons, however, and they will be strong and will have spiritual properties. Both options are fraught with danger and some of you will perish, but if we are to defeat our enemies and rescue our loved ones then sacrifices must be made." He paused for a moment and looked at them sadly. "Please make your choice."

The Great Lord withdrew so that the spirits could talk among themselves and choose which path they wished to take; however, he could hear their thoughts and waited patiently.

"If we take the first option, we will never be safe," said Felicia. "We will be constantly looking over our shoulders, frightened of everything and everyone in case it is them in disguise."

"We must try to get Jessica back home. We owe it to Zoth. He would do this for one of us," said Verda.

Many of the higher beings looked at her. She was only a first level spirit, but she had a special warmth about her.

"She is right," said Bellure.

"We must think carefully as to whether we can fight," said Petra. "Remember what the Great Lord said, many of us will perish, that means die!"

"It will not require everyone to take part in the battle," said Felicia. "There will be a role to play for spirits who choose to stay here. There will be no shame in that. We cannot all be fighters."

There was a general murmuring among the spirits and Felicia said, "It is time to vote. We will first vote on option one or option two. Those who wish to choose the first option should enter the Spirox now."

A few of the lower level spirits entered the Spirox. Then to the Great Lord's surprise Dorias and Petra joined them.

"I must presume that everyone else chooses option two," said Felicia. "You must all be prepared to fight, but initially we need volunteers who will go down to Hades. You cannot vote yes and expect someone else to put their lives in danger for you. We will need others who can be counted on to support the first wave if necessary."

A few more spirits entered the Spirox.

Felicia lifted her arms and said, "All those spirits who have voted not to fight will be given tasks here in Celestina. You will be charged with protecting our kingdom and caring for the injured, but for now gather together in the Celestial Hall while we consult with the Great Lord."

The Great Lord of All returned to receive the spirits decision. It was only a formality as they all knew that he was aware of what had taken place in his absence. Now it was a matter of picking the army that would go down through Hades Gateway to fight the demons and fiends and rescue Jessica.

The Great Lord assembled everyone in the Hall of Judgement and picked his white knights that would go down to the kingdom of the damned to fight for righteousness.

"I hope you are all ready," he said. "No time is the right time for a fight such as this. I bestow you with strength of fortitude and abundant energy. Felicia, to you I give the power to create a vortex; however it will only travel between the Hall of Judgement and Hades. I cannot risk demons and fiends entering Celestina. Gabriel, to you I give the power of the shield. You will be able to create a shield for an injured spirit to rest behind, but it will not remain indefinitely. Sorcell, to you I give the power of healing. When you use it in conjunction with Gabriel's gift its effects will be tripled. To all of you I give a mystical sword, which will kill a demon with one stroke. You will find it more difficult to kill a fiend as they are your bad counterparts, but they will have no weapons, just their brute strength. The sword cannot harm anything good, so use them with impunity. A word of warning; do not let the demons touch you as they are pure evil and will sap your strength."

The Great Lord stretched out his arms and goodness flowed through them into the assembled spirits until they glowed with an inner strength. Gabriel opened the Gateway and the sprits descended into Hades, the city of the damned, the womb of all evil.

Chapter 53

The good fight

Most of the demons and fiends were in Neo-lunar when the spirits entered the first level of Hades. Hax had been left in charge of the stolen souls and he was in a panic as most of them seemed to be disappearing. He dreaded Vorce returning, as he knew that he would be blamed and harshly punished. As he stood in the cavern he glanced through the doorway into the Arrivals Hall as it was suddenly filled with light.

"Now what's going on," he shouted. "As if I haven't got enough to worry about!"

He rushed into the hall, brandishing his stick, to be confronted by a huge army of spirits.

"What are you lot doing down here?" he snarled, suddenly very afraid. Felicia approached him cautiously, her sword raised high in the air.

"You will tell us what we want to know or you die," she said.

The demon looked at her and knew that this was no time to prevaricate.

"What do you want to know? I'll tell you anything, just don't kill me," he whined.

"Who are you and where is your master, Lucifer?" Felicia asked, looking around hoping to catch sight of Jessica, but she was nowhere to be seen.

"I am Hax, the Gateway Guardian and Lucifer is in Hell, I suppose," said Hax, relieved that it was an easy question. "But he's not my master anymore."

Too late, he realised that was the wrong thing to say, as Felicia stepped forward menacingly.

"Who is your master then?" she demanded.

"My Lord Vorce is my master," said Hax, "And he will kill you with his 'goodness' if you don't leave."

Felicia looked puzzled. "What do you mean? A demon hasn't any 'goodness'," she said.

"My Lord Vorce does," replied Hax, sneering. "He collects it and does all manner of things with it."

"Show me?" said Felicia and followed Hax into the cavern where the 'goodness' was slowly revolving in its cage at the back of the cavern. Felicia had never seen anything so pitiful. With one stroke of her sword she smashed the cage and grabbed hold of the 'goodness', taking it back to the Arrivals Hall.

"My Lord Vorce won't like that," said Hax, defiantly. "Just you wait till he gets back."

At that there was a dreadful screeching noise in the cavern.

"Now you'll see," said Hax.

He rushed into the cavern to warn his master of the spirit invasion and suddenly the hall was full of screaming, vicious demons and fiends. Hax laughed gleefully.

"Now you'll be sorry!" he said, gloatingly.

Felicia shouted to her army, "Be on your guard. Use your swords."

The spirit swung their swords this way and that, hacking and slashing fiends and demons alike. Hax raised his stick and hit out at anything that moved, but to his annoyance it swept through the spirits, hitting a fiend or demon instead.

Hax abandoned his stick and tried to grapple the spirits instead. It was painful, but he found that he could bring them down if he held on.

"Don't let them get too close," shouted Gabriel, as Hax tried to grab another spirit.

Hax managed to move slowly round towards the door to the cavern and suddenly saw a gap. The cavern was in darkness, now that the spirits had taken the ball of 'goodness' so he managed to dive through the doorway and join Vorce, who was encouraging his minions to scratch and gouge, bite and punch the enemy. The spirits were winning the battle, forcing the demons and fiends back into the cavern.

"Can't you make some weapons, my lord," said Hax. "We are losing the battle!"

"I need my ball of 'goodness' and it is in the Arrivals Hall behind the spirits," he said.

Hax watched as Vorce crept along the wall until he was next to the doorway, waiting for an opportunity to grab the ball of goodness, but the spirits were fighting right in front of it. There were still a few stolen souls in the cavern, who were cowering in one corner and Vorce grabbed hold of one, holding the soul in front of him. He let out a great roar and the fighting paused for a moment.

"I can cause great pain to this soul, and I shall if you continue to kill my servants," he said.

"Who are you?" demanded Felicia.

"I am Lord Vorce. Very soon I shall rule the universe and you will be my servants. Even as I speak my followers are preparing for my triumphant arrival," as he spoke he moved slowly towards the doorway and suddenly sprang into the Arrivals Hall. He was now right under the 'goodness' and Hax stood open mouthed as his lord summoned a vortex and leapt through in one smooth movement, closing it behind him.

For a moment there was silence as Hax and the other fiends and demons stared at the place where their lord and master had been standing, then mayhem ensued. Hax was angry. He had been betrayed and this made him as mad as hell itself. Although he was a demon, he had principles. When he was created, it was to serve Lucifer and he did this steadfastly and whole-heartedly. His reward was to be banished to the Arrivals Hall and never to set foot in Hell again. When Vorce offered him freedom in exchange for loyalty he grabbed it with both hands. He had done all that was asked of him, and more, but again he was abandoned. He may be rough and bestial, but he believed that one should look out for each other and Vorce had abandoned these demons and fiends as easily as Lucifer had done.

He rushed at the spirits determined to make someone pay for his discomfort. Screaming and shouting, he grabbed hold of Felicia, and as he held her close he could feel her energy flowing into him. It was exquisite! He had never felt this way before and he was intoxicated. He saw Sorcell raise his sword and as he slashed it down at Hax, Hax clumsily rolled out of the way, narrowly missing the swords edge.

"Quickly, help Felicia. She is nearly spent," he heard Sorcell shout.

Two other spirits nearby rushed to Felicia's aid and the three attacked Hax. He was hurting inside and out. His lord had deserted him and now he was in dire straits. He had no option but to let Felicia go, but not before he had almost sapped her energy completely. Hax crawled away to hide from the spirits lest they finish him off and watched the fighting from a safe distance. Although he was mortally wounded, the energy that he had taken from the spirit sustained him and began to heal him.

"Gabriel, Gabriel, where are you?" he heard Sorcell shout.

Gabriel was fighting in the Arrivals Hall and did not hear Sorcell calling. Verda rushed to Gabriel side wielding her sword like a veteran.

"You are needed by Sorcell. Go quickly. I will finish these off," and her sword flashed as it sliced through the air and slew the first demon. Hax winced as the demon fell. The fiend was more difficult, but the little spirit swung her sword this way and that and finally the fiend lay dead.

"Where is Vorce throughout this battle," Hax said to himself. "Certainly not here where he should be. No! He's safe and snug in his little kingdom!"

Hax managed to drag himself into the darkness of the cavern and now he appraised the situation. Most of the stolen souls had disappeared, but there were still many demons and fiends left, all of whom were gallantly fighting. Although the spirits had weapons, they lacked the viciousness and amoral qualities of the evil beings. It was not in the nature of a spirit to hurt and so they were at a disadvantage, even so, Hax had to admit that the spirits were doing well. As he was thinking, three spirits rushed into the cavern and surrounded him. He knew that he did not have the strength to fight so he lay where he was and waited for death.

"Hax," one of the spirits said. "Do you wish to live?"

Hax looked at him, astonished. He had expected to be run through by the spirits sword, not questioned. He slowly nodded and waited for the catch!

"In exchange for life, you must give us some information," continued the spirit.

As the battle continued to rage Hax lay in the corner of the Arrivals Hall waiting to hear what the spirits were going to do with him.

"We need to get him back to the Hall of Judgement," he heard one spirit say, "and we must send Felicia back."

Hax watched as Felicia rallied round and raised her arms. A small, bright light appeared that hung in the room like small sun, accompanied by a musical note reverberated throughout the hall. Then it was gone!

"Felicia has not enough energy to make a vortex," cried one spirit anxiously."What are we going to do? We will be trapped down here!"

"Why don't you use the 'goodness' as my lord Vorce does," asked Hax quietly.

The spirits looked at Hax.

"He is right! There is plenty of energy there," whispered Felicia. "Bring it down to me. I can use it to give me strength."

Sorcell rose up and pulled the goodness down to Felicia.

She tried again and this time the light appeared, getting brighter and brighter. The musical note was strong and suddenly the vortex formed. Two spirits carried Felicia to the entrance and all three were sucked up and away.

"Gabriel you must place a shield around Hax before we send him to the Hall of Judgement, or he will contaminate everything there with his evil," said Sorcell.

Hax was suddenly surrounded with light and he could feel a tingling sensation that was not unpleasant. He was directed to crawl to the mouth of the vortex and as he approached it he was sucked up, swirling and twisting, to land in a heap at the feet of several spirits.

He was moved into an ante-chamber and told to wait there until he was escorted to Michelus.

"While you are in here you will be healed," a spirit said to him. "You have been spared as it is believed that you have valuable information that may help our cause. The eventual conclusion to our investigation will be influenced by your conduct, so think long and hard as to what you hope your future will be. Ultimately, our Great Lord will decide your fate and you will be unable to hide your thoughts from him."

Hax looked round the room and was enthralled by the peace and space around him. Never had he been in a place so beautiful. He had only ever resided in Hell or Hades so, to him, this was heaven! He did not mind how long he had to wait, as each moment was a source of wonder and incredulous joy!

Chapter 54

The winning hand

Now that Sorcell and Gabriel were no longer distracted by Felicia's health they could go back to the battle. The hall was not as crowded as it had been. Many fiends and demons lay on the floor either dead or mortally wounded. There were still a few battles going on, but not as many as before. The situation in the cavern was a different matter. Because of its properties, as the occupants decreased so did the size of the room. It was dark and the ceiling was low, making it difficult to fight effectively. Many of the injured fiends could crawl away into the dark corners to recuperate.

"We need some light in here," said Sorcell. Gabriel looked around and said, "What about the ball of 'goodness'. Can we bring that in here?"

"As long as Vorce does not send a vortex back and grab it," replied Sorcell. "We must keep an eye on it."

He went back into the Arrivals Hall and flew up to the ceiling, grabbing the 'goodness' and taking it into the cavern. The room was at once flooded with light. The fiends and demons blinked, blinded momentarily by the 'goodness'. The spirits took advantage of this and slashed at their enemy with renewed vigour. A demon rushed at Gabriel, screaming like a banshee. Gabriel raised his sword and swung it at him, slaying him as he charged. Soon the room was full of fighting groups.

Sorcell was very busy healing as many spirits as he could, but it was impossible to keep up with the constant stream of injured beings. His attention was drawn to a noise in the hall. He looked up from his task and saw, to his relief, more spirits pouring through the Gateway.

He saw Roxall and Bellure among them and shouted, "Over here! We need you over here!" and they came, bringing many other spirits with them.

"Another sixth level spirit is with us, Xylem," said Bellure. "He has been given the power to create a vortex. We have advised him to stay away from the fighting, lest he is injured and we are trapped."

Meanwhile Roxall was taking in the scene around him.

"Oh, my!" he said. "This is dreadful. So many spirits killed." And he raised his sword and joined the unholy mass of screaming demons and fiends. The extra spirits were just what the battle needed. There were more dead fiends and demons now and fewer and fewer left to fight. Just as Sorcell thought they must win, a screeching noise started up in the far end of the cavern. Everyone stopped fighting and watched the vortex form. Out of the gateway came demons, many demons, but they did not move to fight, but stood still, forming a wall in front of the vortex. Then Vorce appeared half carrying, half dragging a spirit.

Bellure gasped, "Its Jessica!"

"You seek to kill me and rescue this spirit, but you can do neither. I am far too clever to fall into your traps. This spirit is mine, you cannot have her," said Vorce. "You can kill every one of the fiends and demons in Hades, but I have many more that are eager to fight for my cause."

Some of the spirits moved towards him, their swords at the ready, but as they did so the demons raised their arms, each one brandishing a black scimitar.

"Beware," cried Vorce. "These are no ordinary swords. They are forged from evil and created by 'goodness'. You cannot defeat them. Take your dead and dying, and leave Hades now or I shall make the life of this spirit too painful to bear."

Sorcell knew that they were beaten. He could not afford to lose any more sprits and he would be putting Jessica's life in danger if they fought on.

"We will leave, but do not consider this the end. We cannot allow you to endanger the universe in this way, nor can we allow you to steal lives that do not belong to you. Be warned therefore, that we shall defeat you eventually and rescue the souls that you have taken." Sorcell was referring to Alvienne and Kusami as well as Jessica, but Vorce laughed a deep roaring laugh that shook the very foundations of Hades. Vorce turned and entered the vortex with Jessica, and his demons followed him, carrying their injured comrades. The vortex closed and there was a hushed silence in the cavern.

Sorcell looked around. There was carnage in the cavern. Dead fiends and demons lay everywhere and injured spirits lay groaning quietly where they had fallen.

"We must collect up our dead and injured before they are absorbed into the walls of Hades," said Sorcell. "Bellure, where is Roxall? Get him to help the other spirits move the injured into the hall."

But Roxall was not able to help. He lay by the doorway of the cavern, mortally wounded by the fiend that he had so bravely slain. Bellure found him and took him in her arms.

"Roxall, Roxall! My love! You cannot die. We have been together too long to have it all destroyed by a fiend."

Roxall stirred in his soul-mates arms.

"You must be brave," he whispered. "My energy will remain in Celestina for ever. I will become part of its very fabric, with you for all eternity."

Bellure began to wail, "No! No!" she cried. "You cannot leave me! You are part of me! You cannot die! Sorcell do something, help him, please."

But there was nothing Sorcell could do. There was nothing anyone could do. Bellure wept for her lover, for her loss and for her pain. Sorcell gently helped Bellure to her feet and the spirits carefully carried Roxall up to Celestina.

The spirits arrived exhausted in the Hall of Judgement and the first priority was to heal the sick and lay out the dead. Slowly the spirit energy was absorbed into the very heart of Celestina itself and everyone mourned at their loss, but celebrated their lives, knowing that their friends would always be with them.

The Great Lord had questioned Hax and now Sorcell knew about Neo-lunar and Vorce's plans. They still did not know where Neo-Lunar was, as Hax had not been involved with its creation, but he had been able to describe what it was like.

"What is to happen to him?" asked Sorcell. "After all he had no choice in his behaviour. It was his destiny, to be evil. Can we change his nature? Is that possible?"

The Great Lord heard Sorcell's question and said smiling, "Anything is possible when you are God!"

Sorcell looked at the demon within the ante-chamber and felt sorry for him. He was changed since being in Celestina and meeting the Great Lord and would never be welcome in Hades again. He could not be put into the primordial pot as he was pure evil and this would taint the neutral energy, but Sorcell knew that the Great Lord could do anything, so he asked, "Could you merge him with some 'goodness' and grant him a life? I know that he would have to battle with his two sides, good and evil, but most beings do that all the time."

"Would you be prepared to mentor him, be his guide?" asked the Great Lord.

When Sorcell agreed, the decision was made; Hax would be infused with goodness and await the beginning of a new life as a mammal. When Sorcell gave Hax their decision, he was overjoyed. Sorcell warned him that it would not be easy, but also charged him with the enormity of the occasion.

"Remember that this is a priceless gift. It has never been given to another demon, so guard it well and never give us cause to revoke it."

Sorcell was encouraged by the way Hax accepted his new circumstances and apologised for any pain and suffering he had inflicted on the spirits. Sorcell left Hax in the Primare Talis, awaiting his new life.

He slowly returned to Celestina. He was as grieved as the other spirits about the loss of their friends, but he was as determined as them that this was not the finish of their battle for Jessica.

They may have been defeated for the moment, but once they had rallied, they would rise up again and attack the very heart of Vorce's strong-hold; Neo-Lunar.

Chapter 55

The miracle

Back on Earth, Michelle and Lars arrived at Hazelwood Cottage. Lars dragged her from the car and into the hall. At that moment Michelle heard the familiar thud from the bedroom above and knew Thomas had jumped off the bed in the spare room. The door of the room opened slightly and Thomas walked onto the landing. Michelle saw his face appear as he stared down through the banisters and into the hall below.

Michelle knew that Lars was aware of Colandra's presence, but she also knew that Lars could not see or hear him. She, on the other hand, could do both, and now she heard him in her mind trying to reassure her, but she was still very frightened.

She had many questions that demanded answers, so she said to the demon, "My mother was in that hospital wasn't she?"

Lars stepped away from the front door, but did not let Michelle go.

"Why do you want to know that? You never knew your mother," he said.

"No, I didn't know her," Michelle replied. "But I would have liked to. I was never given the chance. She left before I was old enough to know her."

Lars relaxed just enough to adjust his grip and said, "I knew your mother very well. We were together for twenty five years. You could say, I knew her intimately," he said, laughing uproariously. "I was present at your birth and you would have been mine then, if it wasn't for your stupid mother."

Michelle squirmed in his grip and turned around until she faced him.

"What do you mean," she said.

"My Lord Vorce, who even now prepares our new home, was to prepare your body so that I could take it over, but your mother killed him and thus I had to use your mother as my host. She knew that I would eventually merge with you and so she fled with me inside her, to protect you from me. Where is she now, your mother? Certainly not here protecting you. She can't help you now. You are mine!"

Michelle knew instinctively what he meant to do. He would vacate Colandra's body so that he could merge with her. She froze in his grip, terrified at the very idea. She now knew why he had seemed familiar when he had tried to merge her in the Evangelical Hall, because he had tried before, when she was hardly a few months old.

Her thoughts were interrupted when he said, "I know that the soul who belongs in this body is here. You! Whoever you are! Can you hear me?"

"Yes he hears you," said Michelle. "What is it you want of him?"

"You want this body back, don't you? Well you may have it. I have my prize, right here," said Lars, directing his words to Colandra. "When I vacate your body you must merge with it immediately or it will die and end up in the cronkel pot. You will not be able to help your friend from there," he continued, sarcastically.

Michelle heard Colandra shout, "Zoth! Trego! We need you, now!"

But nothing happened.

"Michelle, pretend to faint. I need some distance between you and Lars." Colandra said, urgently. At his words, Michelle went limp and gracefully slid down Lars body and onto the hall carpet. Lars stood transfixed.

"Get up, you stupid woman," he shouted, prodding her prone body with his foot. Michelle did not move. Lars bent down over Michelle, just as Thomas let out a long howl. Frightened, Lars jumped back in alarm and now stood in the centre of the hall. Michelle opened her eyes to see two shimmering figures hovering in front of her.

'At last,' she thought. 'Trego and Zoth are here to help.'

Lars was now caught between Thomas above him and the spirits in front of him.

Michelle heard Colandra saying, "He means to merge with Michelle. He has wanted to from the moment she was born. That was the connection! That's how our lives were linked!"

Michelle crawled away from Lars back towards the front door..

She could not hear the spirits speaking but she knew that they would be planning their next move.

"Michelle," said Colandra. "Zoth has told me that Lars was in the body of your mother when my bus blew up. She was very badly injured and Lars had to vacate it. He found my body by accident and has been in it ever since. Your mother was our Jane Doe and Lars took her to the hospital just a short while ago. Unfortunately she perished with the other patients in the fire."

Michelle was devastated, but she had no time to grieve, there were other more pressing things to be done.

"Lars," said Zoth. "I will make my voice low enough to allow you and Michelle to hear me. You cannot continue to use Colandra's body, nor can you take over Michelle's."

"Colandra! So that is what he is called," said Lars. "Well, Michelle is mine! I shall have her eventually. You cannot be here protecting her forever!" he asked.

"I propose a truce, while you leave Colandra's body and move away from this place," said Zoth. "However, you will only have a few moments before we seek you out and destroy you. Now that we know you are on Earth it will only be a matter of time before you are caught."

"I have no option but to agree," said Lars. reluctantly. "Colandra, I now know who you are. I shall be looking out for you, don't think I shall not. Michelle, you have not won. I will still merge with you eventually. It is your destiny"

Michelle shivered as she heard his words.

As Lars the demon started to rise from Colandra's body, Zoth raised his arm in readiness to strike. At the same moment, Thomas, who was tottering on the top of the banister handrail above Lars head, leapt off, a ball of angry fur, claws and teeth, spitting and snarling as he went. As he flew through the air Colandra's body fell to the floor and a black shadow rose up, colliding with the body of the cat. Thomas landed on all four feet in the middle of the hall carpet, shook himself, and with a howl, bolted into the kitchen. Zoth slowly lowered his arm and sighed.

"Missed!" he said quietly.

Michelle heard the 'Clack!' of the cat flap, and rushed to the kitchen window as Thomas streaked across the garden and disappeared into the woods beyond.

Michelle returned to the hall to hear Zoth shout to Colandra, "Stop! You cannot merge yet. The demon has been in your body too long. It will be full of evil. We must prepare it first and then the Great Lord must work his miracle so that your thread can be re-attached."

"His miracle. What miracle?" said Colandra. "Surely I just need to re-enter it."

"No," said Zoth. "Your thread was completely detached. It does not re-attach itself. The only way is for the Great Lord to enter your body and re-attach it, but he cannot enter it while it is full of evil. Trego and I must purify it first. It will be as if this is a whole new body. When all is ready you will know."

Michelle had listened to the spirits and now watched in awe as the body of Colandra rose up into the air. It hovered in the middle of the galleried hallway. Slowly it took on a vibrant, healthy glow and the harsh features that Lars had etched on its face relaxed and disappeared. Suddenly a golden globe appeared in the eaves above the landing and the body rose to meet it. A shaft of light burst from the globe and the whole house was enveloped in its aura.

Colandra had been in the presence of the Great Lord once before, but for Michelle it was all too much. She fell to the floor in ecstasy, her whole being transported to a blissful state of rapture. The goodness poured into the very fabric of the house and garden, protecting it forever. As Michelle crouched on the hall carpet she heard a voice, deep inside her being. She knew that it was the Great Lord.

"Michelle," he said. "You have been unselfish in your efforts to help Colandra and have put your life in danger for him. You have been instrumental in stopping Lars from conquering the Earth. In recognition of yours and your mother's sacrifice I bestow upon each of you a gift. To your mother I give her life and to you I give you your mother. Together you will help each other follow your destinies."

Michelle suddenly became aware of a woman slowly walking down the stairs. She was beautiful and surrounded in a purple aura. Her face radiated joy and as she reached the hall, she stretched out her arms to enfold her daughter in a mothers embrace.

Again Michelle heard the Great Lord as he addressed Colandra.

"Colandra, you have been stalwart and strong, never wavering in your desire to save mankind. Without you we would never have known about the great threat that Lars and Vorce posed. For that you deserve our greatest respect and thanks. When you merge with your body you will remember what has taken place since the accident and you will retain all the knowledge that you have acquired as a cronkel. Use this knowledge wisely, but guard it well.

To all three of you, be on your mettle. Lars will not stop trying to conquer Earth and one day we may have need of you once more. This house and all the woods surrounding it are now hallowed ground. You are safe as long as you are here. Take care of each other. Colandra are you ready?"

"I am ready," said Colandra and he stepped forward until he was directly beneath his body which still hovered above the landing. Michelle watched his shimmering form rise up and slowly rejoin his body. The moment that she had waited impatiently for was about to become a reality. She and Colandra would be in the same world together, but she knew that she would miss the intimacy that had been afforded her when Colandra was a cronkel!

The light in the cottage was seen for miles around. Some people said it was caused by a sunburst. Others said it was a meteorite. Yet more people thought it was a shooting star.

But many people shook their heads sagely and said, "It is a sign from God!"

Epilogue

December 2008

    The cat sat at the edge of the forest and watched the back door of the house through the trees. He had tried to get closer, but every time he got within a certain distance he experienced excruciating pain, so now he contented himself with sitting and watching.

    The sudden invasion of his body was a shocking experience, but now he had managed to subdue the demon until it was pushed to the back of the cat's subconscious mind. There was no way he would permit it to control any part of him. Lars had chosen the wrong host this time; for Thomas the cat, with his cronkel soul Sirtis, was no ordinary cat.

    He should be a human now, and but for his own stupidity, he would be. He had seen the tear at the bottom of the cronkel pot and gone to investigate it. Before he knew what he was doing, he had slipped through the hole and found himself outside the pot, adrift in space. He could not find the hole again and panicked. He tried shouting, but no-one heard him. The only thing for him to do was to go back to Earth and start again. By chance he saw an escort spirit leading a group of souls up to the Celestial hall and he latched onto them. Unfortunately for him they had been a group of sheep and when they entered the Celestial Hall they were automatically transferred to the mammal compartment of the cronkel pot. He tried to protest, but his protestations fell on deaf ears, so here he was, back as a cat.

'I suppose it could be worse,' he thought. 'I could have ended up as a sheep!'

He knew about the demon from Colandra, and that it wanted to possess Michelle, but he was not going to let that happen. As much as he wanted to be with his mistress, he also wanted to protect her. He began to wash himself. He always thought better after a grooming session.

Book two:

Michelle's Mission

The guardian watched anxiously as Michelle placed the bowl carefully on the grassy knoll. He could see the cat hiding at the edge of the tree line and sense the evil demon within its body, but he knew that as long as he remained by Michelle's side, she was safe.

A guardian is created by the spirits to look after vulnerable humans. They are spiritually connected to their creator, who is instantly alerted should anything untoward happen to them. The guardian has no power as such, but the goodness that was used to create them, protects them from evil and deters unwanted attention.

Michelle's guardian had been most diligent for the past two years, but never had there been even the slightest hint of danger. Recently he had allowed himself to relax and experience the wonders that surrounded him here on Earth. There was so much to see and hear that he was sometimes a little distracted.

Michelle had only just started to leave food for the cat and it was the first time that their feline friend had ventured so close. The guardian had never been near the animal before and he could feel the evil emanating from him.

As Michelle bent down, the cat began to call to her. She looked up quickly as Thomas started to walk out of the trees about twenty yards away. For the first time since he had fled the house two years ago, he appeared quite normal. In the past he had remained hidden in the woods, but they had heard him, spitting and snarling as if to warn the humans away.

"Hello Thomas," she said and immediately the cat's tail went up in greeting.

Michelle moved slowly towards the cat, her hand outstretched, ready to pet him. The guardian stiffened and placed himself between the cat and his human charge, but still Thomas continued to approach Michelle.

"You recognise me then," she went on. "Who's a good boy then? It looks to me as if you have got rid of that nasty demon."

"No, no!" shouted the guardian, even though he knew that she could not hear him.

The cat looked at the guardian, licked his lips and moved forward purposely.

Lightning Source UK Ltd.
Milton Keynes UK
10 December 2009

147340UK00002B/14/P